Read what people are already saying about

CORRIE JACKSON

'Gripping . . . crime with a side order of chic'
GLAMOUR

'It's original, amazingly written and tense. A cracker . . .'
SUN

'Crime meets couture in this gripping story'
MARIE CLAIRE

'A fast-paced, punchy, self-assured thriller from a writer who's bound to go
from strength to strength'
RED

'The dark underbelly of the modelling world is a gritty setting . . . *Breaking Dead* rushes
along at a feverish pace, with a feisty heroine'
GOOD HOUSEKEEPING

'An edge of your seat thriller'
HELLO MAGAZINE

'If you like your holiday reads fast-paced and edge-of-your-sun lounger, this one's for you'
BRIDES MAGAZINE

'Jackson hits the ground not just running, but sprinting in a fast-paced, atmospheric
story . . . Brimming with angst, anger, anguish and action, this is just the start of what
promises to be an enthralling new crime series'
LANCASHIRE EVENING POST

'*Breaking Dead* has the feel of a noir movie, with up-market hotels, seedy
flats and the brightly-lit newsroom. It's tightly-plotted, fast-moving and
I devoured it greedily in two sittings'
CRIME REVIEW

'Deliciously well drawn, intriguing . . . a pacy, intelligent and bang on thriller, darkly
observant and grimly realistic . . .'
LIZ LOVES BOOKS

'It did NOT disappoint at all. I can't wait to r___ ___ ___ his author because
she kn__ws exact___ ___ ___ ___al and l believable
characters and with___ ___ ___ n exciting and fresh
re___ ___ ___ ___h'

Corrie Jackson has been a journalist for fifteen years. During that time she has worked at *Harper's Bazaar*, the *Daily Mail*, *Grazia* and *Glamour*. Corrie now lives in Greenwich, Connecticut with her husband and two children. *Breaking Dead*, her debut novel, was the first in the journalist Sophie Kent series and was described by *Glamour* as 'Gripping ... crime with a side order of chic' and by the *Sun* as 'Original, amazingly written and tense'.

THE
PERFECT
VICTIM

CORRIE
JACKSON

ZAFFRE

For my mum and dad

First published in Great Britain in 2017 by
ZAFFRE PUBLISHING
80-81 Wimpole St, London W1G 9RE
www.zaffrebooks.co.uk

A CIP catalogue record for this book is
available from the British Library.

ISBN: 978-1-78576-182-9

also available as an ebook

1 3 5 7 9 10 8 6 4 2

Typeset by IDSUK (Data Connection) Ltd
Printed and bound by Clays Ltd, St Ives Plc

MIX
Paper from
responsible sources
FSC® C018072

Zaffre Publishing is an imprint of Bonnier Zaffre,
a Bonnier Publishing company
www.bonnierzaffre.co.uk
www.bonnierpublishing.co.uk

2 April 1988

His mum is sleeping.

Her spidery limbs are tucked into the folds of the sofa. Her jeans button is undone, and the green shirt she's worn for three days straight is untucked, exposing a roll of white porridgy flesh. The yellow light from the lamp in the corner illuminates the sticky trail leaking out of her mouth. Her throat catches, and every breath sends a sour cloud towards him. The boy reaches forward to touch her chestnut hair, then pulls back, swallowing his tears.

He chews his fingernail down to where it hurts, stares at his trainers, scuffed, with a hole in the toe. He has small feet for his age. Small *everything* for his age. Puberty has fucked him over. There are hints, a deepening voice, baby-fluff on his chin, *urges*. But he's lagging behind. He pretends not to care, but the weight of it sits in his stomach like a stone.

The boy shivers and pulls his grey tracksuit top tightly around him. He glances at the candy-pink record player in the corner. His mum saved up for months to buy it. He can see her whirling round the sitting room in her grubby blue dressing gown, singing that pop song, '99 Red Balloons', at the top of her voice. She didn't know he was watching as she reached for the bottle of Blue Nun and downed the last two inches of rancid wine. Nor when she sank to the floor and retched into her hand.

The boy glances at the clock: 11.48 p.m. He creeps to the fridge and snaps open a can of Coke. As the bubbles hit the back of his throat, he runs his eyes over the crayon picture taped to the fridge door. It's been there for so many years the edges are curled and yellow. A woman with jagged brown hair and loopy legs, one longer than the other where the green crayon slipped. A little boy, whose feet are larger than his head. He stares at the scribbled blue heart between them and his breathing quickens.

A shriek pierces the air outside and he looks nervously towards the window. A brick wall runs around the edge of a garden, and beyond it are fields. The washing line flaps in the breeze. The breeze, he thinks. *Perfect.*

He crunches the Coke can between his small hands and leaves it on the counter. Then he pads towards the cellar door and lifts it to stop it scraping against the stone floor. The smell hits him in the face – wet-rot mixed with something else. Salt. Their cottage is only three miles from the sea and the briny air permeates everything: your house, your clothes, your skin. The boy doesn't need to turn on the light. He feels his way down the wooden steps taking care to miss out the fourth step, which has broken away. As his feet hit concrete, something scuttles away. A mouse, probably. He sees them down here all the time.

His heart bumps against his ribs as he pulls a torch from his pocket and shines it into the space behind the washing machine. He pulls out a brick and his fingers close around something feathery. The baby bird is as light as dry leaves. He's amazed it's still alive. It's been in there for days. There are others buried deeper in the wall that haven't been so lucky.

He folds one hand round the bird and, with the other, he opens the laundry basket and digs around. The Blue Nun bottle is at the bottom, where his mum hid it. He waits a beat, then springs up the steps to the kitchen.

As he tiptoes past his mum, a car shoots past, its headlights turning the sitting-room shadows cartoony. He freezes, not used to seeing cars in this remote place. His mum shifts, snorts, rubs her stomach with a stubby red fingernail. He counts to fifty. The bird quivers, soft and sick, in his hand. He places it on the carpet, beside his sleeping mum, where it twitches, then settles. It looks peaceful but its eyes are milky with death.

The boy unscrews the bottle lid. Then he pours the liquid on the carpet, trails it around the sofa, over the cigarette butts, the ashtray, the empty wine boxes, the remains of a congealing pizza. It splashes onto his shoes, drips down his wrists. He saves the final drops for the baby bird.

The boy takes one last look at his mum, then flicks the green lighter. The tiny flame shivers and he realises his hand is trembling. He cocks his head to one side, then snaps the lighter shut. His trainers squeak as he lurches – a childish zig-zag – across the kitchen and rips the crayon drawing from the fridge door. He rolls it into a cone then lights one end and tosses it onto the carpet. As the flames shoot forward in an angry orange stripe, words fill the boy's head: *He himself will be saved, but only through fire.*

The boy waits, his eyes watering, lungs filling with smoke as he watches the fire swallow up the bird. Then he drops to his knees and crawls into the hallway. He is about to open the front door when he hears coughing. It's coming from the sitting room. His mum is awake. His hand hovers over the door handle. Then he remembers the crayon drawing.

The woman. The boy. The heart.

He opens the door and darts out into the dirty moonlight.

1

Present Day

The dewy grass was wet against my ankles as I stood in the sunshine listening for signs of death. There, through the whine of a low-flying aircraft, I heard it: the staccato fizz of a police radio. I raced towards the river, kicking through drifts of pink blossoms. The Thames was mirror-flat and sparkled in the Monday-morning sunlight. I paused to glance at a trio of women with buggies. The one nearest me scratched her thick neck and squawked into a mobile phone. The other two balanced snotty toddlers on their hips. I could tell by their loose, easy gestures that they weren't part of the story. A good crime reporter knows that the difference between a page-one splash and a shitty page-five is timing. On a fresh crime scene, I'm dealing in moments. Flashes. I never know how long I've got before the scene shuts down. Before yes becomes no.

As I scanned the crowd, I stretched out the stiffness in my neck, trying to shrug off the weekend from hell. I'd crawled into bed on Friday evening and switched my phone off, and the world out. Three minutes in and my heart was galloping. Five minutes, my palms were on fire. Eight minutes, the negative thoughts thrashed against my ears like bats in the attic. I counted my breaths, just like my therapist, Dr Spado, taught me. Dr Spado is a new addition to my life. It was the *London Herald*'s policy that I check in with him, following a close shave with a serial killer, and a stint in Chelsea & Westminster hospital. I didn't argue. To be frank, I could do with the help. But during my weekly visits to a stucco-fronted house on Leamington Row, it hadn't taken long for Dr Spado to realise that my big black nightmares had very little to do with my run-in with death. You see, not long ago, my younger brother's scrawny, filthy body washed up under Albert Bridge. Tommy was my lifeblood, my reason to get up every day. He was also a homeless drug addict. His death cut me in half. Suicide was the official story, but I'd recently discovered the truth, well, part of it.

Tommy was murdered.

I hadn't got any further, and each day that Tommy's killers walked free was a day I was failing him. Guilt and grief are toxic companions. They fill my head, my heart, my lungs until I can't breathe. Nights are the worst. Without the thrum of day, there's nowhere to hide. So, Dr Spado recommended 'managed relaxation' as a way to ward off the panic attacks that hit when I turn out the lights. Mostly, I resort to next-level help, 'emergency measures', he called it. Sometimes I stagger the sleeping pills. Other times, I throw them down in one, welcoming the slide into oblivion. Last night was a three-pill night, and those always make me feel hollowed-out.

My phone vibrated in my pocket and I sighed. I'd only turned it back on this morning and was paying for the forty-eight-hour technology blackout. A flood of emails and voicemails that I hadn't even begun to sift through.

As I rubbed my gritty eyes, a woman in a red gilet, cradling a black terrier under her arm, shuffled towards me. The breeze whipped her chalky-grey curls around her face.

'Don't go closer, love. Trust me, you don't want to see it.'

'See what?'

'A body. In the river. They just pulled it out.' She pressed the dog into her ample chest, squashing a pair of thick librarian glasses.

'Did you get much of a look?' I pulled out my notebook, then caught her frown. 'I'm a reporter.'

The woman cocked her head to one side. 'Which paper?'

'The *London Herald*.'

She shifted onto the toes of her flip-flops and sniffed. 'I prefer the *Post*.'

I smiled politely, nodded towards the river. 'Can you describe what you saw?'

The woman clucked at the squirming dog and her neck skin wrinkled like baggy tights. 'This going in the paper?'

'If it's useful.' I realised how rude that sounded, and cracked a smile. 'Sorry, my boss just gave me an earful. If I don't phone in with details . . .' I mimed slitting my throat.

She gave me a sharp look. 'Perhaps you ought to find a different vocation.'

I laughed and risked a glance at my watch. I wasn't lying about my boss. Mack Winterson, the *Herald*'s News Editor, had called ten minutes ago.

'Drop what you're doing and get to Bishop's Park. There's a body.'

I had just finished interviewing a member of Hammersmith ambulance crew who had collided with the number 14 bus on the corner of the Fulham Road. Mercifully no one was hurt but, even so, it looked bad ditching the guy mid-interview.

'There's something else.' Mack sounded distracted. 'We've got to fill a double-page spread.'

'Why?'

'Rowntree verdict is delayed. Jury member emergency.'

'Fuck.'

The national media was on high alert waiting for the outcome of the Eric Rowntree court case. Rowntree was a fifty-four-year-old plumber charged with killing his wife and three young sons. With large black sideburns, an oily ponytail and a small pouting mouth, Rowntree looked as if he'd aced an audition for 'deranged killer' in the kind of trash-movie that has critics sniggering into their fists. Apparently fed up with being the proverbial punchbag, his wife, Linda, kicked him out just before Halloween. Rumour has it she'd been shagging a local cab driver, Allen Holmes. Rowntree allegedly repaid her by slaughtering them all in their Battersea maisonette. *Allegedly*. Who was I kidding? Rowntree was guilty. Everyone knew it. But the prosecution had had a hard time proving it. The CCTV camera in the petrol station opposite Linda's house was on the blink that night. Had it been working, it would have shown Rowntree slipping into the house. Still, they were making progress. We were just waiting for the confirmation. But the verdict was due at 5 p.m. yesterday, then at 9 a.m. this morning and now . . .

I kicked the ground with the heel of my boot. 'What else is on the bubble?'

'As of this moment: sweet FA. No one's been paying attention to anything else. We're screwed.'

I rolled my eyes. Mack wasn't known for his grace under pressure. I could picture him pacing up and down by his desk, shiny black brogues scraping away what little of the blue *Herald* carpet was left by his desk, or 'Mack's Patch' as it was dubbed in the office. Mack was a hard taskmaster, but his drive came from a place of fear. Fear that he wasn't good enough, fear that he'd get found out. I pulled my jacket around me as the sun dipped behind a cloud. To say Mack and I had history was an understatement. Screwing my married boss was one of the more messed-up things I'd done lately. When your life blows up and you can't see a way out you tend to make stupid decisions. A smarter one was ending the affair. Mack disagreed, but eventually he saw sense. He was divorcing his wife and, since then, we'd reached a delicate truce; agreed to put the past behind us and act like grown-ups. But there was nothing grown-up about the casual way we picked fights with each other. To be honest, I think we both missed the stress release. Losing yourself in someone else can be addictive.

'Growler's calling an emergency conference this morning. Do not come back empty-handed.'

Growler was the *Herald*'s Editor, Philip Rowley; so-called for his high-pitched nasally voice. But he was as formidable as he was short. I liked to think we shared that, at least.

A loud shout punctured the air. An officer leaned over the railings, one hand on his hat, the other pointing at something we couldn't see.

'What do you think it is?' The dog lady's voice was breathless.

I strode towards the knot of people, notebook in hand, ready with my opening line but a female officer blocked my path. She was slim and neat with a chin that looked as if it had been chiselled in a pencil sharpener. She thrust it towards me, crossing her arms in front of her chest. 'Can I help you, Miss Kent?'

I recognised PC Debbie Waters.

'Nice morning for a walk.' I grinned at her, but she didn't smile back. Waters was too smart to get sucked in, and I respected that about her. I'd heard on the grapevine that she was struggling to make the policing job work around her little boy's schedule after the recent split with her boyfriend. And by 'grapevine', I mean me leaning on every source I had. I like to know as much as possible about every new recruit. In my job, information is currency. I knew PC Waters was fast becoming DCI Sam Durand's righthand officer. And where DCI Durand is concerned, I make it my business to know. We've worked together for years. Durand is a first-class police officer with the right amount of dirt on his hands. We'd grown close in recent months. Close enough to make me wonder if there was something more between us. I shook the image of Durand's rugged face and auburn hair out of my mind. It was easier to tell myself that our relationship was based on scratching each other's backs. Nothing more. At least, not in this lifetime. I've learned the hard way that mixing work and pleasure was the fastest route to a P45. If there were rumours about anything more between Durand and PC Waters, I put it down to idle gossip. The same noise that follows any vaguely successful woman in a male-dominated industry.

'I'm not trespassing.' I gestured towards the blue and white police tape.

Waters glanced towards the river. Her long brown plait swung over her shoulder. A crimson ribbon was tied to the end. I pictured her that morning; the extra few seconds she'd spent fastening it to her hair. Precious seconds she could have spent with her little boy.

'How's life on the Force?'

'Glorious. How's life at the *Herald*?' Her eyes scanned my face, taking in the bloodshot eyes, dark circles and unwashed hair. I knew she wanted to ask more. Waters had seen me at my worst. The days I had lain in a hospital bed, unshowered and pale, my stale breath filling my nostrils, unable to look in the mirror at the purple bruises dotting my neck. When Waters took my statement in that stark white room, she pretended not to notice the tremor in my voice, or the way I gripped the bed. I found out later that Waters called the *Herald* a couple of times to check how I was doing. It was a kindness I wouldn't forget.

'I saw your piece on the Edgware Road riot,' she said. 'Nicely handled.'

I smiled, nodded towards the river. 'So, what have we got?'

'Sophie, listen, there's something you need to kn—' She spotted something over my shoulder, flicked her plait behind her and drew herself up. 'I was just asking Press to stay behind the tape, Sir.'

A man appeared beside us with a ferocious look on his young face. Tufts of sandy-coloured hair sprouted out of his head like the top of a pineapple. A cheap charcoal suit hung off his thin frame.

'Waters, go and check the logbook,' he said in a curt voice.

I stepped forward, plastering a smile on my face. 'I don't think we've met. I'm–'

'I know who you are.'

I frowned. 'Are you in charge of this scene?' When he didn't respond, I pointed to the police tape. 'I'm a crime reporter. This is a crime scene. I'm doing my job.'

'And I'm doing mine.' The man's hand wandered to his earlobe and his aggression spilled out in a short, sharp pinch.

I studied him, trying to read the situation. Being disliked by police is not something I lose sleep over. There are a million reasons why coppers hate reporters. We don't do as we're told, for one. We hold police accountable, for another. But this man's hostility was so potent, I could taste it in the air.

Suddenly, a tinny voice rattled out of the radio in his hand.

'Sir, we've just found a handbag hooked on the railings. Must be hers.'

I raised my eyebrows. 'It's a woman, then.'

He scowled, then leaned towards me, belching coffee breath in my face. 'No comment. Now, piss off.'

'Lovely to meet you, too,' I called out as he stomped away. But my bravado vanished along with him. A CID officer with a personal grudge was very bad for business.

I heard Rowley's voice in my head: *Find me ten ways around the word no, Kent.*

A police van crunched along the path and parked beside the railings. I pulled out my phone to snap pictures and a message blinked at me on the home screen: a voicemail from Charlie Swift, the *Herald*'s Business Editor and one of my best friends. I shut it down and took more photos of the two figures emerging from the police van and pulling on white protective suits.

At that moment, a line of reporters began streaming towards the crime scene. I recognised Stuart Thorp from the *Post* grilling the trio of mums. I nibbled my fingernail. Had I missed something? My eyes slid right and I spotted a figure slumped on a bench by a large oak tree. He was wrapped in a foil blanket and might as well have had a target tacked to his back.

I glanced over my shoulder, then hurried towards him. He was in sportswear: a tight black tank-top and lime-green running shorts.

'Are you thirsty?' The man's head jerked up and I reached into my bag for the unopened bottle of water I hadn't had time to drink. 'Here.' I handed it to him, then sat down on the bench. He pulled his leg away from me for a second, then let it fall back where it was. The leg was smooth and hairless. As he gulped down the water, I stole a glance. Early twenties, blond stubble, white marks around his hairline where sweat had crusted onto his skin.

'I'm guessing you found her,' I said. The man nodded and dug his elbows into his muscly thighs. 'Can you tell me about it?'

He fingered his leather necklace. It was threaded with beaded letters that spelled out S-O-U-L-W-A-R-R-I-O-R, the kind they sell in cheap shops on the Southern Hemisphere gap-year-circuit. 'Are you the police?'

I hesitated then shook my head. 'Press. The *London Herald*.'

'Should I be talking to you?'

'Do you often run in Bishop's Park?'

'I'm training for the marathon. Twenty miles a week.' He coughed again – short, wheezy clicks – and the foil blanket rustled. 'Ran it last year but my hip was playing up. If I can do it sub-four hours I'll be happy.'

I nodded, chewing the inside of my cheek. I didn't want to rush him, but I didn't want to blow the opportunity either. I gazed towards the river. 'What's your name?'

'Adrian.' He cleared his throat. 'Adrian Bronson.' He slid off his glasses and wiped them on his top.

I pulled out my notebook and watched Adrian's eyes flick nervously towards it.

'I'm just after a few facts,' I said, as Adrian twisted the bottle cap in his hand. 'I don't want to do the victim a disservice by getting anything wrong. How did you spot her?'

Adrian thought for a moment. 'I only stopped to take a breather. By the railings there.' He pointed to the spot where the forensics team were setting up a white tent. 'I noticed something in the water. At first I thought it was a coat. Then I saw hair,' he pulled an inhaler out of his pocket, 'lots of it. Red. With things stuck in it. Leaves. And other stuff. I climbed over the railing to get a better look. And that's when I saw the rest of her.'

Adrian shoved the inhaler in his mouth and sucked hard. I didn't speak, wanting him to take his time, knowing how hard this was. In my experience, drowned corpses are among the worst.

The first post-mortem I witnessed was a thirty-eight-year-old homeless woman who'd been found in a canal behind Swiss Cottage Tube station. Police caught her killer; a spineless mouth-breathing drunk with an inferiority complex. When I wrote up the piece, we ran the last-known photograph of the woman. A delicate face with small, pointy teeth and a schoolteacher fringe. She was pretty. Not that it mattered, but I couldn't reconcile that photo with the bloated mess on the coroner's table. Water can do that to a face. So I knew exactly what Adrian was going through.

'What time did you find her?'

He glanced at his shiny watch. 'About an hour ago. I called the police the moment I realised what it was. Waited here. I didn't want her to be alone. Or float away or whatever.' He ground the heel of his trainer into the dirt, and coughed again.

'What was she wearing?'

Adrian licked his lips, trying to unstick his words. 'Black coat. Skirt. No shoes.' He swallowed. 'Her right hand, there was something wrong with it.'

'What do you mean?'

'Like it had been hacked at, or something.'

A wave of nausea burned my stomach, catching me off-guard. I wasn't squeamish. I took a long breath, not wanting to interrupt his flow. 'Did you see anything else?'

Adrian coughed into his hand and took another hit on the inhaler. 'Do you know how long I'll have to hang around?'

I closed my notebook, then handed him my business card. 'Has anyone taken a statement?' He shook his head. 'Speak to that female officer over there. The one with the plait.'

He stood up, but his legs failed and he slumped back down. He gave me a wry smile. 'Sorry, I'm not usually so . . .'

I smiled. 'Her name is PC Waters.'

As he stumbled away, my phone rang.

'Well?' Mack's bark wrong-footed me.

'It's a woman. Just interviewed the jogger who found her. And a bag has turned up; police think it's hers.'

'So who is she?'

'I haven't got that far.'

'Chop chop, Kent. You're almost out of time.' He hung up and I collapsed against the bench, closing my eyes as the adrenaline seeped out of me.

I sighed and scrolled down to Charlie's voicemail. When I needed cheering up, Charlie was the man to do it. Laid-back, popular, Charlie was known for his dry one-liners and infectious smile. Which is all the more impressive when you consider the double tragedy he had suffered. I never met his late wife, Lizzie, but I knew they hadn't been married long when she was diagnosed with leukaemia. In the end it wasn't the leukaemia that killed her. Lizzie went for a swim in the Serpentine Lido and never made it back. Charlie took a fortnight off and returned to the office, deflecting people's condolences with a tight smile. Gradually his smile became larger; the charisma returned. Most people soon forgot. But I wasn't most people. The closer we got, the more I understood how deeply Charlie buried his pain. I knew the effort it took to plaster the smile in place because I was doing the same thing myself. Over the years we picked up each other's pieces – and many long nights in the newsroom led to a friendship I'd come to cherish. One evening, three years ago, Charlie told me he'd started seeing Emily, the young pretty wedding planner who'd organised his wedding to Lizzie. He raised his chin and waited for me to judge him, but I'm the last person to judge anyone.

I hit 'play' and Charlie's deep voice filled my ear. 'Hello? Is that the great Sophie Kent, reporter extraordinaire?' I rolled my eyes at his naff American accent. 'Call me when you get this. I need to talk to you about something . . . personal.'

I pressed 'call back' and put a hand over my ear as a plane whistled low overhead. Charlie's phone rang out to voicemail: *'You've reached Charlie Swift, leave some words.'*

I dug my nails into the wooden bench. 'Here are some words for you: Mondays suck. I'm on a crime scene and the officer in charge wants me dead. I swear, dude. The look in his eye. Also: he looks like a demented pineapple. That reminds me, can you pick me up one of those radioactive smoothies from the canteen? And, yes, I want whipped cream on top. Like I said: Mondays suck. Back in the office soon. Can't wait to hear the personal news. Are you finally coming out of the closet? Because, FYI, your sock choice has been betraying your secret for yea—'

The beep cut me off. I glanced towards the railings where PC Waters was resting a hand on Adrian's arm. She held my

2

I wedged my phone under my ear as I watched the *Herald*'s City Editor, Spencer Storey, lob balls of paper into the bin by his desk. He scored just as DCI Durand picked up and a jeer went up from the City desk.

'What's that noise?'

'The office toddlers. Where were you this morning? The body in Bishop's Park. It's your patch.' I heard the tinny tones of daytime television in the background. 'Where are you?'

Durand's deep voice grazed my ear. 'This isn't a good time, Sophie.'

I drummed my pen against the desk, ignoring him. 'Who's the new guy?'

'What new guy?'

'Prince Charming.'

There was a pause. 'So, you met DCI Toby Golden.'

'Why do I know that name?'

Durand cleared his throat. 'His dad. Paul.'

My pen froze mid-air. 'Fuck.'

DCI Paul Golden was retired now, but in 1994 he oversaw the Amanda Barnes murder case. The teenage model who was strangled in the woods near her home in Liverpool. Police uncovered DNA evidence in the shed at the bottom of her garden that pointed to what looked like an open-and-shut case. And when more DNA evidence was found, it was ignored, because those in charge felt they had their man. It was a decision that led to two more women suffering a similar fate. The man behind the decision was DCI Paul Golden. When I revisited the story recently, the *Herald* outed Golden. It was harsh – and the news team had argued late into the night about whether to withhold his name. A situation like that is rarely black and white. As another copper pointed out to me, forensic testing is expensive; you have to prioritise. Golden made a judgement call. The wrong one. And Rowley wanted justice. Except Rowley's name wasn't on the piece.

'So he's not a *Herald* fan.'

I regretted my flippant tone the moment I heard the disapproval in Durand's voice. 'It's more than that. His dad has really suffered. Graffiti on the house, hate mail, that kind of thing. People in that neighbourhood don't need any more excuses to mistrust the police.'

I bit my tongue, not wanting to get drawn into an argument about who was to blame for the public's loss of faith in the police. It was hard enough working the system without curveballs like this being hurled at my head.

'So Golden is holding me personally responsible?'

Durand turned off the TV. 'Look, Golden is young. Aggressive. He has a great track record but, when he gets the bit between his teeth, it's hard to stop him.' He paused and I heard the smile in his voice. 'Remind you of anyone else?'

I laughed, in spite of myself, and the tension in my shoulders eased a fraction. 'How do you do that?'

'Do what?'

'Talk me down off the ledge so easily.'

'You think this is easy?'

A warm silence stretched between us. I pictured the slow smile spreading across Durand's face and my cheeks flushed.

I cleared my throat. 'So Golden is the new you?'

'For the moment.'

I debated pushing it, then changed my mind. 'Are you involved at all?'

'Let's just say I'm being kept in the loop.'

'So the identity of that woman in the river–'

'Hasn't been released. Nice try though.'

'Come on, Sam. I'm way behind, especially now DCI Dickhead is stonewalling me.'

Durand paused and I felt the air go still. The way it does when a game-changer is about to come my way. 'I can tell you this, and only because it's you,' he said quietly. 'The victim was a lawyer. One of the Big Five firms.'

'And her surname rhymes with . . .' I was only half-joking, but Durand had already hung up.

I opened my drawer and fished out a snack bar. I'd skipped breakfast and was paying the price for hitting a crime scene on an empty stomach. I craned my neck to look for Charlie but he was nowhere to be seen. Sighing, I pulled up LegalAid's league table of the country's top law firms, then started scrolling through photographs of their employees, looking for women with long, red hair. Ten minutes later I stretched my arms above my head, then dropped them to my side with a sigh. I yawned and a mug appeared in front of me. I could taste the coffee without even touching it. Kate Fingersmith's brew was like liquid speed in a mug.

'Voila! Strong and black. As I like my–'

'Former Presidents, yeah I know.' I forced a smile. Kate launched herself into her chair, cackling. She was still obsessed with Barack Obama. Photographs of him were sellotaped all over her computer. 'It's the swagger,' she once told me. 'He can press my nuclear button any time he wants.'

I shuffled forward in my chair. 'What's going down?'

Kate wrapped a brown curl round her finger. 'Same shit, different day. There's been a development on the Rowntree verdict. My source tells me there are rumours he's going to walk.'

'But he's guilty.'

Kate snorted into her mug. 'You've been around the block enough times to know that means nada. Something to do with inadmissible DNA evidence. I'm heading down to the courthouse after Conference.'

I nodded, shuddering as a mouthful of coffee stuck to the back of my throat.

Kate rolled her eyes. 'Don't pull that face, you ungrateful cow. You can make your own next time.'

I swivelled back to my computer. Twenty minutes later, I had two leads: Laura Bradley at Thorman & Gray, and Sabrina Hobbs at Hamilton Law.

I dialled the first number.

A robotic voice. 'Thorman & Gray.'

'Could you put me through to Laura Bradley?'

'One moment, please.'

I bobbed my foot up and down in time to the pip pip pip.

A bright voice. 'Laura Bradley speaking.'

'Sorry, wrong number.' I hung up and punched in the second number.

'Good morning, Hamilton Law.'

'Sabrina Hobbs, please.' I rifled through my notebook while I waited, feeling faintly nauseous as I recalled what the jogger had told me about the victim's hand.

'This is Sabrina's assistant, Rachel Cornish. Can I help you?'

'Is Sabrina in?'

'I'm afraid not. She's in a meeting.'

'Do you know what time she'll be finished?'

'Who is this, please?'

'It's a personal call.' I added a dose of authority to my voice hoping to shut down her questions.

'Right, well. I was expecting her in already but she's been held up. I'll let her know you called.' It was smoothly done but her words ran together too quickly. *She's lying.*

I hung up and stared at the photograph on my screen. Sabrina's red hair fell a couple of inches below her collarbone. She had a heart-shaped face; a small chin with a cleft in the middle and a smile that showed no teeth. She looked like the sort of woman who would pretend-order a gin and tonic at the office party and substitute it for sparkling water. She was a Partner at Hamilton Law. A First from Edinburgh University. No Facebook account but that didn't surprise me. My flatmate Poppy Reynolds was a lawyer and she once told me that employees were warned off social media.

On a hunch I searched for Sabrina's assistant, Rachel Cornish. Evidently that warning didn't stretch to admin staff. I clicked through her photographs. Rachel twirling around a dance floor in a peach bridesmaid dress; reclining by a swimming pool with sunburned shoulders; giving a bleary thumbs-up in a Santa's hat. The caption read: *Hamilton Law knows how to parteeeee.*

I zoomed into the tangle of people behind Rachel. On the right of the group was Sabrina, wine-glass in hand, leaning against a dark-haired man who was kissing her neck. I raised my eyebrows. Maybe she wasn't as buttoned up as she looked. I hovered the arrow over his face and a name flashed up: Bert Hughes. A Junior Partner at Hamilton Law. Almost as an afterthought, I pulled up Twitter. There she was: @SHobbsLaw. Sabrina mainly retweeted news nibs and court verdicts. Then my eye caught on something. Five days ago Sabrina had 'liked' a tweet posted by Charlie Swift. I scanned the feed. Sabrina was often the first to respond to Charlie's tweets, and vice versa.

I drained my coffee and wandered over to the Business Department. Charlie's deputy, Adam Gamble, was on the phone. I perched on Adam's desk, distracted by a commotion coming from Pictures. Austin Lansdowne, the *Herald*'s Deputy Editor and 'bad cop', was tearing a strip off a picture researcher.

'We want people to *pick up* the newspaper, you fucking moron,' he said, slamming his palms on the desk and machine-gunning the terrified woman with saliva. 'Legs. We want to see *legs.* If I see one more photograph of Middleton from the waist up, I'm going to lob you off the roof.' Lansdowne stalked off, looking for his next fight.

Adam held up a hand, mouthing 'two minutes', and I killed time by thumbing through yesterday's edition. ROWNTREE VERDICT: COUNTDOWN. Underneath the headline was a family snap of Rowntree's three sons taken last Christmas. Harry, Danny and Jamie were sitting round a table; all shaggy hair, pimples and teeth. Harry's party hat had slipped down his head making his ears stick out like a mouse. He leaned against his eldest brother, Danny, who was on the cusp of growing into his ratty features. Except none of the Rowntree boys would grow into anything now.

'What can I do for you, Kent?'

I tore my eyes away from the front page. Adam's black moustache was coated in coffee froth and his top button was undone behind his tie.

'I need to speak to Charlie.'

'He's not here.'

'Where is he?'

'Fucked if I know.' Adam gave his horn-rimmed glasses a quick wipe with his sleeve, then caught my expression and sighed. 'He's probably at a briefing.'

'Where's your chart of doom?' I was referring to the multi-coloured timetable tacked to the wall above Charlie's desk. Lansdowne had recently forced one on every department; his way of keeping tabs on the staff. No one liked it. Rowley gave his reporters a long leash. The less we were in the office the better; he wanted us out in the wild, chasing stories. But times were changing. I glanced at the Business chart. Today was blank.

I pushed myself off Adam's desk. 'When his Lordship gets in, tell him to get his arse over to News. And tell him he owes me a smoothie.'

Back at my desk, I dialled Charlie again. '*You've reached Charlie Swift. Leave some words.*'

A shadow passed over my desk.

'Kent.' Mack's voice vibrated somewhere between irritation and desperation. 'Rowley's leaning on me hard for content. Where are we with the Thames body?'

'A tentative ID, but nothing concrete.'

Mack tugged at his sleeve and I caught a glimpse of his cufflink; round and silver, with a 'W' engraved in the middle. 'Where's Kate?' he said. 'How's she getting on with the M4 lorry crash?'

'Ask her yourself.'

Kate appeared at his shoulder, and pulled a face. 'What's kicking chicken?'

Mack's expression darkened at the sight of her. Kate took great pleasure in ruffling feathers. Her poker-face was so good that people often mistook her for a bitch. Not that she cared. Kate was a ballsy news veteran with a sharp tongue and no off-switch. Mack didn't know how to handle her. It didn't help that his sense of worth was tied up in other people's respect for him, and he didn't get that respect had to be earned. He'd perfected the hand-wringing knack of looking busy, particularly in front of Rowley, but it had been months since he'd brought in a story.

I suspected it really boiled down to a lack of confidence; the result of reaching the dizzy heights of Desk Editor through the art of office politics, rather than hard grind. It was a mystery to me that Mack had been promoted above Kate.

Mack opened his mouth to speak but was interrupted by Lansdowne bellowing across the office. 'Conference . . . NOW.'

We jumped up and filed into the meeting room next to Rowley's office. The heating was on the blink and the 'sudden surge in Spring temperatures' meant it was even hotter than usual. Someone had improvised by sticking a fan in the corner that blew our pages across the table. It also wafted a stale sewage smell into the room and I covered my nose with my hand.

'Bloody Bannerman,' Kate said through a pinched nose, as Douglas Bannerman, the *Herald*'s Managing Editor, shuffled to his seat. In his early fifties, Bannerman sported the ash-like complexion of a man who's spent too long indoors. And his sluggish digestive system was office lore. Each morning he drank a double espresso, disappeared into the toilet with a copy of *What Car?*, then trailed the smell around with him all day.

An emergency conference called for skeleton staff: the top dogs and the news team. Rahid Sawney, the *Herald*'s junior reporter, was rifling through his notes with a shaky hand. He caught my eye and gave me a small, dry smile. I smiled back encouragingly. I'd been at the *Herald* for years and Conference still reduced my insides to liquid. Pitching an idea was the moment you stuck your head above the parapet, and I'd watched too many heads get blown to smithereens. Pressure to perform was rocketing as newspapers battled falling readership, limited resources, and social media stole what little impact we had left.

'Right,' Lansdowne punched through the door, 'Rowntree has shafted us. Woe betide anyone in this room who does the same.' He threw himself into a chair with such force that his notepad skated across the table and plopped on the floor. He glared at Rahid who picked it up and handed it back.

The door opened again and Rowley strode in. His round stomach poked through his unbuttoned jacket as he sat down at the head of the table. His bald head was the colour of pine-wood. He had just got back from a week in the Seychelles, where, judging by how many emails the department heads received, he spent the entire holiday glued to his laptop.

'Let's make this quick,' he said in his high-pitched voice. 'I have a meeting with the Board at midday.'

There was a collective fidget around the table. Ever since the first lot of grim-faced suits streamed into Rowley's office a month ago, rumours had been circulating. Was it a merger? A takeover? The apocalypse? Rowley had become increasingly absent and Lansdowne's behaviour even more extreme. The whole newsroom was on high alert. Men in suits never brought good news.

Rowley glanced at the ceiling, then at Mack. 'Your top three, please.'

Mack flipped open his notebook and patted his shiny black hair. 'We're fleshing out the Coventry lorry crash. Four people are in a critical condition, three Poles and a Brit. Rahid is pulling together background on the driver.'

'Cause of crash?' Lansdowne's razor-sharp gaze belied his bored tone. He liked to pretend he wasn't listening so you didn't see the right hook coming.

'Possible DUI. We'll know more soon; we're close to securing an interview with him. If we get the lorry driver to talk, that could make a page, right?' Mack worked his fingernail with his teeth.

Rowley mmmhmmed, which meant 'stop wasting my time'.

Kate took a deep breath. 'Two words: Tube strike.' Kate was a great jazz-hander. One of the only staffers who didn't seem to feel the pressure. A bomb could go off in the newsroom and Kate would simply dust herself off, grab her notebook, and help everyone down the fire escape while recording eyewitness accounts and writing the headers.

'The bastards are planning a Bank Holiday assault on the capital.' She paused dramatically, knowing full well that Rowley's in-laws were visiting from South Africa and he was being forced to stay in London.

Rowley's jaw clenched as the nightmare of a grid-locked, tourist-clogged weekend bloomed before his eyes. 'What's the angle?' he said.

Kate leaned forward. 'Word is the Transport Secretary approached them for talks but the union leader kept it from the union. I doubt they'll be too chuffed to hear it.'

Lansdowne slammed a fist down on the table. 'Yes, yes, yes, but where's the death? Are you telling me with sixty million people currently residing in this country, that we don't have anything more exciting than a Tube strike and a lorry crash on the M4?' He held up a thick hand. 'What people really want is sex and death. So unless any of you have a sex scandal you'd like to get off your chests . . .'

I rolled my eyes, then wished I hadn't as Lansdowne's eyes speared me to the chair. He gave a menacing smile. 'Is there something you'd like to contribute, Sophie? Do tell us if you disagree with the collective sixty-plus years of experience sitting at the head of this table.'

Adrenaline coursed through me, unsticking my tongue from the roof of my mouth. 'I have a murder. A woman's body in the Thames this morning.' Lansdowne tipped his chair back, crossed his arms, momentarily placated by the prospect of a dead body. Female, too. *The best kind*, I thought spitefully. I filled them in on my progress so far.

Rowley tapped his phone against the table. 'So, we have a name and a workplace.'

'The name is unconfirmed,' I said, hearing – and hating – the apology in my voice. 'But I'm going to her law firm and I found this on Facebook.' I pushed the Christmas party photograph towards them. 'I'm interested in this guy, Bert Hughes. Plus she's been in contact with Charlie Swift on Twitter so that could be another route into her life.'

Mack, encouraged by Rowley's expression, placed his forearms on the table and leaned forward. 'I really think this could work. Off the back of the PM's speech about crime rates decreasing. Trying to attract women's votes.' I held my breath, willing Mack on. 'Her death sticks a rocket up that. And anything that makes those Tory twats look bad, right?'

My goodwill towards him deflated. Mack kept his private schooling and second home in Wiltshire on the down-low, thinking it eased the path up Rowley's arse. Rowley was a York-shireman, a die-hard socialist, the first in his family to finish school, let alone go to university. He liked to moan about capitalism but we all knew it was half-baked. It's hard to preach socialism when you're chauffeured to work in the back of a glossy Mercedes.

Rowley cleared his throat. 'Order of priority is this: dead lawyer, lorry crash, Tube strike. Mack, email me an update at 4 p.m. And if Rowntree comes good before then we can all breathe a sigh of relief.'

He closed his notebook and we all stood up, desperate to escape.

'Sophie, hold on a moment, please.'

When everyone had left, Rowley peered at me over his half-moon glasses. 'How are you?'

'Eager to get on with the job.'

'How did therapy go?'

I pictured my final session. Dr Spado, in his trademark polo-neck sweater, fingering his glasses and failing to hide his irritation as I dodged his questions about my parents. My fractured relationships with a narcissistic mother and a bully of a father were my business, not his.

'How are you sleeping?' Dr Spado had asked, his small brown eyes scanning my face.

I chewed my fingernail. Recently, I'd allowed my personal life to cloud my brain. I made a mistake – a lapse in judgement – that put the *Herald* in a difficult situation, and so Rowley fired me. Just like that. I realised then that the *Herald* wasn't just a job, it was my lighthouse in the dark. Although I was eventually reinstated, fear of losing everything had coiled itself around me like a vine. If I told Dr Spado the truth, he would never have given me the all-clear to return to the *Herald*. So I told him the nightmares were loosening their grip. Then I showed him a photograph of me and my brother, Tommy, that I'd started carrying around in my purse. I told him how I could look at Tommy's shy smile and freckled nose without my mind skipping directly on to the next thought: that my little brother was murdered, and he'd called me for help but I was mad at him and didn't pick up the phone so he died thinking I didn't care, and how that thought no longer made me want to climb into the space between my bed and the wall and never come out. I repeated it over and over, smiling until my face hurt. Dr Spado sighed and scribbled out a prescription with his black fountain pen. That night I went home and counted out the pills, counted out the sleeps.

I cleared my throat. 'Therapy made a big difference.' The chatter in my brain was loud – *blink, smile, smile, blink*. 'I'm sleeping, working. Recovering. Really, you don't need to ask.'

Rowley gave me a shrewd look, then gestured to the door. 'I'll keep asking until you tell me the truth.'

3

Hamilton Law, a tall red-brick building on the north side of Manchester Square, was hidden under scaffolding. I dodged a group of anorak-clad tourists and pushed through the revolving door into a reception area that smelt of peppermint and expensive perfume. The lobby echoed with the tinkling sound of a waterfall cascading into an oval pond. Bright orange fish zigzagged through the black water.

I paused at Reception where large copper letters spelled out HAMILTON LAW on the marble wall.

A pretty Asian woman peered up at me, a blank smile on her face. 'Can I help you?'

'Is Bert Hughes here?'

'Do you have an appointment?'

'I'm a family friend. In the area. Thought I'd surprise him.'

'I'm afraid I can't let you up without permission.'

I leaned on the desk and smiled at her. 'Not even for a surprise?'

The woman gave me a cool look, then picked up the phone. 'Louise, it's Dawn downstairs. I have a lady here for Mr Hughes. Says she's a family friend.' She drummed her fingers on the desk. 'Right, I'll let her know.' She hung up. 'Mr Hughes is in

New York right now. Won't be back until tomorrow. Can I take a message?'

As I opened my mouth to speak, the lift doors opened and a slim brunette woman appeared. She was rifling through her tote bag, a scowl on her angular face. I watched her glide through the lobby; her movements balletic and graceful.

'Rachel Cornish?' I followed her to the revolving door.

She spun round, dark eyebrows raised. 'Yes?'

She'd scraped her hair into a tight bun that pulled at her temples. Her eyes were red, as if she'd been crying. Did she already know Sabrina Hobbs was dead?

'Could I take up a few minutes of your time?'

'Who are you?'

I hesitated, then shot for the truth. 'Sophie Kent. I'm a reporter with the *London Herald*. I'm working on a sto—'

Rachel held up a manicured hand. 'Yeah, I know. Bullying in the workplace. I don't want to be involved. Even though this place can go to hell.' She shouted the last part over her shoulder and the receptionist's eyebrows twitched.

I fell in step with Rachel as she pounded the street with sharp, angry strides. 'Can I buy you a coffee?'

Rachel didn't object. After a moment, she sighed. 'Have you ever worked somewhere that – I don't know – no matter how hard you work, the fact you don't have a penis is all that matters?'

I snorted, then caught myself when I saw the serious expression on her face. 'I work at a newspaper. The ultimate sausage factory.'

The corners of Rachel's mouth rose. 'I'll take your sausage factory and raise you a law firm. Honestly, if only–' She stopped, remembering who she was talking to.

We reached a small café with two chairless tables outside, a red canopy and a laminated menu tacked to the greasy window.

I followed Rachel inside. 'What can I get you?'

She leaned elegantly against the counter. 'Americano. Black. Cheers.' She pulled out her phone and pecked at the keyboard with red fingernails.

I got in the queue, debating how to tackle Rachel. She wasn't behaving like she'd just found out her boss had been murdered. Which meant I had an awkward conversation coming my way. Breaking bad news went with the territory. I never enjoyed doing it, but I also didn't enjoy screwing up a lead.

I held out her coffee. 'Fancy getting some air?'

Rachel stuffed her phone into her bag and followed me outside. We wandered back towards Manchester Square in silence.

Eventually Rachel spoke. 'I'm sorry. About before. One of those mornings.'

'What happened?'

Rachel sat down on a bench and sipped her coffee. She winced as it burned her lip. 'I really don't want to be involved in the sexism story, you know. Not my style.'

I wondered what she was talking about, and was about to ask when she glanced at her watch. 'I don't have long . . . sorry, what was your name again?'

'Sophie.' I nodded. 'In that case, I'll cut to the chase. It's about your boss, Sabrina. I'm afraid I have some difficult news.'

I cleared my throat. 'She's dead. I don't know much more than that right now.'

'Sabrina's dead?' Rachel jolted her cup and coffee splashed over the side.

I grabbed it from her and she shook the hot liquid from her hand. 'Are you OK?'

'No. Wow. Sabrina's *dead*?'

I nodded slowly, giving Rachel a moment. I knew she'd have questions and I didn't want to interrupt her flow.

Rachel blew on the raw skin. 'How did it happen?'

I hesitated, then softened my voice. 'Her body was found in the river this morning. I was there covering the story. I'm so sorry.'

Rachel looked away. We sat in silence for a moment watching an overfed pigeon peck at the remains of a burger. I could feel Rachel struggling to keep herself afloat so I threw her a lifeline in the form of a bland question.

'How long have you worked at Hamilton Law?' I said, handing Rachel her coffee.

'Three, no, four years.' She stared at the ground, her voice wobbling. 'Before this I was a dancer. I went to London Dance Academy, graduated top of my class.'

That explained her dancer's posture. 'What happened?'

'I did one show. Chorus line of *Cabaret*, took a tumble and this happened.' She thumped her knee. 'Torn ligament. Bye bye, dance career.'

'So now you work at a law firm.'

She gave a tight smile. 'Secretary. Bit of a comedown after the bright lights of the West End.'

'Have you always worked for Sabrina?'

Rachel shook her head. 'No. Mr Whitaker first, until he left. Then Mr Hughes, then Sabrina.'

I frowned. 'Mr Hughes? As in Bert Hughes?'

'Yes. But only for a couple of months.'

'Why?'

Rachel looked away. 'We weren't a good fit.'

I drained my coffee and shoved the empty cup in my bag. The slant of her jaw told me I wasn't getting any further. I leaned forward and took a breath. 'Rachel, it's my job to write up Sabrina's death. I don't want to let her down. Can you tell me about her? Anything that gives me a sense of who she was.'

Rachel shifted her weight. 'Listen, I don't want to get in trouble. I don't love HL, but I also don't want to get fired.'

I nodded. 'I won't name you.'

Rachel took a deep lungful of air. 'This is crazy. I only spoke to her Saturday morning.'

'How did she seem?'

'Sabrina-ish.'

'What do you mean?'

Rachel sighed. 'She called me from her acupuncture appointment. Sabrina was very into alternative therapy. Acupuncture, reiki, crystals, that kind of thing. I had to carve out space in her diary for regular appointments.'

'So the call on Saturday . . .'

'. . . was because I'd muddled up her dates. I'd booked her in for reiki instead of reflexology and she was pissed off.'

'Right.'

Rachel caught my tone and smiled. 'Look, Sabrina is – was – high-maintenance. Attractive, successful, rich, fit. But, aside from work, she didn't have a lot else going on in her life. Her wellbeing became something of a hobby.'

I nodded. 'Not much else going on. Does that mean no love interest?'

Rachel fell still. 'I can't comment on that.'

I could tell the shock was subsiding and it was dawning on her that she was sitting with a reporter answering sensitive questions. It was time to up the stakes.

I smoothed down my trousers. 'You know, the *Herald* runs a law supplement every year. A round-up of the fifty best and worst firms to work for. I can mention your concerns to the team. No law firm wants to be outed for inequality these days. It might help shake things up a bit.'

Rachel gave me an odd look. 'You're too late.'

'What do you mean?'

'Hamilton Law is already being exposed. By your own paper.'

I frowned. 'The *Herald* is writing about Hamilton Law?'

Rachel smiled sadly. 'Sabrina wasn't one to take it lying down. She knew the best way to fight bullying was by exposing it.'

'You mean in the press?'

Rachel nodded. 'She's been meeting someone. A guy. I don't know his name, but I know he was interested in the story.'

The penny dropped. I logged on to Twitter and pulled up Charlie Swift's photograph. 'Is this the journalist she spoke to?'

Rachel peered at my screen. 'Yeah. That's him. Good-looking guy.'

I nodded, used to the reaction. Half the women at the *Herald* secretly fancied Charlie, the other half openly did. Years ago Charlie inadvertently caused mass hysteria by pitching up to an office fancy dress party as Spider-Man. I've never let him live the red Lycra down.

I leaned back against the bench, irritated that my carrot had been taken off the table. 'What was Sabrina actually fighting?'

Rachel flexed her toes. 'She was promoted to Partner recently, beat off stiff internal competition to get it, too.'

'But doesn't that disprove your sexism theory?'

'Sure, on the one hand. But it's what happened since that upset her. Have you heard of LegalLens.com?' Rachel drained her coffee cup and crumpled it between her small hands. 'It's the legal industry's gossip website. Who's moving where; who got hired and fired. There's a "Wicked Whispers" section. Anyone can upload things to it.' She sniffed. 'Recently there has been stuff on there about Sabrina.'

'What kind of stuff?'

'That she was on antidepressants, mentally unstable, not fit to practise, that sort of thing.'

'Was she on antidepressants?'

Rachel narrowed her eyes. 'That's not the point.'

I'll take that as a yes. 'Was she ever named?'

'No, but there aren't many red-headed Partners at London's Big Five firms.'

Rachel had a point. It hadn't taken me long to track Sabrina down. A siren shrieked down the road next to us and I waited for it to pass.

'Why didn't Sabrina complain?'

'She did. The comments got taken down. But then more reappeared.'

I knew what Rachel meant. As a female journalist, I came in for my fair share of 'below the line' comments. Male colleagues were usually pulled up on their choice of phrasing, I was pulled up because my boobs weren't big enough or because I was 'asking for it'.

'Did Sabrina know who was posting the comments?'

'No idea.' Rachel kicked the toe of her court shoe into the gravel.

I knew she was hiding something but I didn't want to scare her off. I pulled out my phone, and brought up Rachel's Facebook page. 'Can you tell me about this photograph?'

Rachel shielded the screen against the sun's glare. 'The Christmas party? What do you want to know?'

'Behind you, there. Sabrina and Bert Hughes. Was something going on between them?'

She shrugged. 'You know what Christmas parties are like.'

'I thought you said she was too busy for a relationship.'

'Define "relationship".' There was a bitter edge to her voice.

'You didn't approve of Bert?'

'What can I say? He's a charismatic guy.' Rachel rolled her eyes. 'Look, I don't know the ins and outs. The whole staff went on one of those cringeworthy bonding trips in February. Sabrina and I had too many cocktails on the first night and she admitted she was involved with someone. Didn't give me much. Just that she was trying to get out of the relationship.'

'Why?'

'He was unsuitable.'

I frowned at the photograph. 'You think she meant Bert?'

'Wouldn't be the first member of staff he's shagged, put it that way.'

I nodded, studying Rachel out of the corner of my eye.

Rachel's phone rang and she glanced at the screen before cancelling the call. 'Shit, I have to go.' She stood up, then hesitated, looking unsure of herself. 'What do I tell the office? About Sabrina.'

I put a hand on her arm. 'It's up to you. There's a good chance the police have already informed the CEO. The cat won't be in the bag for long.' I handed her my business card. 'You've been so helpful, Rachel but, please, if there's anything else.'

She nodded, then glided off, looking more ballerina-like than ever.

For a second I closed my eyes and turned my head towards the sun. Then I fired off an email to Charlie.

Seriously, stop playing hard to get. I need to talk to you about Sabrina Hobbs and Hamilton Law. CALL ME.

A peal of laughter made me look up. A group of schoolchildren filed across the square, holding onto a rope, bumping and jostling like ducklings. My eyes landed on the tiny boy at the end. His cap fell off revealing a head of fluffy white hair. Just as my throat started to close, my phone rang.

I pounced on it. 'Charlie?'

'I wish. It's Kate. Can you talk?'

'Yep.' I took a shaky breath, then slung my bag over my shoulder and walked towards the road.

'Listen, the police have been here.'

'What?'

'They were in with Growler. Two of them. Man and a woman.'

'A blond man?' An image of DCI Golden's ferocious expression flashed through my mind. Was I in trouble?

'Growler's having a pow-wow with Lansdowne now, but Sophie,' Kate lowered her voice, 'I think it's about Charlie.'

I stopped walking. 'Charlie?'

'Mack overheard them asking about his connection to Sabrina Hobbs.'

I pressed myself against the railing as a group of office workers sidled past. 'I'm still trying to get hold of him,' I told her. 'But listen to this.' I relayed what Rachel had just told me.

'So Charlie was working on a story with the victim.'

'Apparently so. Can you ask Adam about it?'

'Ask him yourself. He wants me to patch him into the call.'

A moment later I heard Adam clear his throat. 'Soph? Listen, don't be mad but I wasn't entirely honest with you this morning. Charlie . . . this isn't the first time he's disappeared lately.'

'What do you mean?' A lorry rumbled past, its brakes squealing. The sound cut straight through me.

Adam was still talking. 'Ever . . . died . . . acting.'

I put a hand over my ear, willing the lorry to move on. 'What? I didn't hear that.'

'Ever since Charlie's mum died. He's been acting weird.'

I raced back towards the lawn where it was quieter. 'What did you just say?'

'Charlie's mum died.'

'When?'

'Recently, I think.' A pause. 'I thought you knew. Um. Look, I don't think he broadcast it to everyone.'

'I'm not everyone, Adam.'

I bent forward, feeling winded. For Charlie not to have told me his mum died was unthinkable. Vanessa was an alcoholic. It was one of things we bonded over. We both understood what it meant to have an addict in your life: the anxiety, the guilt, the lows, the even lower lows. 'The last favour she did me was four decades ago when she squeezed me out of her you-know-what,' Charlie once told me, a scowl on his face. As far as I knew he had very little contact with Vanessa, but even so, her death must have hit him hard.

Suddenly, Adam's earlier comment hit me. 'What do you mean this isn't the first time Charlie's disappeared?'

Adam sighed. 'Look, I don't want to get him in trouble. I'm only saying this now because Rowley is asking for him and I don't know what to do.'

I nodded. Charlie was the kind of guy you wanted to cover for. The kind who always had your back.

'I remember the day his mum died because our junior, Greg, was off with a vomiting bug and we were short-staffed,' Adam continued. 'I was secretly relieved when Charlie said he'd come in anyway.' He paused. 'At first he was OK. But he's been acting more and more weirdly. Coming in late, biting our heads off. Which isn't like him, as you know. Sometimes he doesn't even show up to work at all. I've been doing my best to cover his tracks but now Rowley is on my case and–'

'Adam.' I could hear the rising panic and cut him off. I knew exactly what he meant. Charlie had been struggling with something lately, but he clammed up whenever I broached the subject. *How could he not have told me his mum died?* 'Listen, don't drop him in it with Rowley yet. Give me a chance to find him.' My voice sounded stronger than I felt.

'Where are you?' Kate sounded distracted.

'Manchester Square,' I said, as another siren howled in the distance setting my teeth on edge. 'Has anyone contacted his wife, Emily?'

Kate sighed. 'That's another reason I'm calling. Emily's not answering her phone.'

'You want me to try their flat?'

'She'll talk to you, Soph. At the very least she can give us a steer. Call me in an hour.'

I emerged from Regent's Park Tube station and scampered along Albany Street, past rows of white-stucco Georgian terraces that resembled a BBC period-drama set. The sun was high in the sky and I shielded my eyes as I scanned road names trying to remember Charlie and Emily's exact address. Ten minutes later, I gripped the black railings on the corner of Delaware Street, my heart thudding in my chest. I took a moment to let the adrenaline dissipate. I didn't want to worry Emily.

While Regent's Park was a lofty, leafy part of London, the Swifts lived at the shabby end. Made worse by the state of their apartment block. It was built in the sixties – short and squat, with small windows and grimy yellow bricks – and was in the process of being modernised. A developer bought the block next to theirs and was joining the two buildings, except someone didn't dot the 'i's properly on the planning application and it got rejected after building work started. Now it was in a grim state. Half under scaffolding. A large tarpaulin flapping in the breeze. 'It's been like this for months,' Charlie told me in the canteen queue one morning. 'A total shit-show. Builders made bloody great holes all over the building, then patched them up and buggered off.'

As I waited for my heart rate to slow, I thought back to the first time I visited the flat. A house-warming party two years ago, before Emily and Charlie were married: all gin cocktails, Michael Bublé and a thousand candles. As I stood next to the makeshift bar in the sitting room, Charlie had sidled up.

I pointed to the enormous flamingo-shaped ice bucket and Charlie whispered, 'Emily doesn't do things by halves.'

That was the first night I met Emily. A pretty blonde with huge, blue eyes that gave her a startled look. She smelt of lemons and, after I kissed her on both cheeks, she pressed her business card into my hand. Thick white card, letterpressed with black script: *Emily Danson: wedding planner.*

'Charlie's told me all about you,' she said in a high-pitched voice. 'I'd love to plan your wedding one day.'

I swigged my drink. 'Can you find me a groom too?'

'Surely you don't need any help. Look at you!' The bridge of her nose wrinkled.

Emily told me her plans to branch into eco-weddings – 'the next big thing' – and how her two-year stint in California gave her a renewed respect and awe for the planet. 'People over there are so much more enlightened. One bride got married in a dress made entirely from toilet paper.'

'Handy for the pre-wedding jitters,' I said as my martini hit the back of my throat.

Charlie snorted and Emily laid a hand on his chest. 'You're too funny. Charlie told me how much you make him laugh.' This time the smile didn't reach her eyes.

Later that night she pulled me into a lemony hug and I could feel her spine through her chiffon blouse. 'We must get together soon. If only we could find you a date. Charlie thinks of you as his little sister. He'd be thrilled to see you settled.'

Since then our paths had crossed often. Once Emily realised I had no interest in sleeping with Charlie, she'd thawed. I had a lot of time for her. Some of Charlie's friends had been less than welcoming. Many felt it was in poor taste, hooking up with the woman who'd planned Charlie's first wedding. My attitude is that you have to meet people somehow. And if Emily put an end to Charlie's long, lonely nights at the *Herald*, she was good enough for me.

I buzzed apartment 1B, glancing over my shoulder for any sign of the police. No answer. I buzzed again and was about to leave when the door opened and a tall man in a navy jacket slipped past, brushing me with his rucksack. I darted inside and paused as my eyes adjusted to the darkness, breathing in the stranger's trail of aftershave. I crossed the hallway to Charlie and Emily's green front door and knocked. All was quiet. When I called Emily's mobile, I could hear it ringing through the door. I pulled out a business card and scribbled on the back 'Call me urgently, Sx' then slid it under the door.

As I hauled open the front door, I collided with someone.

DCI Golden's face soured; beside him, PC Waters widened her eyes.

'What are you doing here?' he demanded.

'Visiting a friend.' I leaned against the door and blinked the grit away from my eyes. I heard Kate's voice in my head: *Play to his ego. You can't miss it.* 'Listen, DCI Golden, I think we got off on the wrong foot earlier. Perhaps this doesn't have to be so difficult.'

Golden's laser-blue eyes brushed across my face. 'What do you have in mind?'

'Charlie is a friend. I can help you find him. And I've uncovered a link between him and the victim.' Waters fiddled with the ribbon on her plait, not meeting my eye. 'But I need something in return. Why are you looking for Charlie?'

He cocked his head to one side. 'You first.'

'OK, Sabrina was being harassed at work. Charlie was working on a story with her. That's how they know each other.'

Golden waited a beat, then leaned round me and pressed the buzzer.

'Hang on,' I stepped towards him, 'what about your end of the deal?'

Golden spun round, his eyes on fire. 'I don't make deals with hacks. Go spread your legs for titbits elsewhere.'

His words forced me backwards and I stumbled down the steps. Waters raised a hand to help, then drew it back in sharply. At that moment, the door opened and a tall woman emerged, pulling a suitcase. She glanced at us, then hurried down the steps.

Golden was almost through the door before he turned to me. 'A word of advice: if you do manage to get hold of your *friend*, ask him how he really knows the victim.'

Golden's barb rang in my ears as I strode through the marble lobby of Premier News. I knew it was aimed at my relationship with DCI Durand. Implying I was a slut was the laziest accusation in the book. I punched the lift button feeling furious with myself. I rarely give anything away without getting something in return.

Kate glanced up as I approached, then frowned when she saw my expression. 'Still no Charlie?'

I shook my head, told her what happened.

She perched on the edge of my desk, her cologne tickling my nose. 'What did he mean, how Charlie really knows the victim?'

I shrugged, feeling the weight of the day on my shoulders. 'No idea. Did Rowley fill you in on his tête-a-tête with the police?'

Kate pulled her curls into a low ponytail and lowered her voice. 'The police were vague. All they said to Rowley was they've found evidence that Sabrina was in touch with Charlie on her mobile phone.'

I rolled my eyes. 'He. Was. Working. With. Her. On. A. Story.'

Kate gave me a long look. 'Yep, that's probably it.' She pushed herself off my desk and sat down.

I couldn't let it go. 'What are you saying?'

'Nothing.'

'If you're implying something was going on between Charlie and Sabrina, you're nuts. He's been married to Emily less than a year. He wouldn't do that to her.'

Kate sighed. 'If you say so.'

'You're wrong about Charlie.'

Kate cricked her neck loudly. 'So where is he then?'

4

Emily: 49 weeks before the murder

The wooden bench is digging into her legs and Emily breathes through her mouth to stop the teriyaki fumes turning her stomach. She doesn't want anything to spoil this moment.

'I really think we're onto something here,' says her publisher, Libby Stone, right before jamming a spring roll into her mouth. 'Do you know how much the wedding industry is worth right now?'

Emily shakes her head. All she can think is, *Weeeeee, I'm going to be published!*

Libby pushes a cup of sake towards Emily. 'And a wedding expert who's just got married is even better. You can empathise with your readers. The way I see it is that you write the book exactly like your blog, *Something Borrowed*. Same tone – sisterly, insider-y.'

Libby leans forward, her elbow in a puddle of soy sauce.

'The Instagram photos look *gor*-geous, by the way. We'll use them in the book if that's OK? Show the readers how it's done. It's important that you build your brand. Your website gets a lot of traffic but we can increase that. Social media, obviously. Then there's the publicity campaign and . . .'

Emily tunes out Libby's voice as a snapshot of 'schoolgirl Emily' flashes in her head. The itchy green uniform stretched tightly over her short, pudgy body. Hardly surprising given that Emily's mum let her eat whatever she liked; her way of making up for things at home. At one point Emily was sinking a family-size Dairy Milk bar en route to school. She used to jam the wrapper into her pencil case, trying to hide the evidence, but teenage girls have a nose for weakness. And Emily was at the bottom of the school food chain. Her breathing quickens as she pictures the rows of girlish faces, aimed in her direction, their features arranged into sneers. 'Dumpy Danson' they called her. *Well, look at me now, Form 3a. Dumpy Danson's got a bonafide book deal.*

'Emily?' Libby leaned forward, frowning. 'Is everything OK?'

'Yeah, sorry.'

'So, how was the big day?'

Emily picks up her glass and focuses on the feel of it between her hands. *Well, Libby, funny story: it was both the happiest* and *the unhappiest day of my life.*

There was a moment in the hotel, right before Emily left for the wedding ceremony, when she was all alone in the bathroom. She stared at herself in the mirror: at the vintage, long-sleeved dress falling in ripples down her body, at the diamond-studded 'E' pendant that Charlie had sent to her room that morning as a gift. As a wedding planner, she was used to being on the other side of the glass. This felt weird, and thrilling. But, as she smiled at her reflection, an icy feeling swept through her. What if Charlie didn't show up? That happened to a client once: a leggy lawyer arrived at the packed-out church in her twenty-thousand-pound dress to find the groom had done a runner through the back door. She can still picture the bride's face as it dawned on her she'd been jilted. 'But, this only happens in movies,' she wailed, collapsing on Emily's shoulder.

Emily knew she had a lot to prove. There were mixed feelings about this wedding. Charlie's camp hadn't accepted her, not really. Most were still in thrall to his dead wife, Lizzie. They were protective of Charlie; weirded out by the fact that Emily had organised Charlie and Lizzie's wedding. His friends tolerated her for Charlie's sake, but she caught the eye rolls. The only one who hadn't given her a hard time was Sophie Kent, Charlie's friend from work. Emily pictured Sophie: all elfin features and white-blonde hair. Emily could have done with Sophie being a degree or two uglier. *Still, beggars can't be choosers.*

Standing in that bathroom, decked out in ivory silk, Emily's skin had started to hum. She snatched a pair of nail scissors off the counter and pressed the point into her thumb. What did Charlie's friends expect? That he would spend the rest of his life alone and miserable? She sucked the blood as it blossomed on her thumb, picturing their gleeful expressions if Charlie did a runner. She half expected him to flee herself. Even she couldn't believe Dumpy Danson had bagged a man like Charlie.

Emily wipes her mouth with a paper napkin as a waft of soy sauce threatens her stomach. 'It was perfect.'

Emily closes the door behind her and kicks off her heels. Her long blonde hair is wet with rain. As she pads through the hallway, she feels the draught whistling through the cellar door and shivers. *Bloody builders*, she thinks, pulling her black cardigan round her. The scent of jasmine from the diffuser on the table hits the back of Emily's throat and she wobbles into the bathroom, wincing as her knees hit the cold tiles. The rain drums on the skylight, her heart thuds in her ears. She retches but nothing comes out. Her wedding ring grazes the porcelain. She taps it – *plink plink plink* – waiting for her stomach to settle.

Eventually she hauls herself up and sits on the side of the bath. As the nausea passes, she puts a hand to her stomach. Her sleeve falls back, exposing the whisper-thin lines along her wrist. She traces them with a finger.

A key turns in the lock. Emily forces herself to her feet and glances in the mirror. Her face is ashen; she pinches her cheeks to give them some colour. The lights are off, and Charlie is silhouetted against the kitchen window.

Emily's heart lifts at the sight of him, but then she frowns. Something is wrong. He's swaying.

'Baby, what are you doing home so early?'

Charlie doesn't answer. He's looking at something outside. Emily crosses the room and puts a hand on his shoulder.

Charlie flinches and a sour waft of booze hits her. 'Have you been *drinking*?'

Charlie mumbles something as he crashes against the kitchen counter. Emily stares at him. In the eighteen months they've been together Charlie has never touched a drop of alcohol. They'd served it at their wedding, but Charlie toasted his new bride with a champagne flute filled with Appletiser. He made a joke of it but the guests who'd known him the longest hadn't laughed. It pissed her off at the time. Emily doesn't really like to think of people knowing Charlie before her.

'Baby, talk to me.'

Charlie swivels round to face her. There's a trail of vomit down his suit and his eyes are bloodshot. 'What's there to talk about?'

He ricochets off the counter and, as Emily reaches out to steady him, Charlie shoves her against the wall.

'Is it . . . has something happened with Vanessa?' she says, momentarily winded. She can tell by the way Charlie's shoulders tighten that she's said the wrong thing. Emily fills the kettle with shaky hands and switches it on. 'Baby, please. Sit down, I'll make coffee.'

She takes two porcelain mugs from the cupboard. One has 'Mr' printed on the side, the other 'Mrs'. Emily had spotted them at an upmarket pottery shop on Westbourne Grove and snapped them up before Charlie even popped the question. When he proposed, she uploaded an image of the mugs to her blog alongside the headline: *BREAKING NEWS: I SAID YES #pinchme.*

Emily closes her eyes as she waits for the kettle to boil. She'd bet any money Charlie's relapse was triggered by Vanessa. His mum is a liability, a drunk. Emily first heard about their fractured relationship when she was organising Charlie's wedding to Lizzie. She remembered the debate they had about inviting Vanessa to the wedding. In the end, Charlie won and his mum remained firmly off the guest list. But Emily hadn't realised quite how deep the scars ran. On Charlie's birthday, a month ago, a card arrived from Vanessa. It was sealed under wads of sellotape and she'd drawn a wonky birthday cake in one corner. Charlie glanced at the envelope, then threw it in the bin unopened. She sent one every birthday, but he stopped reading them years ago. When Charlie left for football practice, Emily fished the card out of the bin. Vanessa's tiny blue scrawl covered every inch of the white space.

Charlie, my love. I'm thinking of you. Always. Always. Today I walked round Sandhurst Park and sat on our bench and remembered that time we fed the geese and one charged at you and you leaped into my arms. I'm getting better, Charlie, clearer – haven't had a drink since Tuesday. Will you help me with that thing I asked at your wedding? Please help me I need you when can I see you have I been good enough yet. I love you Charlie I love you Charlie I love you.

When it was her turn to marry Charlie, Emily thought she was doing him a favour by secretly inviting Vanessa. Charlie's dad died when he was a baby and she really wanted him to have family there. In her mind, the wound would be healed and Emily would have succeeded where Lizzie failed. *Misjudged that one, didn't you?*

Emily pours coffee into the mugs then sets them down on the table. She watches Charlie drag his hands over his face. He hasn't shaved; he looks like he hasn't slept for days. His nightmares are getting worse. *Fire. Always about fire.* Emily blames herself for allowing Vanessa to inch her way back in. And she feels the unspoken accusation levelled at her; Lizzie would never have put him in that situation.

Across the table, Charlie sips his coffee. The normality of the action seems to calm him. After a minute, he raises his gaze to her face. 'Hospital called. Vanessa fell down the stairs. Postman saw her through the window.'

Emily reaches across the table and squeezes his hand. 'Is she OK?'

'Define "OK".' Charlie snatches his hand away.

'Well, is anything broken?'

'Nothing that can't be fixed with a short hospital stay and a bottle of Smirnoff's finest.' He gives a thin laugh and Emily catches a glimpse of the hurt little boy and a childhood scarred by empty promises. Over the months, Emily has tried to piece his broken past together. Charlie almost never speaks about Vanessa. The most she got out of him was six weeks into their relationship when a midnight walk along Embankment loosened Charlie's tongue. He talked of the wine bottles stashed in his toy box, the accidents caused by a selfish mum who cared more about her next fix than her struggling son. He dealt with things no kid should have to. And then, he said, something happened when he hit his teens that destroyed their relationship forever. When Emily pressed him for details, Charlie had clammed up.

Emily sits forward in her chair and opens her mouth to speak. To point out the irony that Charlie's response to his mum falling off the wagon is to fall off the wagon. But Charlie needs her love, not her judgement.

She sighs and puts on a bright voice. 'I had lunch with a publisher today. She wants to go ahead with the book.'

Charlie says something into his mug and Emily feels tears prick the back of her eyes. Their marriage is only thirty-six days old and it's unravelling. *Perhaps I should tell* that *to my publisher.*

She stands up too suddenly and a wave of nausea engulfs her. For a split-second, Emily wants to grab Charlie by his perfect hair and tell him that Vanessa's death wish isn't the only thing that happened today. Then she looks at the broken figure in front of her. The man she's vowed to love in sickness and in health, in good times and in bad. The centre of her world.

Emily's hand brushes her stomach. Now is not the time to tell him the news.

5

Present day

'Hello? Is that the great Sophie Kent, reporter extraordinaire? Call me when you get this. I need to talk to you about something . . . personal.'

The sun was setting and the newsroom lights took on a migraine-inducing hue as I played Charlie's voicemail for the millionth time. Over the past hour, I'd deduced two things. One: Charlie's voice dipped on the final word, 'personal'. Two: I was a terrible friend. Charlie left me this voicemail on Friday evening. *Three days ago.* What on earth possessed me to turn my phone off? I swigged my cold coffee not wanting to admit the answer to myself. I heard Dr Spado's voice in my head: 'Think of these tablets as a short-term fix to take the anxiety away.' Truth is, they took away more than that, but I hadn't really cared . . . until now.

I sighed. Text, email, Twitter, Facebook. I'd tried them all. I left a message with Charlie's best friend, Dominic; the man Charlie once referred to as 'the man who knows too much'. Still no word from Emily, either. We hadn't been able to hide the situation from Rowley anymore. When he got back from a board meeting, Kate and I came clean and told him that Charlie was missing. Rowley nodded curtly and disappeared into his office. We hadn't seen him since.

I stared out of the window at Kensington High Street in rush hour. From the eighth floor, people looked like wood-lice scurrying along a forest floor. I envied their journey home. I wouldn't be getting out of here any time soon.

I turned back to my computer and pulled up LegalLens.com, the gossip website Rachel Cornish had told me about earlier. The headline story was about a law firm, Medly & Flynn, poaching a powerhouse American lawyer. No mention of Sabrina's murder anywhere.

I clicked on the Wicked Whispers section and scanned the page for any mention of Sabrina. Mostly the posts were about which lawyer was shagging whom. Then I saw it, 6 May, ten days ago.

– Which flame-haired Partner has been overdosing on happy pills?

And another, the following day.

– Rumour has it this gingernut takes it up the arse.

This thread sparked off a debate about which law firms employed the least frigid women. I pictured Sabrina staring at the screen, feeling each comment like a punch in the chest.

'What's eating you?' Kate slumped down next to me, wafting spicy cologne in my direction.

'Cretins who hide behind their computer screens.'

'I've told you. Ignore the fucktards. Wouldn't know a sentence structure, or a great pair of tits, if their lives depended on it.'

I snorted. 'Not my reader comments. Sabrina Hobbs. The Thames victim. Looks like someone was waging a smear campaign against her.'

Kate studied my screen over my shoulder. 'Christ, look at that one. *Which crimson-haired lawyer deserves everything she gets. Sticking her beak in will only end in tears.*'

'The username changes each time. Look, there it's *in_the_know*, but that one is *cuckoo_crusher*.'

Kate sighed. 'Goes with the territory. Yesterday someone called *ovary_killer* commented under my piece on female crime rates that I looked as if I hadn't got laid for decades and I needed to be raped by a thousand men.'

I raised my eyebrows. 'Nice.'

'I told him thank you very much for the concern, and that yes, meticulously researching and campaigning for justice does play havoc with your libido so I was greatly looking forward to all the sex.'

I slapped her on the arm. 'Don't engage with them, you idiot. They're nutters.'

'They're spotty shitgibbons who still live at home with Mum.' She reached into her drawer and pulled out a miniature bottle of whiskey. 'Today has been the worst.'

'What's the latest on Rowntree?'

She shrugged. 'Wish I knew. Radio silence from the courthouse. It's unlikely anything will be decided tonight. If they need to replace a jury member, the whole trial has to start from scratch.' She unscrewed the lid, took a large swig and held out the bottle. I hesitated, remembering my therapist's warning not to mix alcohol with antidepressants. Then a vision of the ugly sleepless hours ahead of me made my fingers twitch. I snatched the bottle out of Kate's hand.

Kate cleared her throat, the way she does when she's uncomfortable. 'Were you telling Growler the truth earlier? Did therapy help?'

'You were eavesdropping?'

Kate ignored me, digging her teeth into the end of her pen. 'This place is so frenetic, Soph, we don't always catch each other. Look, we don't have to talk about things. The *Herald* is your safe space. I get that. But I'm not a mind-reader. If the tide is pulling you out, wave a sodding hand. I can't spend all my time worrying you're going to drown.'

I didn't trust myself to speak. Instead I pulled Kate into a fierce hug and her hair tickled my nose. 'No need to deploy the life ring yet, I promise.'

She squeezed me back, just as I heard an awkward cough behind me.

'Sorry to ruin the moment, ladies.' Charlie's deputy, Adam, was chewing his fingernail. 'Could you take a look at something, Sophie?'

I cleared my throat. 'Shoot.'

Adam perched on the side of my desk. 'I went through Charlie's files looking for clues.' He caught my expression and gave a tired smile. 'What, you think you're the only sleuth in town? I found this in his bottom drawer. A bunch of research into something called Christ Clan. A religious organisation. Down in Bournemouth.' He handed me a file. 'Charlie stuck your name on the top so I wondered if . . .' he shrugged.

I looked at the Post-It note. Charlie had scribbled my name and the word 'urgent' in his loopy handwriting.

'Thanks, Adam, I'll take a look.'

As Adam walked away, Kate cast me a glance. 'It's late, you should get out of here.'

'But–'

'Sophie, you look like hell. Go home, take a break.'

I hurried up my road just as the sky turned from smudged charcoal into black. Number 7, Bywater Street was a pastel-pink Victorian terrace nestled in a Chelsea cul-de-sac. I closed the door behind me, soaking up the silence. My flatmate, Poppy, was in Texas working for an oil baron client and wouldn't be back for a fortnight. I wandered into the kitchen; a snug room with a large window that overlooked my unkempt garden. I still hadn't got around to decorating the house, even though I'd lived here for four years. Working the crime beat for a national newspaper doesn't leave much time for picking out curtains. Still, it was much better than my previous digs. Poppy and I had lived together since we were students at Oxford University, but when she relocated to New York for a year, I moved in with a friend of her brother's. A guy called Rick, who had a penchant for video games and crack. I didn't last long. Dipped into my trust fund to get my foot on the property ladder. Timed it perfectly; Poppy was back in time to help me house hunt.

'But why do we need a third bedroom?' she'd asked, brow furrowed as we leafed through property details. When I didn't answer, Poppy rolled her eyes. 'Tommy doesn't need a room, for God's sake.'

Poppy was far less sympathetic to my brother's plight. 'You both had the same parents, right? So what's his excuse?'

She thought Tommy needed to pull himself together. Do a stint in rehab and sort himself out. I understood where she was coming from, but she didn't know Tommy the way I did: the scribbles outside the lines.

The first time Tommy's boarding school summoned my parents to a meeting, he was thirteen and called me at university.

'Did you hear the news, Sops?'

Tommy had smoked his first joint, which went straight to his head. He fell in the river and – being a sliver of boy – caught pneumonia and spent the night in hospital. Tommy didn't sound remotely worried about his fate. His voice was light, breathless; as if he couldn't believe our parents were making a two-hundred-mile trip on his behalf. Of course, when the day came, my mother couldn't get out of bed, so my father arrived alone. He must have made a 'donation' to the school because Tommy escaped with a rap on the wrist. Tommy learned two important lessons that day: that money could make your problems go away, and he'd need to try harder to get our mother's attention.

I grabbed an apple and padded through to my office, glancing at the almost-empty whiteboard above my computer. At the top was Tommy's name. So far, information about his death had been thin on the ground. My eyes instinctively went to the phone number on the blue Post-It note tacked to my screen. It belonged to Damo: a former addict who knew Tommy from the streets. I'd only met him once, at a Narcotics Anonymous meeting I'd attended for research. But that day, I got a whole lot more than I bargained for. Damo was the one who put me straight about Tommy's death: that it was murder, not suicide. He'd promised to give me more information, but that was a long time ago. I'd dialled the number every day until our mutual acquaintance, Violet, rang me to warn me off.

'Stop boiling bunnies,' she said in her trademark blunt manner. 'Damo's at a delicate stage of recovery. You hassling him ain't helping.'

'He said he would help.' My words came out in a strangled whine.

'And he will. But addicts . . . they keep to their own timetable. I'll work on him. But you need to give him space.'

How much space did he fucking need? As I fired up my computer, I drummed my fingers on the desk, picturing Sabrina's lifeless body lying in the morgue, her flame-red hair knotted with leaves. I couldn't settle. Not with Charlie still out there ignoring my calls.

I stared at the blackness outside the window thinking back to my first encounter with Charlie.

I hadn't been at the *Herald* long and was learning the art of fire-fighting on multiple levels. Mentally drained, I'd snuck out to the café opposite for a breather. While I waited in the queue, a stout man in a baggy pinstripe suit bowled in behind me barking orders down his phone. Every so often Pinstripe leered into my personal space, dousing me in a cloud of rank aftershave. When my turn came, he stepped round me and barrelled up to the counter.

I opened my mouth to speak but the day was already kicking the shit out of me, and I didn't have the energy for another fight. I didn't even notice the tall, handsome man with a heap of dark curls on his head, swaying in time to the music in his earphones. The next thing I knew, Pinstripe had stumbled and dumped his coffee down himself. People in the café twitched, trying not to laugh. He wheeled round accusingly, chins quivering, his eyes landing on the man at the counter.

'You fucking pushed me.'

The man pulled out one earphone. 'Sorry?'

'Just then. You pushed me. Look what you did.' He jabbed his finger in the man's face, like he was groping for a switch in the dark.

'I was nowhere near you, mate,' he said, sliding his phone into the pocket of his navy suit jacket.

Pinstripe's face turned crimson, a vein bulged in his forehead. He flung his coffee cup onto the counter, splashing me in the process. 'I felt you push me. And now you're going to apologise, prick.'

The man pushed his hair out of his eyes. 'You're making a scene. This lady here, the pretty one.' He gestured towards me. 'Her name is Sarah. She's got a big interview today. With Amaro Intel. Huge tech firm. I'm sure a man of your stature knows it. Anyway,' he grabbed a paper napkin and handed it to me, 'poor Sarah has coffee all down her shirt. You were on the phone – doing a huge deal by the sounds of it, congrats, mate – and lost concentration. Easily done. But poor Sarah now has to run home and change. Will you even make your interview, Sarah?'

I bit my lip, rearranged my face. 'I think I have a spare shirt in my office.'

'Well, that's lucky, mate, isn't it?' He slapped Pinstripe on the back.

The man looked at us, doubt clouding his eyes. 'Amaro Intel? Yes, good firm.' Then he shifted his weight and looked at me. 'Will you make your interview?'

I feigned irritation. 'I've missed my spot in the queue now so . . .'

He raised a fat hand, then leaned towards the barista and mumbled something over the counter. Moments later, he handed me a large coffee. 'Please accept my apologies. Good luck with the interview.' He slunk out of the café, leaving a trail of aftershave in his wake.

I watched him, stunned, then raised my eyebrows. 'Did you push him?'

'Did you hear the way he was talking to his assistant?' He unravelled his earphones and grinned.

I laughed. 'Amaro Intel?'

'Made it up.' He held out a hand. 'Charlie Swift. Business Editor at the *London Herald*.'

I shook it. 'Sophie Kent, junior reporter.'

Charlie winked. 'I know. Come say hi some time.'

That was two weeks before his wife, Lizzie, died.

I grabbed my phone and dialled his number again. *'You've reached Charlie Swift. Leave some words.'*

'Charlie, it's me. Listen, I heard about your mum. I get that you're freaking out.' I glanced up at Tommy's name on the whiteboard. 'Believe me, I know how ... messy it is. I wish I could say take all the time you need. Only,' I squeezed my eyes shut, 'can you just let me know you're OK? That's all I need. To know you're OK. Please.'

I sighed. I knew something had been on Charlie's mind lately. 'You've lost your sparkle,' I told him over coffee a couple of months ago. Charlie fluttered his eyelids at me in a bid to laugh it off, and I'm ashamed to say I didn't push him. I figured he'd tell me when he was ready.

It was almost 11 p.m. but I made myself baked beans on toast and settled down at the kitchen table. It wasn't so long ago that Tommy had sat across from me. Small and pale and twitchy. I lay my cheek on the table, ran my hand across its surface. I could smell the wood. I could smell Tommy: peppermint and cigarettes; could hear his fingers drumming the table, his foot tapping the floor. It was easier to picture the edges of Tommy: his dirty fingernails, his white-blond hair, the feel of his spine when he hugged me. Any more than that, and I went to a different place.

Half an hour later, I climbed into bed and knocked back two blue pills, my cheeks wet with tears. As I drifted off, Kate's words were whisper-soft in my head.

If the tide is pulling you out, wave a hand.

Wave a hand.

Wave a hand.

6

I opened my eyes and fumbled around for my phone. Nothing from Charlie. Then I saw the time. It was 7.34 a.m. I scrambled out of bed, head spinning. Did I sleep through my alarm? *Did I even set it?* Ten minutes later I flew out the door and up the King's Road towards Sloane Square Tube station. The metallic-blue morning sky stretched over the city like a pane of glass.

As I waited on the platform, my phone beeped.

Got your message. Will call later. Em x

I responded.

Have you heard from Charlie?

I waited, but she didn't reply. Emily still hadn't replied when I reached my desk twenty minutes later. I decided to try my luck with my general pathologist contact, Dr David Sonoma. Like DCI Durand, Sonoma was more tolerant of the press. He understood the role we played in the big picture. I worked hard on our relationship because a source inside the coroner's office is every reporter's Holy Grail. I never printed anything sensitive, and I made it my life's mission to ensure that if Sonoma was ever going to talk to a reporter, that reporter would be me.

'Sophie?' Sonoma's voice was early-morning gruff. He was in his late fifties and had a schoolmasterly air about him. Bushy grey eyebrows, small, round spectacles and a fine line in sleeveless cardigans. But I never let his mild manner deceive me. Sonoma was the sharpest scalpel in the box. 'Give me a moment, I'm just finishing up.'

I heard rustling down the phone and chewed on my pen lid. I'd only been to Sonoma's office at St. George's Hospital a handful of times and I was struck by how tidy it was. Rows of neatly stacked papers and identical ballpoint pens, all facing the same way. When I sat down, I inadvertently nudged a wedge of papers and Sonoma pounced, neatening the lines with steady hands. He chuckled when he caught me staring. 'Restoring order wherever I can.'

He didn't need to elaborate. It was bad enough writing about crime victims. Sonoma cut them open, scrutinised their injuries, then pieced together their final brutal moments. If an OCD relationship with stationery brought him a fraction more peace, who was I to judge?

'Sorry, it's been a busy morning,' he said.

'How was the Iron Death concert?'

'Sublime.' I heard the smile in his voice. Sonoma was a die-hard heavy metal fan, and I bagged him tickets whenever I could. 'It was worth waiting a decade for them to reunite.'

I opened my notepad and cleared my throat. 'Can you confirm some details about Sabrina Hobbs?'

'I don't have long, Sophie.'

'I've heard she was on antidepressants.'

Sonoma paused. 'I can confirm that Diazepam was found in her system. Along with alcohol. Not huge amounts but enough to blur the edges of a woman that size.'

'Size?'

'She was petite. Five feet one – about your height, in fact.'

I scribbled down notes. 'Her body was found in the Thames. Did she drown?'

Sonoma sighed. 'Yes. The blow to the back of her head was my first thought. But I don't think it killed her. My guess is the killer stunned her, then threw her in the river, where she drowned. Police found rocks in her pockets, so there was an attempt to hide her, but not a successful one. And I don't think she put up much of a fight. She was wearing earrings, silver four-leaf clovers, and they survived the attack, and the tide. A fibre under her fingernail is being tested, but not much else.'

I nodded, pen flying. 'Can you estimate when she was killed?'

Sonoma coughed. 'Not an easy one. The tide can play havoc with a corpse. I'd say somewhere between 8 p.m. Saturday and 8 a.m. Sunday. It's a big window, I know, but I wouldn't like to be more specific than that right now.'

I thought back to the jogger's grim observation. 'A witness said something about her right hand.'

Sonoma hesitated and I heard the sound of a door closing. 'A carving of some kind on her wrist. Hard to be specific because of the water damage. Some kind of shape, perhaps?' A chorus of voices erupted in the background and Sonoma sighed. 'Sophie, my eight thirty is here.'

He hung up and I logged on to Sabrina's profile on the Hamilton Law website. A year at the Sorbonne university in Paris, three years at Cambridge. A passionate interest in pro bono work: Sabrina had supervised a research team working for the Red Cross in 2010. She qualified at Hamilton Law, worked her way up from trainee to Partner, which didn't fit with the inequality angle. I thought back to the Wicked Whispers campaign. Did a few comments signal a sexism epidemic at the law firm? But Charlie would have done his research before agreeing to expose Hamilton Law. Wouldn't he?

Ask your friend the real reason he knows the victim.

I spun my chair round to the window. Sunlight streamed in, pooling on the grey carpet beside me. I dipped my foot in, allowing the sun to warm my ankle. Was Charlie involved with Sabrina?

Without thinking I dialled his number again.

'You've reached Charlie Swift. Leave some words.'

As I tossed my phone onto the desk, I spotted the file Adam gave me yesterday. I glanced at the Post-It Note. *For Sophie. Urgent.* It wasn't unusual for a colleague to stumble across something juicy and pass it on. Was Charlie directing me to a potential story? But if it was so urgent, why was it stashed in his bottom drawer? I glanced at the top sheet. It was a news cutting from the *Bournemouth Bugle*, May 2012.

The Christ Clan Reborn?

Can the religious group ever break free of its sordid past, asks Jeff Johnson.

The photograph showed a young man with wavy brown hair and a cherubic face that seemed at odds with his guarded expression. I read the caption:

> Hector Marlon, thirty, the tech-genius son of the original First Leader Laurence Marlon, dubbed the Shepherd, who disappeared in 1988.

I scanned the piece.

> The bulk of Christ Clan members are made up of society's most vulnerable: homeless, drug addicts, former criminals. 'The new Christ Clan is nothing to do with the organisation my dad ran back in the eighties,' says the younger Marlon, who made a fortune last year through his Pocket Church smartphone app. 'The religious cornerstones are different. My goal is to help society's cast-offs, to give them a safe place to turn.' When pressed about the rumours that surround his father's organisation, Marlon–

My phone rang and I picked it up, eyes on Marlon's face. 'This is Sophie Ke—'

'Sophie, it's Emily.' The panic in her voice made me forget all about Christ Clan.

'What's wrong?'

Jagged breathing. 'The police. They're here. At the flat. With a warrant.'

Alarm swept through me. 'Are you there now?'

'Yes, but–'

'Stay where you are. I'm coming.'

The heavy black door to Charlie and Emily's building was propped open and I found Emily sitting on the bottom stair in the hallway. Her ash-blonde ponytail hung limply from the crown of her head and she was dressed in black leggings, a long-sleeved Lycra top and bright orange trainers.

She looked up when she heard me; her eyes were rimmed pink. 'Thank God.' She pulled me into a tearful hug, and I caught the scent of lemon mixed with sweat. I was surprised by how much weight she'd lost.

'How long have the police been here?' I asked, looking round. Evidence of long-abandoned building work was everywhere. A large tarpaulin sheet hung from the bannister, piles of timber lay along one wall. I could taste the dust in the air.

Emily's voice tremored. 'Half an hour. They arrived just as I came back from a run.'

I squeezed her hand. 'Did you get the name of the person in charge?'

She brandished a business card.

Toby Golden
Detective Chief Inspector

My heart sank, and I sat down beside Emily. 'What have the police told you?'

Emily wiped her nose with the back of her hand. This was the first time I'd seen her without make-up; I'd never noticed her freckles before. 'That a woman was killed in Fulham on Saturday night. She had a phone in her bag. Pay-as-you-go. Apparently police tracked messages she received from another pay-as-you-go phone.' Emily took a deep breath and exhaled shakily. 'Both phones were paid for with Charlie's credit card.'

I chewed my fingernail. That didn't mean anything. I already knew Charlie and Sabrina were in touch. *Maybe Charlie was taking precautions by using untraceable phones.*

I opened my mouth to speak, but Emily got there first. 'There's more. Charlie sent the victim a text arranging to meet her at Bishop's Park on Saturday night.'

I stared at her. *Bishop's Park. Saturday night.*

'Listen, Em,' I said, forcing the concern out of my head, out of my voice. 'Charlie and the victim were acquainted. They were working together on a story.'

Emily clutched my hand, her voice sounded faraway. 'Who was she?'

'This is her.' I pulled out my phone and logged onto the Hamilton Law website. 'Sabrina Hobbs.'

Emily twisted her ponytail round her hand and pulled sharply as she peered at the screen. 'Do you think they're making a mess in there? I need to photograph my bedroom today. For my blog,' she added. '*Something Borrowed.* My book is due out later this year. Marriage advice for millennials. My publisher wants me to post every day. Today's topic is "inside other couples' bedrooms".'

I pocketed my phone, wondering at the change of subject. 'Emily, where's Charlie?'

'You mean he hasn't come running to you?' The bitterness in her voice took me by surprise. Emily rested her elbows on her knees and picked at her leggings. 'I'm sorry, Soph. I . . . I don't know where he is.'

'I've left messages. Hundreds of them. Emails. The works. He's not responding.'

Emily hunched further over her knees. 'That's because he's gone.'

'What do you mean "gone"?'

Emily chewed her lip, refusing to meet my eye. 'Wallet, phone, holdall. Gone.'

The way she said it triggered a memory in my head. It was a few months ago, a Saturday, I think, and Emily called me to ask if I'd seen Charlie. She hadn't been able to get hold of him. When I rolled into work on the Monday and Charlie was at his desk, I meant to ask him about it. But I'd got sidetracked. Then forgot all about it.

I leaned back against the bannister trying to process my thoughts. 'When did you last see him?'

'Friday. We . . . rowed. I drove to Norfolk that night. Had a client getting married Saturday morning so I stayed overnight. I got back early hours of Sunday morning and Charlie wasn't in bed. I assumed he was in the spare room. But when I woke up later . . .' her words tailed off and she shrugged.

'You haven't heard from him since?' I asked, panic creeping into my voice. Charlie's voice in my head: *I need to talk to you about something . . . personal.* I cursed myself again for switching off my phone.

Emily's phone beeped. She glanced at the screen, frowning, then she typed out a message. My gaze drifted to the diamond pendant round her neck. I remember Charlie showing it to me in the office a week before the wedding.

'What do you think, Kent?' he asked, biting his lip as he handed me the red box.

I stared down at the diamond 'E', nestled against the black velvet lining. 'They say diamonds are a girl's best friend for a reason, dude.'

He frowned. 'I bought Lizzie something similar for our one-year anniversary and she never wore it. Told me the initial made her feel like she was being "branded".'

I glanced at the diamond letter, then back at Charlie. 'Charlie, this isn't the same necklace, right? Tell me the E stands for Emily and not Elizabeth.'

I'd been joking but the way Charlie snapped the box shut made me wonder if I'd hit a nerve.

I cleared my throat. 'Em, I've only just found out about Charlie's mum. I had no idea.'

Emily slid her phone into her pocket. 'You know, the last time Charlie went to Vanessa's place, he poked his head round the door of his old bedroom. First time he'd set eyes on it since he left home as a teenager. Apparently it looked exactly the same. *Star Wars* duvet cover. West Ham posters on the wall. Vanessa hadn't touched a thing. She'd even lain out a pair of his pyjamas on the bed.'

I whistled, and Emily shook her head. 'But Vanessa could also be cruel. I mean, she was a drunk. So out of it by the end that we had to get her mail redirected to us. When I met Charlie he'd barely spoken to his mum in decades. I encouraged him to reconnect with her. That's why I invited her to our wedding. I was trying to build bridges.'

Emily picked at her leggings, her eyes large and sad.

'I thought once Vanessa died, Charlie would be free of whatever grudge he's been holding onto all these years. But she did a real number on him. I mean, I get it; she was an addict, a waste of spa—' She stopped and gave me an embarrassed smile as she realised what she said. 'I'm sorry, Sophie. No offence. I didn't mean all addicts are a waste of space.'

I nudged her leg with mine. 'None taken. You're right; addicts are tough to love. They blow up your life at a moment's notice.'

Emily sighed. 'You weren't at our wedding, were you?'

I twisted the button on my cuff as I tried to push the memory out of my mind. The night before Charlie's wedding, Tommy turned up with a black eye and a swollen jaw. He crawled silently into bed and I lay in the room next to him, listening to his nightmare through the wall. When I found his scrawny frame curled up on the sofa the following morning, I knew I couldn't leave him alone. I left a message on Charlie's phone to say a family emergency had come up, knowing he'd understand.

'Well, you missed the fireworks,' said Emily, running a finger over her eyebrow. 'I can't believe I'm actually saying this but I'm glad Vanessa's dead. For Charlie's sake.'

Emily's phone beeped in her hand. She glanced at it, then quickly shut down the screen. We sat in silence for a moment. It was odd being together without Charlie.

A noise in the stairwell above made us look up. I didn't know how much longer I had. I turned to Emily, urgency varnishing my voice. 'Em, that time you called me when Charlie disappeared. He did the same thing then? Charlie's deputy, Adam, also said this isn't the first time Charlie has done a disappearing act.'

Emily pulled at her shoelace. 'Look, every marriage has its moments. I'm not going to pretend ours is any different. If one of us needs space, the other lets them go.'

'Do most marriages need space after a year?' The words slipped out before I could stop them.

Emily's eyes flashed. 'It's none of your business.'

I regretted pushing her. I knew Emily well enough to under-stand that this was her worst nightmare. She worked hard to project the perfect life on social media. To have her marriage picked apart by others must be torture. I took a breath, know-ing I was on shaky ground. 'Look, I'm on your side, but I'm groping in the dark. If you know anything that could help me find Charlie, you have to tel—'

Footsteps pattered towards us. DCI Golden appeared, followed by PC Waters and three other officers.

His forehead glistened with sweat. 'What an unpleasant surprise.'

I forced a smile, damned if I was going to let him under my skin. 'Just keeping Mrs Swift company.'

He glanced at Emily. 'You know she's a reporter.'

Emily ignored Golden, her eyes on the box in his arms. 'What's in there?'

Golden handed the box to PC Waters. 'Does Charlie have a laptop, Mrs Swift? We couldn't find one.' Emily shrugged, her eyes on the carpet. Golden gave her a long look. 'Right, we'll be in touch. And if you do hear from your husband, tell him things will go more smoothly if he cooperates.'

They filed out and the door slammed, plunging us into darkness.

Being back in her apartment, surrounded by her things, seemed to have a calming effect on Emily. She strolled over to the fridge and pulled out a pink smoothie. 'Do you want one?'

I shook my head, watched as Emily took a sip that left a pink smudge above her lip. Behind her, shelves were artfully filled with cookery books. Charlie loved to cook; he joked that his Beef Wellington had hooked legions of women over the years. Often, when things hit the skids with Tommy, Charlie brought Tupperware filled with homemade casseroles into the office for me.

I followed Emily into the small sitting room that was flooded with light. A thick, floral scent hung in the air along with something else I couldn't place. Damp? I passed piles of glossy magazines that stood in columns along the back wall. Large photographs of Emily and Charlie adorned every available surface. Mainly black-and-white shots from their wedding.

The magazine-vibe was blighted by evidence that the police had rifled through their stuff. Drawers hung open, boxes were scattered across the carpet. I turned a chair the right way up, sensing Emily's distress, and glanced at the space where the mosaic coffee table and shagpile rug used to be. In their place was a glass table. In fact, lots of the colourful decor I remembered had disappeared in favour of whites and greys.

'Have you decorated since I was last here?' I said, laying my jacket on the sofa. Emily waited a beat, then squirrelled it away in a hallway closet.

'I had an epiphany right after the wedding. Things were ... hectic. I decided to take it down a notch at home. Creating a sanctuary within your home is so important. The first thing I did was install double-glazing. Isn't it peaceful?'

Emily's beatific smile was freaking me out. I wandered over to the window and glanced at the ugly grey street outside. Scaffolding poles lay abandoned on the pavement. 'Charlie said the building work has been a drag.'

Emily slumped on the sofa, kicking off her trainers. She curled her feet underneath her and shivered. 'The draughts in this place are *the worst*. I haven't been able to get warm for months. Nothing we can do about the building work. We can't sell, because who the hell would want to live on a building site? We're stuck here waiting for the planning officials to reach an agreement. Meanwhile the building is falling apart.'

I pointed at the wedding photograph on the wall behind her head, the one where Charlie was kissing Emily's cheek. 'Wow.'

Emily followed my gaze, her voice quiet. 'Feels like a long time ago now.'

I leaned forward. 'I'm sorry about what I said earlier. About you guys needing time out. It wasn't fair.'

Emily fiddled with her necklace. 'I'm sorry too, Sophie. I didn't mean to sound like a bitch. But it's always unsettled me out how close you and Charlie are. Call me old-fashioned, but I've always thought the woman closest to a man should be his wife.'

'You don't honestly believe–' I stopped. It was true that Charlie and I were close. Grief binds you together in ways you can't explain. So does a shared experience of fucked-up families. But my friendship with Charlie had nothing to do with attraction. It ran deeper than that.

I shifted on the sofa and, at that moment, a cloud swept in front of the sun, swallowing the light in the room.

'Did Charlie ever tell you he crashed Tommy's wake?'

I coughed, my throat squeezing painfully as the memory pierced my mind. The coffin, the stares, the way people licked their lips as they clutched my hand. My insides felt as if they'd been scorched. I ricocheted from one conversation to another, barely registering words as they came out of my mouth. The only reason I put myself through the torture of making the eulogy was because my father didn't show up and my mother was drunk. Someone had to remind the congregation that there was more to Tommy than a sweaty, paranoid slide into drugs. The wake was held at my family's Surrey estate, Redcroft. My mum lasted twenty minutes before staggering upstairs. I was topping up wine glasses, gripping the bottle so hard my fingers ached, when I overheard a family friend tell another guest that Tommy's death was a relief. 'There's one in every family,' she said, raising thin eyebrows.

I took a breath, then ducked into the library. It took less than a minute to smash every pane of glass in the antique bookcase. My hands were cut to ribbons but I felt nothing. When my knees gave way, I collapsed on the floor; a broken, bloodied mess howling into my sleeve. The next thing I knew, Charlie was standing in the doorway.

My voice wobbled as I focused on Emily's shadow. 'I hadn't told a soul about Tommy's funeral. I knew I wouldn't survive the day around people who knew what Tommy meant to me. But the relief of seeing a friendly face . . .' A tear spilled down my cheek and I flicked it away. 'The bugger tracked me down. Drove all the way from London. Told me he knew how important it was not to face things alone. That you'd taught him how to share the burden.'

I cleared my throat and sat forward, fixing my gaze on Emily.

'I don't know if I'd have made it through that day without Charlie. And I have you to thank. Charlie showed up, because of you.'

Emily dug her stubby fingernails into the plastic bottle, her voice almost a whisper. 'You honestly think he did it for me?'

We sat in silence for a moment, then Emily stood up and coughed. 'I need to take a shower. I'm still sweaty from my run.'

I followed her through to the bedroom. The walls were covered in a shimmery grey wallpaper and cream shutters hung at the window. Police had stripped the bed and piles of fluffy grey cushions lay scattered across the carpet.

Emily sloped off to the bathroom and I wandered over to the wardrobe. The doors were open and Charlie's suits were giving off a faint smell of sandalwood. I spotted a wooden tray filled with cuff-links and loose change. Beneath it, half hidden, was a red velvet pouch. I glanced over my shoulder then tipped the contents into my palm. A silver ring with the inscription 'Forever yours, Charlie' carved on the inside. I frowned. I knew what Lizzie's wedding ring meant to Charlie. On a slow night in the newsroom we'd played 'What three things would you save from your burning house?'

'I'll go first,' I'd said, leaning back in my chair, ankles dangling over the desk. 'My *London Herald* printing plate, obvs.' Every *Herald* reporter was awarded the printing plate of their first front page and mine took pride of place in my downstairs toilet. 'Also, my first edition copy of *The Hound of the Baskervilles.*'

'You're such a dork.' Charlie flicked a rubber band at me. 'What's the third?'

I pulled a photo out of my purse. It showed Tommy and me standing on the doorstep of Redcroft on the first day of term. Me, a skinny adolescent, in a green pinafore and straw boater hat; Tommy barely eight, wearing charcoal shorts that gaped around his spindly white legs. That morning Tommy had refused to go to school. He was already being bullied by that stage. But, right before that picture was taken, our mother knelt down and hugged Tommy. Tommy gazed at me with wide eyes. She wasn't a hugger. As the photo was taken, Tommy squinted into the autumn sunlight, beaming like a lunatic. I can still feel his small, dry fingers between mine.

Charlie reeled off his three items without pausing to think: a West Ham shirt signed by the team, a football his stepfather, Gordon, had given him, and Lizzie's wedding ring. 'It will go with me to the grave,' he told me, tugging on his fringe.

Emily appeared in the doorway, wrapped in a dressing gown. I dropped the ring back in its pouch, storing away what I'd seen, and turned to face her.

'Do you mind if I ask you a personal question, Em?'

Emily sat on the bed, running her fingers through her wet hair. 'That depends.'

'What did you argue about on Friday that means Charlie hasn't been in touch since?'

Out of the corner of my eye, I saw Emily's chest rising and falling. 'It was nothing. Barely a row.'

'But you said–'

'I know what I said, but I'm telling you it was nothing.'

I nodded, sensing the shift in mood. 'Em, you know the *Herald* has to cover this, right?'

She closed her eyes. 'I was afraid of that.'

'Don't be.' I put my hand on hers. 'I'm sure this is a misunderstanding. He'll be home soon.' I pulled out my notebook. 'But, look, for the purposes of our write-up. If you could send a message to Charlie, what would it be?'

Emily rubbed her hair with a towel, thinking for a moment. Then she cleared her throat. 'I'd tell him: I love you, and I'm here for you. No matter what.'

It wasn't until I was halfway down Delaware Street that I realised Emily never asked me a single question about Sabrina Hobbs.

7

Rowley drained his mug as he listened to my update. 'You're sure Emily's happy for us to print her quote?'

I nodded. 'It's on the record.'

Mack, Kate and I were sitting around the square table in Rowley's corner office – a large room overlooking Hyde Park. From his desk, you could see a sliver of Kensington Palace.

He slid off his half-moon glasses and pinched the top of his nose. 'And there's nothing at all from Charlie?'

I shook my head. 'I spoke to his best friend, Dominic, on the way here. He hasn't heard from Charlie, either.'

Rowley sighed and opened his notebook. 'What do we know about the victim?'

I scooted forward, wanting to get this right. 'I'm building up a picture. Sabrina was smart, Cambridge-educated. Conscientious, too. Took on a lot of pro bono work. Not much of a personal life to speak of. But she earned a good salary. I get the impression she spent a fair whack self-medicating.'

'What do you mean?' Rowley rested his elbows on the table.

'Acupuncture, homeopathy, osteopathy, reiki.' I counted out on my fingers. 'And that's just appointments she's made in the past month. Also she was a regular at the Fit Fit Fit gym on Brewer Street. The receptionist remembers seeing her there Saturday lunchtime.'

'Where does she live?' asked Mack.

'Fulham. Not far from Bishop's Park . . .'

'. . . where her body was found,' said Kate, doodling on her pad.

Rowley nodded thoughtfully. 'Friends? Boyfriends?'

I shrugged. 'So far, the closest thing I've found to a friend is her assistant, Rachel. And she told Rachel recently that she was involved with someone. She was trying to extricate herself from the relationship.'

'No confirmation yet as to who he is?'

I shook my head, and the unspoken question hung heavy over the room.

Rowley cleared his throat and closed his notebook. 'Let's not jump to conclusions. Keep pushing your leads, Sophie.' He turned to Kate. 'Where are we with Rowntree?'

Kate threw her pen onto the desk, groaning. 'Stalemate. My source at the courthouse has confirmed that a jury member has been dismissed. We're waiting to find out whether the Judge will order a retrial.'

Mack tapped his fingers on the desk irritably. 'If Rowntree comes off, no one's going to give a shit about Serena.'

I flicked him a look. 'Sabrina.'

'Whatever. The national press is gearing up for a Rowntree extravaganza. You think we're the only ones itching to print what we know? I say we use Sabrina's murder as a back-up, but be prepared to drop everything the moment Rowntree moves.'

I scratched a deep line into the page with my pen. Having a story pulled in favour of a bigger story goes with the territory. What bothers me is how easy it is for everyone to forget that we are dealing with people's lives. In newspapers, it's bad enough that priority is given to the killer. What compels someone to kill makes for interesting copy, and the victim is often depicted as just that: a victim. I understand, but I don't agree with it. So I fight hard to tell their stories. To prevent them from being defined by their final, brutal moments.

Rowley stood up and moved to the window. His navy suit billowed around his legs. 'You said there's a colleague of the victim you want to interview?'

I nodded. 'Bert Hughes. He's due back from New York today. I'll doorstep him later, if that's OK?' I glanced at Mack. As my department head, he had to sign off on my movements. But Mack was staring straight ahead, his mind on something else.

Rowley turned to face me. 'As far as we know, all the police have on Charlie is the two pay-as-you-go phones?'

'And the fact he arranged to meet Sabrina in the area her body was found,' I said. 'Although there's no evidence he actually met her.' Rowley nodded, but his long face was pensive. 'Can we ask Jasdeep to look into the gossip website, LegalLens?' I asked. 'I'd love to know who's behind the smear campaign.' Jasdeep Chopra was the *Herald*'s IT whiz.

A knock at the door. Adam poked his head around, brandishing a file. 'I'm sorry to interrupt but I thought you should see this.' Rowley beckoned him in and he sat down next to me. 'I've just printed off the email trail between Charlie and Sabrina.'

Adam laid out the pages. 'There isn't a lot but, look, the last email is dated a week ago.'

I pulled the page towards me and read it out loud.

Dear Sabrina, I'm happy to confirm our meeting. Before we meet, please send over the figures relating to the company contract.

Best wishes, Charlie

Dear Charlie, I really enjoyed our lunch yesterday. I'm thrilled you're taking on the story. Let me know if you need anything else.

Kind regards, Sabrina

I sat back in my chair, chewing my lip. Something wasn't right.

I turned to Adam. 'Does this sound like Charlie to you?'

Adam's mouth was pulled tight. 'It sounds very formal. Like he's trying to . . .'

'. . . not sound like he's shagging her?' Mack's voice was laced with sarcasm.

I opened my mouth to defend Charlie when my phone beeped. It was an email from the Met. I scanned it, then scrambled to gather my things. 'Shit, the police have called a press conference relating to Sabrina's case.'

As we filed back to News, I glanced at Mack. 'You were quiet in that meeting.'

'Didn't think my opinion would be very popular.'

'That's never stopped you before.'

Mack gazed past me at Charlie's desk. 'Did it ever strike you as odd that he ended up marrying his wedding planner?'

I shrugged. 'People have to meet somewhere.'

Mack tugged at his sleeve. 'I know you and Charlie are close now, but you hadn't known him long when his first wife died. It always surprised me that he was able to slap on a smile and banter in the office.'

My voice struck a warning note. 'People deal with grief in different ways.'

'But it points to a certain mentality, don't you think? What do they call it? Compartmentalising.'

I shrugged. 'He was widowed in his thirties, for Christ's sake. In that scenario, you get through the day however you can. What's your point?'

Mack's dark eyes dropped to my mouth and he blinked. 'Only that, when Charlie returned to work, he didn't look like someone drowning in grief.'

I leaned against the desk, mentally running through my to-do list. 'Oh yes, and what does someone drowning in grief look like?'

He held my gaze. 'Like you.'

The conference room at New Scotland Yard was brightly lit. A makeshift stage containing a table, three chairs and three microphones had been erected at the far end. Behind me I could hear the scrum of TV news crews jostling for space. I fanned my face with my notebook and a sharp hit of BO wafted towards me from the man on my right. I shifted up a seat.

'If you get any closer, you'll have to buy me dinner,' said a nasal drawl.

I swung round to find a leering Eliot Sampson, Chief News Reporter at the *Post*. He was potato-shaped, with a black beard and shrewd blue eyes. He was also a seriously talented journalist and had won more Scoops of the Year at the National Newspaper Awards than any other reporter. A fact he never let anyone forget.

'You know what this press conference is about?' I asked, pulling my Dictaphone out of my bag and testing the batteries.

'You don't?' He hooted with laughter and saliva splattered my chin. If Sampson was a colour, he'd be a brash Ferrari red. His phone beeped and he looked at the screen, licking his lips. 'How are things over at the *Herald*? Sinking in shit, I hear.'

I smiled sweetly. 'I saw the *Post* got a rap on the knuckles for the Edgware Road riot.'

Sampson didn't seem fazed. 'Did wonders for our circulation, though. Survival of the fittest and all that.'

'Fittest?' I looked pointedly at his wide girth and Sampson's lip curled.

The door at the side of the room opened and DCI Golden strode in flanked by two officers. His blond hair was gelled into an aggressive side parting and his young face was set rigid. He sat down and cleared his throat.

'At 7.30 yesterday morning a woman's body was found on the banks of the Thames in Bishop's Park, Fulham. The woman has been identified as thirty-three-year-old Sabrina Hobbs from London. Our initial investigation has led us to a suspect, a forty-two-year-old male.'

Golden paused and clasped his hands on the table.

'We have taken the decision to release his name and his photograph because we believe the suspect has absconded. We ask that you circulate his image to the public. His name is Charles Swift. He is a journalist at the *London Herald* and I'm sure is known to many of you here.' A murmur rippled through the room and Golden raised his hand, calling the room to order.

I gripped my voice recorder with a damp hand, ignoring Sampson's hard stare.

Golden took a sip of water, his eyes scanning the room. They stopped for the briefest moment on my face. 'I've got time for one or two questions.'

Everyone put their hands up and Golden nodded towards a chestnut-haired reporter in the front row: Lindsay Thackery from the *Daily News*.

'Do you have any leads as to Swift's whereabouts?' she asked in a loud voice.

'We believe he is still in the South-East, but I can't be more specific than that.'

I raised my hand higher. Golden's eyes found mine then kept going.

At that moment, Sampson gave me a sideward glance and cleared his throat. He rarely waited to be asked. 'DCI Golden, the *Post* has spoken to a Dr Anne Lack, an obstetrician on

Harley Street. She confirmed that the victim had an abortion recently. Can you confirm whether Charles Swift is the father?'

I felt the room go still, bright; like the vicious split-second of silence after a bomb detonates.

Golden's eyes narrowed. 'I can't comment on that yet, or on any other evidence. A forensics team is currently at Swift's flat so we will update you soon if there's anything further.' He gave a final sweep of the room, then stood up. Yanking down his jacket, he, and the other officers, filed out.

People charged past me, eager to file copy to waiting editors. I couldn't move. My feet felt as if they were glued to the floor. I clutched hold of my chair. *An abortion? Forensics?*

Sampson sidled over. His face was red and sweating. 'Didn't see that one coming, did you?'

A scream bubbled in my throat. I hurtled towards the exit, knocking over a chair in my haste. Outside, the sun cast a brittle light over the city. I staggered down Broadway, fumbling with my phone, and leaned against the wall of St James's Park Tube station.

Kate picked up after two rings. 'What's up, butterc—'

'Sabrina was pregnant had an abortion is he the father forensics are–' My words tripped over themselves.

'Slow down, Soph. What the fuck?'

'Sabrina had an abortion.' I stopped, squeezing my eyes shut as the full force of reality hit me. 'There's a forensics team at Charlie's flat.'

'I – fuck.'

'What do we do?'

I sensed a shift in gear as Kate pulled herself together. 'Right, Growler's due back any moment. I'll grab the team. We need a strategy.' A pause. 'Do you want off this story?'

'What? Why?'

'You know why.'

I slammed my palm against the wall, wincing as my thumb hit a sharp edge of brick. 'Are you mad? Charlie isn't a killer. This is all a stupid misunderstanding.'

'Right.'

The doubt in Kate's voice made me forget the pain in my hand. 'You don't honestly believe Charlie did this? There's no motive.' *That we know of.* I could hear Kate's thoughts.

She sighed. 'Have you spoken to Emily about any of this?'

'Not yet.'

'Do it now. She's front and centre.' I nodded, hearing the subtext. If Emily was going to become part of the story, the *Herald* might as well be the newspaper she spoke to.

I started towards the steps when a thought hit me. 'Kate, tell me my piece hasn't gone live. The one with Emily's quote. If the media know she's spoken out, she'll become their number one target.'

I heard the sound of Kate frantically tapping away on her keyboard. 'It's live. And, shit.'

'What?' I tried to quell the rising panic.

'It's been picked up.'

'Already? Who by?'

Kate whistled. 'Everyone. Listen to this headline on the BBC website: *Murder suspect's wife sends message: I love you. No matter what.*'

My voice dropped to a whisper. 'Fuck, we've thrown her to the wolves.'

8

She opens the café door and breathes in the scent of croissants and coffee. Charlie is sitting in the corner, his head dipped low, his thick fringe swept over one eye. Emily watches the nearby table of yummy mummies nudge each other and point at Charlie. One wipes her baby's milky chin with a muslin and flicks her hair back, laughing too loudly to try and catch his attention.

Emily sighs, remembering the first time she saw Charlie, striding up the path to her front door. He was dressed in a navy peacoat and jeans, looking as if he'd stepped out of a Burberry campaign. She was living in Chiswick at the time, operating her fledgling wedding-planning business out of her ground-floor flat. Emily spotted them out the window. Lizzie was pixie-pretty, with short blonde hair that showed off a slender neck. Charlie's arm was slung around the shoulders of her suede coat and he whispered something in her ear as they waited on the doorstep.

Emily had made up her mind about Charlie before he even rang the bell. She'd met his type before. Sexy, self-absorbed and totally uninterested in the wedding. But Charlie had surprised her. So had Lizzie, who threw herself on the sofa and stretched out her long legs, resting one biker boot on the coffee table. Sensing Emily's discomfort, Charlie gently nudged his fiancée's foot off the table. Normally the bride-to-be led the way in these consultations, but Lizzie was indecisive and easily bored. *A pain in the arse,* Emily decided. A pretty girl who was used to getting things her own way. Lizzie hadn't had to work at life like she had. Emily ended up directing most of her attention at Charlie. He laughed when she asked him about flower displays ('Um, pink ones?') and had been surprisingly patient as she ran through the checklist ('Invitations, music, food; load me up, I can take it!') After they left, Emily ran her hands over the imprint he had made in the sofa, lost in the trace of his woody scent.

Emily weaves through the cafe, sensing the yummy mummies' eyes on her. Charlie is reading something. She catches a glimpse over his shoulder. A letter. Vanessa's childish scrawl.

My darling darling son, forgive me this letter is over forty years late but–

Charlie senses her presence and spins round. He plasters a smile onto his face and pats the chair beside him. 'I've ordered for you,' he says, stuffing the letter in his pocket.

Emily fixes her gaze on the red-checked tablecloth as the café sounds fill her head. The clink of cutlery, the hum of Tuesday-morning voices, a baby's howl.

A baby.

Emily covers her face with her hands.

Charlie's hand is on her shoulder, his voice soft in her ear. 'What did the doctor say?'

'That it's nature's way.' She feels the doctor's cold hands on her stomach. 'It was only the size of a grain of rice. Barely worth bothering about.'

She forces a smile, but the anguish is building inside her. That tiny sack of cells had lit her up in a way she hadn't thought possible. She had already planned the Instagram announcement: three pairs of Converse trainers in a row. Charlie's, hers, and a tiny pair no bigger than her palm.

Emily has always wanted kids but when she fell in love with Charlie, a primal instinct took over. She wants Charlie's child so badly it scares her. In her darkest moments, she wonders whether it's really the baby she wants or what the baby symbolises. Everything Charlie and Emily share, he has shared before. With Lizzie. Charlie has popped the question before, bought the ring before, kissed the bride before. But a baby? Lizzie never got that far. Perhaps a baby will make Charlie forget.

Charlie squeezes her arm, mutters, 'Give God your weakness, and He'll give you his strength.'

'What?'

Charlie shakes his head. 'I'm sorry, Em. I know how much you wanted this.'

'How much *we* wanted this.' She gazes at him through tear-sodden lashes, suddenly unsure of everything. They've never really had the 'kid' conversation. Not properly. She raised the topic once or twice at the start of their relationship but Charlie's lukewarm response put her off asking again. Once, at a party, a friend of Charlie's – Ashley something? – announced she was pregnant. When Emily asked if she had any names picked out, Ashley grinned.

'Current frontrunner for a girl is Arabella,' she said, pinching Charlie on the arm. 'You don't mind, do you? I know that was one of yours.'

Charlie put a hand on his heart in mock indignation, but Emily could see the tightness around his eyes. *Arabella.* That night she asked Charlie about it, but he just shrugged.

'It was Lizzie's choice. You know how it is.' But she didn't. She and Charlie had never got as far as discussing baby names. That night she locked herself in the bathroom and carved an 'A' for Arabella into her thigh.

A reedy waitress with spiky hair sets a mug of tea down in front of her. Her gaze lingers on Charlie and Emily feels like slapping her.

'How long will it take to . . . you know,' Charlie says, chewing his lip.

'He wasn't too specific. Says I need to take it easy.'

Charlie nods, rubs his eyes with the heel of his hands. Emily studies his face. Did he sleep at all last night? The nightmares are getting worse. Last night his screaming woke her in the dead hours; he dreamed he was being burned alive.

Emily sips her tea, feeling a stab of irritation in her chest as she watches Charlie tap out an email on his phone.

'I've emailed Sophie to say I'm taking the rest of the day off,' he says. 'She'll cover for me at work.'

She can't hide her surprise. 'Are you sure?'

Charlie hesitates, then cups her cheek in his hand. His warmth spreads through her. As the chasm between them closes a fraction, she feels a shift inside her.

She puts a hand on his. 'We're going to be OK, aren't we?'

'This was just the first attempt.'

'I don't mean the baby. I mean us. You and me.' Emily sees the shadow flit across Charlie's face and regrets her words. She stares down at her tea. 'I want to go home.'

Charlie lays a tenner on the table. 'You go ahead, I'll meet you there. I have to run an errand first.'

Emily pushes her mug away. *Please don't leave me alone.* 'I'll come with you.'

'No, you need to rest.'

Charlie slips his jacket on and kisses her cheek. Over his shoulder the yummy mummies narrow their eyes.

The sitting room curtains are half-drawn and the air is heavy with the caustic reek of wilting flowers. Emily curls up on her sofa and picks up an interiors magazine, trying to quieten the noise in her head. She flicks to the photographs of a beautiful Georgian farmhouse in Bath. The interior is arctic-white: walls, rugs, curtains, furniture. The owner, an elegant woman with grey hair that hangs as straight as rain, gazes serenely at the camera. 'My life was so hectic but, after my encounter with God, everything made sense. Part of my epiphany involved chucking things out, stripping them back.'

Emily drums her fingers against the chair. Where is Charlie? It's been three hours since she got home.

It's just nature's way.

The doctor had peeled off his latex gloves and shrugged, like he was apologising for the weather. Emily dials Charlie's number again but it goes to voicemail.

'Baby, where are you?' she says, her voice high and pleading. 'Please come home.'

She throws her phone onto the coffee table. She shouldn't have to be alone, not today. Doesn't Charlie realise that? Doesn't he love her? Her skin starts to vibrate. Emily glances at the abstract painting on the wall and its garish colours shout at her. The panic lodges in her throat. Too much noise. Too much colour. Too much everything. *What did you expect, Dumpy Danson? That you were going to live happily ever after?*

All of a sudden, Emily can't breathe. Her skin screams. She lurches forward and rips the painting off the wall, then she shoves the mosaic coffee table and kicks the striped rug to one side. Feeling giddy, Emily stumbles over to the window and yanks down the purple curtains. Sunlight streams through the window. She opens the cellar door and staggers down the steps, returning with a wedge of bin liners.

An hour later, Emily has torn through the entire flat filling the hallway with bin bags. She's ordered a glass coffee table, a white rug, white curtains. *An encounter with God.* But it's still not enough. She crawls to the bathroom and picks up her nail scissors.

The relief is instant.

Emily slumps on the toilet lid, watching blood dribble out of her hip. Four cuts, one for each hour she's been alone. She waits for the noise in her head to die down, then busies herself tending to the cut.

The key turns in the lock, and Emily winces as she pulls up her knickers.

Charlie has to shove the door open to get past the rubbish bags. He stares at the sitting room open-mouthed. 'What the hell happened?'

Emily feels dazed. 'Where have you been?'

Charlie strides towards Emily and pulls her onto the sofa beside him, nuzzling her hair. The smell of him makes her dizzy. She wants to ask again where he's been, but the desire to hold on to this moment, on to his warmth, is too strong. She has to trust Charlie. Her eyes grow heavy and she sinks into his chest.

Emily pictures her parents. Middle-class, ordinary. That's what everyone thought. But she grew up watching the trust dissolve between them. Even now the smell of Sunday roast flings her right back to family meals spent in itchy silence. She vowed her own marriage would be different. No secrets. No suspicion. Her marriage will be perfect.

Charlie flicks on the TV, she knows without looking it will be football. Emily clings to her husband, and drifts off to sleep. She sleeps so soundly, she doesn't feel Charlie slide out from under her, or hear the front door close as he disappears into the darkness.

9

Present day

I emerged from London Bridge Tube station and pulled up Google Maps on my phone. Rain was falling like a silver veil from the sky and, as I hurried along the cobbled street that ran through Butler's Wharf, I was struck with a heady mix of river tang and wet tarmac. Tea Trade Wharf was an eighteenth-century brick building dotted with glass balconies. Once the dirty hub of city life, this former warehouse had been hollowed out and polished up, and now rich City kids rubbed shoulders with ghosts of the Industrial Revolution.

I ducked into the marble lobby and a bald man looked up from behind the reception desk.

'Can I help you?'

'I'm here to see Bert Hughes. Apartment 7A.'

A shadow passed across his face as he picked up the phone. 'Your name, please?'

'Sophie Kent,' I said, leaning against the desk and listening to the sound of rain pelting against glass. I wondered if Bert knew Sabrina was dead, given he'd just returned from New York.

'Mr Hughes, there's a lady in reception. A Sophie Kent.'
I could hear the squawking from where I stood. The man
replaced the receiver and gave me an apologetic look. 'Mr
Hughes isn't available right now.'

I glanced at his name badge. 'Would you mind calling him
again, Seth?' He blinked rapidly, his mousy brown eyebrows
knitting together. I smiled. 'You don't have to speak to him.'

Seth hesitated, then dialled again and handed me the phone.

Bert answered on the first ring. 'Listen, you prick. I told you–'

'Mr Hughes, it's Sophie Kent. Please don't hang up.'

'How did you–'

'Mr Hughes, I'm a reporter from the *London Herald*. I've
uncovered an issue at your law firm. In connection with your colleague, Sabrina Hobbs's, death.' Silence. *He knows.* 'I'm approach-
ing you first because I've heard that you and Sabrina were close.
I understand it's a difficult time.' I paused, choosing my words
carefully. 'I'm happy to leave you out of the loop and go directly to
your boss. We can get the whole thing out in the open.'

Out of the corner of my eye, I saw Seth's jaw slide open.

Bert's voice was pure ice. 'For Sabrina's sake, you have five
minutes.'

The line went dead and I handed the phone back to Seth. 'Can
you point me to the stairs?'

Bert Hughes scowled in his doorway. His charcoal sweater
stretched tight over his biceps and he was wearing sunglasses on
top of his head; the pink cord hung down behind his large head.

He raised his chin at me. 'I don't take kindly to threats.'

'I appreciate you seeing me, Mr Hughes.' I waited awkwardly for Bert to invite me in, but he didn't. 'You want to do this in the corridor?'

Bert shot me a look, then pushed himself away from the door frame. I followed him into a large, open-plan room. The far end of his apartment was all glass and looked out over Tower Bridge. In the centre stood a granite-coloured L-shaped sofa; the black marble floor was edged in LED lights.

Bert prowled into the kitchen; his aftershave, a cloying musk, laying down an overpowering track wherever he went. I watched him gulp down a glass of water, then dump it in the sink.

'I'd offer you a drink, but I want you gone,' he said.

I shook off my jacket, buying some time. I didn't take Bert's hostility personally. I've developed a thick skin over the years. A reporter is a lightning rod for people's emotions. You appear in their lives at the worst possible moments. The least you can expect is a bad attitude.

'I'm very sorry about Sabrina.' I wandered over to the window. The flat light made the Thames look solid, like a sheet of metal.

Bert perched on the edge of the sofa. 'Let me be clear. Nothing I say is on the record. Don't even think about stitching me up. I know my rights and, believe me, I'm fucking good at my job.'

I nodded, registering the accent, a gruff North-Eastern twang. 'How long have you been at Hamilton Law?'

'Four years.'

'And you're a Junior Partner, right? And Sabrina was a Partner.'

Bert traced a circle in the air with his bare foot. 'Promoted just before Christmas.'

'Sabrina must have been good, then. To get the promotion.'

'Must have been.'

I heard the sarcasm in his voice but I held my tongue, biding my time. Knowing when to pull back and give a person space is the difference between a killer quote and a slammed door.

I nodded towards the drum-kit in the corner. 'Your neighbours must love you.'

'I had the place sound-proofed.'

'You any good?'

'What do you think?'

The smirk on Bert's lips hardened my stomach. 'Are you aware your firm is being investigated for sexism?'

Bert spread out on the sofa and put his bare feet on the coffee table. 'How do you know about that?'

'I'm also good at my job.' I waggled my eyebrows, earning a smirk from Bert. 'What can you tell me about the website, LegalLens?'

He shrugged. 'It's for time-wasters. A joke.'

'I don't think Sabrina found it funny.'

'I wouldn't know.' As Bert stretched his arms up, his gold Rolex glinted in the light.

'So, you weren't aware of the smear campaign against Sabrina?'

Bert raised an eyebrow. 'I hardly think a few spiteful comments constitutes a smear campaign.'

'So you have seen it.' I crossed the room and sat in the armchair opposite Bert.

'Sabrina asked me for advice about what to do. I told her to ignore it. She was always too sensitive.'

I narrowed my gaze. 'So your advice was to accept the abuse. Move on.'

Bert tapped his finger against his thigh and rolled his eyes. 'Look, Sabrina was smart, a brilliant lawyer. But outside work it was a different story. She wasn't right. In here,' he tapped his head. 'She was on the happy pills because she got herself all worked up about stuff.'

'What kind of stuff?'

Bert crossed one leg over the other, and ran a finger along his jawline. He was shooting for nonchalant, but the tension around his eyes gave him away. 'She showed up here back in February. Tears, the lot. She thought she was being followed. That someone had broken into her flat.'

I fidgeted in the chair, trying to get comfortable. 'Did she report it?'

'I doubt it. Sabrina was cuckoo. Struggled with reality some-times. I thought she was making it up.'

Something was bothering me. I stood up and wandered to the window, giving my brain space to breathe. *Happy pills. Cuckoo.* Both had appeared in those poisonous posts on LegalLens.

Suddenly, there was a click and the front door opened. A bundle of fur scampered across the flat and leaped into Bert's lap.

'Thanks, Bridget,' he called out, nuzzling the dog, as the door closed again. He glanced at me. 'This is Butch.'

My mouth twitched. I definitely hadn't pegged Bert as the owner of a Yorkshire Terrier.

Rifling through my bag, I pulled out the picture from Facebook and joined him on the sofa. 'This photo was taken at your office Christmas party,' I said, as Butch licked my hand with his small pink tongue. 'Not long after Sabrina was promoted, right?'

Bert was stroking the dog, his eyes on the floor. All of a sudden, he turned to me and his jaw tightened. 'The *London Herald*. Your colleague is the man who killed Sabrina.'

'The man suspected of killing Sabrina,' I corrected him.

Bert gave me a cool look. 'Well, he was sleeping with her.'

'He wasn't the only one.' Bert twitched and the dog looked up at him.

'Did you know about Sabrina's affair with Charlie Swift?' I asked.

'Why would I know about it?' He rubbed his eyes with a fist and dropped his head. I knew Bert's alpha-male ego had taken a beating over the promotion, but there was something else, something deeper.

I turned my head and watched Bert's reflection in the gigantic flat-screen TV hanging on the wall. 'Were you in love with Sabrina?'

Bert's gaze hardened, then he threw the dog off his lap and stalked into the kitchen. This time he poured himself a proper drink. 'What does any of this matter now? Sabrina's fucking dead.' Finally, the mask slipped and I saw pain in his eyes. But I also saw something else. *Fear.*

I slid forwards on the chair, and kept my voice level. 'Bert, whether you realise it or not, you've given me two strong motives for Sabrina's murder. Jilted boyfriend with an axe to grind. Bitter colleague who lost out on a promotion. Your relationship with Sabrina could play out a thousand ways in the press.'

Bert raked a rough hand through his hair and his sunglasses clattered onto the floor. He stared down at them, his voice as hoarse as a rusty saw. 'You're forgetting one thing. The police have their man.'

I shook my head. 'They have a suspect. There's a difference. Where were you on Saturday night?'

Bert drained his glass. 'Are you fucking serious?'

'Come on, it's good practice for when the police show up.'

'And why would the police show up?'

'Because you're not as good a liar as you think.'

Bert's face twisted into a snarl and he thumped the glass down on the counter. 'I'm a fucking great liar. I just happen to be telling the truth right now.'

I nodded towards the window. 'I was there, you know. When they pulled Sabrina's body out of the Thames. I'm going to find the person who did this.'

I use that line a lot. It makes an innocent person feel as if we're on the same side. Only a person with something to hide hears it as a threat.

I waited a beat, then picked up my bag. 'Thank you for your time, Mr Hughes.'

'It must be pretty tough on his wife.' The words were so quiet, I almost missed them.

I glanced over my shoulder, frowning. 'Whose wife?'

'Your colleague.'

'You mean Emily?' I turned to face him. 'Yeah, she'll be happier when Charlie turns up.'

Bert followed me to the door and scooped the dog up in his arms. 'You don't think Charlie did it?' His eyes swept across my face and that's when I spotted it; a flicker of something in his eye.

I sighed, my mind still on his question about Emily. 'Innocent until proven guilty. You should know that more than anyone, right?'

He looked as if he was going to say something else. When he didn't, I handed him my card, then slung my bag over my shoulders.

As I marched towards the stairs, Bert's eyes burned a hole in my back.

10

I knew something was wrong the moment I stepped out of the lift.

It was eerily quiet, as though a blanket had been thrown over the newsroom. Clusters of people were gathered around computer screens. I darted towards News, tension coiling in my stomach. Kate, Mack and Rahid were glued to Kate's computer screen.

Kate looked up when she heard me, her face pale and drawn. 'Where have you been?'

'Interviewing Sabrina's ex. What's going on?'

She shifted to the left and I caught a glimpse of her screen. The *Post*'s homepage displayed a photograph of Charlie and Lizzie on their wedding day. It had been photoshopped to look as if it was ripped in half. I read the headline, and felt the blood drain from my face.

BREAKING NEWS: JOURNO BEAT UP LATE WIFE
By Eliot Sampson

The *Post* can exclusively reveal that Charles Swift, Business Editor at the *London Herald* and the prime suspect in the murder of Sabrina Hobbs, was arrested for assaulting his late wife, Elizabeth, in July 2007. Charges were dropped after Elizabeth decided not to pursue the matter charges. A source remembers how Swift's assault left his wife needing twenty-eight stitches in the back of her head.

A smaller photograph of Lizzie's head injury showed a red gash oozing stickiness.

I blinked rapidly, unable to process the image on the screen with something Charlie had done. 'It says ... it says Charlie wasn't convicted.'

'Are you fucking blind?' Mack rapped the screen with his knuckles. 'Look at that photograph. Shit, did she have cancer when he did this to her?'

We all stared at the computer screen, the atmosphere plummeting fast.

'Rowley is going to hit the roof.' Mack rounded on me, dark eyes flashing with anger. 'We missed this, Kent. And you know why? Because we've spent the last twenty-four hours trying to keep a lid on Charlie. We look like we've been caught with our dicks in our hands.'

I leaned against the desk, feeling light-headed. 'Let's not get carried away. This assault doesn't prove Charlie murdered Sabrina.' I waved my notebook in the air. 'I've just come from Bert Hughes's apartment. He has a motive, two actually. Then there's the smear campaign and–'

'Enough!' Mack's voice cut through me. 'If you can't be objective, you're off the story. I will not let you screw it up.'

'Hear hear, fucktards.' A shadow passed across my desk as Lansdowne bore down on us. 'You are officially the most useless news team on the planet.'

I opened my mouth to speak, but Kate shook her head.

'You have two hours to pull this back from the brink and come up with something new,' said Lansdowne. 'Or I will march over to the *Post*, poach every one of their staff and nail you lot to the wall by your genitals.' He kicked a wastepaper bin, spilling the remnants of Mack's quinoa salad across the floor, then stalked off.

Mack buttoned the jacket of his custom-made suit and smoothed down his tie. Under the newsroom lights, his overly gelled hair looked shiny and fake. 'Kent, I want you to pass Bert Hughes over to Rahid.'

'But–'

'No buts, Kent. I need you on Charlie.'

Kate glanced at her watch. 'I'm out of here in fifteen minutes. My Rowntree source says news is imminent.'

'Good, maybe a verdict will kick this off the front page,' I said, then hated myself for the comment.

Mack was pacing up and down beside his desk. 'Emily. That's our angle. Second wife commenting on first wife. Get a quote from her and we're golden.'

Kate snorted. 'Are you mad? There'll be a ring of fire around Emily now. Wouldn't surprise me if she's signed with a PR firm.'

If that was true, Emily could name her price for the exclusive sit-down interview. The *Herald* couldn't afford to join a bidding war.

Mack leaned forward and tapped my notebook. 'Charlie. Where is he? We need to think like him. Pull together everything we know about his background, friends, family. Police sources – what's the latest? Any sightings of him, CCTV. Has he used his phone, his bank card? Anything that points to–'

'Listen up, everyone.' Spencer Storey, the City Editor, strode into our circle, his gut hanging over his belt like a sack of flour. 'We're clearing space in the print edition. Legal are drawing up a statement. We need to cover our arses.'

'Thanks for pointing out the fucking obvious,' said Mack, squaring up to Spencer.

I left them to their pissing competition, forcing myself to tune out the noise. One of the first things you learn in the newsroom is that facts don't necessarily sell papers. Although it was pretty hard to argue with the evidence on Kate's computer screen. I dragged my eyes away as Rahid picked up a tray and collected our mugs.

The picture of Lizzie's injury made me feel sick. I slid down my chair, sifting through my brain for clues to Charlie's violent streak.

A memory took shape in my mind. Charlie and I in a bar last November. It was coming up to the one-month anniversary of Tommy's death. I'd been at an awards lunch and, like every other journalist, had taken advantage of the free bar. That afternoon I kept my head down in the office but, at the end of the day, Charlie spotted me barrelling into the lift. He tried to steer me to a cab. Instead I staggered into a bar, where my red high heels and pencil skirt combo proved beyond my levels of coordination, and I promptly fell over.

I ordered a vodka tonic and Charlie pulled up a stool, frowning. 'Take it from me, booze isn't the answer.'

'You know what's worse than an alcoholic,' my words were already slurring together, 'a reformed alcoholic.'

As I signalled to the barman for another round, Charlie sighed and pushed a menu towards me. 'At least eat something.'

I shook my head, and jabbed my finger in his chest. 'Eating's cheating.'

Charlie scowled. 'You think Tommy would want to see you like this?'

'What the fuck do you know about Tommy?' I glanced down and noticed the holdall by Charlie's feet. 'Going somewhere nice?'

'Geneva. For work. Flight leaves tonight.'

I slumped against the bar, looking at him. 'Ge-nee-va. Emily going? Dirty weekend away, is it?' I waved my glass in front of his face, feeling mean. 'You sure you don't want one?'

'I'll pretend I didn't hear that,' he said, shooting me a look. He picked up a beer mat and turned it over in his hands. 'Soph, listen. When Lizzie died, I was face-down, frozen. Couldn't understand why someone so beautiful and kind was taken, when deadbeats like Vanessa get away scot-free. It was as if a light went off. I was crawling around in the dark, wondering what happened, and why I couldn't do the most basic things like toast my bread, or tie my shoelaces.'

The barman slid me a drink and I sucked greedily on the straw. 'Let me guess, a year went by and the light came back on.'

Charlie gave me a tight smile. 'The light has never come back on.'

I stared at him. 'What, never?'

He shrugged. 'I've learned to feel my way in the dark. I don't need to see the toaster to know how it works. And now I wear slip-ons.' He gestured towards his brown loafers.

I blinked a couple of times. 'So, you're saying I'll never get through this.' I watched Charlie fold the beer mat in half, a muscle working in his jaw. 'But what about Emily?'

'What about her?'

The bar flashed in and out of focus and I clutched my stool. 'Can I let you into a secret, Charlie Swift? I don't want to get through this.' And I meant it. Grief was suffocating, but it was addictive. I'd made a pact with myself that I would hold on to the pain. The more it hurt, the closer I was to Tommy's death, closer to when he was alive. I didn't want time to pass, or the hurt to ease. I wanted it raw and recent. Recent meant I couldn't forget him.

Charlie tossed the beer mat on the bar and faced me, his thick dark fringe swept low over one eye. 'You think if the pain fades, so will Tommy.'

'Got it in one, buster.' I gripped the glass so tightly I was amazed it didn't shatter. I signalled for another drink, but Charlie stopped me.

'Look, I've got to get to the airport, but I'm not leaving you here alone. You're wasted.'

I ignored him, and lay my head on the bar. It was wet and smelt sour but I didn't care. 'How have you done it? How have you found happiness again?'

'Who says I have?'

All of a sudden I felt the meanness twist inside me like a living, breathing thing. I leaned towards Charlie and whispered, 'A new wife, a new life. Charlie's got all the answers. Maybe I'll take a leaf out of your book and find a new brother.'

The hurt in Charlie's eyes sobered me up a fraction.

'Fuck. I'm sorry, I didn't mea— You're a good husband. You deserve it. All of the happiness.' I waved my arm around, unbalancing myself.

Charlie grabbed my arm to stop me sliding off the stool and, as he bent towards me, his voice was harsh and unfamiliar. 'Can I let *you* into a little secret, Sophie Kent? I'm not a good husband.'

I blinked. 'You're right. The brown loafers, for one.'

Charlie rolled his eyes and pulled out his wallet. 'Time you went home.'

Home. The night narrowed before me like a tunnel.

Charlie saw the look on my face and sighed. 'Why don't you stay at mine tonight?'

'Thanks, but you're not my type.'

Charlie's mouth twitched. 'Emily's at a wedding show in Paris. You'll have the place to yourself. Might do you good to have a change of scene.'

I sagged against him. 'Charlie, the bar is spinning.'

After that, my memory dims. A nauseating taxi ride. Tripping up stairs. A sickly smell of jasmine. Charlie pulling back the duvet. A bitter taste in my mouth. I woke up the next morning with a splintering headache. Something felt off. I stared down at my half-naked body, wondering for one awful moment if Charlie and I had crossed a line. Then I remembered he was in Geneva. The rest of the day was taken up piecing together the night before, praying Charlie would forgive me for the hateful things I said.

I'm not a good husband. I'd forgotten that comment until now. According to reports, Charlie was already cheating on Emily by then. Two months after that night in the bar, Sabrina would be pregnant. Five months later she'd be dead.

I rapped on the divider between my desk and Kate's to get her attention. She looked up and I pressed a finger to my lips, then lowered my voice.

'You know what else happened in 2007? Charlie gave up drinking. He never told me why. Just said that he'd behaved like an arsehole.'

Kate folded her arms. 'Hospitalising your wife's a pretty big sign you're an arsehole.'

I shook my head as the teeth of a headache started to bite. I forced myself to look at the computer screen. At Lizzie's head wound. 'I just can't imagine Charlie doing this. It doesn't fit with the friend I know.'

Kate eyed me carefully. 'You know, years ago I interviewed a woman called Daisy Brent. A total pop tart, all hair extensions and silicone implants. Daisy was married to that Z-list reality-TV star. Jez something. Good-looking but the sort of guy you want out of the gene pool.'

Kate stood up and stretched her arms over her head.

'Anyway, the TV network held their Christmas party at the Randall Hotel but Daisy was struck down with flu so Jez went alone. By midnight, he'd taken so many drugs he was bouncing off the ceiling, trying his luck with anything with a pulse.

When no one gave the loser the time of day, he spiked a camera assistant's wine with Rohypnol.' Kate pulled her curls back into a ponytail, the memory hardening her eyes. 'Except Jez wasn't even a competent rapist. He doubled the dose for luck. By the time he dragged his victim into the disabled toilet, she was foaming at the mouth. Instead of calling for an ambulance, Jez unbuckled his belt. She slipped into a coma. Was brain-dead for months.'

I stared at Kate in horror. 'I hope they chopped off his nuts.'

'He's holed up at Pentonville and a pretty little thing like him is bound to be in demand. But listen, after Jez's conviction, Daisy told me that even with the stack of evidence against Jez, her mum didn't believe he was guilty. Her mum was a for-mer porn star, a regular in the trashy magazine party pages. A famous son-in-law was good for business so she chose to see what she wanted to see.'

Kate's words sunk in and I arched an eyebrow. 'Am I Porno Mum in this scenario?'

Kate sighed. 'All I'm saying is: keep an open mind.'

I spun back round to my computer, wishing people would stop telling me that. *I'm not a good husband.* I picked up my phone and dialled Emily, cursing as it went to voicemail. I left a message, then logged onto her blog, *Something Borrowed.*

'Er, guys?' I glanced over at Spencer and Mack who were still arguing and raised my voice. 'Guys, take a look at this.'

Emily's latest post was called *My Husband.* She'd uploaded it thirty minutes ago.

Dear friends,

I can call you friends, can't I? And friends tell each other stuff, right? Well, I've thought long and hard about what I'm going to do, and I've decided I can't bottle it up any longer.

If you haven't heard the news, my husband Charlie has been accused of murder. I feel like I'm stuck in a bad movie. The police think Charlie had an affair with a woman called Sabrina, got her pregnant, and then murdered her. For Christ's sake!!!

My heart is so full of . . . everything. I can't unpack my feelings. Would Charlie cheat on me? Regular readers of *Something Borrowed* know Charlie as PC. *Prince Charming*. Prince Charmings don't cheat, right? They also don't murder helpless women. I don't buy it. And he got her pregnant? I don't think so.

You see, Charlie wouldn't do that to me. *deep breath* We've been struggling to have a baby. I've kept this buried because, you know: emotional wreck. But this feels too relevant not to share. I've had three miscarriages in the past year. That's *three times* our hearts have been smashed to pieces.

What is one of the things I harp on about in this blog? Marriage takes WORK. You can't throw in the towel just because life gets hard. So, until Charlie gives me his side of the story, I'm standing by my PC. Innocent until proven guilty, right?

Judging by the number of offers I've had from media outlets, you're interested in my story. But I'm not going to let my words get twisted. What's the point of having a blog if you can't talk directly to your readers? I've decided instead to blog daily about my experiences, thoughts and emotions.

This will be my story, in my own words.

Keep checking in for updates. And thank you soooooo much for your support and kind words. It means a lot.

Love,
Em xx

P.S. By the way, the *Post*'s article claiming that Charlie assaulted his first wife, Lizzie? Charlie was a different guy back then. He was an alcoholic and did many things he wasn't proud of. Not that it excuses his actions, I know. For what it's worth, I've never known Charlie to touch a drop of alcohol, nor has he ever been violent towards me.

I leaned back in my chair and whistled. 'Put away the cheque-book, folks. Emily's just blown us all out of the water.'

11

Emily: 28 weeks before the murder

A rustling noise wakes her up. Emily rubs her eyes and sees Charlie pulling on his jeans through the gloom.

'What time is it?' Her voice is thick with sleep.

He whips his head round. 'Shhh, go back to sleep. It's early.'

'Where are you going?'

'I . . . uh. Bournemouth.' He glances round as if searching for something.

Emily sits up sharply. 'What? Why?'

Charlie's face is in shadow. 'It's – complicated. Vanessa. She left a voicemail. I need to . . .' Charlie pulls a burgundy jumper over his head and ruffles his fringe.

Emily sighs. Since the wedding, there has been a steady stream of phone calls. Vanessa doesn't keep to normal hours. She often rings in the middle of the night, leaving endless messages. Sometimes telling Charlie she loves him, or that she wishes he'd never been born, depending on how much booze she's sunk. Lately she's been begging Charlie to help her find something. *'Charlie Charlie Charlie don't let me down this is so important I need your help find him find it.*' What or who she wants Charlie to find, Emily has no idea, Vanessa never says. And Charlie brushes off her questions with an impatient flick of his hand. All this time Charlie has never rung back; he's certainly never paid her a visit.

'What did Vanessa's voicemail say?' she asks. When Charlie doesn't answer she sighs. 'Baby, she's drunk. By the time you get there she probably won't remember she called.'

Charlie mumbles something then moments later Emily hears the tap running in the bathroom. She swings her legs over the side of the bed. Cold air swirls around her ankles. She hits the light and looks at the clock: 5.46 a.m.

Emily pulls on her leggings, fighting down the nausea in her stomach. She's learned to embrace the sickness, welcome it. *If I'm sick, the baby is still in there.* She puts a protective hand over her stomach, *Hi, peanut,* and slides a grey hoody over her head.

'What are you doing?' Charlie is in the doorway, frowning. There's a smudge of toothpaste on his lip.

'I'm coming with you.'

Charlie's face darkens. 'Em, you need to rest. Like you say, it's a fool's errand.'

'So we can be fools together.' She lightens her voice, but Charlie doesn't smile. 'Baby, you can't deal with Vanessa on your own. You know what happens.'

Charlie sighs, then sits beside her on the bed, far enough away so that their legs don't touch. 'This isn't a good idea.'

Emily stares at the space between them and her skin tingles. Then she shifts round to face him, her gaze direct, challenging. 'I'm coming.'

Charlie gives her a curt nod and thunders to the door.

Emily rests her head against the rain-streaked window of the car. The road runs parallel to the beach and she watches the wind whip the waves into a frenzy.

Charlie takes a hard right turn and Emily grips the door handle. 'So, are you going to tell her?'

'About what?'

'The baby.'

Charlie rips the gearstick into a lower gear and puts his foot down. The car shoots forward, leaving Emily's stomach behind. 'Vanessa is having nothing to do with this baby.'

'But she's going to be a grandmother. Maybe it will give her an incentive to . . .' Her words trail off and she tears her eyes away from the waves skidding across the sand. Emily draws the letters 'C' and 'E' in the condensation on the window, wondering what their lives would look like without Vanessa in it. Hatred binds Charlie to his mum in a way Emily can't understand. Since Vanessa reappeared in their lives, there's a hardness to Charlie she doesn't recognise. The more he pulls away from her, the worse Vanessa's drinking gets.

Emily's phone vibrates in her bag. She fishes it out and glances at the screen. A shot of adrenaline spikes through her. She thrusts it back in her bag, her knuckles white.

The car rolls to a stop at some traffic lights and Charlie flicks the radio on. A perky pop song fills the car and Emily switches it off.

'It's time I saw her,' she says, quietly. 'It's been seven months since the wedding.' Emily closes her eyes as she remembers the low point of their big day. Her dad was making a speech and had just reached the anecdote about Emily's career rock-bottom working in a pet food factory aged fifteen, when there was a clatter from the back of the room. Everyone turned to see Vanessa trip over a flower display. Her cheeks were crimson and she had the wine-glazed look of a woman who'd been drinking since breakfast. Charlie, who'd been on edge all day, half-rose from his chair but Emily put a firm hand on his thigh. Not now, not during the speeches. She wouldn't let anything ruin their day. Instead she flung a desperate look at her bridesmaid, Sinead.

Moments later a screech rang through the banquet room. 'Don't touch me! How dare you. Who do you think you are?'

Emily's dad laughed nervously. 'Is everything OK back there?'

She could see Sinead trying to steer Vanessa out the door. Then Vanessa lashed out and caught Sinead's chin, her words loose and slurred.

'Don't shush me, you slut. Charlie, are you going to let her treat me like this?'

Horrified, Emily jabbed Charlie in the ribs. He leaped up and propelled his mum towards the door but Vanessa was on a roll.

'This wedding is a farce. My son is already married. Why should we celebrate *her*?' She thrust a finger at Emily before Charlie managed to bundle her out.

No one spoke. Emily's cheeks burned. As her dad soldiered on with his speech, Emily felt the weight of the empty seat beside her. Later that day she saw Charlie and Vanessa fighting outside the restaurant. The hatred on Charlie's face had turned her stomach.

'Why are we bombing down here at the crack of dawn?' She hears the pleading note in her voice and wishes she could stop. Charlie opens the window and a blast of cold, salty air drowns out her words. ' 'Baby, I'm your wife. You shouldn't have to deal with this on your ow—'

'Just STOP.' Charlie slams his fist against the steering wheel making her jump. She feels his anger down to her bones. Charlie glances at her, his eyes softening a fraction. 'Christ, you make things ten times worse for yourself.'

Emily puts a hand on her stomach, blinking back the tears. After the miscarriage, things briefly improved between them and Charlie became more like his old self. He researched which foods boosted fertility and stocked the fridge with homemade smoothies filled with weird things like Maca Root and wheat grass. 'Consider me the fertility fairy,' he laughed when he caught her eyeing the green gloop. And, when she clung to him at night, her body wracked with sobs, Charlie stroked her back until she fell asleep. But she knew it was over the morning she woke to find Charlie's side of the bed cold. He only ran at dawn after a nightmare. And the nightmares meant one thing: he would slip through her fingers again. Things crashed quickly after that. For the first time she can see the effort it's taking Charlie to stay sober. Before their wedding, he was going to one AA meeting a week, two tops. But now it's daily, sometimes twice daily. Last week, when they argued, Charlie called her Lizzie by mistake. She slapped him, then shut herself in the bathroom and sliced the skin on her thigh until her breathing evened out.

The car reaches the end of a dirt-track and pulls up outside a shabby cottage called The Ridings. The windows are crusted with salt; paint is peeling off the exterior walls in a way that makes it look as if the house is shedding its skin. On the front patch of lawn, beneath the Horse Chestnut tree, is a sculpture of a boy sitting on a swing and gazing up at the heavens.

Charlie pauses for a moment, both hands on the steering wheel, looking lost.

Emily is about to put a hand on his leg when he clears his throat. 'I think you should stay in the car.'

'But–'

Charlie leans his head against the steering wheel and for an awful moment she thinks he's going to cry.

'So I'm just supposed to sit here and wait? After driving all that way?'

'I never asked you to come.' Charlie's voice is soft but final.

Emily watches Charlie scorch up the garden path and disappear through the front door. The car still smells of him. Emily breathes him in as she watches a flock of seagulls land in a line on the thatched roof.

Emily's phone beeps again and she slides it out of her bag. Tinder is already open on her phone. Emily scrolls through endless faces and her breathing quickens. *Charlie loves me.* Swipe. *He loves me not.* She knows it's a dangerous game to play. Emily closes her eyes, remembering all those times in the past when the hot, furious touch of a stranger took her to a white space in her head. A space that didn't hurt. She thought that was all behind her. But Charlie is giving her no choice.

The noise in her head grows louder, and her skin starts to buzz. A loud screech pierces the air and she jumps, wondering for a moment if it's inside her head. Above, the seagulls sail through the air and vanish. It's enough to break the spell. Emily shoves her phone in her bag, feeling guilty. She hesitates, then opens the car door. The wind howls around her ears, throwing a briny scent into her face. She pulls her hair into a bun and creeps towards the cottage. What could Vanessa have possibly said in her voicemail to make Charlie drive all the way here?

Emily peeps in at the sitting room window, careful to keep her face from view. She can see Vanessa's pink slipper dangling off the sofa; the rest of her is obscured by Charlie. His back is to the window and he's waving a piece of paper in the air. He's shouting but she can't hear what he's saying over the wind.

Then Charlie moves to the fireplace and she gets a view of Vanessa lying on the sofa. Her dark hair is fanned out across the cushion; her face bloated and washed-out. She's wearing grey tracksuit bottoms and a black fleece and Emily can tell she's drunk. Her head lolls to the side and her eyes struggle to follow Charlie round the room. There are wine bottles around her feet, an overflowing ashtray on the side table.

Vanessa heaves herself up to sitting. She's trying to talk. She gropes around for the nearest bottle but, before she can lift it to her mouth, Charlie snatches it out of her hand. Vanessa picks up an empty bottle and hurls it at Charlie. He ducks and it smashes. Emily watches as Vanessa lunges for another bottle and a memory of her childhood flickers in her brain: the gloopy moment before the smash or the hit, when you know it's coming and there's nothing you can do to stop it.

As the second bottle smashes, Emily slams her hand against the window. Charlie is crouched down, scooping up splinters of glass, and doesn't hear but Vanessa glances at the window. When she sees Emily, her face contorts in fury. Emily stumbles towards the car and trips over the boy sculpture, landing hard. Hauling herself up, she half-falls against the car as a pain twists in her stomach. The pain is familiar. Emily moans. She glances down at the mud smeared across her jumper. She feels the leaking sensation between her legs. *Please no please no please no.*

Tears blinding her, Emily lurches towards the cottage.

At that moment, the front door opens and Charlie appears. His eyes flash. 'I thought I told you–'

'Charlie, I need a bathroom.'

'Fuck's sake, Em. Do you have any idea what–' He spots her expression and he slows down. 'What's the matter?' Emily shakes her head, the tears falling fast. She watches the realisation dawn on his face. He holds her gaze for a moment, then helps her to the car. 'There's a petrol station a mile away.'

Emily sobs. 'Can't I just go in her house for a second?'

Charlie's jaw clenches. 'Put your seatbelt on.'

Emily does as he says, then doubles over trying to calm her breathing. As Charlie pulls away from the kerb, he squeezes her thigh. Emily stares at his hand; it's the first time he's touched her in weeks.

They pull into the garage forecourt and Charlie turns to her, his eyes unreadable. 'You want company?'

Emily bites her lip. 'No, I'll be back in a minute.'

She limps to the toilet and shuts the door behind her. Then she unbuttons her jeans. The blood has already soaked through her pants; the metallic, meaty odour makes her gag.

As she sits on the toilet she traces a hand over her thigh. The patch of skin that Charlie touched is warm.

It feels like heaven.

12

Present day

I woke to find Emily at the centre of a media storm. Her blog had gone viral. Radio 4's *Today* programme featured a segment called 'Standing by your spouse' and a panel on *This Morning* were debating the merits and pitfalls of Emily speaking out so publicly. She was fast becoming a divisive figure. She also wasn't answering her phone.

As I sloped towards Green Park, shards of sunlight bounced off windows, spearing me in the eyes. The bright, cloudless morning was amplifying my headache. Even after a cocktail of sleeping pills I couldn't get the image of Lizzie's smashed skull out of my mind.

A crowd of joggers sprinted past, spraying water over themselves. It was only ten o'clock but the sun was already warming the air. I slid off my jacket and tramped across the grass, looking for Dominic Randall, Charlie's best friend. I spotted him stretched out on a bench beneath an oak tree, one leg crossed over the other, a newspaper spread out on his lap. The sleeves of his electric-blue shirt were rolled up, and he was wearing a red bow-tie.

I strolled over. 'The *Post*? Are you kidding me?'

Dominic's face broke into a grin. 'So sue me, I like a quality paper.' His mock American accent made me smile. Dominic folded the newspaper and stood up, kissing me on both cheeks. 'Long time no see.'

His cheek was clammy and he'd shed a few pounds since I last saw him. I sat down, breathing in the sunbaked, polleny air just as a Jack Russell dog trotted up and cocked his leg against the bench.

Dominic arched an eyebrow. 'See, he's not a fan of the *Herald*, either.'

I've always liked Dominic. I first met him a few years ago when I stumbled upon their boys' night out. I was annoyed that a piece I'd put my heart and soul into had been spiked at the last minute and needed to let off steam in the Anchor & Hart, an old man's pub tucked in a leafy square behind the *Herald*.

I ordered my drink, ignoring the chubby guy who was throwing peanuts into his mouth. He missed and one caught me in the forehead.

'Allow me to make it up to you. The next drink is on me.' He flicked his tawny fringe and waggled his eyebrows. 'You're a friend of Swifty, right? I'm Dominic.'

'Sophie Kent.' I held out my hand, then glanced past him to where Charlie sat with a group of guys. 'Looks like fun.'

Dominic put his hands on his hips, his pea-green shirt straining across his stomach. 'I'd ask you to join us but we're on a boys' night out.'

'I wouldn't join you anyway. I'm on a girl's night.'

'You're meeting friends?'

'Nope.'

Dominic belly-laughed and pushed the wine-glass towards me. 'Well, if you get bored, I'm sure we could make an exception.'

Charlie told me the next day that Dominic had kept him out till four in the morning singing eighties ballads in a karaoke bar, even though Charlie didn't drink. 'Dominic was so pissed he puked in the water taxi.'

'Water taxi?' I said, incredulously.

Charlie rolled his bloodshot eyes. 'Blame Dominic.'

I'd seen Dominic a handful of times over the years. He always played the joker but Charlie once told me it was a front. Dominic came out to his working-class parents while he was at university and was still paying the price. 'They call him a poof, to his face,' he said, curling his lip. So Dominic hid the hurt by becoming the life and soul of every party.

A skateboarder zoomed past and I watched him carve a trail in the path. 'How have you been?'

Dominic brushed the hair out of his face. 'I'm a therapist now. Part-own a practice. Very grown up.' He clutched a roll of fat and put on a camp voice. 'You know the personal training gig just wasn't working out for me. Too many bored housewives trying to get into my Lycra thong.'

It felt good to laugh, but then I remembered why we were here and I sighed. 'Have you seen him, Dom?'

He held the coffee cup to his lips and I saw his jaw tighten. The lightness disappeared from his voice. 'He won't return my calls.'

I closed my eyes. 'Where the hell is he?'

'I wish I knew.'

'Did you know? About the affair?'

'I knew things weren't great at home, but these days Charlie-boy plays his cards close to his chest.' I detected a hint of sourness in his tone, which was very unlike Dominic.

I laid my jacket over the arm of the bench and fiddled with my collar. 'I saw the *Post*'s piece, about Lizzie.'

Dominic threw the newspaper onto the bench and leaned forward. 'Did you ever meet Lizzie?'

I shook my head. 'Before my time.'

He stared straight at the ground. 'She was lovely. Gorgeous, funny – a terrible dancer though. Two left feet. Luckily her face made up for it.' He scrunched his empty cup between his hands then lobbed it towards the bin. It missed and he sighed. 'Story of my life.'

He dumped the cup in the bin.

'Lizzie was good for Charlie. Bolstered him up, kept him grounded,' he said. 'Charlie's always had a tendency to spiral. Still, it's in his genes.'

I leaned back against the bench, closing my eyes into the sun. 'You know, Charlie never told me Vanessa died.'

Dominic cleared his throat. 'He didn't tell me either. I found out through a family friend who still lives in Bournemouth. Not that thirty-five years of friendship counts for much.'

I raised my eyebrows. Not telling me was one thing, but *Dominic*?

He straightened his bow-tie. 'You know Charlie was there when it happened, right?'

'When Vanessa died?'

'No, Lizzie. She was swimming in the Serpentine while Charlie was on the phone to his mum. She called him out of the blue that day; naturally, she was plastered. Charlie was so engrossed in their fight that he never saw Lizzie go under. She was so weak after all that chemo; she must have got tired.'

I stared at Dominic, open-mouthed. 'So he blames his mum?'

Dominic shrugged. 'Put it this way, that was the only time Charlie spoke to his mum since he was a kid. And look what happened.' He gave me a wry smile. 'Christ, this is laugh-a-minute, isn't it? Sure you don't want to talk about my new boyfriend, Zayn? He has a tiny little bottom that looks like a peach.' I put my hand on his arm, and Dominic gave it a squeeze. 'Sorry, serious isn't my forte.'

I smiled, knowing how hard this was for Dominic. He was the closest thing Charlie had to a brother. They'd been friends since primary school, ever since Charlie defended Dominic's right to wear a sparkly tie to school. He got beaten up anyway, but Dominic never forgot the fact that Charlie had stood up for him.

'Vanessa was nuts. I know you shouldn't speak ill of the dead, but she was a wack-job,' said Dominic. 'A real hippy. Joined a religious cult in the seventies. It went pear-shaped and she escaped but I think part of her was brainwashed. She used to spout Bible quotes at us when she was drunk, which was most of the time. Always about fire. *Depart from you cursed, into the eternal fire.*' He gave a sad laugh. 'I can't believe I can still remember that.

My mum caught Charlie lighting matches in the attic once, went ballistic.'

An elderly couple shuffled past us, wrapped up in winter coats, despite the balmy temperature. We watched them walk perfectly in sync with each other, then Dominic sighed.

'Vanessa believed she could bring things back to life by submerging them in water. Took the baptism thing a bit literally. Poor Charlie; he believed it too. He was such a weirdo when we met. We once found a bird with a broken wing in his garden. He told me he could revive it by filling the sink with water and holding it under.' Dominic rolled his eyes. 'Funny enough, the Lord didn't reveal himself. We buried it in a matchbox under the rhododendron bush.'

'Charlie once told me he spent a lot of time at your house.'

Dominic nodded. 'For a couple of years he went back and forth, yeah. His house was a bit drinky-drinky-shouty-shouty. Anyone who knew them could see how much Vanessa loved him. She lit up when Charlie was around. And she was always frittering away what little money she had on him: a new bike, a Lego set, the latest clothes. But what Charlie really craved was stability, and when she drank . . .' Dominic rolled his eyes. 'He bore the brunt of it. Vanessa had a string of men, unsavoury characters. Charlie got good at making himself invisible. Used to take his sleeping bag and camp out in the airing cupboard, poor sod. The other kids used to tease him about her. Called her Vomiting Vanessa because she pitched up drunk at the nativity play and puked during the first half. Charlie used to make her park down the road when she dropped him off; booze made her unpredictable and he was worried she'd do something to embarrass him.'

I stared at him. 'She drove him drunk to school?'

'It was the early eighties. In Bournemouth. Enough said.' He picked up an acorn from the ground by his foot and turned it over in his chunky fingers. 'You know, we used to find her empties stashed under the teddies in his toy box.'

A flash of anger coursed through me. 'And no one did anything?'

'No one knew the full extent of it. Charlie protected her. When Vanessa crashed her car, Charlie supported her statement that a cat ran out in the road. He was always getting into trouble, though. Once he fell out of a tree and got concussion. Another time, the brakes went on his bike and he ended up in A&E. We used to call him Charlie Cat because he seemed to have endless lives. Although,' Dominic swept his hair over his shoulder, 'now I look back on it with my therapist's hat on, I wonder if it was a cry for attention. Getting himself into scrapes hoping his mum would notice. Like how he used to disappear. The Lost Years, I call them. No one had any idea where he was. Eventually the school got tired of him and booted him out.'

'Christ,' I kicked the ground with my heel. 'Charlie did a serious 180. University, career, marriage.'

Dominic twisted the acorn round in his hand. 'Things improved for Charlie when Gordon came into his life.'

'His stepdad?' I'd heard Charlie mention Gordon before.

Dominic gave an exaggerated roll of his eyes. 'Two prawns short of a cocktail. Not quite all there, if you catch my drift. He and Vanessa were only together for a couple of years; they split when Charlie was still in primary school. But, to his credit, Gordon stayed in Charlie's life; helped him get back on the straight and narrow. Especially once Charlie cut his mum out of his life.'

I rested my elbows on the back of the bench, mulling over Dominic's words. Some of it was familiar; the scraps that Charlie had chosen to share. But hearing the sordid details of his childhood laid out by someone who witnessed it was hard to stomach.

'You didn't know much of this, did you?' said Dominic, giving me a wry smile. 'Charlie learned to cover it all up with an easy smile. His way of coping.'

A warm breeze rustled through the trees and I rested my head back against the bench. 'What was the final nail in the coffin between Charlie and Vanessa, anyway?'

Dominic sighed. 'There was a fire. At the house, when we were just kids. Charlie never spoke about it, not even to me. All I know is something snapped in Charlie that day. The fire changed everything. He was done with Vanessa, and that was that. Over the years I've asked Charlie if he'd give his mum another chance, but he never budged. All roads lead back to that fire.' Dominic threw the acorn on the ground and crushed it under his suede brogue. 'What little light that existed inside

Vanessa was snuffed out the day Charlie left home. She gave up on everything.'

I recalled Emily's words yesterday. *That's why I invited her to our wedding. I was trying to build bridges.*

'So, Vanessa turning up to Charlie's wedding . . .'

'Was about the worst thing that could have happened to him. Honestly, what was Emily thinking?'

'She was only trying to help.'

'Yeah, well, look where her meddling has led. You know, Charlie told me that Vanessa cornered him at the wedding. Told him that Lizzie went to visit her, not long after her leukaemia diagnosis. Apparently she begged Vanessa to stop drinking; to patch things up with Charlie. She and Lizzie never had a relationship, but I guess Lizzie wasn't sure if she'd have long left and it was worth a shot.'

'How did Vanessa react?'

'She called Lizzie an interfering cow, said she didn't deserve her son.' Dominic paused, trying to keep his voice calm. 'Ever since the wedding Charlie has slowly retreated into himself. Don't tell me you haven't noticed. He's been weird, distant. Vanessa inching her way back into Charlie's life has dredged up old wounds: his childhood, Lizzie's death.' He leaned forwards and exhaled loudly. 'Christ, I mean Lizzie's death absolutely crucified Charlie.'

'Do you think he'll ever get over it?'

Dominic toyed with the hem of his shirt; he looked as if he was debating something in his head. 'A year after Lizzie's death, I went round to Charlie's place. He hadn't thrown out a thing.

Lizzie's clothes were in the wardrobe, her make-up in the bathroom cabinet, he confessed he sprayed her perfume on the pillow every night before bed. I gave him some tough love, told him he needed to move on, for his own sake. We played loud music and had a cry together. You know the way boys are.'

Dominic forced a grin, but I could see the strain around his eyes.

'I helped him separate Lizzie's things into piles. Charlie could barely touch her stuff so I told him to put the kettle on, desperately wishing we could neck something stronger, but he was off the booze by then. So I'm in their bedroom alone, going through their cupboards, feeling like an intruder and I come across a shoe-box.' Dominic paused. 'Inside is a pile of bones.'

'Bones?'

'Loads of them. Tiny little things. I was totally freaked out. I showed it to Charlie and you know what he said? *That box is to go in the "keep" pile.*' Dominic shook his head. 'He used to make Lizzie chicken soup. When she was going through chemotherapy, it was all she could manage. Charlie saved the chicken bones.'

'Why?'

'Because he's Morticia Addams. I don't know. I think because it was another link to Lizzie.'

'Christ.' I ran a thumbnail along the crease in my trousers, trying to process Dominic's words. 'So, even though he's remarried . . .'

'. . . he's not over her. Look, I think Emily started out as a distraction. Charlie's way of trying to stay afloat. But you know what they say about a square peg and a round hole.'

I raised my eyebrows. 'Poor Emily.'

Dominic's eyes flashed. 'I wouldn't feel too sorry for her.'

His brittle tone took me by surprise. 'You don't approve?'

Behind us a group of school children gathered for a PE lesson. I watched their teacher empty a net of footballs onto the grass.

Dominic sighed. 'Lizzie thought she was odd. Told me Emily made her feel uncomfortable. Stuck with her because she couldn't be arsed to find a new wedding planner. The irony that she ended up marrying her husband.' Dominic sighed and flicked a fallen leaf off his knee.

I pictured Lizzie, and my mind shifted to the photograph of her head injury and stuck there.

Dominic sighed. 'I know you want to ask me about it.'

I held his gaze, trying to ignore the flutter in my stomach. 'Is it true?'

Dominic reached into his rucksack for a water bottle. He uncapped it and took a long slug. 'The day Lizzie was diagnosed with leukaemia was the beginning of a very dark period for Charlie. He was so angry with the world. Like his mum, he turned to drink. And the drink turned him into someone he's not.'

I closed my eyes. 'What happened?'

Dominic didn't speak for a while. When he did, his voice was flat. 'Lizzie was furious with him. She hated it when he drank. She got sick of it and found comfort in a guy she met at the hospital.'

I turned to face him. 'Lizzie cheated on Charlie?'

Dominic gave a sad smile. 'First woman ever to do it. When you look like Charlie, girlfriends generally count their blessings. Anyway, he found out that night. They rowed, he lost his temper.'

'So that's the reason he stopped drinking.'

Dominic took another swig; his face was sweating. 'Never touched a drop again. Became the model husband. To Lizzie, anyway. Doesn't look like he extended the same courtesy to Emily, does it?'

I rubbed my eyes. 'If Charlie's so unhappy why doesn't he just admit the marriage isn't working?'

'I have no idea. Charlie's been so secretive lately. If I had to hazard a guess, I'd say it's the baby thing. As the world now knows thanks to Emily's blog, she's miscarried three times. Charlie isn't that much of a shit that he would leave his grieving wife.'

'So he just cheated on her instead.' The words came out of nowhere. I was shocked at the bitterness I felt.

'Listen to me, Sophie. Charlie's a good guy. Deep down he's–' Dominic's voice cracked. He bent down to zip up his rucksack and I saw him wipe his eyes. 'He's a good guy. I just . . .'

Dominic slung his rucksack over both shoulders and stayed like that, gaze on the ground for the longest time. When he eventually turned to face me, his eyes were pink-veined and wet.

'You know what keeps me awake at night?' he said. 'Lizzie drowned because Charlie wasn't paying attention. Soph, what if we weren't paying attention to Charlie, and he drowned too?'

I stared at Dominic, the dread building in my chest. 'Dom, you don't actually think Charlie might have done this?'

Dominic kissed me on the cheek and hurried away without a backwards glance.

13

'Brace yourself, Kent.' Spencer Storey leaned over my desk and drummed his fat fingers on my computer. 'My brother-in-law works for Bournemouth CID. Owes me a favour. He just called to say Charlie used his credit card last night.'

'Where?'

'Global Bank on Orchard Street.'

I stared at Spencer, trying to quell the queasiness in my stomach. 'But Charlie knows police can track ATM use.'

Spencer shrugged, his beard was flecked with foam from his morning coffee. 'People get desperate. You know that. Charlie will have grabbed a wad of cash, but it's been four days. My brother-in-law says Dorset Police are scouring CCTV of the area. Net's closing in. He thinks an arrest is imminent.'

'Spence!' Lansdowne's booming voice reverberated down the office and Spencer stiffened.

'Fucking now what,' he muttered, sloping off towards Conference Room 3 where Lansdowne was waiting with a face like a rabid Pitbull.

I lay my head back against my chair, still haunted by the look on Dominic's face.

Ten minutes later, I'd called Charlie's stepdad Gordon and Emily's friend Sinead. Both went to voicemail. I felt itchy, boxed in by dead ends. I glanced at the clock on the wall. Five o'clock. The time was dissolving into nothingness as it always does when I'm in the thick of a story.

Why was Charlie in Bournemouth? He grew up there; it was such an obvious place for him to go. But if you know an area well, you know where to hide. Dominic's words rang through my mind: *Charlie got good at making himself invisible.* But where would he go? He was a mess, he was vulnerable. As I stretched my arms above my chest, something flickered in a distant part of my brain. I rifled through the piles of paper on my desk until I found the brown file Adam had given me; the one with my name tacked to the front. Opening it, I ran my eyes down the *Bournemouth Bugle*'s article on Christ Clan until I found the quote from its leader, Hector Marlon.

'My goal is to help society's cast-offs, to give them a safe place to turn.'

Why had Charlie been researching Christ Clan? Why had he drawn my attention to it? Was he trying to send a message? Dominic had mentioned Charlie's childhood brushes with God but did that stretch into adulthood? I couldn't remember a single time Charlie mentioned God, but I was learning a lot of new things about Charlie. I fired off a quick email to Jeff Johnson, the journalist who wrote the piece, asking for five minutes of his time, then settled in to read the rest of the article.

The original Christ Clan was formed by local man Laurence Marlon in the mid-eighties. Marlon, a former teacher, believed himself to be a direct descendent of Jesus Christ. Thanks to his charismatic personality, members flocked to join his religious group. At its height, 750 members, mostly young and male, lived on the forty-two-acre commune in rural Dorset. Rumours of abuse, both physical and psychological, spread and, in 1987, Mark Miller, a teenage member of Christ Clan was hospitalised after suffering severe injuries. The following year, the body of a female member, Samantha Hartley, was found in a stream on the commune grounds. She was believed to have overdosed and drowned. Marlon fled before police could question him, and Christ Clan closed in December 1988. Reports that Marlon absconded to Spain are unconfirmed. When asked if he has stayed in contact with his father, Hector Marlon remains tight-lipped.

The repackaged Christ Clan, which launched in 2012, displays its motto: Love, Strength, Sacrifice on the–

My phone buzzed on my desk. It was a Twitter alert from the TV news programme, *London Today*. I read it once, then re-read it in disbelief. I jumped up, looking around for Mack and Kate, but only Rahid was there, hunched over his desk.

'Rahid, check this out.'

'What?' He was furiously scribbling in his notebook and didn't look up. I darted across to his desk and shoved my phone in his face. Moments later he stared at me with wide eyes. 'Are you kidding me?'

I looked at the tweet again.

@LondonToday LIVE on the 6 p.m. show: Emily Swift, wife of prime suspect in #SabrinaHobbs murder

I started pacing up and down. 'Spence says Dorset Police are confident about an arrest.'

Rahid frowned. 'You think that's why *London Today* have pulled Emily in?'

'Well, the timing fits.' I glanced at the congealing pizza slice that lay half-eaten in his in-tray. 'You finished with that?'

Rahid shrugged, his eyes back on his notebook. I grabbed the pizza and took a bite. It was cold and chewy but it tasted good, and I needed something to line my stomach before the next call.

The phone almost rang out, but Durand answered, sounding breathless. 'If you're ringing about the Sabrina Hobbs story, I'm not the DCI you need–'

'Sam, why have *London Today* got Emily Swift on in fifteen minutes? Has Charlie been arrested?'

Durand sounded weird, distracted. 'I have no idea. I'm not in the office.'

I paused. In all the years I'd known him, Durand had rarely taken time off. Even when his wife, Jen, left him in November, he barely broke step. I thought back to the first time I saw Durand after I heard about the marriage breakdown. The Met held a press conference to update the media on a burglary gang who were smashing their way through London's high-end jewellery stores. Durand looked the same. Handsome face, auburn hair. But his eyes were blank, and he stumbled over his words a couple of times. I was going through my own personal torment. Tommy had died three weeks earlier, and I was seeing the world through a thick layer of glass. Still, I knew Durand well enough to spot a man in pain. So I sent him a bottle of Scotch and a CD of Gloria Gaynor's hit single, 'I Will Survive', with a scribbled note:

Turn this up to eleven. Sophie x

A few days later, a padded envelope landed on my desk. Inside was the empty whisky bottle and a note that read:

I'm surviving. Thank you. Sam x

I picked the varnish off my nails, watching the sugar-pink flakes settle on my desk. Should I push Durand? Let him know I was there for him, like he'd increasingly been for me? I didn't want to overstep, and I certainly didn't want to jeopardise our working relationship. *Yeah, right, your 'working' relationship.* An image of Durand's grey eyes slid into my head and my insides tightened. I shifted my weight. *What the fuck was wrong with me?*

I opened my mouth to speak when I spotted Mack and Kate filing out of Conference Room 3, their expressions grim. They were followed by Spencer, Rowley and Lansdowne.

I forced myself to focus. 'Rowley is about to launch me off the roof for missing the story about Charlie assaulting his first wife, Sam.'

There was a pause. 'How well do you know Charlie?'

'Clearly not as well as I thought.' I flicked my nail against the desk, not sure what to say, but not wanting to hang up. Just knowing Durand was there made me feel better.

'Look, the last I heard, there was some debit card activity and a possible sighting,' he said. 'If an arrest has been made, it hasn't filtered through to me yet.'

I heard a thud in the background and a woman's voice calling his name. 'Oh, sorry. I didn't know you had company.' An odd feeling twisted in my stomach.

'Sophie . . . listen. I've got to go.'

The line went dead and I stared at the phone trying to make sense of the heaviness in my chest.

I distracted myself by ringing Emily's number but it went dead after two rings. *Great, so now she's screening me.*

Mack and Kate appeared by my desk and I could tell by the way Kate was fidgeting with her sleeve that she was building up to telling me something.

I pushed Durand out of my head and took a breath. 'What is it?'

Mack perched on the side of my desk, tension pulling the corners of his eyes. He picked up my pen and twirled it round his bony fingers. 'Rowley got a heads-up an hour ago that Emily is going on TV.'

I nodded. 'I've just seen the Tweet. How much do you reckon *London Today* forked out for her?'

'Sweet FA. Ugh, there's mould growing in my mug.' Kate picked up her coffee mug and examined its contents, her nose wrinkling in disgust. 'Emily called *London Today*, set it up herself.'

I stared at her. 'What? Why?' Kate flicked a glance at Mack, and opened her mouth to speak but I saw him shake his head. A sick feeling tugged my stomach. 'Guys, what's going on?'

My phone vibrated and I glanced at the number. 'Shit, this is the *Bournemouth Bugle* reporter, I need to take this.' I pressed the phone to my ear. 'Thanks for calling back, Jeff.'

'What's this about, then?' Jeff's voice was gravel-low.

'Christ Clan. More specifically, the article you wrote about the original organisation and Laurence Marlon. It was a great piece.'

'Why the interest from the dizzy heights of the *London Herald*?' he said, and I heard the murmur of a TV in the background.

'I have a possible crossover with another story I'm working on. Was there anything you dug up that didn't make the feature?'

Jeff coughed down the phone. 'Put it this way, you read the watered-down version. My Editor was a pussy. Too scared to libel anyone. The things I uncovered, it could have changed everything for me.'

I nodded, debating how to handle the enormous chip on Jeff's shoulder. 'That must have been galling after all your hard work.'

Jeff growled. 'Don't fucking patronise me, love. I've been doing this longer than you've been alive. Just because I haven't got my feet under the desk at a national paper–' He dissolved into a hacking wet cough that sounded as if it was coming from the depths of his stomach.

I waited, cursing myself for reading him wrong, then decided to try the opposite tack. 'Shall we cut to the chase, Jeff?' I heard the flick of a lighter and the sound of him inhaling on a cigarette. 'You responded almost immediately when I emailed you. And now you're giving me the runaround. So I assume you want something; something you think I can deliver. Why don't we stop wasting our time, and you tell me what it is so we can get on with it?'

Jeff gave a hoarse laugh. 'You're a piece of work.'

'Yeah, I've heard that before.'

'He never believed the things I found out, you know. The Editor.' He coughed, then spat it up. 'Guess how old he was. Go on, guess.'

'Jeff, I don't have time for this.'

'Twenty-fucking-two. Can you believe it? The Board decided the *Bugle* needed some fresh blood. I've had fungal infections older than that weasel.'

I shook my head exasperatedly. 'You want a wider audience? Well, here I am. What did you dig up?'

'Things I'd rather forget.' The sound of cigarette smoke flowing out of Jeff's mouth; another cough. 'You know what's so evil about Christ Clan? The leader, Laurence Marlon. The Shepherd, they called him. He went out of his way to target vulnerable young kids. Kids who had no place else to turn.'

'What are we talking?'

There was a pause. 'You seen that film *The Hunger Games*? Christ Clan made that look like a garden party. Marlon used to pit the kids against each other. Think cock fights, but with half-starved kids. He was a sick man. Sadistic and bored. To understand him, you have to go decades back. He started a religious group called the Saviours of Christ. He believed he was the Second Coming and he was put on earth to procreate. Got himself a harem of women, planned to flood the earth with hundreds of mini-Marlons. But there was one flaw in his plan.'

'He wasn't the Second Coming,' I said, arching an eyebrow.

Jeff snorted. 'Make that two flaws. Marlon was virtually impotent. Couldn't impregnate a woman to save his life. Apart from the time he conceived Hector; the toe-rag who's set up a new Christ Clan on Rockwell Road. Just what the world needs, by the way. Anyway, Marlon senior didn't cope well with his failing manhood; it wasn't long before he was taking it out on the world. On women, especially. Seems it was everyone else's fault except his.'

I fiddled with the phone cord. 'So what happened to this cult?'

Jeff coughed again. 'Depends who you talk to. Marlon went underground for a while, then resurfaced in the eighties. Set Christ Clan up in 1984. Only this time the angle was all about purifying your soul, or some bollocks. Marlon believed people were put on this earth unclean and the only way to regain God's love, was to purify their souls. And, don't doubt that when he meant God's love, he meant his own.'

I heard the snap and fizz of a bottle being opened.

'There were three stages of baptism: water, fire, blood. The purest souls were cleansed by all three. According to my source, it started out as symbolic but the more twisted things got in the commune, the more literally Marlon took it. He came to believe that true purity could only be gained by sacrifice.' Jeff took a long gulp and belched. 'If you ask me, it was just an excuse to fuck around with indefensible kids. Most thought it was a small price to pay for a roof over their heads and a hot meal. Some of them ended up in bad shape.'

I glanced down at Jeff's article. 'Tell me about the two kids you named.'

Jeff sniffed wetly. 'Mark Miller. I tracked down his dad, Les, but he wouldn't speak to me. Used to knock Mark around. But that was nothing compared to what happened to him at Christ Clan. He was beaten to a pulp. Hospitalised. Samantha Hartley wasn't so lucky.' He paused, letting that sentence sink in. 'Police said her death was accidental but that's bullshit. I think she was killed by someone at Christ Clan.'

Out of the corner of my eye I could see Kate and Mack deep in conversation. Every so often, one would glance my way. *What was going on?* 'So why was there never an investigation?'

'Because no one would speak out. Police didn't have the budget or time to look into a bunch of homeless drug addicts. I only know this much because I got to someone fifteen years after Christ Clan closed, and only then it was because his quotes were off the record. My editor wouldn't run them, called him an "unreliable witness", the fucking foetus.'

My mind was working overtime. 'Why are you so sure that Samantha Hartley was murdered?'

'Because I did my homework. Marlon believed the fastest route to the Holy Grail was through sacrifice.'

I glanced down at the article again. 'You think someone sacrificed her?'

'I don't think it's a coincidence that she ended up dead in a river. And there's something else about her death–' He stopped, and I heard him talking to someone in the background. 'Listen, I have to go.'

'Wait.' I hadn't even asked him about Charlie. 'Jeff, please. We need to finish this.'

A hacking cough, then silence.

I threw my phone onto the desk, but before I could work through the conversation in my mind there was a loud bang as Rowley's door was flung open.

'News Fuckers!' Lansdowne bellowed across the room and we all jumped. 'The boss's office. Now.'

As we scurried across the newsroom, I caught Spencer's eye and he jokily mimed slitting his throat. I heard someone yell out that *London Today* was about to start and the wall of TV screens on my left flickered to an identical picture of the credits rolling on a cookery programme.

Rowley was sitting behind his enormous desk, his eyes glued to the TV that hung on the opposite wall. Lansdowne was sprawled out on the black leather sofa, his shirt half untucked from his trousers and a cigarette tucked behind his ear. He reeked of cigarettes. When the smoking ban was enforced, Lansdowne learned to smoke cigarettes twice as fast. On a particularly stressful day in the newsroom, he'd been known to smoke two at once in the alleyway behind Premier News.

Lansdowne gave us a thin smile, gesturing to the sofa next to him. 'I've got a special treat for you today, folks. A front-row view of your latest fuck up.' He swung his beady eyes towards me. 'Sophie, aren't Swifty and Emily your mates? Why the hell isn't she coming to you with this? We should be fu—'

'That's enough, Austin,' said Rowley, his nasally voice sounding even more pinched than usual.

I ignored Lansdowne's glare and squeezed onto the sofa between Mack and Kate. Rahid perched on the arm, fiddling with his shirt sleeve. As the *London Today* theme tune resounded around the office, I glanced through the glass wall and saw the newsroom come to a standstill.

The newsreader, Jillian Snowdon, reeled off the day's headlines in her trademark velvety voice. She was known in the industry as 'Sniper Snowdon' for the ruthless way she attacked her interviewees. My fingers found a loose thread on the sofa and I twisted it.

Jillian blinked slowly at the camera, a sombre expression on her face. 'Five days ago, thirty-two-year-old Sabrina Hobbs's body was discovered in the Thames by Bishop's Park.' Jillian paused as a photograph of Sabrina flashed up on screen. 'The prime suspect, *London Herald* journalist Charles Swift, who is believed to have been in a relationship with Miss Hobbs at the time of her murder, has not been seen since she died.'

A photograph of Charlie flashed up on the screen. The producer had used a shot of him mid-blink so he looked slightly deranged.

'Where the fuck did they get that photo?' Lansdowne's voice was strained.

'I am joined in the studio tonight by Charles's wife, Emily.' The camera panned out to show Emily. Her white blouse was undone at the neck exposing a flash of blotchy skin, and her blonde ponytail was pulled so tight, it gave her a faintly surprised look. She was blinking fast.

Jillian cleared her throat and gave a breezy smile that didn't reach her eyes. 'Emily, first things first. How are you holding up?'

Emily's fingers went straight to the diamond 'E' around her neck. 'Well, Jillian, I can't lie. It's been a really tough few days.'

Jillian nodded and the studio lights picked out the light grey in her bob. 'Have you had any contact with your husband?'

Emily glanced at the camera, licked her lips. She clasped her hands together as if she was praying. 'I haven't spoken to Charlie since Friday evening.'

Jillian's smile never faltered. 'We have heard in the last hour that your husband drew money out of a bank in central Bournemouth, and that members of the public have called the police helpline to say they've seen a man matching his description in the area. Why Bournemouth?'

Emily pulled at the cuff of her blouse and her voice wobbled. 'I guess because he knows the area? Charlie grew up in Bournemouth, you see.' She reached for her glass of water and took a long gulp.

'You wrote a very public blog post earlier today responding to claims that your husband physically assaulted his first
wife,' said Jillian, a smile pulling at the corner of her mouth.
'Many people are asking why you've chosen to speak out so
publicly. Do you worry that by adding fuel to the flames, by
whipping up public interest, that you're in danger of harming
the investigation?'

Emily's nostrils flared a fraction. 'Listen, I'm not revealing
any details that aren't already in the public domain. I just ...
I want to show the people who write these stories, and read these
stories, that those of us caught in the middle are human beings.
That I'm a victim, too, and I'm doing the best I can under the
circumstances.'

Jillian's eyes narrowed and she glanced at her notes. 'In your
blog, you also touch on the fertility issues that you and your
husband have faced. What was the feeling behind sharing that
information?'

Something flickered across Emily's face, but she fought to
keep it in check. 'My decision to talk about my miscarriages
was one that I didn't make lightly. But people are reading a
bunch of stories about my husband, and I want them to know
that nothing exists in isolation. It's been a very tough period
for us and–'

'It sounds to me like you're making excuses for your husband.' Jillian's expression hardened. 'Let me ask you this: what
has the response been to your blog?'

Emily shifted forward and winced as if she was in pain. 'Um,
it's been mainly positive. My approach isn't for everyone. I'm

not trying to blaze any trails here. I'm . . . just, like I said, I'm just doing the best I can.'

Jillian rested her elbows on the desk. 'We should make viewers aware that you called *London Today* yourself, and asked to come on the show. Why is that?'

Emily ran a hand over her ponytail, the colour in her cheeks rising. She looked terrified. 'Because I want to send Charlie a message.'

Jillian waited a beat, her eyes on Emily's face. Then she glanced at the studio. 'OK, camera five, go ahead.'

Emily shifted round to face the camera and the bright lights accentuated the dark circles under her eyes. She chewed her lip, composing herself. Then she took a deep breath. 'Charlie, baby, please stop running. Whatever happens, I am here for you. We can fix this together. Please, make contact with me.'

'Do you think she's been briefed by police?' asked Kate.

'Doubt it,' I said. 'The Met must be hating this even more than us.'

Jillian shuffled the papers on her desk. 'Many people will be surprised to hear you say that. Given everything your husband stands accused of: infidelity, assault and battery, murder.'

An odd expression swept over Emily's face. 'Charlie and I made a vow. For better or worse. And it doesn't get much worse than this, right?'

'So the fact Charlie got another woman pregnant . . .'

'Sorry, I can't talk about that yet. It's too . . . painful.' Emily's chin creased and, for one awful moment, I thought she was going to cry on live TV. 'I'll blog about it when I'm ready.'

'Of course she will,' said Mack, folding his arms.

'And in case viewers don't know,' continued Emily, 'my blog is called *Something Borrowed*, and my book is due out later this year.'

Lansdowne dragged his hands over his face. 'Tell me she didn't just plug her fucking book.'

'How do you answer the critics who say you are deluded?' asked Jillian. 'That you're simply refusing to face up to the harsh truth that your husband is a killer?'

Emily's eyes flitted down to her hands and her voice dropped. 'I would say that you know nothing about me, or my marriage.'

Jillian blinked a couple of times, and I could tell by the look on her face that she was building up to the big one. 'Emily, what if I told you that *London Today* has managed to obtain a copy of the forensic report police filed after the search at your flat yesterday.' Beside me Kate stiffened. 'The report showed that fibres found on the hammer used in the attack on Sabrina match fibres found in a rug in your apartment, leading them to conclude that the weapon came from your home.' Jillian leaned forward, her voice like brushed velvet. 'Do you still think Charlie is innocent?'

I groped for Kate's hand, feeling as if the air had been sucked out of the room.

Emily had gone white. Her eyes darted across Jillian's face and I could see them glistening under the studio lights. 'This is – I can't . . .' She stopped, took a breath. 'I need to speak to him. Charlie, please. Get in touch. I love you. I can't believe you're capable of hurting anyone.' She turned to face Jillian and stuck her chin out a fraction. 'I just don't believe it. Any of it. You may call me deluded, or perhaps I'm just a victim of–'

'It's interesting you keep using the word "victim",' Jillian's smile was icy, 'because, of course, the real victim here is Sabrina Hobbs.' The camera switched angle and Jillian squared her shoulders. 'Unfortunately we'll have to leave it there.'

We sat in silence for a moment.

Eventually Rowley stood up and wandered to the window, breaking the tension in the room. 'Emily was ambushed. But that's what happens when you court attention.' He turned to face me. 'Sophie, you know her best. What do you think?'

My mind was whirling. I stared from one to the other. 'The hammer. Did you all know about that?'

Rowley's expression hardened. 'An old friend gave me a heads-up.'

'Why didn't you–' A rush of panic engulfed me. I needed air and space, and not to be in a room of people raising their eyebrows at me. I jumped up, climbing over Kate in my desperation to get out. Wrenching open the door, I raced towards my desk, feeling the stares from every direction.

Do you still believe Charlie is innocent?

My mobile was ringing and I pounced on it, hoping, for one lunatic moment, that it might be Charlie. I held my breath and hit 'answer'.

'Soph, it's the call you've been waiting for.' A dark, husky voice. 'I'm with Damo.'

I sat down heavily in my chair. 'Violet?'

'I told you I'd work on him.'

I rubbed my forehead, trying to focus. 'Where are you?'

'The Den. Tufnell Park. Listen, I dunno how long he's got. Can you come here now?' I glanced back at Rowley's office. The door was closed. I couldn't justify leaving the office. Not when things were blowing up all around me. 'Sophie, you there?'

I closed my eyes. 'I'm on my way.'

14

The Den was located in the basement of a low-rise block that housed a sports shop and a Lebanese fast-food joint called Bistro Beirut. The stone stairwell wasn't lit, and I skidded down the steps and slammed into the wall. I bent over to catch my breath, swallowing the bile in my throat. I'd waited so long for this moment, but now it was here, I was terrified. I counted to ten, drew myself up and opened the door.

The smell almost floored me: a claustrophobic dankness, old hot dog grease and cigarette smoke. An electric guitar hung on the wall behind the bar next to a neon sign that spelt DRIVE THRU, except the 'R' and 'V' were missing so it read DIE THRU. A naff jukebox peppered out a Johnny Cash song. The bar was almost empty, apart from two figures huddled on a mangy sofa in the corner.

I forced the nerves to the bottom of my stomach. 'Violet?'

She looked just as I remembered. Short dark hair cut close to her head, and inky-black eyes rimmed with kohl. She half-rose from the sofa and gave me a hug. But my eyes were on the figure behind, who was hunched over, tracing a pattern on the table with a heavily ringed finger.

I held my hand out but Damo just stared at it so I eased off my jacket and sat down on the leather sofa next to them.

'Damo's been volunteering at a shelter in Glasgow, haven't you, love?' Violet's voice was light and breezy, as though she were talking to a child.

When Damo didn't reply, she nudged him in the ribs.

'Yeah. Temporary gig,' he said. His voice was small and slight, with a soft Irish twang.

'When did you get back?' I asked, trying to ignore my galloping heart rate.

'Monday.'

I threw a glance at Violet, who gave a tiny shake of her head. *Give him space.* Damo's leg bobbed up and down and he flicked his finger against the table. I thought of Tommy. The more the drugs attacked his mind and body, the twitchier he became.

'Do you want a drink?' Violet stood up. 'It's my round.'

'Coffee, please. And load up the caffeine.' I blinked, trying to push Charlie and the murder weapon bombshell out of my head. I turned to Damo. 'So . . . do you mind if I ask you about Tommy?'

His wary grey eyes darted over my face. He licked his dry lips and I caught a glimpse of uneven teeth.

'I want you to know that I'm not here as a reporter. Everything is off the record. I just want to–' My voice cracked and I glared at the ceiling. 'I want to find out what happened to my brother.'

Damo scratched beneath the lank curls that were poking out of his red cap and looked at me for the first time. 'He was a good guy, Tommy. You were his guardian angel. Did you know that? He talked about you all the time. About your house. Christ, I didn't know Tommy was from such a rich family.' He paused. 'The big tree in your garden, that's what he liked to talk about.'

I closed my eyes, willing back the tears. Ever since we were children, the oak tree at Redcroft was our special place. I told Tommy it was the Magic Faraway Tree from Enid Blyton's adventure story. Tommy used to watch the tree from his bedroom window, long after dark, waiting to catch a glimpse of the fairies. We used to climb it together, knees stinging-red from the bark, and sit in the knotted branches throwing acorns at birds. The day before Tommy was sent away to boarding school, he hid up there for hours, only coming down after my father threatened the tree with a chainsaw. The following year a freak storm brought the tree down. The last time I was at Redcroft was at Tommy's wake and I'd sat on the tree stump in the rain until my hands turned blue.

'I hadn't seen Tommy for a while.' My voice was flat, robotic; the only way I could get the words out. 'We fell out after he stole from me.'

As Violet returned with the drinks, Damo picked at the ripped knee of his jeans. 'Tommy wasn't well,' he said.

'I know. Addiction is an illness, not a choice.'

'No, listen to me, Sophie. Tommy was ill in here.' Damo pressed a finger to his temple, just like Bert had done earlier when he'd described Sabrina's mental issues.

I sighed, glancing at the cigarette machine that had an OUT OF ORDER sign taped to the front. 'Look, my brother was a teenager when he first did drugs. A decade of narcotics must do things to your brain.' Damo's eyes flickered to Violet and I saw her shrug. 'Sorry, am I missing something?'

Damo plucked the slice of lemon off his glass and sucked it. 'Have you heard of High Place Phenomenon?'

'People who are afraid of heights?'

'They're not afraid of falling, they're afraid of jumping. Like lemmings.' Damo's leg jerked so fast, he jogged the table and my coffee spilt everywhere. 'I knew a guy once, on the streets. Flat out refused to cross any bridge in London on foot. He didn't trust himself not to jump.'

I soaked the puddle up with a paper napkin, wondering where this was going. 'So, Tommy was scared of heights?'

'I couldn't tell you about heights, but sharp objects. He was scared of those.'

'Sharp objects?'

Damo nodded, twisting his ring round his thumb. 'Had a phobia. Knives, screwdrivers, glass, even pens at one point.'

'That's ridiculous.'

Damo gave me a long look, clearly debating how to tackle this. 'When Tommy ate in front of you. Near the end. Did he use a knife and fork?'

I threw the sodden napkin on the table. 'What the hell are you talking about? Of course he–' But as I said it, I realised Damo was right. Tommy ate with his hands. At least he had the last few times I saw him. I didn't push it; I didn't push many things with Tommy. I was always so grateful to see him that I indulged whatever quirk he displayed. Especially when it came to food.

It was hard enough to get him to eat. So, I fed him sandwiches, chicken legs, burgers.

Damo leaned forward and clasped his hands together. His fingernails were jagged and bitten. 'The truth of the matter is, Tommy didn't trust himself with anything sharp.'

'In case he hurt himself?' I asked, glancing at Violet. She was picking the label off her beer bottle and wouldn't meet my eye. 'Can someone tell me what the fuck is going on?'

Damo rubbed his temples. 'Tommy wasn't worried about harming himself.'

Laughter bubbled in my throat. 'You mean Tommy could have hurt someone else? Are you serious?' I pictured my brother, frail and thin as a dying leaf.

Violet drained her glass, then scooted along the sofa and nudged my leg with hers. 'Mate, you have to understand. Tommy was ill.'

'Yes, yes, so you both keep telling me.' Suddenly I'd had enough. I lunged for my bag, desperate to get out of this place and away from people who acted like they knew all about Tommy but really knew nothing at all.

Damo blocked my path, his scrawny frame drowned by a baggy Adidas jumper. 'Negative thoughts are fucking powerful, man. Tommy's were profound. He was paranoid. Yes, the drugs made things worse, but . . .' he broke off, shaking his head. 'The first time I saw Tommy, he was shivering in his sleeping bag in a doorway on Baker Street. A nice African lady took pity on him and gave him her leftover lunch. First thing Tommy did after thanking her was throw the plastic knife and fork in the bin.

I was curious. But I didn't know the kid. It was only later that I asked him why. He told me that sharp things called out to him. They made him want to do things. Bad things. The only way he was safe, was if he kept clear of anything sharp.'

Violet inched closer; I could smell her vanilla lip balm. 'Tell her about Phil.'

Damo poured water from a dirty jug on the table, then swigged it down. 'Phil was another lad on our turf. Welsh, angry. He had a cruel streak and, after a couple of nights in Tommy's company, Phil decided to play a trick. One morning, Phil told Tommy that Tommy had killed someone the night before. It was just a joke but Tommy lost it. Fell apart. He was convinced Phil was telling the truth. I felt bad for the kid so I came clean but Tommy didn't believe me. He ripped his backpack apart looking for the knife. Scoured his hands for blood. Picked up every stray newspaper looking for news about the body. He almost turned himself into the police. Took him weeks before he let it go.'

I put my hands over my face, swallowing the lump in my throat. 'But Tommy wouldn't hurt a fly.'

Damo shrugged. 'Doesn't matter. He believed he could, that's the point.'

The honeyed tones of Johnny Cash drifted from the jukebox in the corner.

'It got worse after Phil's stunt,' he went on. 'You remember how Tommy only ever stayed with you for a few days at a time? That's because he didn't trust himself.'

I stared at Damo. 'You mean Tommy wanted to hurt *me*?'

All of a sudden, Tommy's quirks flew at me thick and fast. Tommy aged eight, cramming food into his mouth in suffocating amounts because he had to eat the meal in a certain number of bites. The time on holiday he wouldn't leave his room because his clothes didn't 'feel right'. When I asked him about it he'd stiffened. 'Just keeping a lid on things,' he told me quietly. His behaviour got worse during the summer of 2000. The family doctor diagnosed him with Obsessive Compulsive Disorder and prescribed him medication. I closed my eyes. *The medication.* He wouldn't have had access to it on the street.

'Fuck.' I slumped forwards, tears dropping onto my lap. 'Why didn't he tell me? I could have helped.'

Damo sighed. 'Can you imagine living with this? Wanting to harm the person you love most in the world? Give the kid a break. Tommy was always searching for relief, acceptance, salvation; he bounced with different crowds, all over the place. City, coast, wherever he could disappear to.'

I was gripping my knees so tightly my fingers ached. My whole body felt as if it would shatter if someone touched me. 'So that last time I saw him. When he stole–'

'The urge was so strong, he needed an escape. But benders cost money.'

I closed my eyes, thinking back to the hours leading up to that day. The way Tommy shrank from me when I hugged him. His twitchiness had been out of control but I blocked it out, pretended to myself he was no worse than normal, that a miracle was still within our reach. Would he really have hurt me? The little white-haired boy I loved more than myself.

Damo seemed to read my mind. 'Listen, Tommy's illness flared up around you precisely because he loved you so much. Made him even more paranoid. You were the most important person in his world.' Damo leaned forward and took my hand between his damp palms. 'You know the only thing I ever saw that didn't trigger off his paranoia? The badge you gave him. The one he wore on his coat.'

The pain was coming in big, dark waves. I raised my eyes to Damo's, willing him to stop talking.

'For some reason, that was sacred. Didn't matter that it had a bloody great needle attached to it. Tommy said it didn't count. He lost it once. It fell off his jacket and he went nuts. Retraced his steps for four miles until he found it half-hidden under a bin near Oxford Circus.'

I put a hand up to stop Damo, gulping down air. The rusty Care Bear badge I'd given Tommy when we were little, and which Damo had passed on to me when Tommy died. Violet put her arm round me as great big sobs shook my body until there was nothing left.

I took a juddering breath. 'If that badge was the only sharp object Tommy could handle, how did he inject himself with heroin?'

Violet stiffened. I felt the air around me go cold.

The corners of Damo's mouth twisted downwards and his voice dropped to a whisper. 'I didn't like to see a mate in pain.'

It started in the pit of my stomach: white-hot rage, twisting, writhing, boiling, until the fire burned behind my eyes. '*You* injected him?'

Damo glanced at Violet, licked his lips. 'I'm not proud of what I did. But out there, the rules are different. You do what you can to–'

'Survive.' I rounded on Violet and the bitterness in my voice forced her eyes to the floor. 'Yeah, I've heard that before.'

I hated them both. For knowing Tommy's secret. For reaching corners of Tommy's mind I never had. I hated my brother for not telling me the truth. For cheating me out of the chance to save him. But the blackest, vilest, most potent degree of hate: that was for me alone. For missing this, for failing him, for letting Tommy die.

Suddenly I was standing, stumbling away from the table. Violet came at me, her dark eyes flashing with concern. But I slammed her hand away and staggered out into the night.

15

Emily: 20 weeks before the murder

She is close enough that she can smell the shower gel on his skin. It mingles with the dusty scent of library books. The man is shorter than his Tinder profile suggests, but his crew-cut hair and doughy jawline are unmistakeable. As Emily brushes past him, the hairs on her arm stand up. The man turns his head, catches her eye. She is about to say something, then stops. *What am I doing?* At that moment – the moment when it counts – all she can think of is Charlie. Emily keeps walking, past Nineteenth-Century Novels, through World History and down the stairs to the exit.

The afternoon is crisp and bright. The skin on her bare legs puckers. Emily tosses her ponytail over her shoulder and hurries along the street, her heart hammering in her chest. This is the closest she's come. Her legs feel lighter than air, but her elation is short-lived. This time she resisted. Next time, she's not so sure.

Up ahead, a man in a camouflage bomber jacket leans into the wind and the music from his headphones drifts towards her. Emily crosses the road and turns right into Delaware Street. Her footsteps slow as she approaches her building. She leans against the railings breathing in the odour of builder's dust and dog shit. The builders abandoned the site a month ago, but the scaffolding is still here. As she stares at the criss-cross shadows it casts across the brick façade, she wonders how many other newlyweds dread going home.

It's been two weeks since Charlie called her, tears choking his voice, to say Vanessa was dead. She'd fallen down the stairs in yet another drunken stupor. The blow to her head knocked her out, which was a relief because the cigarette she'd been smoking set fire to her booze-soaked dressing gown. Half the ground floor went up in flames; hardly surprising given that the carpets in Vanessa's home were drenched in alcohol. The pathologist suggested a closed casket. Her funeral was small: just Emily, Charlie and a white coffin in a cold church.

Emily glances over her shoulder, towards the line of parked cars, and shivers. She first noticed it a week ago. The prickly, creepy sensation of being watched. Even at home she doesn't feel safe. *Especially at home.*

The cold is nibbling her toes. Emily drags herself up the steps and opens the door. Her eyes go straight to the postbox, the letters are still in their cubby hole. Charlie isn't home yet. *Thank God for that.* Emily stands there for a moment, wondering how it's come to this.

I know exactly how it's come to this, she thinks. Charlie is losing his mind.

It started with small things. Charlie would tell her he was working late so Emily would make plans without him. The gym, mainly. Or a quick mooch around the shops. Then Emily would come home to find clothes left on the floor and food missing from the fridge.

Last week she came home to find her new silk pyjamas – the ones she bought to kickstart things in the bedroom but hadn't actually taken out of the carrier bag – perfectly laid out on her side of the bed. Charlie looked at her as if she was a lunatic when she brought it up.

Recently, as she cleaned their bedroom, she found an old Bible in Charlie's bedside drawer. An inscription: *My darling son, God is with you always. Love, Mum.* Emily was shaken. Vanessa was religious, in a nutty, fanatical way, but Charlie had turned his back on that world when he was a teenager, hadn't he? She didn't know anymore.

The final straw had been three days ago when she found two empty vodka bottles stashed at the bottom of the laundry basket in the cellar. When Charlie claimed he didn't know how the bottles got there, Emily felt the anger rise up in her chest, and keep rising until it filled her whole body. The feeling had terrified her, and she locked herself in the bathroom with her nail scissors for an hour, pretended to Charlie she was having a bath.

Emily crosses the hallway and sighs. She grew up in a violent home, but not in the way people think. An image of her parents flashes in front of her eyes. It's the day her mum swipes her dad round the face with a scalding iron. Emily is hiding behind the door and she watches her dad drop to his knees, blood running down his blistered face. She sees the fevered look in her mum's eyes the moment it's over. Her mum's temper is absolute; the rage eats her alive. She throws glasses, plates, book ends, once even the goldfish bowl. That day, Emily had cowered under the kitchen table, transfixed by the sight of her pet fish flapping and quivering on the linoleum as it suffocated to death. Her mum's fury is never aimed at Emily, always her dad. As far as she knows, he's never retaliated or reported her. *Probably didn't want to admit he's being beaten up by his five-feet-four wife.*

'Your mum is highly strung,' he once told her. 'She loves me but sometimes she has a hard time expressing herself.'

In her bleakest moments Emily worries she's inherited her mum's rage and she'll lose control. At fourteen, the tension at home, along with her spiralling hormones, turned Emily's body into an alien space. So she learned the art of release. A cut here, a slice there. Soon, her body was a patchwork of wispy lines. Since then, she's become better at hiding it.

As Emily trudges to her door, she resolves to sort things out. *You are nothing like your mum. You hear me?* Her escape in the library is the wake-up call she needs. It's time to take control, to fight for this marriage. What does she always tell her followers on *Something Borrowed*? Marriage takes work. *A true marriage is two imperfect people refusing to give up on each other.*

Emily turns the key in the lock.

The smell hits her instantly: vanilla with a musky undertone. *Why do I know that smell?*

'Hello?' Her voice carries down the hallway into nothing. 'Baby, you home?'

Frowning, Emily hangs her jacket in the cupboard, then wanders into the kitchen and throws the post onto the counter.

She switches on the kettle and opens the fridge. She is going to make dinner, a peace offering. She isn't the greatest cook but she's started cutting out recipes from the Sunday paper and sticking them on the fridge as inspiration. Tonight is lamb chops, Charlie's favourite. As the kettle hisses and steams, Emily hears something.

She pours her tea and takes it through to the sitting room.

That's when she spots the TV. An image, black and white, frozen. Charlie dressed in a morning suit, leading his beaming bride out of the church. Only the bride isn't Emily. It's Lizzie.

Emily's knees give way. She collapses onto the sofa, barely noticing the tea burning her skin.

'Charlie!' Emily hauls herself up and stumbles through the apartment. 'Where the fuck are you?'

As she reaches their bedroom, Emily stops abruptly. The vanilla scent fills her nostrils, catches in her throat. She follows the trail all the way to their wardrobe. She opens the door, stares at Charlie's suits. Then she starts yanking things out: his shoes, his belts, his ties. Breathless, she spots a box, half hidden beneath a pile of shoes. She picks it up with trembling hands. Inside is a pink perfume bottle. *MoonFlower*. Emily staggers backwards, sinking onto the bed. That's why the smell is familiar. It's Lizzie's perfume. She remembers helping Lizzie hunt for it on the morning of her wedding. Emily stares wildly at the door. That sound she heard before. Was that Charlie leaving? The perfume bottle feels like a grenade in her hand.

Emily stifles a sob. She charges into the kitchen and hurls the bottle in the bin. Adrenaline forces her chest up and down.

She grabs her phone, about to dial her dad, then hesitates. She knows what he will say. That Emily chose this path; she chose to marry a man who was still in love with a ghost. Emily squeezes her eyes shut. One day this will all be worth it; one day Lizzie will fade in Charlie's mind, and Emily will fill his whole heart.

The vanilla scent is embedded in her nostrils. Jumping up, she hurries to the bathroom and fishes the nail scissors out of the drawer. She slips down her knickers. The ivory skin below her hipbone is criss-crossed with lines. She pauses for a moment, then makes the cut. The relief takes her breath away. Emily holds on to the pain, counts to ten. In the mirror a fat, round school-girl face stares back at her. When the bleeding stops, she pulls up her pants and hobbles through to the sitting room. Even after she switches off the TV, Lizzie's radiant smile is seared on her eyelids. Emily throws herself on the sofa and picks up her laptop. She's received a question via her blog, from a woman with pre-wedding jitters.

How do you know if he's Mr Right?

Emily's fingers hover over the keys. Then she begins to type.

You never know, babe. That's the magic of love. But ask yourself this: can you imagine life without him? If the answer is no, then my advice is this: grab onto him with both hands and never let go.

Emily senses something, someone. She turns her head sharply. The room is empty. Pain sears through the wound on her hip. She swivels back round to her computer and taps away at the keyboard.

No matter what it takes. Never. Let. Go.

16

Present day

I run, stumble, run. The carpet scratches my feet. The moonlight pours in through the large Georgian window, illuminating the small boy with milky-white hair. He runs, too. Away from me. His bony elbows slice through the air and he glances over his shoulder, his eyes wide with terror. I call out but he slips away like a shadow: round corners, up stairs, through doorways. I race after him, my breath loud in my ears. I need to touch him, to feel the heat on his bones. I stumble round the corner. He puts a finger to his lips and beckons me towards him. With each step, he becomes brighter, as though someone has flicked a switch inside him. The light blinds me. I put a hand up to shield my eyes and that's when I see it. A mountain of knives, all shapes and sizes, thrown together like a giant Jenga tower. The boy raises his hand. He is holding a carving knife that's dripping with blood. I look down. Blood spills out of my stomach and I press my hand over the wound. It's warm and sticky. The boy raises the knife to his mouth and licks the blade. The tower is growing, filling the space so fast that the knives cascade to the floor. The jangling sound fills my head.

The boy's eyes turn red. The ringing noise drags me upwards, to the surface.

I woke up wet and hot and twitching. The noise was real. I snatched my phone off my bedside table. A number I didn't recognise. 'Yes?'

'I can't believe you'd do this to me.'

I forced myself up to sitting. The sleeping pills made me feel like I was at the bottom of the sea. 'Who is this?'

'You're such a two-faced bitch.' The voice was slurred, female, familiar.

I rubbed my eyes. 'Emily?' I spun my legs over the side of the bed and groped for the light switch. 'Slow down, what's going on?'

'I found it. Charlie's other phone. You must think I'm so stupid.'

'Emily, please.' I dragged myself up to standing. 'What time is it?'

'All along you've pretended to be my friend, you've been *screwing my husband*.'

My legs went from under me and I collapsed on the bed. A clink, the sound of a drink being poured. I lurched towards the pile of clothes on my armchair and starting pulling on my sweatpants. 'I don't know what you think you've found but–'

'Liar!' Emily let out a strangled cry.

I squeezed my eyes shut, trying to get a handle on my thoughts. 'Em, talk to me. What's on the phone?'

'As if you don't know. You must have thought this was Charlie ringing.' I heard her take a gulp. 'You can go to hell, Sophie. Your dirty little secret is out in the open.'

'Please, let me come over,' I said, scanning the room for my bag. 'We can talk this throu—'

There was a bang in the background, like the sound of a door slamming. Emily's voice faded.

I pressed the phone to my ear. 'Em, can you hear me?'

Another bang.

Emily's voice. 'Charlie? Thank God.' Then louder. 'Where have you be—?'

There was a scream. A thump.

The line went dead.

I skidded through the automatic doors into UCLH's Accident & Emergency and raced towards reception.

I smiled at the large black lady with braided hair. 'Can you help? I'm looking for a patient, Emily Swift.'

She scanned the clipboard in front of her. 'Are you a family member?'

'A friend. I called the ambulance, I was on the phone to her when she collapsed.'

The lady sighed. 'If you take a seat, someone will–'

'Is she OK?'

'Like I said, if you take a se—'

I threw my hands in the air as the stress hit me. 'I just want to know if she's OK. Is she alive? Can you manage that?'

She raised her eyebrows, hardened her voice. 'I'm sorry, ma'am. You need to take a seat.'

I gave an exaggerated sigh, then shuffled to the waiting area. It reeked of antiseptic and panic. Opposite, a man with a grizzled face and unruly grey eyebrows gave me a sympathetic look.

It wasn't busy, but it was only five thirty in the morning. I sat down on the plastic chair, regretting losing my temper with the receptionist; she could have proved useful if handled in the right way.

I fished out my phone and sent a group text to Mack, Kate and Rowley.

> At UCLH. Emily's here. I think she's been attacked. Trying to get more details.

I scrolled through my emails and messages. Emily's friend Sinead had texted to say she could meet me after 9 a.m. Just as I replied to say I'd be there, two police officers strode past me. The receptionist directed them along the corridor to the right. I waited until she looked down at her clipboard, then I followed them to a room marked '12'. The female officer knocked on the door and a nurse answered. She shook her head then closed the door again. One of the police officers disappeared and came back moments later with two chairs, which they positioned outside the room.

I pressed my back against the wall and waited. I heard footsteps squeaking down the corridor and peeped round. It was the same nurse. She rounded the corner and I stepped out.

'I'm sorry to bother you but is Emily Swift in that room?'

She frowned. 'I'm sorry, who are you?'

'Her friend. I was on the phone to her when . . . it happened. I was the one who called the ambulance. No one will tell me anything. Please.'

She darted a glance behind her. 'Listen, love, I really can't say much. She's had a fright but I think she'll be OK.' She patted my shoulder. 'Why don't you go and wait in reception? Get a cup of tea in you. You look washed out.'

I peeked around the corner again. The police officers had vanished and the door was ajar. There was a panel of glass in the door and I inched closer to have a look. They were standing at the end of the bed, talking to Emily. She was hooked up to a drip and looked small and frail, her blonde hair spread across the pillow.

It was as if she sensed me there. She turned her head and a look of anguish swept across her face.

'Get her away from me!' Emily's shriek rang down the hallway. She thrashed her head and the nurse bustled past me and put a hand on her forehead.

The male officer pulled me out of the room. His beady eyes pinned me to the wall. 'Step away, miss.'

'Please, I need to speak to Emily.'

'Miss, I'm asking politely, but I can make this more formal.' He gestured towards the handcuffs on his belt.

'Brays, what's going on?' A voice boomed down the corridor and my stomach dropped. DCI Golden appeared, his sandy hair even more dishevelled than usual. He was clutching a bottle of water.

He gave me a dark look. 'Does my officer need to escort you from the premises?'

I shook my head. 'Emily's got the wrong end of the stick.'

Golden gave me a tight smile. 'It appears you're more involved with the Swifts than you let on.'

'I've never slept with Charlie. I don't know what she's talking about.'

Golden gave me a hard look. He threw back two antacids, slugged some water, then took two more. 'And I suppose those photographs on his phone just appeared by themselves, too.'

'The . . . photos?' I leaned against the wall, feeling faint.

'Well, we'll find out soon enough, Miss Kent. The phone is with forensics.'

For a moment, all I could hear was the hissing sound of my brain overheating. 'Listen, someone is setting me up.'

Golden blinked slowly. 'You can tell us all about it when we take a statement. Now scram. You're upsetting the victim, and she's had enough for one night.'

He turned away but I put my hand out to stop him. 'Please . . . on the phone. I heard Emily say Charlie's name. Did he do this to her?'

Golden gave me a flat look. 'No comment.'

Outside, the sun rose and spread its light across the city. I sat on the hospital step sifting through my thoughts. *Charlie hurt Emily. He put her in hospital.* If it was true, it changed things in ways I didn't feel equipped to deal with. Not on so little sleep. Sighing, I dialled Rowley's number.

He answered immediately. 'I got your text. Are you still at the hospital?'

'Just leaving. There's a wall around Emily. I can't get to her.'

'What the hell happened?'

A bus driver leaned on his horn and I pressed the phone against my ear. 'I think Charlie attacked her. At home.'

There was a pause. 'How badly hurt is she?'

I pictured Emily's face, her eyes burning with hate. 'Philip . . . there's something else.'

I filled him in about the phone Emily found.

'So, there's a photograph of you on it,' he said.

I closed my eyes, feeling the exhaustion seep into my bones. 'No one will tell me anything.'

Rowley cleared his throat. 'Sophie, are you sure you're telling me the whole truth? Whatever has happened between you and Charlie, it is better for us – and for you – if I know the truth.'

For us and for you? Was Rowley distancing himself from me already?

'Philip, I'm being set up.'

An ambulance wailed past and Rowley waited until it had disappeared before he spoke. 'I'll find out what I can.'

He hung up and I sat there, breathing through the panic, staring up at the cruel, blue sky. I could still hear Emily's scream inside my head. I focused on it, sharpened it, inflated it until the big red sound reached every part of my head. Only then could I tune out the sounds of my nightmare. *Tommy, with a knife.*

17

I stood outside Sport First on Holborn, draining the dregs of my coffee. Sinead's Body Blitz class finished at 9 a.m. and I was grateful I had somewhere to be. I couldn't face going back to the *Herald*. Word would have spread about the night's drama and the adrenaline that got me through the last four hours was fizzling out. I'd nipped into Cos to buy a change of clothes and hoped the new threads would go some way to mask my exhaustion.

I tossed my cup in the bin just as a stream of Lycra-clad women with cerise faces filed out of the door. I wrinkled my nose as the dank waft of raw sweat hit me and scanned the group. I hadn't seen Sinead since September, when I'd joined Charlie and Emily's friends for dinner. I'd missed the scoop on a violent burglary in Crystal Palace and Lansdowne had balled me out in front of the whole newsroom. After my second glass of Pinot Grigio, I felt the day roll off my shoulders and I turned to the plump woman on my right. Her translucent skin was crying out for powder and her small, blue eyes were slightly pink. I briefly wondered if she'd been crying. She introduced herself as Emily's oldest friend, which at the time I thought odd, considering they were sitting at opposite ends of the table and hadn't spoken all night.

The gym door opened and Sinead appeared wearing a black pencil skirt and a polka-dot blouse. She'd cut her hair just below her jawline and had lost a ton of weight.

She gave me a shy smile. 'Sorry, have you been waiting long?'

'Wow, you look amazing,' I said, kissing her on both cheeks. 'Good class?'

'Hell. But I'm getting married in three months so it's all about getting into the dress.' She waggled her ring finger in my face and the solitaire diamond glinted in the sun.

'Who's the lucky guy?'

'Oliver. An accountant,' she rolled her eyes. 'I know. But it's a myth. He's one of the funniest people I know.'

I fell in step with her. 'How long do I have you for?'

'Twenty minutes or so. I've got a meeting at half nine. Let's head to my office.'

We stopped at a pedestrian crossing, waiting for the lights to change. 'So, is Emily planning your wedding?'

Sinead looked straight ahead. 'I'm doing it myself.'

Something about her tone made me wonder, but I didn't push it.

The lights changed and, as we crossed Shaftesbury Avenue, I turned to Sinead. 'Where are you getting married?'

'Family church. My mum would have killed me if I'd chosen anywhere else. She's already having palpitations that Oliver is an atheist.' Sinead crossed herself and grinned. 'Here's my office.'

'Shall we have a coffee over there?' I pointed to a café on the corner.

A shadow passed across Sinead's face, but she nodded.

I opened the door and the heady scent of freshly baked croissants and cinnamon made my stomach growl.

'Christ, look at that pastry counter,' I said, pointing to the display, but Sinead had already marched over to a table by the window. She was rearranging her face into a smile as I sat down.

'Are you OK?'

Before she could respond, a svelte lady with thinning silver hair shuffled over to take our order. Her face was wrinkled and brown, like a walnut. When she saw Sinead she smiled, exposing lipsticky teeth.

'Miss Sinead, where you been?' Her low-pitched voice had an Eastern European twang. She turned to me. 'She is best customer, but not here for long, long time.'

I glanced at Sinead, whose fixed smile wasn't reaching her eyes. 'I've been busy, Magda.'

'And no eating by look of things,' said Magda, running a disapproving eye over Sinead. 'I help with that. You want croissant? Danish? Cinnamon bun? I bring you.'

'No.' Sinead blurted the word out, then gave a shrill laugh. 'I've eaten already. Just a fresh mint tea, please.'

'A cappuccino for me, please,' I said.

Magda frowned, then scuttled off.

Sinead let out a sigh as if she'd been holding her breath. 'I haven't been here lately.'

'I gathered,' I said, stifling a yawn. 'Sorry.'

Sinead twisted her engagement ring round her finger and raised her eyebrows. 'Not getting much sleep with this Charlie story, I'll bet.'

Magda returned with our drinks and a plate of croissants. She held her hands up. 'I know, I know. But you are wasting away. Is on the house.'

Sinead's expression darkened. I was desperate to eat one, but sensed it wouldn't be the right thing to do in front of Sinead. 'You know who'd love these,' I told her. 'My office. Do you mind if I wrap them up and put them in my bag?'

Sinead gave me a grateful look. 'Just don't let Magda see. She might bring more.'

I bundled the pastries up and shoved them in my bag. 'Have you spoken to Emily today?'

Sinead poured her tea, dribbling water over the table. 'Emily and I haven't spoken for a while.' She mopped up the puddle with a napkin, not meeting my eye.

'So, you don't know that Emily is in hospital?'

Sinead looked up. 'What?'

'She was attacked at home. Last night.'

'By who?'

I hesitated, not wanting to say Charlie's name out loud. I didn't need to.

Sinead's eyes widened. 'Is she OK?'

I wrapped my hands around the coffee cup; the china burned my skin. It was a welcome distraction. 'The details are sketchy. I was hoping you might have spoken to Emily.'

Sinead pressed her lips together and folded her paper napkin into a fan shape. 'I gave up smoking recently and now I don't know what to do with my hands. No booze, no fags, no caffeine, no red meat.'

'And no fun, right?'

She gave a tight smile. 'Bridal bootcamp. All in pursuit of dewy skin and visible collarbones.'

I leaned towards her and softened my voice. 'When did you last talk to Emily?'

She sighed. 'A couple of months ago.'

'Did something happen between you two?'

Sinead kept her eyes on her paper fan. 'Did you see Emily on the news yesterday?'

'Who didn't?'

'The social media stuff is . . . intense.'

I nodded. Memes of Emily popping up in random places to plug her blog were going viral. The last one I saw showed Emily's image photoshopped between the Queen and Prince Philip at the Grand National. The words *Screw the race, let's talk about my blog* were plastered across it. #SomethingBorrowed was trending. Some people thought Emily was brave for rewriting the rules of news journalism. Taking the wind out of the media's sails by going it alone. But, for every positive reaction, there were ten negative. She was publicity-hungry. Unlikeable. Fake. A doormat. And worse. I was worried that by putting herself out there, she'd unwittingly put herself in danger. It couldn't be a coincidence that Charlie attacked her the day after she appeared on *London Today*.

I sipped my coffee. 'I wonder if the haters would hate quite so much if Emily wasn't a pretty blonde.'

Sinead opened the fan out and smoothed it on the table. 'You know, if I showed you our school photograph you wouldn't be able to pick her out. Emily had mousy hair. Same as mine. We hung out every day. Ate our lunch in the science lab. Emily was bullied. We both were. Back then, things were difficult. Her parents–' Sinead paused, choosing her words carefully. 'We went to private school. Everyone's parents were doctors, lawyers or bankers. Respectable. Law-abiding. Emily's parents were all that but, behind closed doors, it was a different story.'

She hesitated, but I kept quiet, giving her space to think.

'Domestic violence didn't exist at our kind of school,' she said quietly, her eyes on the table. 'Well, you know how bitchy girls can be. There wasn't much sympathy. And it didn't help that Emily was the size of a house. Oh yes, didn't I mention? We were the fat girls. So we'd sit in the empty science lab and work through the pain with chocolate bars and iced buns. The worst thing about it is that I didn't even have an excuse. I did it to keep her company.'

The memory coloured Sinead's cheeks, and in that moment I saw the lifelong battle she fought to find comfort in her own skin.

'We both got into Eastford College for our A-levels, a co-ed boarding school down by the coast. The summer before we started, Emily went to France with her parents. Spent six weeks out there. When term started, Emily was . . . well, she was basically someone else.'

'How do you mean?'

Sinead gave a sad smile. 'She'd lost three stone, got blonde highlights, learned the art of eyeliner. It was a miracle. To Emily's credit, she never dropped me. And in return I never blew her cover.'

'Her cover?'

'She invented a new family. Told everyone her dad was an international property consultant and her mum was a travel writer. They needed jobs that took them abroad so they never had to show up to school functions. She created a new past and it worked. Her new attitude had the boys running circles around her. Where the boys lead, the girls follow, right?'

I sipped my coffee, kicking over Sinead's words in my mind. 'But didn't people know the old Emily?'

Sinead shook her head. 'Emily covered her tracks. And Eastford College was miles away from our old school. She got away with it, mainly because she talked the talk. And she was beautiful. Under all that puppy fat. You know what it's like at school: beauty is currency. Emily's life was one big façade. It's no surprise she's ended up selling the idea of love and happiness to other people.'

The door opened and a group of suited men trooped in. Sinead ducked down, her cheeks flaring.

'What are you doing?' I said, frowning.

'I don't want anyone from the office to see me in here.'

'Why not?'

Sinead gritted her teeth, but didn't answer. At that moment one of the guys spotted her and she swore under her breath as he marched over, wrinkling his pug nose. 'Hi, David.'

'I knew you didn't have the will power. You need to be stronger than this if you're going to hit that target weight, right?' He turned to me. 'Sinead's on a diet. We call her Sinead the Sink. Because she eats everything . . .'

'. . . but the kitchen sink!' The chorus of men guffawed in the background.

Sinead froze. David pointed to the empty plate. 'Come on, how many have you eaten?'

I spun round in my chair and gave him a wide smile. 'David, is it? Lovely to meet you. I'm Sophie.'

David raised his eyebrows, and leered towards me. 'You single, Sophie?'

'I am single, David. Are you interested?'

He glanced at his crew, taken aback by my brazenness. 'Er, yeah.'

I leaned back in my chair, sizing him up. 'Do you know what I do for a living, David? I'm a reporter, which means I spend a lot of time reading people. Do you know what I see when I look at you?'

David licked his lips nervously.

'I see a phony, a dud. The fake gold signet ring on your little finger screams pretentious. Your suit is at least one size too small, so either you're not as trim as you think or, more likely, you've put on weight. Probably driven by the fact you can't get a girlfriend because who in their right mind would want to date a spiteful little man with halitosis and a receding hairline? And that snug suit definitely won't help your erectile dysfunction. What do they call you behind your back? Dickless Dave?'

The sniggering in the background grew and David took a step back. 'How do you know my ring is fake?'

'The skin on your finger is green. Now, piss off.'

David slipped away to the cries of 'Dickless Dave' from his jubilant friends.

I swung back round to face Sinead and rolled my eyes. 'Fucking moron.'

Sinead grinned. 'That was awesome.' Then she glanced at her watch and the corners of her mouth dropped. 'Damn it, I haven't got long.'

I signalled to Magda for the bill. 'Do you mind if I ask a couple of questions about Emily?'

'After that performance, I'll tell you whatever you need to know.'

'What did you think of her and Charlie? As a couple, I mean.'

'Look, the thing you need to know about Emily is that she tries really hard to maintain a certain image. The Instagram-life, the perfect relationship, these things are important to her. It takes a certain kind of person to reinvent themselves, right? Many schoolgirls dream of that, but Emily actually did it. It takes strength of character. Some might say control freak.'

Magda appeared with the bill and Sinead waited until she'd gone.

'But that makeover she underwent at school? It's all surface. Underneath she's the same insecure, fat girl peddling the perfect lifestyle. And Charlie is her Achilles heel. The one thing that bothers Emily more than anything is Lizzie.'

'Charlie's first wife?'

'Yep, Emily's paranoid she can't live up to her memory.'

I put a fiver on the table, not meeting Sinead's eye. After what Dominic told me about the bag of chicken bones he found, I wasn't surprised.

'So, the fact everyone knows Charlie cheated on her with Sabrina must be killing her,' I said.

Sinead chewed her lip. 'Look, if there's one thing I know about Emily, it's that she'll come out swinging. Have you found it weird that she's been so public about everything? She wants to control the situation. Just like she did at school. She didn't like the story, so she rewrote it. Charlie's cheated on her, he's got another woman pregnant, possibly killed her, and has left Emily to pick up the pieces. You think a woman like Emily is going to take this lying down? If she can't play the role of the perfect wife anymore, she'll play the perfect victim.'

I drained my cup, considering Sinead's words. 'Can I ask you a personal question?'

Sinead raised her eyebrows. 'It had better not be about my weight.'

I smiled. 'Why haven't you spoken to Emily for so long?'

Sinead pushed her mug away and sighed. 'She overstepped the line.'

'How?'

'The last time I saw her she told me she was pregnant.'

'When was this?'

Sinead screwed her face up trying to remember. 'I don't know . . . February, I think. Anyway, she seemed nervous about it. Not psyched in the way I thought she'd be.'

I did the mental calculations in my head. 'But she'd had two miscarriages already by then. Maybe she was worried she'd miscarry again.'

Sinead shook her head. 'No, that wasn't it. I can't put my finger on it. She was anxious, about Charlie. The pregnancy was causing a rift. I got the impression Emily was worried he didn't want kids.' Sinead stared out of the window, her eyes blank with memory.

'So, what happened?'

Sinead gave a tired smile. 'I dared to suggest that they get help. See a marriage counsellor. It was clear something wasn't right between them.'

'And she flipped?'

'She did more than flip. Emily did what she always does when she's pissed off with me.' Sinead's expression hardened. 'She took what was mine.'

I frowned, not understanding. 'You mean . . .'

'Oliver. Well, she tried, anyway. She spent the rest of the dinner flirting her arse off with him. Olly, bless him, was like a deer in the headlights. Didn't know what to do with himself. It's a power thing. You know how pretty she is. Anyway, I was livid. So was Charlie. It was the most awkward evening of my life.'

'Has she done that to you before?'

'Sure. Whenever she feels threatened. Although why she'd feel threatened by me is a mystery.' Sinead glanced over her shoulder, even though there was no one there. 'Look, what I told you earlier about school. Someone did see through Emily's transformation. A girl called Katy Baker. She was a friend of a friend; got wind of the bullshit. Anyway, Katy confronted Emily in front of a crowd of people outside the Dorset Arms one night. Really embarrassed her. Two days later Emily told a teacher that Katy's boyfriend raped her.'

I raised my eyebrows. 'You're not suggesting . . .'

'. . . that she made it up? Well, put it this way, I was in the pub with her the night the alleged rape took place. I mean, there's a chance it happened. Emily never went into details with me but she stuck to her story. The school took it seriously. Steve was expelled, right before his A-levels. And Katy was so devastated she flunked her exams.'

Sinead shrugged but I could see the tension in her face.

'Emily's always blurred the lines between reality and fantasy. She plays the "little girl lost" character but she knows exactly what she's doing,' she said, draining her cup and giving me an odd look. 'What you have to understand, Sophie, is this: Emily has been spinning a story her whole life.'

18

I stood outside 30 St Mary Axe – the skyscraper affectionately known as the Gherkin – staring at my haggard reflection in the blackened glass. I had a million other places to be but, somehow, I'd ended up here, at the place I'd vowed never to come to.

The lift swept me up to the sixteenth floor where a woman with a platinum bob and snaggle-toothed smile glanced up from the marble desk.

'Can I help you?'

I squared my shoulders. 'Is Mr Kent in his office?'

'Do you have an appointment?'

'I don't.'

She frowned. 'Do you mind me asking why you want to see Mr Kent?'

'Because I'm a masochist.'

'Excuse me?' She pushed her hair behind her ear, exposing three small diamond studs in each lobe. 'That's not really – he doesn't like to. Uh, what's your name?'

'Sophie Kent.' I waited for the penny to drop. Which it didn't. 'As in *Kent* Industries. I'm his daughter.'

A flush spread across her cheeks and she put a hand to her throat. 'I'm so sorry. It's only my second day. Wow, that's embarrassing.' Her eyes darted left and right as she tried to work out how to play this. I regretted making her feel uncomfortable but being in the vicinity of my father played havoc with my ability to function like a human being.

I shook my head, wondering how young she was. 'Don't worry. Where's Ramona?'

Ramona was my father's secretary. A severe blonde with a lifelong smoker's voice. She guarded him fiercely, and he returned the favour. One year my father bought her a vintage Mercedes. Another year, he put her son through private school. If my father was busy, Ramona wouldn't let anyone near him, not even me. *Especially me.* Ramona once confessed that I was one of the few people who could ruffle Antony Kent's feathers. Unlike everyone else in his life, I couldn't be bullied or bought and I drifted in and out of his orbit like a rogue satellite.

'Ramona is out on a personal appointment.'

I leaned my elbows on the table. 'Can you just tell him I'm here? Look, I'll just sit over here. I'll be quiet, I promise.'

I shook off my jacket and looked out the window, trying to ignore the queasiness in my stomach. Far below, London spread out like a child's Lego city, coloured yellow in the morning sunshine. Kent Industries moved into the Gherkin five years ago. In his speech at the opening party, my father announced the move signalled a new era for the company. I'd stood in the corner, in a black velvet dress, nursing a glass of champagne, and smiling until my face hurt. At the time, I was piecing together a story about corruption at a private German bank, and I knew the CFO would be at the party. That's how I justified accepting the invitation. By that stage, I needed an excuse. When I was younger, I used to attend the same parties as my father because a photographer would inevitably ask for a picture of us together. I had stacks of these photographs. I couldn't bring myself to throw them away. One night I lined them up in a row. Identical silvery-blonde hair, pale blue eyes and fake smiles. In every picture my father's arm is around my waist. Except, what you can't tell from the photographs, is that he's not actually touching me.

I thumped down on the angular leather sofa, underneath the gigantic letters spelling out my own surname, and stared up at the painting of my father that hung on the far wall. Since it was taken, his tan had deepened and the years had dug more lines into his face, but he hadn't really changed.

'Does your dad have an ageing portrait in the attic?' Kate once asked me, in a tone that bordered on flirtatious. 'What's his secret?'

'Feasting on the blood of newborns,' I said, shooting her a look.

Even though I hadn't seen my father since our disastrous dinner where I blamed him for Tommy's death, last night's drama with Damo had strengthened my resolve. As much as it pained me, I'd track Tommy's killers far quicker with my father on board.

My phone beeped with an email from Kate. The subject line:

Have you fucking seen this fucking hell fucking hell fucking hell

I was about to click on the email when the receptionist cleared her throat. 'Mr Kent is ready for you.'

I paused for a moment outside my father's office, mentally preparing myself, then knocked. I didn't bother waiting for a reply.

This was the first time I'd set foot in his office. I inhaled the scent of leather and money. At the far end stood a table the size of a pond. To my right was a large built-in dresser, which contained rows of photographs. I was curious to see who'd made it into the Antony Kent Hall of Fame but couldn't see from where I stood, and I didn't want my father to know I cared.

My father sat behind a large teak desk, with his back to the view. His steely eyes followed me as I approached his desk. 'To what do I owe this pleasure?'

I sat on the chair opposite his desk. 'Sorry, I should have called first.'

'My 11.30 is running late.' His face darkened and I already felt sorry for whoever that was. 'You look terrible.'

I wrapped my arms around my bag. 'Late night. Lots going on.' I glanced at the window. 'Nice view.'

'I don't get much time to look at it. How are things at the *Herald*?'

'Busy. How's life at the top of the world?'

'Busy.'

There was a pause.

'Right,' I said, opening my bag. 'Now we've established we're both busy people, I'll cut to the chase.' I fished out a document and handed it to my father. It was Tommy's post-mortem report. Durand had given it to me a while back, as a favour. I'd read it so many times, the paper had practically disintegrated.

As my father scanned the page, I spotted more picture frames on his desk. I shifted my weight to get a better look but they were obscured by a plant.

My father tossed the piece of paper onto his desk and steepled his fingers together.

'Don't you have anything to say?' I said, when I couldn't bear it any longer.

'I'd like to hear your thoughts first.'

I rested my hands on the arms of the chair to steady myself. 'Well, there's the evidence that Tommy didn't kill himself.'

My father peered at the page. '*Cause of death: inconclusive.* That's not quite the same thing.'

I sat forward on the edge of my seat. 'I met a guy who knew Tommy from the streets. He was there the night it happened. He says two men came for Tommy, held him down and forced a needle into his arm. They left the syringe in his hand to make it look like suicide.' My words ran together and I took a gulp of air.

My father stood up and strode to the mahogany sideboard. He poured himself two inches of whisky and drank it in one.

I raised my eyebrows. 'Bit early to open the bar. You taking a leaf out of Mum's book?'

It was cruel, even for me. I sighed, opening my mouth to apologise. Not least because I needed him on side.

My father tapped his finger against the crystal tumbler. 'Tell me, Sophie, when you're interviewing a witness, how far up the reliability scale would you place a drug addict?'

I twisted the handle of my bag. 'It depends what they've taken.'

'Well, let's assume this source is more advanced than your entry-level addict, you trust his word?'

'Why would he lie?'

'He knows who you are, I suppose.'

'What do you mean?'

My father waited a beat. 'Presumably, he's done his home-work. He knows you're not from ordinary stock.'

'Christ, you make me sound like a cow. Not everyone is as motivated by money as you.' I glanced towards the window, not wanting him to see how much his words unsettled me. What was it Damo had said last night: *I didn't know Tommy was from such a rich family.* Was that why he agreed to meet me? He was hoping for some kind of financial reward?

I dragged my gaze back to my father. 'Or he could be telling the truth, that your son was murdered.'

He strolled back to his desk and sat down. 'It was night-time, yes? Dark. Under a bridge. It couldn't have been very clear. He could have hallucinated this for all we know.'

I shook my head incredulously. 'So that's your answer, is it? To dismiss this as the unreliable word of a junk—' I stopped, as a piece of the puzzle slotted into place with a thud. When I asked Durand why there hadn't been an investigation into the cause of death, he told me: *the whole thing was quietly dropped.*

'You knew.' I closed my eyes, and for a second, I almost laughed. 'You're the dead end.' Tears burned the back of my eyes. 'Do you know what it's been like? Living with the guilt since he died?'

I heard a sound and opened my eyes. My father was shuffling his papers, a grim look on his face.

I slowed my breathing. 'What possible reason could you have for shutting this down?'

My father's voice was unnaturally harsh. 'Do you really think I would risk airing our dirty laundry on the word of a drug addict?'

'Our dirty lau—' I stared at him, fury rising in my chest. 'Your son was murdered.'

'So you claim.'

'I've looked this man in the eye. He knows what he saw. Two killers are walking free because– Why the fuck am I having to argue this? Why aren't you shouting this from the rooftops?'

'You know why.'

'Because of this?' I gestured wildly around his office. 'Your *business*?'

'This business might not mean much to you, Sophie. You've never missed an opportunity to pour scorn on my achievements. Perhaps you share something with your grandfather in that respect. He never believed I was capable of turning the Kent name into a lasting legacy. But empires are built on a knife-edge. I made a call that it wasn't worth the risk.'

Anger coiled in my stomach. 'What possible deal could be worth letting your son's killers walk free? How much money do you need in the bank before you're willing to take that risk? Ten million? Fifty million? A billion?'

My father shifted forward in his chair and fixed me with a cold stare. 'Do you know what Tommy said the last time I saw him? That he was going to kill himself. Three days later he overdosed.'

'That's beside the fucking–' I frowned. 'You saw Tommy three days before he died?'

My father took off his glasses to inspect the lenses. 'One of our bench visits. We used to meet up every now and then. Park benches. Battersea Park, Hyde Park, Green Park. Wherever he was calling home at the time. I'd try and encourage him to get help. Tommy would refuse. I'd hand over money. Then I wouldn't see him again for months.'

I stared at him. 'I didn't know that.'

'I suspect there are a lot of things you don't know.'

I chewed my fingernail. Tommy never mentioned he was still in touch with our father.

All of a sudden the fire left my father's eyes. 'When did you last see your mother?' he said, leaning back against his chair and crossing his arms.

'What's that got to do with anything?'

'Her latest stint in rehab was tough-going.'

'She should try getting out of bed once in a while.'

My father's face darkened, but he didn't rise to the bait. 'You know what's interesting, Sophie. You make endless excuses for Tommy. If you believe his addiction was an illness, why can't you extend the same courtesy to your mother?'

'She's manipulative. There's a difference.'

My father gave me a cool look. 'Doesn't she deserve your compassion?'

I sat back, staring at the view of London behind his head. In the distance, between two glass skyscrapers, I could just about make out the domed roof of St Paul's Cathedral. I focused on it while I waited for my breathing to calm down. My father's question was fair. The truth was, I'd never believed my mother. Deception rose from her like a stench. The mood-swings, the melodrama, the teetering walk. But I knew her secret. Once, I came back from university a day early and she was home alone. Dressed in jeans and a flannel shirt, she was whistling to herself as she chose fabric swatches for the drawing-room curtains. When she spotted me, her face fell. After an awkward hug, she disappeared to her room. By supper time, the shrieking arias she insisted on playing on full volume shuddered through the walls. She spent almost every day of my Easter break in bed, tangled up in a white night-dress like some kind of Gothic hero-ine. Everything was done for effect. She shut herself away from her family *for effect*. Hoping that the more pathetic she was, the more attention she'd get. Except it didn't really work. She wildly misjudged my father's capacity for sympathy. If she wanted his attention, she should have threatened his bank account. The only person who did lavish attention on her was Tommy, but she held him at arm's length and I couldn't forgive her for that.

My father cleared his throat. 'You have a naive view of Tommy. You know, the last time I saw him, he told me he stole money from you.'

'He was desperate.'

My father shook his head. 'When will you realise he wasn't perfect? Look, I know you blame me. I wasn't the father either of you wanted. When you have children, you can choose to be the kind of parent you want. I provided for you both. That was my job.'

'Didn't you do well.'

My father ignored the sarcasm and gave a tight smile. 'When I look at you, at what you've achieved, at what you're going to achieve, I don't think I did badly at all.'

I shook off the compliment, my mind muddy with exhaustion. 'I'm only half the story though, Dad. Your other child is dead. I'd call that a fifty per cent failure rate.'

My father flinched. 'Has it never struck you that while Tommy and your mother have battled depression and addiction, you and I have forged ahead and made something of ourselves? Perhaps we're not so very different after all.'

For one brief moment, an alternative scenario played out before my eyes. One where I reached across the divide towards my father, where we put the past behind us. I was tired of fighting him. But then my eyes drifted from his face to the wrinkled piece of paper on his desk. I pulled it towards me and my heart hardened inside my chest.

'The difference between us is that I loved Tommy.'

My father held my gaze. 'So did I, Sophie.'

'So fucking act like it.' I brandished the post-mortem in his face, my voice rising. 'Now's your chance to do something for Tommy, to finally show up for him, to be the father we always needed you to be.'

He gazed at me, defiant, stubborn, and something else. Something I couldn't read. 'I'm sorry, Sophie. I can't do it.'

I stood up so suddenly, the chair toppled over. My breath was coming in shallow puffs. 'I will find Tommy's killers. And when I do, I want everyone to know you didn't lift a finger to help. You don't get to call yourself his father anymore.'

My father didn't move. His voice sounded as exhausted as I felt. 'Are we done?'

As I strode towards the door, I finally caught a glimpse of the photographs on his dresser. Rows of besuited grey-haired men: politicians, oligarchs, captains of industry. Not a single photograph of his family. I picked up the nearest picture frame and flung it at the wall. It smashed into a thousand pieces.

Then I squared my shoulders. 'Now we're done.'

19

Emily: 15 weeks before the murder

'One ticket for *DragonSlayer*, please.'

A greasy teenage face stares back at her. 'Two o'clock showing?'

Emily nods, hands him the cash and glances over her shoulder. The cinema air is thick with the fatty fumes of hot dogs and popcorn. She wanders over to the pic 'n' mix area and pretends to inspect the sweets. She buys a bottle of water and a packet of chewing gum. She'll need it for after.

Emily makes her way to Screen 4 and pushes open the door. The velvet quietness envelops her. She slips through the darkness, brushing her hand along the seats, until she reaches the back row. The screen lights up, and the music starts. Emily's heart feels as if it's going to lift out of her chest. She closes her eyes, hoping the noise will drown out her thoughts.

She is supposed to be meeting a potential client right now. A South African couple who want to get married in London next summer. Their budget is huge; the bride-to-be has big connections in the magazine industry and could open whole swathes of doors for Emily. But instead of winning them over with her pitch, she's in a cinema in Broad Green, miles from home.

Because today, for the first time, she can't do it. She can't sit across from a couple and sell the happy ever after. She can't talk about soul mates or wedding favours or the Big Day. She can't watch two people in love.

Not when the world is crashing down around her ears.

Emily leans her head back against the chair. She is officially losing her mind. Her failing marriage is turning her into a twitching, paranoid wreck. Again, last week, she found more evidence that Charlie is drinking. A bottle of whisky under the bed; empty beer cans stuffed in his gym bag. The drinking is bad enough, but it's the lying that is killing her. When she confronted Charlie, he gave her a long, cold look then stormed out.

Heartbroken, she turned the flat upside down looking for more evidence that Charlie was lying to her. And that's when she found them. The black-lace knickers stuffed at the back of Charlie's sock drawer. Later that night, when she threw them in his face, he called her a 'bloody maniac' and told her she must have planted them herself, before yanking on his trainers and going for a run. Emily logged on to his laptop and scrolled through his internet search history feeling sick. There were pages and pages of religious searches: biblical cleansing, baptism by fire, by water, by blood. Emily was horrified by the images. The next day, she sneaked a look at his phone when he was in the shower and found a religious app buried at the end of all his other apps. When she asked him about it he claimed he didn't know how it got there. 'Lay off me, Em. Just lay the fuck off.'

The following morning she drove to Oxfordshire to oversee a client's wedding and couldn't get hold of Charlie the whole time she was there. Her voicemails were curt, then furious, then worried, then desperate. She called his two closest friends: Dominic and Sophie, feeling like an utter loser when she called Sophie. '*Hi Sophie, I seem to have misplaced my husband. No worries, he probably forgot to leave a note. You know how scatty Charlie is. Yep, I'll keep you posted. And dinner soon? Would love to!*' She'd hung up, and suddenly the prospect of a normal meal out in a normal restaurant like a normal couple was so preposterous that Emily folded over and sobbed. The moment she could get away, she fled the wedding and sped down the M4 back to London. The flat was empty. Charlie's holdall was gone. Emily huddled under the duvet and cried until she had nothing left. *He's gone, Dumpy Danson. Well, what did you expect?* It was her own fault for pushing him. She always knew this day would come. Once Charlie discovered she wasn't the carefree, upbeat, uncomplicated woman he thought, he'd realise she wasn't worth loving.

She went for a run, and when she got home, Charlie was asleep on the sofa. He leaped up when he saw her; a mortified look on his beautiful face.

'Em, my phone died. I'm sorry. I've only just got your messages. I called you from a payphone. Left you a voicemail. You didn't get it?'

'Where were you?'

'I promise you. I'd never not call you, Em. I just needed . . . space.'

'From me?'

'From everyone.' He pulled his fringe back from his face and she saw the deep lines etched into his forehead. 'I was up North. An old uni friend.'

When he left for work the following morning, Emily checked his jeans and found a train ticket to Bournemouth in his pocket, along with a business card for a divorce lawyer.

That was when she made her first Tinder connection. A mechanic with small hands called GunnersMan23, who met her in a dark Portuguese bar on Dean Street. Afterwards she sloped back to Delaware Street, raw and broken, and discovered she was miscarrying for the third time. *Serves you right, Dumpy Danson. Serves you right.*

Emily leans forward in her seat and traces the scarred skin on her wrists. She knew Charlie wasn't ready for marriage but she pushed and pushed, hoping that the stupid piece of paper would make up for everything. *Dress for the man you want, not the man you have. Fake it till you make it.* The brazen approach had worked for her in the past, but the problem with faking it is that you can only do so much and then one day you come home and find your husband spraying his dead wife's perfume around the flat.

In the quiet hours, when the city slows right down and darkness falls, Emily prays to a higher being that their marriage will be saved. She isn't one to quit. She will fight for the both of them if she has to. Other times, she finds herself fantasising about all the ways she can make Charlie pay for what he's done. Either way, she just needs a plan.

Emily shifts in her seat. She hears the voice in her head: *if you were thinner, prettier, smarter, Charlie wouldn't leave you.*

Or if you were dead, like her.

A surge of adrenaline courses through Emily. Her skin is starting to itch. Her emotions are going to take her down from the inside if she doesn't let them out. The men aren't hard to find. She doesn't care who they are, or what they look like. Only that they can meet when she wants. And they don't expect sex. Because sex isn't what this is about. Today, it's a man called Sternus whose Tinder profile is even starker than her own. He's been bombarding her with messages. At first it was too much, but she's come to appreciate the flattery. She'll do what she needs to do, then block him from her phone. The cinema was Sternus's idea, and she agreed immediately. It's perfect; dark, anonymous.

The door to the left of the screen sweeps open. A figure pauses, then makes his way towards her. Emily shifts her weight, flexes her fingers. Her skin is burning. He slides through the seats and stops beside her. Emily keeps her eyes on the screen and nods. When he sits, she can smell the musty funk of unwashed clothes. As a giant CGI dragon sweeps across the screen, Emily puts a hand on his thigh. She hovers over his zip, then tries to undo it but it sticks. As she reaches across with her other hand, the light from the screen hits his face. She freezes. Something about the slant of his jaw, the arch of his brow, reminds her of Charlie. The light shifts and the likeness disappears. Her mind is playing tricks on her. But she refuses to feel guilty. Not when all this is Charlie's fault in the first place.

Emily frees the man with her hands and bends over, taking him in her mouth. On the screen a battle is raging. The cinema floor vibrates as something explodes. His hand is on the back of her head. She can smell the nicotine on his fingers, see the tattoo on his wrist. As she slides her mouth up and down she pictures the blank look on Charlie's face as she told him another one of their babies had died. Emily closes her eyes, trying not to gag. The man shifts his weight. It won't be long now. Her body is humming. She feels the dark red swirl building in her stomach. She pushes him deeper. She wants it to hurt. She hates oral sex, but that's the point. The man thrusts, the guttural sounds coming from his throat. He pulls her hair. He's close.

Suddenly, a flash lights up the space in front of her eyes. *What the fuck?*

Emily glances up and sees his phone. He's taken a picture of her. She freezes.

'Keep going.' His voice is low, breathy.

Something isn't right. She should stop, demand he deletes the picture. But she's raw, the burning in the pit of her stomach is all-consuming. She needs this to be over. Emily grips harder and squeezes her eyes shut.

The man shudders. Emily swallows, gags, then slips to the floor, her body like a spent balloon. She can hear him breathing hard. He zips up his trousers, puts a damp hand on her head and gives her an awkward pat.

Then he leans down close and whispers in her ear, 'Filthy bitch.'

Emily doesn't respond. The floor is sticky beneath her. As he disappears into the darkness, she clutches hold of the seat and listens to the wet, meaty sound of a dragon devouring a village of people. She feels drunk. She feels euphoric.

Her head is filled with white.

Bright, virginal, wedding white.

20

Present Day

It wasn't until I was in the taxi and almost back at the office that I remembered Kate's email. It was a link to Emily's blog. There was a new post up, entitled *Three Times*.

Dear friends,

I promised you my story, in my words. Well, brace yourselves. Things are about to get ugly.

As I type, I'm propped up in bed lying in a stark hospital room. Last night I was attacked in my home. By the man I love most in the whole world. The fact that Charlie could hurt me makes me want to curl up and cry. But it turns out, I'm not the only one he has hurt. Remember in my last blog post, I opened up about my three miscarriages? This morning, DCI Golden from the Metropolitan Police let me in on a secret. Those miscarriages weren't 'Nature's way' after all.

OK, here goes. The police have found evidence that Charlie has been poisoning me, deliberately causing me to miscarry. I can't go into details but the evidence, it's . . . compelling.

If the police are right, that's three times Charlie has spiked my food and waited patiently for our child to die inside me. Three times I've crouched in the bathroom and watched my longed-for baby slip away. Three times Charlie has held me in his arms afterwards and told me everything will be OK. I find myself replaying everything in my head. The homemade smoothies he made me drink, the dinners he cooked. Am I married to a monst—

'Miss?' The cabbie rapped on the glass. 'We're here.'

I tore my eyes away from my phone and held it together long enough to fling some money at him and slide out the door. Then I staggered to the back entrance of Premier News and collapsed on the steps, rereading Emily's words. Each line cut deeper into my heart. *Poisoning me. Hurt me. Causing me to miscarry.*

A group of tourists meandered past leaving a thick trail of cigarette smoke in the air. I shifted towards the wall and closed my eyes. What was it that Dominic said about Emily's miscarriages: *Charlie wasn't that much of a shit that he would leave his grieving wife.* Had Dominic and I got Charlie wrong? I pictured the hopelessness in Dominic's eyes and felt my insides go cold. My phone rang and I fished it out of my bag.

'Hello?'

'Where the hell are you?' Mack's voice was low and urgent.

'Downstairs. What's wrong?'

'I take it you haven't listened to my voicemail?'

I closed my eyes, feeling delirious with tiredness. 'I haven't had a chance.'

'Clarion call from Rowley. He wants us in his office. Move it.'

He hung up. I had five new messages. One from Mack and four from numbers I didn't recognise. I hit the first one.

Hi Sophie, this is Jemma Williams from the Tribune. *Could you ring me when you get a moment? I'd love a comment about the rumours you've been sleeping with your colleague, Charlie Swift.*

I swore under my breath and stomped across the lobby.

'You sure you're OK?' Rowley's angular face peered at me from behind his desk. 'You're looking a bit . . . peaky.'

I felt Mack and Kate staring and dug my nails into the arm of the chair. What could I tell them? That my father was a sociopath, that my brother was murdered and I was no closer to finding the killers, that everyone thought I was a lying whore, that my friend had jumped off the deep end and left us all shovelling his shit. The walk of shame through the newsroom had nearly finished me off. I'd felt each pair of eyes on my back like an icy wind.

I took a long breath and forced a smile. 'I take it we're here to discuss Emily's latest blog post?'

'Amongst other things,' said Rowley. He slid his tortoiseshell glasses off his nose and rubbed them with his tie. 'Have any of you heard of an app called KeepSafe?'

Kate tapped her pen on her notepad, still looking at me. 'It's a way of protecting files, isn't it?'

Rowley nodded, slipping his glasses back on. 'KeepSafe is the second most widely used data protection app in the UK. It has varying degrees of security; the lowest being a simple password. So if, for example, you download the app onto your smartphone and your wife finds it, she won't be able to access your deepest, darkest secrets.'

The atmosphere deadened. We could tell by the look on Rowley's face that something major was about to go down.

'It turns out the phone Emily found doesn't just contain photographs,' said Rowley. 'There are videos, too. I've pulled in a favour from an old friend on the Force and he's given me a snippet; a heads-up before another press conference tomorrow morning.'

Mack frowned. 'Another press conference?'

I licked my lips, feeling light-headed. Next to me, Kate scratched lines into her page.

Rowley shifted his computer round and clicked on a link.

A screen popped up, flickering briefly then settling on a place I recognised: Charlie and Emily's bedroom. A woman drifted into the frame. Dressed in a dark green coat, she was laughing and looking over her shoulder at someone off camera. Even before she flicked her long red hair away from her face, I knew who she was. *Sabrina.*

Sabrina shrugged off her coat; underneath she was wearing black lacy lingerie and suspenders. She wobbled over to the bed and unzipped her knee-length boots. She was alone on the bed but Charlie had obviously entered the bedroom because she followed him with her eyes. She slipped a bra strap over her shoulder, then put her finger to her lips. In the background, a wedding photo of Charlie and Emily was visible on the bedside table.

We sat rigidly watching Sabrina peel off her stockings and throw them at Charlie. When she was naked, she looped a lock of hair around her finger and peered up at Charlie through her lashes. She blew him a kiss, then beckoned him over. The pout on her face said he was playing hard to get. She rolled her eyes, then slid off the bed and sashayed off camera.

Rowley hit pause.

'No prizes for guessing what happens next,' said Mack, his voice lacking the usual sarcasm.

'When was that?' I asked, still staring at Rowley's computer.

'Fifteenth of January,' he said. 'Four months before her death.'

Kate closed her notebook with a slap. 'A performance like that and not a single glance to the camera? What does that tell you?'

'She didn't know Charlie was filming her,' I said, already drawing the same conclusion. I made a mental note to ask Durand if Forensics found a hidden camera during their search. I glanced at Rowley. 'Are there more videos on the phone?'

Rowley reached for his glass of water. He took a sip, then cleared his throat. 'Mack, Kate, start fleshing out the bones for tonight's edition. Now, please,' he added, his voice shifting into a high whine.

Kate raised her eyebrows at me as she stood up, and I shrugged, praying Rowley wasn't going to subject me to another pep talk.

The door closed and Rowley's shrewd grey eyes darted across my face. He tapped his finger against the rim of his water glass, opened his mouth, then closed it again.

'Are we going to need something stronger?' I pointed towards the silver drinks trolley in the corner, only half joking.

Rowley gave me a taut smile. 'I'm not going to drag this out, Sophie. There's no way to sugar-coat what I'm about to show you. Company protocol is that a member of HR should be present in a matter like this, but I'm choosing to ignore that. I wanted to give you the space you deserv—'

'Just play it, Philip,' I said, hugging my arms around myself.

Rowley clicked his screen.

We were back in Charlie and Emily's bedroom. It was the same scene, but a different time of day. The curtains were drawn and the lamp in the corner bathed the room in a mellow light. A figure darted past the camera. I caught a glimpse of dark hair. He paused by the bedside, and I recognised Charlie's West Ham hoody. He leaned over the bed for a moment, then straightened up. At first I didn't see the woman lying on the bed. She was so small, I mistook her for a pile of cushions. She was lying on her side, eyes closed, arms tucked beneath her. She was fully clothed; still wearing her shoes. I leaned in for a closer look. *Red high heels.*

My jaw clenched so hard it rang through my teeth. 'Is that . . . me?'

Charlie knelt on the bed, his back to the camera, and I watched in horror as he unbuttoned my blouse, yanked down my bra and started kneading my flesh. My hand flew to my mouth and I was vaguely aware of Rowley moving away from the computer. Charlie undid my skirt and slid it down over my legs. Then he stood back to look at me.

He tilted his head, then ran a hand up my leg. As I watched him slip his hand inside my knickers, I curled my legs onto the chair. I wanted to run, scream, hurl the screen at the wall, but I couldn't tear my eyes away. I owed it to the unconscious woman to witness every single thing Charlie did.

Charlie pulled a phone out of his pocket, and held it aloft. The camera flash lit up my unconscious face. Satisfied, Charlie tossed the phone on the bed and buried his face in my hair. Then he unbuckled his belt and reached inside his boxer shorts.

All of a sudden, the screen went black.

A clink, as a tumbler of whisky appeared on the desk.

'Drink it,' said Rowley.

'What happens next?' My voice sounded like it was coming from far away.

'Drink it, Sophie.'

I picked up the glass; it felt as heavy as a rock. I gulped it down, my eyes watering.

Rowley crossed to the window and stood with his back to me, hands in his pockets. 'It's not clear what happens next although I think we can assume–' He stopped, then strode over to the drinks trolley and snatched up the decanter. He poured us both another measure and drank his in one. 'The police want to talk to you, but I've told them you'll need some time. To get your head around things.'

I couldn't speak. The only night I'd ever stayed at Charlie's was just before Christmas. The night Charlie flew to Geneva.

But I would have remembered if he'd ... I stared at the computer screen, at the space where the video had played.

Bleating an apology, I hurled myself through Rowley's door and sprinted to the toilet. I only just made it in time, throwing up over and over until I sank, shivering, onto the floor.

Ten minutes later, I was tucked in a dark corner of the Anchor & Hart and Kate was stomping back from the bar with a tray of tequila shots and a stony look on her face. She shoved one towards me, then downed hers and slammed the empty glass on the table.

'Wait till I get my hands on that fucking pervert.'

I picked the edge of my fingernail, staring hard at the table. I couldn't shake the images from my eyes. Charlie's hand on my leg, my breasts, my ... I swallowed. The parts of my body he'd touched burned and itched. I wanted to tear off my clothes and scorch my skin under a melting-hot shower. I wanted to wash every trace of Charlie Swift off me.

I turned to Kate. 'Charlie was supposed to be in Geneva that night. He gave me a place to crash. I was in a bad way. He looked after me. I–' My voice tremored. 'I've seen him almost every day since then, Kate. How did he do that? Carry on as if nothing happened.'

I pulled my sleeves down over my hands and leaned into Kate as scenes from the past month played out in my head: Charlie sitting on my desk, howling with laughter at YouTube clips of drunk people falling off things (his favourite web channel);

tossing the new J Crew catalogue on my desk so I could pick him out a new suit ('This one's going shiny at the knees.' Mock horror face. 'Do I have shiny knees, Kent?'); taking a detour via my desk most days to bring me a Starbucks coffee, always with a fake name written on the cup, generally someone small: Tinkerbell, Smurfette, once Danny ('Danny?', 'Devito,' he chuckled, sidling off before I could swipe him with my foot). Did this sound like the behaviour of a man who'd sexually assaulted me?

Kate stroked my hair. 'You know, we haven't even discussed the other bombshell. Charlie poisoning Emily. Lansdowne wants to hang Charlie out to dry. His wife lost a baby last year. Almost full term.'

I closed my eyes, only half listening. 'How did I not know it happened? I should have known, right? My body . . . it should have told me. That I was . . . that I was . . .'

'Raped.' Kate's voice was soft but I could see the fire in her eyes.

I clamped my hand over my mouth as vomit slid up my throat. Suddenly, a memory from that night hit me. The bitter taste washed down with water. I thought Charlie had given me paracetamol, but was it something else? A drug to knock me out, and keep me out?

He's been poisoning me.

Emily's words slid through my mind and I dropped my voice to a whisper. 'Kate, I think Charlie drugged me that night.'

An hour later I was drunk. Red-hot, steaming, ugly drunk.

I clutched Kate as we made our wobbly way to the taxi rank. 'Can't go home. Need to work.'

Kate squeezed my arm. 'You need to sleep.'

I waved a finger in the air, then prodded her in the shoulder. 'I can see two Kates, and neither is drunk.'

She wiggled her arse. 'My extra padding soaks up the alcohol. Come on, get in.' She bundled me into the cab and gave the driver my address. 'Sleep this off, then tomorrow we'll make a plan. And call me. If you need anything. I mean it.'

I clung on as the taxi pulled away from the kerb. The images from the video swam in front of my eyes. The sound as Charlie unbuckled his belt. I opened the window and gulped down the warm, sooty air.

My phone rang and I fumbled around in my bag trying to find it.

Durand's voice was soft. 'Sophie, are you OK?'

The cab braked suddenly and I plummeted to the floor and banged my head. 'Fuck.'

'Hello? Are you there?'

'Drunk.'

'Where are you?'

'Cab.' I hauled myself up and took a deep breath. 'Going to be sick.'

Durand sighed. 'Ask him to pull over.'

I rapped on the window. 'Stop the cab.'

The driver took one look at my face in the mirror and hurtled towards the kerb. I fell out the door and vomited. I was still clutching my phone and I held it to my ear. 'Just ruined my shoes.'

'Sophie, get back in the cab. It's late.'

I leaned on the taxi door and waggled my eyebrows at the driver. 'There's a policeman on the phone and he says he'll arrest you if you don't take me home.'

'Don't push your luck, love,' he said, narrowing his small eyes. 'One more and you're out.'

I climbed back into the car; sweat was pooling under my arms.

'Is there anyone at home who can look after you?' said Durand.

I opened my eyes. 'You're still there?'

'You won't be alone, will you?'

I pictured my empty, silent house. 'Loads of people. All the people. Can't move for people.'

'Why do I get the impression you're lying to me?'

'Cos you're a know-all.' I leaned my head against the window, trying to stop the cab spinning.

'Look, I know how you operate, Sophie. You're going to push everyone away and pretend you're fine. But let me help you. Meet me at Florian's café on Marylebone High Street at nine tomorrow. I have a favour to ask. And it might provide a distraction from . . . everything.'

I closed my eyes, lulled by the rocking cab. 'Why are you so nice to me?'

'Because I need a favour.'

'That's not what I mean.' I slid further down the seat.

There was a pause. 'Because we're friends.'

'Friends.' I tried the word out for size. 'Don't friends tell each other things? Real things. Not who left fingerprinty-things on the doorknob. Or which DNA swap was tampered with.'

'Swab.'

'Shut up. I mean, real things. About their lives and stuff.'

Durand cleared his throat softly. 'Do you have a real thing you'd like to share?'

I could picture the suppressed smile on Durand's craggy face and a warm feeling spread through me. 'You go first.'

I heard the sound of a TV being turned down. 'OK. I'm supposed to be at a charity fundraiser tonight but I told the organiser I had food poisoning so I could stay home, watch Alan Partridge and eat an M&S lasagne.'

I raised my eyebrows. 'What charity?'

'I can't say.'

'Friends, remember?'

Durand sighed. 'Starlight.'

'Kids with cancer? Wow, you bastard, I wish I'd never asked.' The taxi swerved and I slid to the right. 'Ow!'

'Your turn,' he said, with a mouth full of food.

I rubbed my head where I'd bashed into the window. 'Are you and Whatsername together now?'

'Huh?'

'You know. Pretty chin. Nice plait.'

A beat. 'You mean PC Waters?' Durand chuckled. 'She's a colleague. A junior. It would be against the rules.'

'Do you always stick to the rules?'

'Not always.'

I opened the window a crack more as my stomach lurched. 'So, who would you date? An astronaut? A tea-lady?' The driver was giving me a death stare in the mirror and I waved at him.

'A journalist?'

'That depends.'

'On what?'

'On whether we're talking Battleaxe Barb from the *Post* or–'

'Or who?'

'That redhead at *The Times*. Christina someone?'

I snorted. 'Christina Gulliver? She's married.'

'She is?'

'Dunno. Maybe,' I said, feeling irritable as I pictured Christina's long legs and swishy hair. 'Would it make a difference?'

'Breaking up someone's marriage isn't my style.' Something about the way Durand said it triggered off a warning bell in the back of my mind, but I was fading fast. We were driving through Knightsbridge and the Harrods fairy lights glittered across my vision.

I slid down the seat. 'It's a no to dating reporters, then. Unless they're Christina Legs-Up-To-Her-Armpits Gulliver.'

'Not exactly what I sa—'

'Got it.'

'You're an idi—'

'Loud and clear, friend.'

Durand made an exasperated sound. 'Soph, can you remember where we're meeting tomorrow?'

'Mmm.' I could feel sleep tugging me downwards.

A sigh. 'I'll text you the details. Get home safe. And call me if you need anything.'

I held the phone to my ear long after Durand hung up, drifting off into the darkness. I was grateful when the cab driver shook me awake because, this time, when I dreamed that Tommy was coming for me, he wasn't alone.

He had a tall, handsome accomplice, with a dark fringe and a killer smile.

21

Florian's was an Italian café chain that fell short of the authentic Italian experience by dint of its weak coffee, Polish waiters and German techno music. I pushed the door open, grimacing as the white lights grated against my eyes. An enthusiastic cleaner had gone overboard with the bleach and I covered my nose, willing my stomach to settle.

Durand sat in the corner, beneath a print of St Marco's Square in Venice. His long legs stuck out either side of the table and the sun streaming in from the skylight turned his hair burned copper.

He was poring over the paper, squinting at something.

I dumped my bag on the floor beside him. 'Just wear your glasses. I won't judge.'

He raised his eyebrows. 'After last night's performance you don't get to judge anyone.'

I felt the colour hit my cheeks as snippets of our conversation ran through my mind. *What possessed me to ask if Durand had a girlfriend? Was I seventeen?*

I cleared my throat and slid onto the chair opposite, just as a short, dark-haired waiter appeared at my shoulder.

He gave me a smarmy smile. 'What can I get you, beautiful lady?'

'Large black coffee. Extra shot, please.'

As he melted away, Durand closed his newspaper. 'Sure you don't fancy a Bloody Mary?'

I shuddered. 'I barely even remember getting home.'

'I take it those aren't the puke-stained shoes,' he said, peering under the table.

The waiter reappeared and set a large mug down in front of me, leering. 'Anything else, bellissima?'

As the waiter disappeared, Durand rolled his eyes. 'Does the brazen approach ever work?'

I gazed out the window, distracted. 'Maybe you should try it some time.'

'Don't need to.' Durand cracked his knuckles and pointed at his hair. 'Gingers are having a moment. Prince Harry is paving the way.'

I forced a smile. 'Ron Weasley is probably more your level.'

'Harry Potter's sidekick? Charming.'

'Who got the girl in the end?'

Durand held my gaze until I dropped my eyes to the table.

I heard him sigh. 'Are you going to mention the tape at all?'

I shrugged. I didn't want to think about that tape, let alone talk about it. I was lying when I told Durand I couldn't remember getting home. It turns out I wasn't drunk enough. I'd thrown myself into bed and pulled a pillow over my head. Alone for the first time, the silence was deafening. The image of

Charlie kneeling over me burned the inside of my eyelids. All of a sudden, the bed tilted and I clutched the blanket as my breath came in short stabs. Then, with no one around to see, every emotion I'd fought to repress came shooting out of me. I stuffed the duvet in my mouth to drown out the noise. That was when I counted out the blue pills, wondering how many it would take to plunge me into a thick, black sleep with no end. For a brief moment, the idea of checking out was so tempting it scared me. I stared at the pills until an image of the small, unconscious woman on Charlie's bed drifted through my mind. I couldn't abandon her now.

'Sophie,' he broke off, emotion colouring his voice. 'For the record, what Swift did to you . . . I want you to know, we're going after him, hammer and tongs.'

I nodded. 'Hammer and tongs.'

'And I've arranged for PC Waters to take your statement. Thought you might prefer a familiar face. You know, pretty chin, nice plait.'

I appreciated his attempt to lighten the mood, but the thought of reliving that night and making a statement turned my stomach.

This morning I'd made a detour to the family doctor on Cadogan Gardens: an olive-skinned Frenchman who'd known me since I was a teenager. I didn't have an appointment, but Dr Betrand ushered me in anyway.

'Everything OK, Sophie?' he said quietly, after I asked for an STD check.

I stared hard out the window, at the red-brick building opposite, and half-shrugged, not wanting to say the words out loud.

Dr Betrand coughed once, then told me he'd rush the results through, and call me later today.

Sensing my distress, Durand scooted his chair forward and cleared his throat. 'Right, shall we talk about that favour before you change your mind?'

'Does it involve nailing my former friend, Charlie Swift?'

Durand's face turned serious. 'Sophie, what I'm about to tell you is so far off the record it exists in another dimension.'

As he tapped his fingers on the table, I noticed that the faint tan line on his ring finger had almost disappeared. I did the mental calculations in my head. Had it really been six months since his wife left him?

'Sophie?' Durand gave me a questioning look. 'Are you listening?'

'Sorry.' I forced myself to focus.

'I want you to keep an open mind, which won't be easy, given what you saw yesterday,' he said. 'But, listen. Certain people working on this case believe the evidence points in one direction – and one direction on–'

'By "certain people", you mean DCI Golden,' I said, picking up my spoon and stirring my coffee.

Durand's eyebrows dropped. 'If you're going to interrupt me we'll be here all day.' He took a deep breath. 'The case against Charlie Swift is compelling. He was sleeping with the victim, the weapon used in the attack came from his apartment, and then there's the fact that–'

'He's a fucking rapist?' I took a swig of coffee, biting down on the china. 'Sorry, won't interrupt again.'

Durand's fingers twitched, moved a fraction closer to mine. 'I'm worried that other avenues aren't being chased because they don't fit the narrative.'

I frowned. 'Other avenues? You mean another suspect?'

'I mean closer to home.'

I shook my head, not understanding.

Durand ran a hand through his hair, then rested his elbows on the table. 'I've been in this game a long time. The guys I work with; they're family. DI James Flynn took part in the police search of Charlie's apartment. The second phone that contained the videos, Emily found it in a shoebox underneath a floorboard in the spare room. Along with the abortion drug.' Durand paused, taking a sip of coffee. Then he fixed me with his shrewd, grey eyes. 'Flynn says that shoebox wasn't there when police searched the flat.'

I leaned back and folded my arms. 'He would say that, wouldn't he?'

'Trust me, Flynn isn't the kind of man who would lie to save himself. Sometimes the police don't catch every detail first time around. It happens. Flynn wouldn't have a problem telling me that. If it was the truth.'

I frowned. 'So what are you saying? That the shoebox was put there after the search? By who? The police?'

Durand shrugged. 'It's possible.'

I gave him a long look. 'But that's not what you're thinking.'

Durand chewed the inside of his cheek, waiting for me to piece it together. *Closer to home.*

My cup slipped, spilling coffee on the table. 'You think *Emily* planted that shoebox?'

'It's a theory.'

I dabbed the coffee with the corner of the paper tablecloth, my mind spinning. 'Why on earth would Emily plant the phone? It only makes Charlie look more guilty.'

'Maybe that's what she wants.'

'Are you seriously suggesting she's framing her own husband?'

'I'm suggesting nothing,' said Durand. 'I'm only asking you to look at the evidence. The powers that be believe the phone was missed in the first search, which fits their Charlie theory. But if Flynn is telling the truth, it throws the whole thing open. It means someone is manipulating the evidence.'

I rubbed my eyes, trying to absorb Durand's words. 'But if Emily planted the phone, it means she's known all along that Charlie was sleeping with Sabrina. And she would have . . .' my voice trailed off. I swallowed hard. 'She would have seen what Charlie did to me.'

'Not necessarily.' Durand's voice was soft. 'The videos were protected by a security app.'

I blinked, trying to slow my thoughts down. 'But couldn't someone else have planted the phone? Someone who broke into their flat after the initial search?'

Durand shook his head. 'We've had a watch on the place, in case Charlie reappeared. I mean, it's possible, but unlikely.'

'But Charlie did reappear. He attacked Emily in the kitchen.'

'So she says.' Durand's voice was calm, measured.

I stared at him. 'You can't possibly think Emily faked the attack.'

'According to Emily's statement, Charlie batted the phone out of her hand. The phone that contained footage of Sabrina, of his assault on you. If Charlie was really there, why didn't he take it with him? Why leave incriminating evidence behind?'

I opened my mouth to speak, then closed it again. Durand had a point. 'What does Golden say to that?'

He shrugged. 'That Charlie panicked when he realised Emily was on the phone, and he ran.'

'That's possible, right?' I thought back to that night, when I answered Emily's call. She'd sounded like she'd had the shock of her life. Could that really have been an act?

Durand sighed. 'Look, all I'm saying is that if Flynn is right and the phone was planted then Emily is lying about a lot of things. She is not the victim she's making out.'

She'll play the perfect victim. Sinead's words drifted into my head and I pushed my cup away, feeling sick. 'Why isn't Golden entertaining this option?'

Durand turned the teaspoon over in his big hands, a muscle working in his cheek. 'He's new. He doesn't know the boys like I do. But if Flynn tells me that shoebox wasn't there, I believe him.'

I studied Durand's face, wondering how close he was to this. Sure, Emily was a possibility. But there was another explanation: Flynn was lying.

'How do you know all this if you're not even on the case?' I said. Durand glanced down at his fingers and something clicked in my head. *PC Waters.* That's why they were so close. 'You're being updated behind Golden's back?' For the briefest, sharpest moment I actually pitied Golden. Then Durand rubbed his eyes and I saw the exhaustion and concern chase each other across his face.

My gaze softened. 'Sam, why are you taking so much time off?'

He pinched the top of his nose and closed his eyes. When he opened them again I saw the struggle, the desire to confess; it was on the tip of his tongue. But he swallowed it down and shook his head. 'You've heard the theory. What do you think?'

'What's Emily's motive? She finds the phone a while back, sees what Charlie's done but sits on it hoping they can work through their problems,' I said, scraping my hair back into a ponytail. 'Then Sabrina is killed, so Emily cuts her losses and pretends to find the phone and Charlie is outed as a baby-killing maniac?' It was possible. It fit with what I'd discovered about Emily's desire to control the story. 'My question is: if she lied about the phone, what else is she lying ab—?'

A thought struck me and I rolled it around in my mind before saying the words out loud. 'Wait, the shoebox. You said the abortion drug was hidden there too?' Durand watched me carefully, absolutely still. 'So, if Emily knew about the phone, she knew about the medication. *She knew Charlie was drugging her.*'

'That's one explanation,' he said and I frowned, wondering how much darker this was going to get. 'Another is that she was administering the medication herself.'

'What?' The word came out half-laugh, half-shriek.

Durand shrugged. 'I have no idea why a married woman would take drugs to force a miscarriage. But, say Charlie was abusive and she felt unsafe. Or she didn't want children but hadn't told him. Or perhaps no one drugged anyone, and it's just what Emily wants us to think.'

I rested my head in my hands, feeling exhaustion sweep through me. 'But all this hinges on Flynn's word. If he's mistaken,' *or lying,* I almost added, 'then Emily's in the clear. There's no reason to believe she's a liar. Also, something else doesn't add up. Where is Charlie while all this is going on?'

Durand tilted his chair back. 'The team have received more calls about possible sightings. Oxford, London, Bournemouth, even as far as Sheffield.'

'But if Emily is lying about the attack, why isn't Charlie defending himself?'

'I can't answer these questions. I'm only drawing your attention to certain anomalies before the press conference.' Durand glanced over his shoulder. 'The feeling at the Met is that Emily needs reining in. Every blog posts whips the public up. Golden is trying to handle her. He's suggested that instead of writing another blog, she makes a televised appeal to Charlie. She's agreed to let journalists ask questions.'

'It's a risky strategy.'

Durand nodded. 'But Golden thinks they're closing in and Emily is his secret weapon.'

'Why is Golden so adamant Charlie is guilty?'

'When you're the Senior Investigating Officer, you have fourteen tons of information thrown at you. It's a skill to sort the wheat from the chaff. Throw in a personal bias and things can get . . . muddled.'

'Personal bias? You mean his father.'

'There's a reason why he's fixated with a *Herald* journalist.' Durand massaged his temples and sighed. 'Look, I need to know whether my theory about Emily has legs, and that's where you come in. At the press conference, I want you to ask Emily if she staged the attack at her apartment.'

I froze. 'Are you nuts?'

Durand shifted forwards in his chair. 'Hear me out. Emily is a blogger; she's good with the written word, good when she has time to think things through. But I want to put her under pressure and it's the only way I can do it without formally bringing her in for questioning. I'm not officially on the case, remember.'

I dropped my hands into my lap and gave a shrill laugh. 'But Emily's my friend. OK, she thinks I'm shagging her husband and won't return any of my calls, but still. I can't do that to her.'

'Firstly, Emily knows what Charlie did to you. Golden has shown her the video. Secondly, I think your involvement in the story might force more of a reaction.' Durand kicked back in his chair. 'Listen, I know it's unorthodox but a woman is dead. Think of Sabrina Hobbs. We owe it to her to get to the truth. If Emily has played any part in the death of an innocent woman, I need to know.'

I clinked my spoon against my cup. Durand knew me too well; appealing to my sense of justice was a smart move.

I sighed. 'I need to run this past Rowl—' My phone rang and I glanced at the screen. 'Sorry, this could be important, do you mind?'

Durand shrugged, and turned to get the waiter's attention.

I hit 'answer'. 'Hello?'

'Hello, Sophie?' A man's voice, softly-spoken. 'It's Gordon Brennan. Charlie Swift's stepfather. Look, I've only just got round to opening all the letters. I've had so many, you see. I didn't realise you knew Charlie. But, of course you do. He's mentioned you before. You're friends.'

I swerved the oncoming image of Charlie pawing at my unconscious body and cleared my throat. 'Thanks for calling, Gordon.'

'Sophie, I need your help. People are making up their minds about Charlie before he's had a chance to defend himself.' A pause while he took a breath. 'Please. They don't know the real Charlie.'

I closed my eyes, wondering if maybe, just maybe, this was the real Charlie all along. 'Would you be willing to talk to me face to face, Gordon?'

I could hear the sound of voices in the background. Gordon's voice shifted, 'What time is it?'

I glanced at the clock on the wall. 'Ten fifteen.'

'I have to go.' He sounded distracted. 'Come to the house, 23 Hindhead Close, Bournemouth. Today if you can.'

'Gordon, I've got a press conf—' The line went dead.

Durand raised his eyebrows. 'Everything OK?'

I nodded; overcome with an overwhelming urge to cry. I dug my nails into the tablecloth and tried to push through the noise in my head: *Charlie, Emily, Tommy.* I was sick of liars, of not knowing the truth. When I looked up Durand was frowning at me.

Suddenly he covered my hand with his and, for a split-second, the air went still.

Without thinking, I snatched my hand away. Then felt like an idiot.

'I'm sorry, I didn't me—'

'Don't mention it, I shouldn't ha—' Durand fumbled with his wallet, his eyes still on the table where my hand had been. 'The coffee's on me.'

Embarrassment coloured my cheeks. I couldn't think of a single thing to say. In the end I settled on an awkward wave, then scurried across the café, and out into the sunshine.

22

'You are not going to believe this.' Rahid sounded breathless.

'Slow down. Start again.' I was standing outside St James's Park Tube station, one hand clamped over my ear trying to drown out the sound of a fight between a pregnant woman and the van driver who'd almost hit her at a pedestrian crossing. I ducked back inside the Tube station, trying to find a quiet spot. My feet were sweating inside my shoes. A Tube journey on a hot day was always a low point in London. Throw in a hangover and it was sensory Armageddon.

'Sophie, are you there?' Rahid's impatience vibrated through the phone. 'Wait till you hear this. I've spent the past three days becoming an expert on Bert Hughes. From the ground up, like you taught me.'

I fumbled around in my bag for a bottle of water, then cursed as I remembered I'd left it on the Tube seat. 'Yep, go on.'

'Two words: Eric Rowntree.'

I pressed the phone against my ear. 'What?'

Rahid's voice rose a notch. 'Remember Rowntree's wife, Linda? She kicked him out in October. There was a rumour she'd hooked up with another bloke.'

I nodded, vaguely remembering the poor sod who'd been chased by every news outlet. 'Allen something?'

'Allen Holmes. Turns out the rumours were true.' Rahid paused and I glanced at my watch. The press conference was due to start in ten minutes.

I slung my bag over my shoulder. 'What's this got to do with Bert?'

'Wait, I'm getting to it. The night Rowntree broke into Linda's house and murdered his family, Allen Holmes was there. He turned up an hour earlier. Probably for a shag. Anyway, when Rowntree pitched up, Allen, being the chivalrous sort, ducked out the back door and legged it over the wall.'

A group of school kids in front of me started shouting at someone across the road and I darted into a doorway. 'How do you know all this?'

'Because there is CCTV footage of Allen entering the house.'

'From where?'

'The petrol station opposite Linda's house.'

Up ahead, New Scotland Yard glinted in the sunlight. I crossed the road, shielding my eyes from the glare. 'But the petrol station's CCTV wasn't working. Everyone knows that.'

'It's all bullshit. Someone paid an employee for the tape.'

'What?' I slammed to a halt.

'It goes like this: Allen assumes he's been caught on CCTV. Even though he's innocent, he doesn't want to get dragged into the Rowntree mess. He panics and turns to his best mate for help. A mate who has connections.'

I shook my head, bewildered. 'I don't follow.'

'His best friend is a guy called Simon Hughes. Bert's dad.'

I'd reached the entrance to New Scotland Yard, but I hung back, letting a TV news crew in. 'You're saying Bert Hughes made that tape disappear? Why would he break the law and risk everything?'

Rahid sighed. 'I've been piecing the guy's background. It's not pretty. A tough Manchester upbringing. Parents split when he was small. Moved South with his dad when he was fourteen. His dad's a bully. Nothing Bert has done is ever good enough.'

'His son becomes a rich lawyer and that's not good enough for him? Christ.' I recognised the fat silhouette of Stuart Thorp sloping towards me. I dropped my voice. 'So you think Bert's dad pressured him to buy up the evidence?'

'It fits, doesn't it? And if Sabrina found out about this . . .'

'It gives Bert the mother of all motives for her murder.' I flashed my press pass at the desk and hurried towards the meeting room, feeling as if my feet weren't touching the ground. What was the Wicked Whisper on LegalLens? *Sticking her beak in will end in tears.*

I hovered outside the door for a moment, looking around for water. 'How did you figure it out?'

I heard the smile in Rahid's voice. 'When I was researching Bert, I found a picture of his dad with Eric Rowntree. It was taken at the Battersea Rise bingo hall in the late nineties. Linda and Allen are in the photo, too. They all know each other. So I tracked down people who know them and started asking questions. Just like you taught me.'

I grinned. 'Then you know what I'm going to say next.'

He sighed. 'I don't have the attendant on record yet. But I'm working on his moral conscience. He feels sick about the whole thing. He knows he's destroyed the one piece of evidence that will convict Rowntree of murdering his family.'

I nodded. 'Keep at him. This is huge, Rahid. You need a good run at this if you're going to make this stick. Does Rowley know?'

'Should I tell him yet?'

A journalist opened the meeting room door; the seats were filling up fast. 'Look, the press conference is starting any moment. And then I'm driving down to Bournemouth to meet Charlie's stepdad. Fill everyone in. I'll see you back at the *Herald* tonight, or first thing tomorrow. And Rahid?'

'Yeah?'

'Great work.'

I pushed open the door and immediately locked eyes with Jemma Williams from the *Tribune*, one of the reporters who'd left me a voicemail asking for a quote about the rumours that I'd slept with Charlie. I ignored her and slid into a row near the back. From the other glances, I could tell that word was spreading fast.

I pulled out my Dictaphone and checked the batteries, still reeling from Rahid's bombshell. His discovery was a potential game-changer. If Sabrina found out that Bert had broken the law, and confronted him, who knows what he might have done to keep her quiet? The link between this and the other story of the moment, Rowntree, was going to blow this sky-high. I needed to give Rahid time to make it watertight.

I closed my eyes, feeling the chair digging into my sweaty back. Twenty-four hours ago, finding out that Bert had a strong motive for Sabrina's murder would have buoyed me up. But then I saw that tape.

A wave of panic swept through me and I inhaled deeply through my nose, counting my breaths, just like Dr Spado taught me. *One*. An image of Charlie, so familiar it hurt. Tugging on his fringe, standing in his usual awkward stance with one leg wrapped round the other. *Two*. The night in the bar: *I'm not a good husband. Three*. Charlie unbuckling his belt.

Panic gave way to anger and I gripped the chair so hard my knuckles hurt. How could he? *How could he?* Even if Charlie didn't kill Sabrina, nothing, *nothing*, would ever make up for what he did to me.

I loosened my grip on the chair and slumped forwards. What was it Rowley always said? *Never let emotion cloud the goal*. That is the truth, it's *always* the truth. As much as I wanted Charlie strung up for assaulting me, if he didn't kill Sabrina, then he didn't kill her. No one should go down for a crime they didn't commit.

Behind me, a desperate cameraman knocked over a chair trying to get a good angle. I craned my neck and could only just see the table at the front of the room. Press conferences weren't always this packed out, but everyone had been given a heads-up that Emily was making an appeal. And Emily was big news. The pretty, blonde wife of an alleged killer who wasn't afraid to speak out had captured the nation's imagination. By blogging her experience, she was sharing her nightmare with people in real time; they were discovering aspects of the investigation as she did.

But the country still couldn't decide if she was a victim, or a nutcase, or both. For some, Emily represented everything that was wrong with modern life. She was too vocal, too ready to overshare; guilty of putting herself at the centre of this story and detracting from the real victim: Sabrina. I didn't entirely disagree. So far, the column inches devoted to Charlie and Emily far outstripped those devoted to Sabrina. Killers trumped victims. And, as the link between the killer and the victim, Emily trod the line separating the two. Which is why the room was packed to the rafters.

Still, feminists hailed Emily as a trailblazer; a woman who was refusing to be defined by the actions of her husband, who was breaking the mould of a spouse caught in the middle of a press gangbang. Many felt protective of her – Emily's vulnerable streak played well with the mainstream media. Sinead's words drifted through my head again: *she knows exactly what she's doing . . . she'll play the perfect victim.* I shivered, looking around for Durand.

I pulled out my notebook and wrote today's date. My mouth was bone-dry and I wished I'd managed to get my hands on some water. I spotted Durand leaning against the wall, his arms folded, his foot tapping the floor. The skin on my hand lit up where he'd touched me and I clenched it into a fist. Durand must have sensed me looking because he glanced over and caught my eye. I resisted the urge to look away, watched as he pulled his phone out of his jacket pocket and started typing. Seconds later, my phone beeped. I read his text message with raised eyebrows, then scribbled down the new information.

I shifted in my chair, feeling uneasy. Was I really going to set Emily up, in front of all these people? An inside tip-off always comes with a risk. It's not unheard of for the police to leak incorrect information on purpose. Rowley wasn't a hundred per cent behind the plan to confront Emily, and neither was I. Emily was a friend. I felt uncomfortable putting her on the spot after everything she'd been through. A little voice in my head piped up: *if you're friends, why hasn't Emily reached out to you after seeing that tape?*

Suddenly, the door opened and DCI Golden appeared, his face set into a stiff mask. He glanced at the audience once, then strode towards the table. Everyone's eyes were on the door, waiting. At last Emily appeared. Her blonde hair was pulled into a low bun and she was wearing a neck brace. She turned her whole body awkwardly to look at the room, her big blue eyes flicking nervously over the crowd. I tried to catch her eye but she didn't see me.

She smoothed down her navy, long-sleeved dress and darted towards Golden who pulled out the chair for her. They were joined by Dolores Robinson, one of the Met's press officers, who tottered towards the desk in a too-tight pencil skirt. A memo had gone out to the media specifying that the press conference would be pre-recorded, not live, which made me wonder whether they were concerned about what Emily was going to say.

When everyone was seated, Golden cleared his throat and leaned towards the bank of microphones on the desk. 'Good afternoon, folks, we've called this press conference to update you on the inquiry into Sabrina Hobbs's murder. Over the past forty-eight hours, we have received an increasing number of calls from members of the public who believe they have seen the suspect, Charles Swift. As you can imagine, it is taking considerable time and resources to follow up each call.

'But,' Golden ran his eyes across the room, 'we believe we have had a breakthrough. At 6.40 p.m. yesterday, the suspect was caught on CCTV leaving a supermarket in Bournemouth and again on CCTV footage at a newsagent's on Rockwell Road nearby.'

My head snapped up. Rockwell Road. Why did that ring a bell? I fumbled through my notebook, stopped at the interview with the *Bugle*'s Jeff Johnson. *The new Christ Clan on Rockwell Road*. That was one hell of a coincidence.

Golden sipped his water, swooshing it round his mouth. 'We will shortly be releasing those CCTV images but suffice to say, we're confident the suspect is in Dorset and we are prioritising calls from that area.' He cast his gaze to the left and gave Emily a quick smile. 'With that in mind, I would like to hand over to Emily Swift, the suspect's wife, who wishes to say a few words.'

For a moment, Emily looked startled, then Golden dipped his head towards her and whispered something in her ear. Emily nodded, then shifted her gaze to the TV camera in the middle and licked her lips.

'Before I start, I'd like to thank the staff at UCLH for taking such great care of me since the attack,' her hand fluttered to her neck brace, 'and to DCI Golden and the team for being so supportive at this difficult time. I'd also like to thank the many, many people who've reached out to me on my blog, or through social media. Your kind words have helped more than you know. And now, I have a message for my husband, Charlie.'

Emily was staring at a spot above our heads, chewing the inside of her cheek. A ripple ran across the crowd while we waited, and waited.

Eventually Golden gave her a nudge.

'Charlie, so much has happened in the past twenty-four hours. I'm going crazy trying to piece this mess together. The only thing I can imagine is that you are suffering. You are sick, and you need help.' Emily reached out a hand to steady herself, her voice wavering. 'I know you didn't mean to hurt me. I know you didn't mean to hurt our babies,' her voice broke and she glanced at Golden. 'I know you are not a bad person. But, please, baby, come home. We will fix this. I am here for you. Never forget: I'm here for you.'

A taut silence settled over the room and I stared at Emily. *I'm here for you.* Where was the fight? Where was the spark? The feminists wouldn't be happy with that. Was Emily really standing by Charlie after everything he'd done? Or was this a tactic she'd agreed with Golden to bring Charlie in?

I glanced over to where Durand stood. He'd moved away from the wall and was staring straight ahead, his jaw tight.

'Thank you, Emily,' said Golden, patting her arm. 'Right, we're going to open the floor for a few questions.'

We all raised our hands and Golden pointed to a grey-haired man in the second row.

'What other measures are being taken to apprehend the suspect?'

Golden moved the microphone a fraction. 'I can't be more specific than I've already been but, rest assured, we are working closely with Dorset Police.'

A sea of hands shot up again. Golden pointed at the woman who was sitting in front of me. She hesitated a moment, long enough for me to seize the moment.

Pretending I thought Golden had pointed at me, I sat up straight and cleared my throat. 'This is a question for Emily.'

Emily's eyes darted in my direction when she heard my voice.

'It's about the attack that occurred at your apartment two nights ago,' I said, steeling myself. 'Emily, could you comment on the rumours that you staged the attack?'

Emily flinched. 'What rumours?'

Golden started to raise his thick hand but I jumped in. 'In your statement, you said the last thing you remember is Charlie batting the phone out of your hand. But if the phone contained damning evidence, why didn't Charlie take it with him?'

I tried to ignore the horrified look on Emily's face and glanced down at the information Durand had just given me.

'Emily, the *Herald* has discovered that the forensic testing on the phone has thrown up only one set of fingerprints: yours. You never mentioned he was wearing gloves. If Charlie had handled the phone like you say he did, where are his prints?'

Golden's anger was as quick as a flame. He yanked the microphone towards him, but Emily put a hand on his arm.

She leaned forward awkwardly and her eyes fluttered close for a moment. 'Sophie, the man I love wants me dead; he wants our children dead. I've been poisoned, attacked in my own home, shredded by the Press. Just,' she covered her face with her hands, and her voice trembled, 'give me a break. I'm doing everything I can to reach out to Charlie. To get through this . . . this . . . nightmare in one piece. For you to suggest any of this is my fault is . . . unspeakable.' Emily sat back in the chair, her whole body shaking.

A brief pause, then the room erupted.

Golden stood up so fast his chair fell over. 'OK, that's all we have time for. Thank you for coming.' He glared at me. 'Dolores will email those images to you and we'd be grateful if you could include the helpline number in your write-ups.'

He guided Emily towards the door and I felt the other reporters giving me quizzical looks, unsure where my curveball had come from.

Durand was deep in conversation with Waters and I threw him a desperate glance, willing him to look at me. *Emily didn't crack under pressure. Now what?*

Behind him, I saw Emily say something to Golden. His shoulders sagged, then he glanced in my direction and beckoned me over.

As I crossed the room, Durand met my eye and, for a split-second, I thought I saw a glimmer of doubt.

Golden glowered at me as I approached. Any chance I ever had of winning him over had evaporated. I hadn't just burned the bridge, I'd shoved the red-hot embers up my arse.

'You actually think I faked that attack,' said Emily, her eyes wet with tears. 'I might have known you'd take Charlie's side.'

'This has nothing to do with sides,' I said.

'I trusted you but you're just like the others. All along you've been biding your time, waiting to stick the knife in.' Emily's cheeks quivered with rage. 'Well, was it worth it in the end? I saw that video tape. You got what you always wanted.'

I stared at her. 'What did you say?'

'Oh, please. All those evenings you made Charlie work late,' she said, brushing the tears away from her red face. 'He might have been fooled, but I wasn't.'

I kept my voice level. It wouldn't help my cause to show I was rattled. 'Em, did you watch that tape with your eyes open or closed?'

Emily gave a thin smile. 'You can spin that video any way you like.'

Beside us, a group of reporters dragged their heels, trying to eavesdrop. I lowered my voice. 'I was unconscious. Charlie assaulted me. Where's the grey area?'

Emily raised a hand to her neck brace and her sleeve slid towards her elbow. She caught me staring at her scars and yanked it back down. 'You know, Charlie always says how desperate you are. How you'll use any excuse to keep him in the office.' Emily's eyes flashed. 'Even your brother's death.'

Any guilt I felt over what had just happened vanished. 'That's bullshit, and you know it. Charlie and I have been friends for years; long before you married him.'

'And that's what kills you, isn't it?' said Emily, her voice rising. 'All those hours you put in, and Charlie picked me. *He picked me.*'

An image of Charlie unbuckling his belt struck me between the eyes and I put a hand on the wall to steady myself. 'Em, listen to me. Charlie told me he was flying to Geneva that night. That I'd have the place to myself. I–'

Emily shook her head, wincing as the movement jarred her neck. 'Listen to yourself, Soph. You think you're the first woman to throw yourself at Charlie? Sabrina did the same thing. He was going through a rough time and you both made it worse.'

Golden moved towards us with a dark look on his face, but Emily turned her back, cutting him out.

'You have no idea what the last few months have been like for Charlie,' she said.

I shook my head, bewildered. 'Aren't you *done* making excuses for him?'

Behind us, the room had almost emptied out. I spotted the *Post* reporter, Stuart Thorp, giving me a sly look.

Emily's voice dropped to a whisper. 'Charlie was sick.'

'Clearly.'

'That's not what I mean. Since Vanessa's he's . . . he's fallen apart. It's not Charlie's fault. None of this is Charlie's fault.' Emily's voice dissolved and her eyes filled with hot, angry tears. She was wound so tightly she looked as if she'd shatter at the faintest touch. For a brief moment, I felt for Emily. I knew what it was like to believe in someone when no one else did. But then I remembered the tape. I'd seen Charlie's fall from grace with my own eyes.

I took a breath, softened my voice. 'Em, listen to me. The Charlie we thought we knew is gone. Maybe he never existed at all. He raped me. He attacked you. He killed an innocent woman. And he's left you all alone to deal with it.'

Emily started to cry openly. 'Don't you see: he was doing it for me. Wiping the slate clean. I'm sorry that woman had to die, but who knows what kind of pressure she was putting him under?' Out of the corner of my eye, I saw Golden watching Emily with an odd expression on his face. 'Without Sabrina, we can start again. That's why he needs to come home.'

'Start again?' I stared at Emily in disbelief. 'Charlie's facing a fucking life sentence.'

'Stop it,' Emily put her hands over her ears, and squeezed her eyes shut. The tears were coming thick and fast. 'It's not his fault.'

'Then whose fault is it?' The words screeched out of me. 'If Charlie didn't kill Sabrina, who did? You?'

I didn't see it coming. But the slap was hard and loud. My cheek stung. For a moment no one moved. Emily's gaze was like

23

Emily: 5 weeks before the murder

The rain pelts down and Emily sprints towards her front door. She misjudges a puddle and lands in it, kicking up filthy water. She is staring down at her muddy orange trainers and doesn't see the man until she hits the top step.

Emily pulls out an earphone, catching her breath. 'Um, can I help you?'

'Are you Emily Swift?'

He holds a newspaper over their heads, but he's so tall that Emily is getting drenched.

She fumbles for her key. 'Who are you?'

'Look, this is going to sound odd, but I have some information about your husband,' he says and Emily's hand tightens around the door handle. 'Can I come in? I'm soaked.'

Emily lets the man into the hallway. She flicks the switch but the light isn't working. She can smell him in the dark; the scent of coffee and cologne is heightened by the rain. Emily puts a hand to her cheek, knowing she's bright red from her run. She has that sort of skin; everything is on the surface. She remembers her first eyebrow wax. Even though the beauty therapist furiously applied calamine lotion, she'd walked around with two pink caterpillars on her forehead for hours. 'I've never seen skin so sensitive,' the woman told her, transfixed by Emily's forehead. Emily felt weirdly defensive. She wanted to peel down her pants, point to the scored skin on her hips and say, *not so sensitive there, huh?*

A faint light filters through the gaps in the far wall, which the builders haven't got round to filling. The man shakes out his overcoat and Emily catches a glimpse of gold around his wrist. 'Look, I'm sorry to be dramatic. If there was any other way of contacting you, I would.'

Emily looks up at him, wincing as she flexes her calf muscle. After the latest miscarriage the doctor told her she needed to lay off the running. Give her body a chance to rest. At first, she'd listened. Every morning she drank the fertility smoothie Charlie made, saying a silent prayer to the imaginary children in her head. *Please stick around this time. Please let me be your mummy.* She's started dreaming about babies. The ones she lost, the ones she's yet to lose. Not that she's going to get pregnant again any time soon. Not with Charlie sleeping in the spare room every night. She's become used to the vicious silence in the flat; the way they both adapt their schedules so they spend as little time together as possible. But Emily carries the weight of their failure inside her like a . . . baby. A dead baby, she thinks savagely, as her eyes flick towards the stranger in her hallway.

She needs an outlet, an escape. Sternus, the man from the cinema, has been bugging her with daily text messages, and

Emily knows it's only a matter of time before she relapses. So this morning, she pulled on her orange trainers and hammered her usual route round Regent's Park.

Emily nibbles her thumbnail. 'How do you know my address?'

The man glances at the carpet. 'I'll explain everything. I–'

He stops as the front door opens and an elderly lady in a cream mac and shiny black boots appears. She gives them a nod, then rifles through her post.

The man lowers his voice. 'Can I buy you coffee somewhere? I just want to talk.'

Emily glances at her neighbour, then down at her sodden running kit and sighs. 'Let's just go inside.'

The flat is cold; a draught shivers across Emily's back. The damp smell has returned, except now it's tinged with sewage. It's worse down in the cellar. It smells like something's died there. She really must get it looked at. Emily gestures towards the sofa, then she spreads a grey throw over the armchair and sits.

The man reaches into his overcoat pocket for something and Emily combs through possible scenarios. Judging by how nervous he is, the news isn't good.

He pulls out a business card and hands it to her. 'Here, this is me.'

Emily takes the card and stares at it. *Bert Hughes: Junior Partner, Hamilton Law.*

'Look, I almost didn't come,' he says, loosening his tie and undoing his top button. 'But I've been going over this in my mind, and I really think it's the right thing to do.' Bert's mannerisms feel exaggerated, rehearsed; it sets Emily's teeth on edge.

She twiddles her diamond pendant, waiting. 'Your husband is sleeping with my colleague and I thought you should know.'

Emily goes still. She pulls her necklace so hard it cuts into the back of her neck. 'Why?'

'Why what?'

'Why do you think I should know?' Her voice sounds weirdly calm; it freaks her out.

Bert frowns. His eyes go to the ceiling. 'Because it's the right thing to do. He's married. To you.' He falters. 'I mean, don't you want to know he's having an affair?'

An affair. The arm of the chair is digging into Emily's ribs. The drab, grey light coming through the window makes her feel as if she's underwater. Emily runs her eyes over Bert's face. His cleft chin reminds her of Gavin Lyle, a boy from school. She lost her virginity to Gavin when she was twelve, in the woods behind the dining hall. The night before, her parents had a huge row about money. Funds were tight in the Danson household but that didn't stop Emily's mum throwing down eighty quid on a novelty teapot to add to her collection. Rows of them cluttered the surfaces in their house. The newest, shaped like a cat curled in a basket, was front and centre on the sitting room mantelpiece. When Emily's dad spotted it after a long day in the office, he lost his temper. Emily remembers trying to get his attention, shaking her small head at him to stop shouting at Mummy because she knew what would happen next. Her dad yelled, called her mum 'profligate' and she hadn't known what it meant. Her mum stomped into the sitting room, returning with the Oxford dictionary. Moments later she flung it at her husband's face, shattering his nose. The following day, Emily sought out Gavin Lyle and led him into the forest. It was only later she found out that Gavin told everyone at school Dumpy Danson's fat arse nearly suffocated him.

For a moment, Emily can smell the heady scent of pine needles and wonders if her mind is playing tricks on her. Then she glimpses the diffuser on the coffee table: Autumn Pine.

Emily shifts her weight, breathes out. 'Um,' she glances at the business card on her lap, 'Bert. Can I just . . . are you romantically involved with this woman?'

'Excuse me?'

'It's just that I don't think you're really here for my benefit.'

Bert fidgets with the metal strap of his watch, as though debating something in his head. 'We've been together since last summer. On and off. It was pretty casual.'

'Casual. Huh.' Emily blinks; her eyes are dry. 'And yet, here you are.'

Bert shakes his head and a lock of hair falls across his forehead. 'I'm not the bad guy here.'

Outside, a screech of brakes punctures the air, followed by a chorus of car horns. Emily would give anything right now to be far away from the city, away from the noise, the dirt, the *disappointment.*

'Who is she?' she says and her voice is almost drowned out by the rain hammering on the window. But she knows Bert has heard her.

'Sabrina Hobbs.'

'And how do you know that she's . . . that she's,' Emily digs her fingernails into the palm of her hand, 'sleeping with my husband?'

A muscle flickers beneath Bert's eye and he rubs it with a tanned finger. 'Because she told me. When she broke up with me. Apparently it's been going on for months.'

Months? Emily fights to keep her face in check. She feels like she's in a movie scene. One of those dramatic moments in life where nothing feels real. *Oh, this is the scene where the heroine finds out her husband is a lying, cheating prick.*

But, amongst the hurt and pain and shock, she also feels something else: relief. There's a real, tangible reason why her marriage is caving in. Proof that she's not going mad. For a moment Emily feels like punching the air: *I told you! I knew it!*

Instead, she massages her ribs where the arm of the chair has been digging in.

'Tell me about Sabrina,' she says softly.

Bert crosses an ankle over his knees and leans back. 'She's a Partner at my law firm.'

'What does she look like?'

The muscles in Bert's face tighten. 'She has long red hair the colour of a winter sunset, and the prettiest smile you've ever seen.'

Emily's throat catches and she pretends not to notice this stranger spreading rain and dirt across her white sofa. 'So, she's your boss?'

'I wouldn't put it like that. She recently got promoted. Why?'

'It probably explains why else you're here.'

Bert's lips screw into an icy smile. 'Do you know what your husband told Sabrina? That your marriage is a mistake and he's going to leave you.'

Emily flinches. She uncoils herself and lurches to the window. The rain is beating down so hard, Delaware Street is deserted. She wants to smash this man's head through a window. But she knows Bert isn't the one she's angry with.

Emily turns to face Bert. She asks again, 'How do you know where I live?'

He hesitates. 'I followed Sabrina.'

'She's been *here*?' For a fraction of a second, the mask slips and Emily's eyes dart around the room, looking for signs of this woman. An image: black-lace knickers crumpled in the back of Charlie's sock drawer. *Of course.*

Emily's skin starts to purr and she clutches hold of the windowsill. 'Um, do you want a proper drink?'

She doesn't wait for an answer; stumbles into the kitchen and grabs a bottle of vodka from the freezer. Emily splashes large measures into two glasses, then knocks hers back neat. She pours another, then plucks a lemon from the fruit bowl and a knife from the drawer. As her hands close around the cold steel, a vibration sweeps through her skin.

Emily leans over the counter, squeezing the lemon between her hands. She breathes in the citrus scent, trying to focus. Bert's words swirl round her head: *your marriage is a mistake . . . he's going to leave you.* All of a sudden, Emily recalls the divorce lawyer's business card she found in Charlie's pocket. She pictures everyone's faces when they hear the news. Her book is due out in three months. *Team Us: How to Go From Newlywed to Forever Wed*, they're calling it. Her publisher, Libby, is thrilled. She wants to use a photograph of Charlie and Emily on the cover. Emily slumps over the counter. She'll be a laughing stock. *Dumpy Danson, the marriage guru who can't keep her own marriage afloat.* Emily slams the knife back in the drawer. She refuses to be shed like yesterday's skin. She will not let Charlie destroy her.

Piss off, Dumpy Danson. I've never liked you anyway.

Emily presses her forehead against the fridge door, listening to the clock ticking on the wall. Then she squares her shoulders and returns to the sitting room.

Bert is flicking through a cycling magazine but he tosses it on the table as she hands him a drink. He slugs half of it down in one hit. Emily's eyes go to the dip in his chin; they follow the line of his jaw, down his neck to his broad shoulders. Her fingers twitch, as though a current is racing through her. She knows Bert has noticed.

The atmosphere shifts and he blinks at her slowly.

Emily chews her lip. The noise in her head kicks up a gear. She looks out the window and fixes her eyes on the slate-grey sky behind Bert's head. Then she sets her glass down on the table. She drops to her knees, and crawls towards Bert. She unzips his trousers. He freezes, his brow puckering. He grabs her hand, then slowly releases it. Emily squeezes her eyes shut and takes him in her mouth. With each thrust, Emily pictures Charlie and the red-haired woman doing the same thing in this exact spot. All this time she's been blaming Lizzie and Vanessa for driving a wedge between them.

But now there's someone else to blame.

24

Present Day

As I pulled into Hindhead Close, I checked my phone. Nothing from Dr Betrand yet. Nor anyone else. Ever since I found out Charlie had been spotted by a CCTV camera on Rockwell Road, I'd been trying to reconnect with the *Bugle*'s Jeff Johnson. Reporters often talk about hunches, or gut feelings. A good journalist has five senses, plus an extra one. The fact that Charlie was spotted so close to Christ Clan was significant. I just didn't know why yet. So I planned to pay the charity a visit while I was in Bournemouth, and I wanted Jeff's counsel first. But it seemed Jeff had other ideas.

I forced the car door open and could just about make out white-tipped waves hurtling along the beach. The howling wind whipped my hair into a frenzy and I dropped my car-key on the wet pavement. Cursing British summertime, I dipped my chin into my collar and crossed the road.

Number 23 was a salmon-pink thirties bungalow that stood behind a threadbare lawn. A broken gutter hung over the lip of the roof and water was gushing down the broken tiles. One of the windows at the front had been smashed and the curtains were drawn across the small, white leaded bay windows at the front, giving it a hostile, closed-up air. But as I scurried up the path, I noticed the flower pots dotted along the front patio were well-tended and filled with scented blooms.

I rang on the doorbell, eyes on the sticker in the window. *Jesus is love.*

Footsteps sounded on the other side and I heard a clank and jangle as a chain was released. The door opened an inch and an elderly man peered out. He had a neat moustache peppered with grey, and wore thick glasses, the kind that magnified the eyeballs.

I smiled. 'Gordon, it's Sophie Kent.'

His face lit up. 'Yes, yes. Come in.'

The hallway was painted green, but the paint didn't quite reach the edges. The whole interior had a distinctly DIY look about it. Gordon led me into a small, dark kitchen. There was a stench, like rotting bins. I scanned the room, wrinkling my nose. Dirty plates were piled on the counter and a fly buzzed over the sink. The bin in the corner was overflowing. Something was leaking out the bottom. Gordon pulled his brown cardigan around him and shuffled towards the armchair in the corner. After a moment, Gordon went back to the newspapers he'd moved to the table, and started piling them back on the armchair. Suddenly he froze. 'What time is it?'

'Almost 2.15 p.m.,' I said, glancing at my watch.

Gordon hobbled across the kitchen and fiddled with the button on a small black radio.

'*. . . But the warm weather is over for now. The worst of the storms will be in the South where severe weather warnings are in force. Torrential rain, flash-floods.*'

Gordon patted his pockets, blinking owlishly. 'My pen and pad, where are they?'

The distress in his voice surprised me. I scanned the room and strode over to a small table laid out with a notepad, pen and magnifying glass. 'Do you mean these?'

Gordon snatched them off me. 'What did he say? Flash-floods. Weather warning. In May. Huh.' He scribbled something down then settled into the green armchair and placed his knotted hands on his knees.

I looked around for somewhere to sit. 'I was very happy when you called, Gordon,' I said, perching on the edge of the armchair opposite him. 'I've been wanting to talk to you for a while.'

'Why?'

I frowned. 'Well, about Charlie.'

Gordon's forehead puckered and he shook his head. 'What's he done now?'

I opened my mouth to ask Gordon if he was messing around when I remembered Dominic's words: *Gordon's not quite all there, if you catch my drift.*

'Tea, dear?' Gordon limped over to the kettle and pulled two mugs out of the sink.

I sighed, and wandered over to him. 'Here, let me do it.' There was mould growing in the bottom of the mugs. I gave them a rinse, then opened the fridge to find milk. The stench knocked me backwards. I clamped my hand over my mouth. Thick, grey gloop puddled along the bottom of the drawer. I spotted a milk bottle, but the milk was practically solid.

I turned to face Gordon. 'Um, you're out of milk. Is there a shop nearby? I can nip out.'

'No matter. I didn't really want one anyway.' He sat back down in his armchair with a sigh.

I held my sleeve up to my nose, trying to get the putrid smell out of my nostrils, and marched over to the curtains. 'Let's get some air in he—'

'No!' It came out as a wail. 'Keep them closed. I don't want to see them.' Gordon started to rock. 'They throw things at the house. Put things through my letterbox.'

'You mean vandals?'

Gordon pulled his glasses off and wiped his eyes. 'Charlie's all over the news. People know who I am. They think I'm hiding him here.'

'Have you told the police?' I asked and Gordon shook his head. I crouched down beside him. 'Does anyone come round to help you?'

Gordon pulled off his glasses and rubbed them on the sleeve of his cardigan. When he slipped them back on, he smiled at me. 'Charlie always told me how pretty you are.'

I squeezed his hand; Gordon's mottled skin was paper-dry. 'We need to talk about Charlie.'

Gordon raised his watery blue eyes to mine. 'Have I offered you a tea, dear? I can't remember–'

'You did, thank you. But I'm fine.' I paused. Up close I could see a patch of white stubble along Gordon's jaw where his razor had missed. 'I'm so sorry about Vanessa. I only found out a few days ago. Charlie never told me she died.'

'Poor Ness,' Gordon rubbed his thumb with a swollen finger. 'She tried but this business with Charlie. She couldn't see it.'

'See what?'

'That he loved her. Underneath it all. All Ness saw was his anger and his hate. Charlie was just a boy when he cut her out of his life. Ness drank, which made things worse. It was a vicious circle.' Gordon gave a small shrug. 'Some people are hardwired for unhappiness. Ness didn't want to stop drinking, you see. She wanted to forget. What is it they say? The first rule of recovery is that you have to want to get better.'

A deep ache settled in my jaw, and I realised I was clenching my teeth. I said that line to Tommy so many times over the years, it lost its meaning.

Gordon pulled his cardigan more tightly around him, his eyes drifting towards the clock on the wall. 'Remind me when it gets to 2.45 p.m. Weather report.'

I settled back against the chair, biding my time. 'Where did you and Ness meet?'

A smile spread across Gordon's face. 'The local picture house was doing a Hitchcock special. We were the first two there and got chatting. Ness was wearing a woolly hat but when she took it off she had the most beautiful chocolatey curls. Took my breath away. At the end of *Rear Window*, I invited her to dinner. A new fish and chip shop had opened across the road. They had two types of vinegar.' Gordon pinched the end of his nose, and his eyes softened. 'We talked all night. She told me I was the first grown-up she'd spoken to in over a month. Can you imagine? She was lonely, adrift. She didn't mention Charlie at first. Kept him secret. She thought it would put me off. His name slipped out while we were feeding the ducks in the park. Charlie was only eight, she told me, and the centre of her world. I was so nervous when I met him. But we hit it off. He was a good kid.'

'And you married soon after?'

Gordon shook his head, his eyes crinkling round the edges. 'Lost count of the number of times I proposed. But Ness wouldn't have it. Said it would be daft to wear white in church when she already had a son. I didn't mind. It was more for Charlie's sake.'

Gordon pushed himself off the chair and shuffled to the old-fashioned bureau in the corner. He handed me a photo frame. It was a photograph of a little boy wearing navy shorts and a green T-shirt. His leg was in plaster and he was sticking out his tongue. A younger Gordon had a hand on Charlie's shoulder. His woody-brown hair swept back off his forehead. Without his moustache his lips looked thinner.

'Always was small for his age, bless him,' said Gordon. 'That was taken just after the car crash. I bought Charlie a bike after that. I didn't learn to drive until later in life, you see, and I thought it would be better for . . .'

As he trailed off, I stared down at the photograph in my hand, remembering Dominic's words: *Charlie protected her in ways a little kid shouldn't have to.*

'Why didn't anyone take Charlie away from his mum, Gordon? Keep him safe. He was just a kid.'

Gordon's eyes sharpened. 'Ness wasn't a bad person. She could be kind and loving. And she worshipped that boy. But when she drank she forgot about everything, and everyone. I saw what it did to Charlie. Why do you think I stuck around?'

He sniffed and pulled out a tissue. 'After we split up, things got worse. Vanessa would call to say Charlie had disappeared. God knows where he went. Then there was the fire . . .'

Gordon drifted off, watching something play out in the air in front of him.

'There was an accident. At their home.' He picked a piece of flint off his cardigan. 'Charlie never spoke about it. But after the fire, he refused to go back. It crucified Vanessa; she tried to kill herself. I found her with her head in the oven.'

'When did you last see Charlie?' I said, pretending not to notice the tears wetting Gordon's eyes.

'He's not been here, if that's what you're asking.' Gordon sighed and glanced towards the window. 'I keep expecting him to show up. I still leave the key under the flowerpot for him. I just want to know he's–' Gordon's voice cracked and he took a long shaky breath. ''Course here is the last place Charlie would come.'

'Because it's too obvious?'

Gordon shook his head. 'Because he hates me. Told me that the last time I saw him, the day Ness died. Charlie turned up here, in a real temper. I figured Ness had done something stupid. But it was me he was angry with, not her.' Gordon closed his eyes and, when he opened them, his gaze drifted towards the floor. 'Made all sorts of demands. Wanted to know why Ness had changed her will. She asked for my help with it, you see.'

'What did the new will say?'

'She wanted to leave some money to a religious group, a charity.' I stared at him. 'What's it called, this group?'

Gordon sighed. 'Charlie got it in his mind that I'd somehow pressured Ness. But it wasn't true.'

I leaned forward, and put my hand on Gordon's, my heart starting to race. 'Can you remember the name of the organisation?'

He gave my hand a squeeze. 'I thought it was odd, you know. The place shut down long ago. Which wasn't surprising. I've lived in this area my whole life. I heard the rumours. But once Ness's mind was made up there was nothing anyone could do about it.'

'Gordon, the name?'

He picked at his sleeve, and I noticed it was crusted with a yellow stain. 'It reopened, you know. Different person in charge now. For the best. The leader was a nasty man. People used to say they sacrificed goats there, or sheep. Bred the poor animals especially for it.' He caught my look and sighed. 'It's called Christ Clan. Which I always thought was a weird name. Clan. Doesn't sound very godly, does it? Reminds me of the Ku Klux Klan.'

Vanessa left money to Christ Clan? I drummed my fingers on the chair, trying to keep the adrenaline out of my voice. 'Did Vanessa say why she was leaving money to this organisation?'

Gordon pulled out a stained handkerchief and blew his nose. 'Ness was a religious sort. Joined a cult when she was a teenager.

She was impressionable. Always searching for something. God knows she needed some lightness in her life. She lived for that boy. It was tragic, watching it play out. They both loved each other, but couldn't show it.'

Something Gordon said earlier struck me and I frowned. 'That was the last day you saw Charlie? You didn't see him at Vanessa's funeral?'

To my horror, Gordon's bottom lip quivered. 'Charlie told me I wasn't welcome.'

'He stopped you going to her funeral?'

Gordon nodded. 'I'm the closest thing Charlie has to family. What is it they say: you hurt the ones you love. Listen, Charlie isn't a bad kid. There have been plenty of times over the years that I've worried about him. But he's proved me wrong every time. And he's had his share of heartbreak.'

'You mean Lizzie?'

Gordon smiled and pointed towards the bureau, to the wedding photograph of Charlie and Lizzie on display. 'Lovely lass, she was. Tragedy what happened to her.'

'I heard Charlie blames Vanessa for her death.' Gordon's shoulders drooped, but he didn't answer. I sighed. 'Have you ever met his second wife, Emily?'

'Once or twice. Seems nice enough, I suppose.'

I waited for him to elaborate but he pushed himself to the edge of his chair, then stood up. He hobbled towards the filthy kitchen and started rifling through cupboards.

'I had a glass in here somewhere. The medication I'm on, makes my mouth as dry as a rag.'

I watched Gordon, feeling a stab of pity. 'I don't suppose you have a pair of rubber gloves, do you?' I said, rolling up my sleeves.

As I ran the taps, I found an ancient bottle with a dribble of soap at the bottom and started wading through the pile of dishes.

'Do you have any family? Anyone who can look in on you from time to time?'

Gordon lowered his eyes. 'When you get to my age, visitors are few and far between.'

I scraped a plate that was caked in something brown. 'When was the last time you saw Vanessa?'

Gordon screwed up his face. 'The day before she died. I took her some bread and milk. She seemed OK. Thin. God knows when she had last eaten. And she'd been drinking, but that was par for the course.' Gordon's hands shook as he dried a plate with a grimy tea towel, and I marvelled that he was able to look after Vanessa when he struggled to look after himself. 'There was a funny smell in the house. I called the gas board and reported a leak.'

Gordon's voice tremored. 'Silly cow fell down the stairs. Knocked herself out. Had a cigarette in her mouth and the house went up in flames. You should see it; a shell. I went round to clear out her things. Charlie refused to go back there, and I couldn't leave her stuff.'

'What happened to the house?'

'The Ridings? It's empty.' Gordon set the mug on the counter and dabbed his eyes with a tissue. Suddenly, he squeaked.

'Quick, I'm going to miss it.' He hobbled over to the radio and turned it up.

I washed the last of the dishes, sorting through his words in my mind, then I wandered into a laundry room in search of bin liners. Piles of clothes blocked the entrance, cardboard boxes, more newspapers. I leaned against the door forcing my way through. I was on the third cupboard when I noticed the box on top of the washing machine was labelled 'Ness'.

Glancing over my shoulder, I pulled the box towards me and flipped open the lid. A red leather photo album lay on top. Inside were pictures: Charlie as a baby, dressed in a blue woollen romper chewing his fist; two shots of Vanessa in hospital, cradling Charlie moments after he was born; Vanessa, wearing a white leather jacket and a glazed smile, next to a glaring Charlie. The table behind them was covered with empty wine bottles. The next page showed Charlie older, already handsome, even with the aggressive haircut. I sighed and peeked inside the box. There was a takeaway menu for a Chinese restaurant, a bunch of letters tied with string. I read the top line: *Mum, I know you won't read this but . . .'* I was just about to slide the letter out when my eyes landed on something else. A piece of paper with a symbol of a blood-red cross stamped in the corner. It was a leaflet on the Christ Clan; old, judging by how tatty it looked.

Love! Power! Sacrifice! Blood! Fire! Water! Covenant!

Cleanse your soul! Water, Fire, Blood. The very life from which the mission of God flows in the world. Join us as

we raise churches of souls amongst the destitute, capture
men from the jaws of hell, conquer the spiritual powers of
darkness. We are soldiers of the Lamb, and we will march
through the country: pubs, nightclubs, red-light districts,
back streets. The Clan will go where others will not go.
We will take the gospel to the forgotten people.

There was a photograph of a pasty-looking man dressed in a
combat jacket and jeans, holding a shovel. In the background
was a cornfield. The caption beneath: *Our Clan Centres are
places of healing! We welcome the downtrodden!* Another
photo showed a group of men, all in combat jackets, sitting
in a circle holding hands. A third was of the leader, Laurence
Marlon, standing in front of a group of teenagers. Marlon had
dark cropped hair and sideburns that swept halfway down his
cheeks. His hands were on his hips, a slight smile on his face.
I glanced at the group behind him, and suddenly the back of
my arms prickled.

'Wondered where you'd gone.' Gordon was stooped in the
doorway, smiling. 'Flash-floods have been upgraded. We're in
for a wet one.'

'Gordon, have you seen this photograph?' I led him over to
the window. 'This guy, he's the leader you mentioned, right?
Laurence Marlon. Look behind him.'

Gordon pushed his thick glasses up his nose and peered at
the photograph. 'But that's Charlie.'

'You told me earlier that Charlie used to disappear. Is this
where he was going? Christ Clan?'

'My Charlie would never have got caught up in that place,' he said, shaking his head. Even so I could hear the doubt in his voice.

I put my hand on Gordon's shoulder feeling his bones poking through the fabric. 'How old would you say Charlie is here? Thirteen? Fourteen?'

Gordon started to rock again. 'You know what they used to call that place round here? Hell Clan.' He folded forward and moaned.

I shoved the leaflet back in the box and led him over to his armchair. 'Gordon, would it be OK if I took Vanessa's things with me?'

He looked up at me, his eyes cloudy with pain. 'Charlie's a good kid. He . . . please, just find him.'

The last thing I heard as I pulled the front door closed was Gordon's hoarse muttering from the kitchen.

'Torrential rain, unsettled weather. Torrential rain, unsettled weather.'

25

The white sign was so small and understated, I almost missed it. 'Christ Clan' written in black beneath a blue graffiti cross. The logo looked vaguely familiar but I couldn't place it. I parked up next to the pair of large iron gates on Rockwell Road, wound down the window and pressed the buzzer on the keypad. I was just bracing myself for a fight to get in, when the gates juddered open. I shifted the car into gear and the road gave way to a dirt-track running through the heathlands. Glancing in the mirror, I watched the iron gates and six-foot fence shrink from view, wondering idly whether the barrier was to keep people in or out.

After I'd left Gordon's house, I'd taken a picture of Charlie in the Christ Clan leaflet and texted it to the *Bugle* reporter, Jeff Johnson, explaining why it was so important we met. Then I sat in the car and pulled up everything I could find on the new Christ Clan. The group allied itself with the Christian Fellowship Church but, as far as I could tell, much of its success was down to one man: Hector Marlon. Hector created his first app aged twenty, then went on to launch Pocket Church – an app that was part social network, part Biblical resource. With over five million users, it was one of the UK's biggest hitters. But last year, Marlon surprised everyone by selling it and moving from buzzy Shoreditch to the Dorset coast. In a statement on his Facebook page, Marlon explained that he was sick of the virtual world. He missed physical contact and a slower pace. His goal was to help real people – and it was only right that he returned to the place where it all began.

I rounded a bend, and in the distance a forest spread to the horizon, beneath a layer of inky black clouds. Beyond it was the sea. I wondered what it would be like to grow up here. The sole child of Laurence Marlon, Hector was only one when the original Christ Clan closed down. And when his dad absconded, all forty-two acres were signed over to him. I wondered how Hector squared his benevolent outlook with the rumours of his father's sadistic legacy.

I cursed as a deep pothole scraped the bottom of my car, wishing Hector's refurb had stretched to the sweeping drive. Up ahead the heathlands opened out into a dark spot of a few acres. Despite the glowering sky, the fields were dotted with people dressed in blue overalls working the land. None of them showed a moment's interest in my car.

I turned a final bend and a white Art Deco-style building came into view. It looked identical to the one in the *Bugle*'s article, except for the enormous blue graffiti cross sprouting from the top. My tyres crunched across the gravel and I pulled to a stop in the driveway, beside a gleaming red Ferrari. In the distance, more people, dressed in the same blue overalls, were on their hands and knees weeding the flowerbeds. I got out of the car and hurried up the steps to the entrance.

As the heavy oak door closed behind me, the roar of the wind disappeared. The brightly lit foyer was almost silent. On the right-hand wall was a huge mural of Jesus Christ and, underneath in large gold letters, were the words: *Everyone's invited, including YOU.* Blowing on my cold hands, I peered through the glass doors, which opened onto a vast room filled with low-slung sofas. A snooker table stood in the corner beneath a giant framed poster spelling out: *Feel the thrill of God's call!*

'Can I help you?' The voice was high-pitched with a Scottish accent.

I glanced round and saw a woman with bright blue hair sitting behind a wooden desk. She was so large, her cleavage stood out like a shelf.

'Sorry, I didn't see you there. This place is amazing.'

She smiled. 'Are you interested in joining us?'

I pretended to consider her question. 'I'm undecided.'

'Well, then let me see if I can persuade you. My name is Dolly Summerville.' She held out a fat hand covered in rings. She was wearing a black T-shirt with a blue graffiti cross emblazoned across the front. 'Let me show you around.'

'You've already seen the Den,' Dolly said, gesturing towards the glass doors. 'The Prayer Pod is through there too. That's a quiet space where we meditate.'

She opened another glass door and led me through a vast library. Our footsteps were muffled by a large cream rug that was thrown over wooden floorboards. An ornate chandelier hung low over a giant L-shaped sofa, and cushions were piled on window seats that opened out to beautiful views across the heathlands.

I pointed to the signpost on the wall. 'A swimming pool? Seriously?'

Dolly nodded and the rolls of fat on her neck jiggled. 'Hector believes that spiritual wellbeing is paramount. And that means a healthy heart and a healthy mind.' She checked her watch. 'I'd take you there but it's being used for Aqua-Zen at the moment.'

We strolled through a long pastel-grey corridor that was dotted with black-and-white photographs of members, along with quotes: 'I'm back on track with my life'; 'Everything is easier when you're walking with Jesus'.

As I caught the mouth-watering aroma of home-cooked stew, I raised my eyebrows. 'This place is nuts. It's like a boutique hotel.'

Dolly rubbed her nose, slightly dislodging a silver stud. 'Isn't it? And this is just the first one. Hector has big plans for more Clan Centres around the country.' I glanced through an open door to a room that was set up like a classroom, with rows of chairs and a whiteboard at the end. 'That's one of our Learning Lounges. There are five in total. We host inspirational talks, run seminars, that kind of thing.'

Dolly guided me through a boot room to a back door that was half glass. She gazed up at the sky. 'Let me show you outside before it starts raining.' The door opened onto a small courtyard that was filled with pots of lavender. She pointed to an outhouse. 'That's the Clan Café. Would you like anything?'

'Just a water, please. Here,' I pulled out my purse.

Dolly shook her head. 'You don't need that. It's all free.'

She ducked into the café and returned with a bottle of water.

'Don't people take advantage of this place?' I asked, unscrewing the bottle and taking a gulp.

'How do you mean?'

'Come on, most people would be happy to walk with Jesus if he led them here.'

Dolly's smile didn't falter, but her eyes hardened. 'Now, that's what Hector would call an "unkind thought". But don't worry, you'll learn to channel your negative energy during your screening process.'

I slid the bottle back in my bag, raising my eyebrows. 'Screening process?'

Dolly tilted her head back, as if unsure how to read me. 'Hector likes to know what makes people tick. The screening divides people into different groups so that those who need more care and attention get it.'

Suddenly Dolly's face fell. 'Who would do such a thing?' She waddled across the gravel path and picked up a Coke can. 'One of our Clan rules is to love and respect our environment. Littering isn't loving.' She crunched the can and slid it in her cardigan pocket. 'I'll find the culprit on the security camera. Hector will want to know.'

We paused by the fence and the wind tossed a wet, briny scent in our faces. 'How many members do you have here? Surely you're going to run out of room.'

Dolly folded her arms; the skin on her chest was puckering in the wind. 'We currently house three hundred members. But Hector is expanding fast. We've been given planning permission to build more dormitories on the land. See those old outbuildings in the distance; Dolly pointed to the horizon where I could just about make out a stack of stone boxes, 'they'll be razed to the ground to make way for a sports centre. And we are going to increase the usable farmland. There's a rota, and we all take it in turns to work the land. We're completely self-sufficient, you know. It's hard work, but rewarding.'

'Do you get paid?'

'Not in the traditional sense. But our payment is protection.'

'Protection from what?'

Dolly kicked the ground with the heel of her Converse. 'Some of our members have been through a tough time. They need protecting from themselves.'

I nodded, watching the clusters of people working in the field beside us. 'Do you mind me asking what brought you here?'

Dolly blinked skywards and her face broke into a smile. 'A friend threw me a lifeline. I travelled from Poole to see what the fuss was about and I never left. It's been the happiest year of my life. We're all grateful to find a community that accepts us for who we are.'

As she spoke, a group of people loped towards us carrying shovels, their overalls smeared with dirt.

A skinny man with a pitted, white face broke away and sidled up to us. 'It's gonna rain, Dolly. Reckon the Lord might see fit to send us a beef stew?'

Dolly snorted and patted his arm. 'I'll ask the chef. There's tea and biscuits in the Lounge.'

As he hurried to join the others, Dolly smiled. 'You should have seen John when he joined us three months ago. A bag of bones. Addicted to crack, in and out of jail. Last week he won the Clan cup.'

'What's that?'

'Hector awards a trophy to the week's most compassionate member. It's a huge honour.' Dolly glanced at her watch. 'You know what? Hector's afternoon sermon finishes in a couple of minutes. If we hurry we can catch the end of it.'

As we crossed the courtyard to a white-brick building, Dolly smoothed down her shirt and flicked up her hair. We stepped out of the whistling wind into a softly lit atrium that smelt of air freshener and paint.

Dolly wrinkled her nose and the silver stud twitched. 'The Chapel block was only finished last week.' She beckoned me over to a dark blue door and opened it a fraction. I peeped inside and saw rows of people sitting in long lines, all gazing towards the front of the room. The room was so packed I couldn't see who they were looking at, but I could hear him. A soft voice amped by a microphone, with a slight West-country lilt.

Dolly dipped towards me and whispered coffee breath in my face. 'Hector's Thought for the Day is our most popular session.'

'Is it possible to meet Hector?' I asked, craning my neck for a view.

Dolly closed the door and guided me towards a padded cream bench. 'You know, one of the great things about Hector is that he always has time for people. You see, what Hector believes is–'

I tuned out Dolly's voice, and yet another soliloquy about the benevolent Hector Marlon. It was time to kick things up a gear.

'I heard rumours that Christ Clan wasn't always such a happy place,' I said, setting my face to 'nonchalant'. 'Didn't it close down in the late eighties?'

Dolly blinked a couple of times. 'I don't know much about that.'

'It was Hector's dad who was in charge back then, right?' A shadow passed over Dolly's face and I hurried on, keen to keep her on side. 'Hector's done an amazing PR job. Like a phoenix rising from the ashes.'

Dolly's eyes brightened when she heard my analogy and she nodded. 'Sometimes you have go through hardship to know who you really are.'

'Are any of those original Christ Clan members back here?'

My phone beeped and I glanced at the screen. It was a text from Jeff.

The Old Goat in an hour. See you there.

I looked at Dolly. 'Is the Old Goat a pub?'

'It's on Farmer Street. Round the corner. Why?'

'I'm meeting someone after this.' I broke off as the door opened and hordes of people silently streamed out, all bearing the same beatific expression. Dolly quivered beside me and I glanced up to see a man standing in the doorway untangling the microphone from his blue robe. His youthful face was tanned and he'd gelled his dark-blond hair into a stiff wave.

When he spotted Dolly, his face broke into a smile. 'We missed you today, Dolls.'

Dolly gave a high-pitched giggle. 'It was my turn for desk duty. Next time, though.'

He held his hand out to me. 'Hector Marlon, leader of Christ Clan.'

I waited a beat, then shook it. 'Sophie Kent, a reporter from the *London Herald*.'

Dolly squealed. 'I'm sorry, Hector. She didn't say she was a reporter. I'd never have–'

'Your name is Kent?' Hector's hand tightened around mine. Then he seemed to recover himself. 'We have nothing to hide here, Dolls. Our doors are open to everyone.'

'If they can get past the six-foot fence and electric gates,' I said, sweetly.

Hector gave me an odd look, then he gestured for me to follow him. 'I'm due a break before I start the afternoon sessions. Why don't you join me? The team has been working on a new Clan cocktail: kale, citrus fruits and cucumber. Dolly, would you mind grabbing us two?'

Dolly smiled but the moment Hector turned away she gave me a filthy look.

Hector escorted me through a glass corridor that led to the main building and to a door at the far end. I followed him into his office; a large white room with an ultra-modern gas fire that kicked out a cloud of heat. As I slipped my jacket off, Hector wandered over to his desk and took off his robe. Underneath he was wearing stonewashed jeans and a cream sweater that clung to his slight frame.

In the centre of the room, two circular wooden chairs hung from the ceiling. Hector gestured towards one and I raised my eyebrows.

'Don't knock it till you've tried it,' he said, laughing as I perched on the edge. 'You've got to commit to the chair. Go on, put your feet up.' I curled my legs up on the sheepskin blanket and the chair swung gently.

Hector kicked back in his chair. 'I take it you're not here to fill out an application form,' he said, studying my face. 'You should consider it, you know.'

'Thanks, but I don't think a religious commune is very me.'

'You know, ever since I was tiny, I knew I was different. I have a gift. Before I was old enough to understand this gift, I used to call it my Colour Code.'

He turned his head to face me and his pale blue eyes glinted in the half-light.

'I see shades of colour around people. Sometimes it's faint, sometimes it's intense – and the colour changes depending on a person's emotional state. Contrary to popular belief, blue doesn't mean sadness. It means peace.'

'Fascinating,' I said, dangling my leg over the side of the chair, wondering how long I had to listen to this drivel.

Hector picked up the sarcasm in my voice and sighed. 'Do you know what I see when I look at you, Sophie? The colour black.'

I rolled my eyes. 'And let me guess, if I sign myself over to Christ Clan, you can spirit the black away.'

'Eventually, yes. But what you've got going on there, isn't a quick fix job.' Hector focused his gaze on me and I went still.

'The pain is streaming out of you. That hole in your life is like a cancer; it's destroying you from the inside.'

Suddenly the room lit up and there was an almighty crash of thunder.

I licked my lips. 'Did you arrange that?'

Hector grinned. 'All part of the service.'

A throng of people trooped silently past Hector's window, their heads bowed against the rain.

'Why doesn't anyone talk here?' I said, grateful for the distraction.

Hector smiled, revealing overly white teeth. 'Silence is under-rated. I wouldn't expect you to understand. Yours is a frenetic, fast-paced world. A lonely one, too, I bet.' Hector slid off the chair and closed the window. 'I used to be part of that world, too. But now I'm here, helping real people with real problems, doing the Lord's work.' He paused. 'I'm sorry about before. I didn't mean to alarm you. I can't switch it off. If I see someone hurting, I'm programmed to help.'

To my absolute horror, I felt tears prick the back of my eyes. I bent down and pulled out the Christ Clan leaflet.

'I'm interested in this person,' I said, sliding it across the desk.

Hector picked the leaflet up. 'Where did you get this?'

'Does it matter?'

Hector sat down in the white leather chair behind his desk and narrowed his eyes. 'I thought all the old propaganda had been pulped.'

There was a knock and Dolly appeared holding two glasses of thick green goo.

Hector smiled. 'This is the cocktail I was talking about. It's going to do wonders for your immune system.'

I took the glass from Dolly, then zoned in on Hector, determined to keep him on track. 'The boy standing behind your dad. His name is Charlie Swift, and he's on the run for murdering his mistress.'

The second glass slid out of Dolly's hand too quickly and juice splashed onto Hector's desk.

'I'm so sorry, Hector.' She patted herself down for a tissue, cheeks flaring.

Hector gave her a smile. 'I've got this, Dolly.'

Dolly went bright red and bustled out.

When the door closed, I leaned my elbows on his desk. 'You must have heard about Charlie Swift in the news.'

Hector pulled a tissue out of his drawer and mopped up the juice. 'I don't follow the news anymore. I imagine that sounds strange to you. Your whole livelihood depends upon the misfortune of others. But here,' he gestured around him, 'is a safe space. A place where outside influences don't matter. What matters is our community.'

'But the outside world impacts your community, doesn't it?'

'Not if I'm doing my job right.' Hector tossed the tissue into the bin under his desk. 'This is a simple place with simple people and a simple message.'

His languid manner was beginning to piss me off. 'Plus it's much easier to control people if they're shut off from the outside world,' I said.

Hector crossed his arms over his chest, and tilted his chair back. 'It's easy to dismiss what you don't understand, isn't it?'

I held up my hands. 'Look, I don't doubt you help people. Whether you need to sink millions into a state-of-the-art health club to do it is up to you. Just don't peddle it in my direction. God, Buddha, UFOs; it's all the same to me.'

Hector let his chair drop forward and the breeziness left his face. 'You know, you remind me—'

'Stop psychoanalysing me.' It came out harsher than I intended. 'Look, I appreciate the thought, but you're wasting your time.'

Hector cocked his head to one side. 'Do you know one of the reasons Christ Clan actively searches for members in rough places? Do you know why we live by the motto: everyone is welcome? Because being Laurence Marlon's son has been one long fuckfest.'

I raised my eyebrows. 'Good word.'

'People here have long memories. No matter what I do, no matter how many people I help, I will always be the Shepherd's son. And until my dad decides to reappear and clear his name, the cloud of suspicion will hang over me.'

'So why return to Bournemouth?'

'Because it means more. People round here have very little respect for me, for my work. But if I can change their minds, perhaps they'll realise the apple can fall a long way from the tree.'

'So that's why you've reopened Christ Clan.'

Hector shrugged, his gaze lost over my head. 'I could have changed the name. But why should I? I'm not my dad.'

'Do you think the rumours are true?'

'When I find him, I'll ask.' The light shifted and suddenly Hector looked even younger. 'Sorry, it's a running joke. I've spent a lifetime searching for my dad.'

'Yeah, well, dads can be overrated.'

Hector's eyes snapped towards mine and an odd look swept over his face. 'If I do find my dad, I'd like to ask him what he thinks of the changes I've made. I don't mean the material stuff. I mean the cornerstone to the Christ Clan's beliefs. His version was all about purifying society's strays. He believed that the soul had to be cleansed by fire, water and blood: the three principles of baptism. I think God created us in a certain way for a reason. You have to find that good inside of you. It is already there, if you know how to set it free.'

'Is there goodness in everyone?'

'No one deserves to be shut out.' Hector followed my gaze to the leaflet. 'No matter what they've done. The past is the past.'

'What if the past catches up with the present?' I said, sharpening my voice. 'Charlie Swift's mum left a wedge of her estate to Christ Clan. And this photograph establishes another link to your organisation. You say you have nothing to hide, but are you willing to have that tested?'

Hector leaned forward. 'What do you want, Sophie?'

'I want to know if Charlie's been here.'

Hector held my gaze. 'He has not. As far as I know Charlie Swift has never had any link to Christ Clan, either now or then.'

I prodded the leaflet. 'How do you explain that photo then?'

Hector shrugged. 'It's an old photograph. It could be anyone.'

'Come on, Hector. You'll have to do better than that.' When he didn't speak, I stared at my fingernails and altered my voice. 'Fine, have it your way. I'll set the team on digging around in your past. Who knows, we might even unearth your dad. You can thank me later.'

Hector scribbled down a number and handed it to me, all the friendliness leaving his voice. 'Any further questions, you can direct them at my solicitor.'

As I reached the door, Hector cleared his throat. 'He wouldn't want to see you in this much pain, Sophie.'

I whipped my head round. For one brief moment I wondered if Hector really was able to see inside people. 'Who are you talking about?'

Hector's eyes were on the window. 'I'm talking about God.'

26

The Old Goat car park was almost empty: two other cars and a huddle of teenagers in caps and high-tops who drifted away as I switched off the engine. I took a moment to steady myself. Hector's perceptiveness had hit me harder than I cared to admit. Suddenly, I caught a flicker of something out of the corner of my eye and a creeping sensation spread through me. Like I was being watched.

My phone rang, making me jump. I glanced at the number and my stomach turned.

'Dr Betrand?'

'Yes, Sophie, hello. I have your results.' I gripped the phone tightly and closed my eyes. 'Everything came back normal.'

I exhaled loudly, as a warm dose of relief spread through me.

There was a pause and I could sense Dr Betrand picking over his words. 'Is there anything else I can do for you, Sophie?'

'Thank you, no. And thanks for getting back to me so quickly.'

I hung up and thumped the steering wheel, thanking my lucky stars that I'd dodged that bullet, at least.

I slammed the car door shut and sprinted across the gravel just as the rain started.

I opened the door and was hit with a waft of beer, bleach and grease. The barman glanced up as I entered, then looked away. A pale, thin man was hunched over the bar studying the front page of a newspaper. I recognised the cough.

I slid onto the stool beside him. 'One of yours?' I pointed to the giant headline: *City on high alert for wanted killer.*

Jeff Johnson peeled off his glasses and grunted. 'I wish. Try page eight.' He licked his finger and flicked to an article about a local nursery teacher strike.

I nodded at his glass. 'Same again?'

I ordered a round of drinks, studying Jeff out of the corners of my eyes. Horn-rimmed glasses, a receding hairline and skin the colour of ham that had been left out too long.

I pulled out the Christ Clan leaflet and slid it across the bar. 'You got this photo I sent?'

Jeff drained his glass, then sat staring at the foam puddling at the bottom.

'I just paid Christ Clan a visit,' I said, handing over cash to the barman. 'Interesting place.'

'That's one way of putting it.'

'Hector Marlon is quite something.'

'He's a prick.' Jeff coughed again, then hoicked up something that turned the tissue red. He caught me looking. 'Stage four. Lung cancer.'

'I'm sorry.'

'What for?'

Outside a roar of thunder split the air. I took a sip of Coke. 'Look, Jeff. Cards on the table. I'm finding connections between

Christ Clan and Charlie Swift all over the place. That photo proves he spent time there as a kid and–'

'There are three things you need to know about that photograph,' said Jeff, pushing his pint glass away and prodding the picture. 'The first is: look what your friend's wearing.'

'You mean, the combat jacket?'

Jeff shook his head. 'The combat jacket, everyone wore. It was Christ Clan uniform, so to speak. I'm talking about the gold epaulettes on his shoulders. Only the magic circle wore those.'

'The what?'

'Marlon called 'em his Golden Flock. Kids, mainly. Groomed them to do what he wanted.'

My grip tightened on the glass. 'Which was what?'

'By the late eighties, Christ Clan wasn't doing so well. Rumours dogged the place. Membership was dwindling. So were the donations it relied upon to operate,' said Jeff, sniffing wetly. 'Marlon used the Golden Flock to keep things ticking over. Made them break into people's houses and steal food, money, whatever they could lay their hands on. Marlon trained them to be invisible. I mean, these kids were *ghosts*. Most of the time people didn't know they'd been robbed until much later.'

Jeff drained half his pint in one go.

'The Golden Flock were damaged goods. Marlon messed with their minds good and proper. Don't forget, these kids had nothing. Society had rejected them; they didn't have the emotional bones to deal with this kind of crap.'

'So what did they do?'

'They did what Marlon told them. I tracked down an ex-member. The details he gave me would make your skin crawl.'

I glanced at the photograph of Charlie. 'What's the second thing I need to know about this picture?'

'The man standing next to Charlie Swift.' Jeff took a long swig, thumped his glass down and looked at the barman. 'You want to take it from here, Fred?'

The barman emerged from the shadows. He was wiry; an angular face spread with stubble. He couldn't have been more than forty-five but the stooped way he carried himself made him seem much older.

I looked from the photo to Fred, frowning. 'That's you? Did you know Charlie?'

Fred leaned across the bar and wiped his nose on the back of his hand. I opened my notebook to a fresh page, waiting, but Fred didn't speak.

Beside me Jeff shifted his weight and, even though we were the only ones in the pub, he lowered his voice. 'Tell her about Samantha Hartley.'

'The girl who ended up dead in the river?' I asked.

Fred's eyes flicked to the floor. 'Samantha got caught up in the crossfire.'

'Between who?'

'Two men you don't want to get on the wrong side of.'

I leaned forward. 'Is one of them Charlie Swift?'

Fred reached behind him for a bottle of whisky. He poured himself a double measure then downed it in one.

I glanced at Jeff for help but he was staring down at the bar, looking sicker than ever.

This was taking too long.

I closed my notebook. 'OK, forget Charlie for a moment. Let's go back: what can you tell me about Laurence Marlon?'

At the mention of his name, Fred went still. 'The Shepherd was the real deal.'

Jeff gave a thin laugh. 'Fred, come on, we've been through this.'

Fred picked up a pint glass and started drying it with a cloth. 'You can mock, but you didn't meet him. He had the voice of the Lord running through him.'

Jeff snorted and Fred worked the cloth faster in his hand.

I reached across the bar to Fred. 'I want to understand. About the Shepherd. About everything. Please,' I gestured to the photograph on the bar, 'I need some details.'

Fred held my gaze, his eyes dark and empty. 'You don't know what it's like to have no one who cares if you live or die. My childhood was– When I was recruited by Christ Clan, it was like I'd found my place. Somewhere I belonged. Mr Marlon cared about us. When he looked at you, you felt it, right here.' He pointed to his heart. 'But when his light moved away from you, it was the worst feeling in the world. You'd do anything to get it back.'

'Anything?' asked, watching Fred closely.

Fred sighed. 'The Shepherd was sick. I realise that now. The sickness made him do things.'

I glanced at Jeff. 'What kind of things?'

Fred didn't answer immediately. He finished drying the glass and set it down, then he looked towards the window. 'It started with Fight Night. The Shepherd used to make members fight in front of the whole commune. The loser would be punished.'

'Punished how?'

'No food for twenty-four hours. Scrubbing toilets, that sort of thing.' Fred chewed his lip. 'But it got worse. Solitary confinement in the Bunker; a shitty, freezing hell-hole in an outhouse. But even that didn't satisfy him. He raised the stakes. The fighters were given weapons: crowbars, hammers, whatever was lying around. People got smashed up but we never went to hospital in case it raised questions. Mr Marlon told us Jesus was testing our stamina and strength.' Fred raised his shirt and turned to the side. A purple scar ran from his ribs to his hip. 'A hammer with a nail stuck to the end of it. Nearly ripped my kidney out.'

'And you didn't get medical help?'

Fred grimaced. 'Vodka, and a needle and thread. I wasn't going to be the Shepherd's first failure.'

Jeff twisted his pint glass round and raised his gaze to Fred. 'The power went to Marlon's head though, didn't it, fella?'

Fred nodded slowly. 'He believed we'd all had a crappy time in life because we were sinners. The only way to atone for our sins was to purify ourselves. We bathed together in the freezing river every Sunday. Lit fires and burned our belongings.'

'Water, fire,' I paused. 'What about the blood?'

Fred waited a beat, then his voice flattened out. 'Once a quarter we sacrificed a sheep and drank its blood. Mr Marlon told us that sacrificing one of God's creatures was the ultimate display of purity.' He caught my shocked expression and his eyes narrowed. 'Look, I know how it sounds. But the rituals . . . they made you forget. They wiped you clean. Trouble was, some people got a taste for the violence.'

Fred reached out for another glass and I saw a tattoo on the inside of his wrist. Two red triangles, one pointing up, the other pointing down.

'Marlon's mark,' said Jeff, following my gaze. 'Tell her.'

Fred traced the shapes with his fingertip. 'The first triangle signifies water, the second signifies fire. And the red is the blood.'

'A badge of honour amongst the Golden Flock.'

Fred's expression darkened at Jeff's sarcastic tone. 'You make it sound a lot more organised than it was. We were just a bunch of scared kids doing what we needed to survive.'

Questions flooded my brain, but I didn't want to overwhelm Fred. I could see the toll this conversation was having on him.

I softened my voice. 'Why didn't you leave Christ Clan?'

Fred's laugh cut straight through me. 'And go where? I had nothing. No money, no food, no prospects. Christ Clan was messed up, but the real world was worse. We had no place to go, and the Shepherd knew that. Towards the end, he was bad. Real bad. Drinking. Drugs. You name it. He could feel it slipping away. He reeked of failure.'

Fred leaned against the bar and scratched his chin.

'Places like Christ Clan, they're smoke and mirrors, mostly. Only work as long as people believe in their leader. We all knew the Shepherd didn't have two pennies to rub together. That's why he sent us out to steal. But nothing we did pleased him. Things got worse. One kid ended up in intensive care after a punishment went wrong. And then Samantha Hartley died.'

I leaned forward. 'What happened to her, Fred?'

He picked up the cloth. 'No idea.'

'You expect me to believe that?'

Jeff flicked a beer mat into the air and it landed in a puddle on the bar. 'My money's on the Starling.'

I turned to face him. 'Who?'

'That's what you called him, right, Fred? The darkest kid of the lot. Think Artful Dodger to Marlon's Fagin.'

Fred glanced past us towards the window. 'Do you know anything about starlings?'

I ran my finger round the rim of my glass. When Tommy and I were younger, an uncle gave us a bird box for Christmas. It was tangerine, with a little wooden roof and a sign that said: *Home Tweet Home*. We hung it on the silver birch outside the back door and would sit on the step, waiting to welcome its first resident. For a while, nothing happened. We threw crumbs on the ground below and eventually a plump brown sparrow moved in. Tommy was delighted. He changed the tiny water bowl every day, and furnished the table with scraps of bread. A pretty female sparrow appeared and the following spring, when Tommy wanted to peep inside, I told him to bide his time. We'd know when the chicks hatched because we'd be able to hear squeaks. Except the squeaks never came. One day I spotted a larger bird, speckled black with a yellow beak, perched on the roof of the box. Later that day, I found the eggs smashed into pieces and the broken bodies of dead chicks. I cleared the mess away, not wanting Tommy to find them. Our gardener told me there was a starling in our midst. *Bloody aggressive creatures. One day you come home and a starling is in your place. They'll do whatever it takes to steal other birds' nests.*

I cleared my throat. 'Actually, I do.'

Fred sighed. 'Then you know how sneaky they are. This kid, he had a talent for stealing into people's homes. They never even knew he was there. Sometimes he'd hide out there for days, just spying and messing with them. Mr Marlon loved him, but gave him the roughest ride, too. He spent more time in the Bunker than anyone.'

He picked at his fingernails, lost in thought for a moment.

'I'm sure that's why he was so sadistic. Although he softened when Samantha came along. They were involved with each other. But something happened between them, no one knew what exactly. There were rumours she cheated. Soon after that, she died. When her body was found, she had Marlon's mark, two triangles, etched into her wrist.'

A memory stirred deep inside my head. Dr Sonoma's describing the mark he found on Sabrina Hobbs's body. *A carving of some kind on her wrist.*

I stared at Fred, my pulse started to quicken. 'Who was the Starling?'

Fred glanced at Jeff, his eyes unreadable. 'We didn't use real names. Mr Marlon encouraged us to shed our identifications when we joined Christ Clan.'

I reached for the photograph. 'Jeff, you said there were three things about this photograph.' I pointed at Charlie. 'The Starling . . . are you telling me that's him?'

When neither of them spoke, I felt the exhaustion come flooding out of me. I jabbed the photograph and raised my voice. 'Is. That. Him?'

A look passed between them, then Fred put the glass down and dropped his elbows onto the bar. 'That's him.'

I stared from one to the other, unable to speak. My shock gave way to despair. 'But it doesn't add up. I've known Charlie for almost a decade. He's successful, for Christ's sake. Respectable.'

'Not anymore though, is he? You know, I once interviewed a kid, born in Christchurch. Matthew Lamberton. Spent his whole childhood watching his dad pummel his mum. Eventually the bastard killed her with a swift right hook to the temple. Anyway, Lamberton finished school, got a job at an estate agent, married a local girl, had a couple of kids.'

Jeff coughed into his fist, his eyes watering with the effort.

'Our interview took place at Guys Marsh prison where Lamberton was serving life for his wife's murder. Beat her so badly, police had to use her dental records to ID her. Lamberton told me he didn't mean to do it; that something in him snapped. He felt like it was someone else crushing his wife's head against the wall.' Jeff rubbed his bloodshot eyes with the heel of his hands. 'People handle the after-effects of abuse differently. And it doesn't sound like your friend had the best start in life from what I've read.'

I stared at Charlie's familiar handsome face on the *Bugle*'s front page. 'Hang on, you said the Starling has a talent for hiding. That explains why Charlie has disappeared into thin air. He could be anywhere.'

Fred shrugged. 'Or he's going to zero in on the place where it all began.'

'You think he's hiding out at Christ Clan,' I said, my eyebrows shooting up. 'But I've just been there. It's a completely different place.'

'You really think Hector is above board?' said Jeff with a sneer.

'Don't you?'

'That monster's blood runs through h—' Jeff doubled over as another coughing fit erupted, worse than before. Fred gave me a look and I nodded.

'It's getting late,' I said, sliding off my stool and picking up my bag. 'I've got a long drive.'

I was about to thank them both when Jeff stopped me. 'Listen, I wasn't entirely honest earlier about having no leads. Didn't know if I could trust you.' He pressed a piece of paper into my hand. 'The kid who ended up in hospital, Mark Miller. This is his dad's phone number. Les Miller. I tried once upon a time but didn't get very far. Something tells me you might have more luck.'

I shoved the scribbled note in my pocket and slid off the stool. 'Thanks for ev—'

'And do me a favour, Miss Kent.' The look on Jeff's face made me pause. 'Blow it apart. Christ Clan. For those kids. Promise me?'

I held Jeff's gaze, then squeezed his arm.

It was dark outside; the rain was blowing in sheets across the car park. I leaped inside my car and shut out the storm. As I slotted the keys in the ignition, I pulled out my phone and dialled Kate. It went to voicemail.

'It's Soph. Listen, I'm leaving Bournemouth now. Be back in a couple of hours. Round up the troops, Kate. I've got lots to–' I glanced in the mirror and the words died in my mouth. In the gloom, two familiar eyes stared back at me. Before I could turn, his arm was round my neck, pinning me to the seat. I couldn't breathe. My eyes watered. The phone slid out of my hand. I clawed for breath. A gurgling sound filled the car. I kicked and thrashed. But he was too strong for me. As the blackness closed in, I raised my eyes to the mirror and met his cold, blank gaze.

Then, nothing.

27

Emily: 2 weeks before the murder

'Ready?' Charlie pulls a grey sweater over his head. It flattens his hair and, without thinking, Emily reaches out to brush it back up. She pretends not to notice the surprise on Charlie's face.

Twenty minutes earlier, Emily had arrived home to find all the lights off and Charlie sitting rigidly on the sofa. Her heart sank; she wasn't in the mood for a fight. But, when she flicked the lamp on, Charlie stood up and cleared his throat. 'Let's go out for dinner.'

His suggestion was so left-field that Emily actually laughed. A few weeks ago, a romantic gesture from Charlie would have sent her straight into his arms. The opportunity for them to reconnect was everything she wanted. But that was before she'd discovered Charlie's dirty little secret.

Your marriage is a mistake and he's going to leave you. As Emily slips on her denim jacket, Bert's words drift into her head like a poison thread.

The affair is still going on, she's sure of it. Yesterday, she found a silver earring under the sofa. It was shaped like a four-leaf clover. Emily crawled onto an armchair and stared at the earring for so long she missed her appointment with the fertility specialist. To punish herself, she carved a tiny four-leaf clover into her hip. She can feel the scab catching on her knickers as she walks in silence along Delaware Street. Next to her, Charlie is chewing the inside of his cheek, the way he does when something is on his mind.

They stop outside Papa Paulo's, their local Italian, and Charlie holds the door open for Emily. The warm, candlelit restaurant smells of bread, rosemary and olive oil. It's so searingly familiar that Emily's eyes mist up and she has to clutch the back of a chair to stop herself unravelling.

She remembers their first time at Papa Paulo's, when their relationship was only a couple of months old. There was a bite to the evening air but they'd insisted on sitting outside. Charlie slipped his jacket around Emily and she peered up at him as if she'd hit the jackpot. It was one of those life-affirming evenings when, in the early flush of lust, each person finds the other endlessly fascinating. Charlie pretended to leave the restaurant when Emily asked for sultanas on her pizza ('Noooo, tell me you're not one of those freakazoids who like fruit on their pizza?!') and she'd laughed at his clumsy Italian ('La bella donna would-o like-o a glass-o of vino'). She loved the way Charlie laughed, a quick snort followed by a sheepish look, as if he was embarrassed by the sound he'd made. Emily opened up about past relationships, minus a few details, of course. Charlie didn't have to know about her need to find solace in a stranger's bed. She knew he was holding back about Lizzie, but she never pressed him. She didn't need to. Emily knew what Charlie had lost; she was there the day he married her. That evening Charlie asked Emily to move in with him. She knew it was sudden, but she didn't care.

Emily takes a deep breath and zigzags through the restaurant. As they settle into a cosy corner, she senses the other diners watching them. She is used to people staring at Charlie. She swears he's the reason she got her book deal in the first place. 'Your husband is so fucking hot. Talk about Instagrammable,' her publisher, Libby, had sighed.

Emily has never really minded being the sidekick; she's always been grateful just floating in Charlie's orbit. As if being with him is validation enough. Tonight, though, she feels the accusatory edge to each stare. As if each person is wondering how a woman like her managed to hook a man like Charlie. Emily feels a bubble of laughter in her throat. She wants to hold her hands up and say, *Don't worry, guys. I still know my place. Hooking Charlie is one thing, keeping him is a whole different ballgame.*

Emily knows the other diners will want to see how in love they are so she reaches across the table for Charlie's hand. A faint crease appears between Charlie's eyes but he doesn't pull it away.

'That's a pretty colour on you,' he says, glancing at her crimson sweater.

'What, this old thing?' She raises an eyebrow and is rewarded with a smile from the elderly woman on the next table. Truth is, this sweater is the only thing that hides how much weight she's lost. The pounds have been falling off ever since Bert Hughes dropped his bombshell all over her white sofa. *Jutting hipbones come at a price, she thinks.*

A barrel-shaped waiter with a shiny black moustache appears with menus and bread. He gives the wine list to Charlie who passes it straight to Emily. The moment Charlie looks down at his menu, the smile falls from Emily's face. She studies her husband. His thick dark hair is even more unkempt than usual but his beauty still takes her breath away.

'Let me guess. You're going to have a Margarita with chorizo and sultanas.' Charlie's voice is teasing.

Emily grips the tablecloth between her fingernails, wondering at Charlie's change in mood. This is the most he's spoken to her, the most he's *looked* at her for . . . Emily doesn't know how long it's been. Days have become weeks. She tries to recall the last time she felt safe and loved. Then she remembers: the last miscarriage. Even if it's brief, Charlie always rallies around her when she miscarries.

Emily unfolds her napkin, trying to think of something to say. 'How was your day?'

Charlie picks up his fork. 'Well, the markets are screwed but my comment on the National Bank of Scotland might make tomorrow's front page.'

He drums his fork on the table in time to the beat of the music and Emily frowns. Charlie seems different, relaxed. As if a weight has been lifted. Emily takes a sip of wine and it starts to dawn on her. The change in Charlie, the intimacy, their restaurant; they add up like a column of figures in her mind. He has something to tell her. He is going to come clean.

The affair.

A knot forms in Emily's stomach. How will she play it? Charlie can't find out that she already knows. It would lead to all sorts of questions about how she found out. Emily closes her eyes. If they are going to make this marriage work, Charlie must never find out about Bert, or Sternus, or the others. She will do whatever it takes. Even if it means burying what they've both done.

Charlie is eyeing her over his glass; she can feel his knee bobbing up and down under the table. He glances out the window, then brushes his fringe back from his face.

Let's get this show on the road.

'Is something the matter?' she asks mildly.

Charlie shifts forward, pinning his eyes on her face with an intensity she hasn't seen for a long time. 'Em, there's something I want to talk to you about.'

Emily bites her lip, her heart fluttering in her chest. She can see it unfold in front of her eyes. Charlie will confess, she'll play the shocked wife, pretend to consider her options, then open her arms to him. Will she cry? Will *he* cry? If things go well, they can start trying for a baby tonight. Maybe this time they'll be lucky. We're due some luck, she thinks, putting her hand on her stomach.

Charlie's phone vibrates on the table and he glances at the screen. Emily shifts in her chair. *Ignore it. Start talking.*

The colour drains from Charlie's cheeks. 'It's work, I have to take it.'

He holds the phone to his ear and darts across the restaurant, but not before Emily has heard a female voice on the other end. Work, really? Sophie, maybe? Although it didn't sound like her.

Through the window, she watches Charlie pace up and down. He jabs his finger in the air and the strength of feeling makes his mouth move in fast forward. A group of teenage girls walk past and Emily sees one of them point to Charlie and fake-swoon to the others. Right before Charlie hangs up, he smiles; a dazzling, volume-all-the-way-up kind of smile.

Moments later he bounds back to the table, eyes still shining. 'Sorry, Em. Looks like work want me in tonight. The Scottish bank drama. Might be a late one.'

Emily tries to ignore the wrenching feeling in her stomach. *It's not too late. Ignore whoever that was on the phone. Do the right thing. I'll forgive you. Please.* 'What were you going to say before your phone rang?'

Charlie twists his wedding ring round his finger and she sees a glimmer of uncertainty in his eyes.

Just say it: I had an affair. It's over and I'm sorry.

Charlie clears his throat. 'Summer holidays. Where do you fancy going?'

Emily freezes. '*That's* what you want to talk to me about?'

'What about Tuscany,' he's glancing over her shoulder, distracted, 'or the Amalfi coast?'

'*Our honeymoon place*?' Emily's voice is barely a whisper. She glances down at the red-checked tablecloth as an image of that sun-baked, lust-filled trip flashes through her mind. A fly is crawling along the edge of the table and she swats it away with her hand.

'Remember the restaurant you could only access by speed-boat. We could see if . . .'

Emily grips either side of her chair, tuning out his voice. Suddenly she understands. Charlie can talk about summer holiday plans because has no intention of following through with them. That's why he seems different, lighter. Emily glances down at his phone.

He is going to leave you.

The thought gives way to a flicker of anger in her stomach. Emily stares at the curve of Charlie's mouth as he fills the silence with hot air; acting as if he hasn't just taken a sledgehammer to their marriage.

Charlie wipes a slick of oil from his chin. 'So, what do you think?'

For the briefest moment a memory hits her. It's raining, she's lying on a beanbag watching *Fraggle Rock*, tuning out her parents' fight. The screams are getting louder, her mum's face is scorched red with rage. Emily tries not to watch the way her dad holds out his hands, placating; tries not to watch her mum pick up one of her treasured teapots, the one shaped like a red pillar box, take aim and–

Emily sets the glass down on the table. 'Sure, I'll look at some travel websites.' Her voice sounds forced but Charlie doesn't seem to notice. 'By the way, I've been meaning to ask,' she holds up the silver earring. 'I found this under the sofa yesterday. Do you know anything about it?'

Charlie turns the earring over in the candlelight, frowning. 'Never seen it before. You sure it isn't one of yours?'

Emily shakes her head, wondering at Charlie's ability to lie so effortlessly to her face. For a moment, she indulges herself, allows herself to believe this is all a huge misunderstanding and their marriage is fine; they're just two people out on a mid-week date night. By the time the pizzas arrive, she almost believes it. But then she spies Charlie pocket the earring when he thinks she isn't looking.

He points at the bottle of water in the ice bucket behind her. 'Can you top me up?'

As Emily's hands close around the bottle, she has to use every ounce of will power not to bring it crashing down on his head.

An hour later she's back in their apartment and Charlie is on his way to God knows where. Emily curls up on the sofa picturing Charlie in the arms of the red-haired woman. She knows now that Charlie is going to leave her. How could she be so stupid to think otherwise? Charlie never had any intention of doing the right thing. He was just biding his time, planning his escape. Emily scratches at the four-leaf clover scab on her hip through angry, exhausted tears.

Suddenly she hears a thud and looks up.

What was that?

Emily pulls herself up and walks unsteadily into the hallway. Other than a distant siren, all is quiet. She's about to turn round when she notices the cellar door is open and the light is on. She frowns. Was that open when she got home?

A prickling sensation creeps down her neck. Emily steps across the hallway and sticks her head round the cellar door.

Nothing unusual. As she thumps down the steps, she gives herself a talking to. Maybe she's misjudged Charlie. His mum just died; he's going through something at the moment. He'll come back to her when he's ready. She just needs to stick it out. Emily steps over a pile of laundry and scans the cellar. She's about to leave when she spots something sticking out from behind the washing machine. It's Charlie's West Ham hoody. His favourite sweater. *What's it doing behind there?*

Emily has a bad feeling, deep inside her bones. She feels inside the pockets and pulls out a piece of paper. Emily looks at the image; the fuzzy background, the speck that looks like nothing but is, in fact, everything. A tiny dot, a baby, a whole life.

That's funny, I don't remember giving Charlie a copy of my last baby sc—

Emily's eyes flick to the words printed in the top left corner. The air around her goes still.

She looks closer, at the three words that change everything.

Patient: Sabrina Hobbs.

28

Present day

The first thing I saw when I opened my eyes was a needle sticking out of the back of my hand. I took a deep breath, inhaling warm, disinfectant-laced air and moaned as a stinging pain sliced through my neck. The dark-skinned man in the white coat looked up from his clipboard.

'Good morning, Sophie.' His voice was warm, and he came towards me with a large smile on his face. 'My name is Dr Chatterjee. I'm an ENT surgeon at the Royal Bournemouth. How are you feeling?'

I opened my mouth to speak but nothing came out.

'Here, drink this.' He handed me a paper cup, then took out a torch and shone it in my eyes. 'We've put you through your paces since you've been here, but you've passed with flying colours. Both the nasendoscopy and the neck CT came back clear. There's no fracture and only minor oedema so we moved you out of the High Dependency Unit.' He glanced towards the shut door. 'Now, there's a police officer waiting outside to take your statement but, please, take as much time as you need.'

I winced as I swallowed the warm, stale water.

'Swallowing, talking and breathing are going to be a little uncomfortable,' said Dr Chatterjee. 'And the redness in your eyes will fade, but it's perfectly normal after what happened.'

I turned my head away as fragments of memory ricocheted through my brain.

The scratch of wool against my neck.

The sound of my throat closing.

The Starling.

Charlie.

I dropped the cup and water splashed across the white floor. 'How long have I been here?'

Dr Chatterjee bent down to pick up the cup. 'Since yesterday evening.' He wrapped cool fingers around my wrist to check my pulse.

When he was done, I hoisted myself further up the pillows. 'You can send the police officer in.'

'Are you sure you–'

'I want to get this over with.'

Dr Chatterjee raised his eyebrows a fraction, then disappeared out the door. I heard the sound of a hushed, urgent conversation taking place and closed my eyes. When I opened them a familiar face was hovering, unsmiling, at the end of my bed.

I stared up at Durand. 'What are you doing here?'

'What do you think?' He strode over to my bed, stopping a couple of inches away, as if there were an invisible wall between us. For a moment, I forgot about the pain in my neck.

Durand tore his gaze away from my face and looked at the window. Raindrops hit the glass like bullets. 'It's been coming down like this all night. Flash-floods all across the South. We'll go over your statement when you're feeling ready but,' he turned to face me, his eyes full of fire, 'what the hell were you thinking?'

I was about to open my mouth to protest when I caught a flash of humour in Durand's eye. 'You're joking?'

He gave me a tight smile. 'Would it help if I told you I wasn't?'

I shook my head and a searing heat spread through my neck. 'Sam, listen,' I said, trying to breathe through the pain. 'The doctor didn't get into the details.'

Durand unbuttoned his jacket. His pale pink shirt was creased. 'Are you sure you want to–'

'Please.'

Durand heard the despair in my voice and took another step towards me. Then he sighed. 'He would have killed you had it not been for the interruption.'

'The interruption?'

'You left your notebook in the pub. The reporter ran out to give it to you. Saw what was happening. He chased your attacker but didn't get very far.'

An image of Jeff's waxen face came to mind. 'He's not well.'

'We owe him a huge debt, though. He rang the emergency service–'

'Wait, my notebook. Where is it?'

'It's in your bag.' Durand gave me an incredulous look. '*That's* what you're worried about?'

I ignored him, pulling the corner of my hospital gown over my shoulder. 'So, my attacker got away?'

'The last twelve hours have been busy,' Durand said, rocking back and forth on his heels. 'Bournemouth isn't my jurisdiction, obviously, but I go way back with the Superintendent. He fast-tracked the forensics on your car.' I picked at the frayed edge of the sheet, focusing on my breathing. 'The perpetrator didn't leave much behind,' Durand continued. 'A single hair, in fact. But a single hair is all we need.'

I raised my gaze and the look on Durand's face told me everything I needed to know.

'I'm sorry, Sophie. I know this isn't–'

'Don't.' I forced a smile that hurt my teeth. 'Look on the bright side, if Charlie wants me dead, I must be getting close to the truth.'

Durand didn't return my smile. 'The question is: did Charlie follow you to the pub, or did someone alert him to the fact you were there?'

I glanced out of the window, trying to piece together those last moments. Jeff, Fred and I were the only ones in the pub. I remember a group of kids hanging around outside as I arrived. Then it hit me: Dolly Summerville. I'd asked her about the Old Goat pub.

My eyes flicked to the ceiling. I didn't want to give anything away until I'd spoken to Rowley.

'So, what's the plan, Sam?' I said, attempting to lighten my voice.

Durand poured a cup of water, then handed it to me. 'The area is on lockdown. Charlie won't get far.'

I sank back into the pillow, wishing I couldn't hear the doubt in his voice. 'Do people know? About the attack, I mean. Is it out there?'

'We tried to keep a lid on it but news travels fast. Especially when a local reporter sees an opportunity to get his name in lights.'

I smiled, in spite of myself. 'Good for Jeff.'

'But not good for us. We look incompetent for letting Charlie slip through the net again. There's call for Golden to resign his post.'

'Wow, things must be bad.' A huge gust of wind struck the window and the casings rattled.

'There's something else.' Durand turned to face me, his grey eyes flat. 'Emily is missing.'

I sat up so quickly the pillow fell off my bed. Durand bent down to pick it up and, without thinking, leaned in close and slid it behind my back. The gesture was so intimate, it took us both by surprise. Durand sprang backwards and I pretended not to notice the colour in his cheeks.

I pushed my hair behind my ear, trying to order my thoughts. 'How long has she been gone?'

'Since the press conference. She told a friend she was going for a run to clear her head and never came home. A blue hatchback was seen speeding away from the area around that time. We're still trying to trace it.'

I scooted up the pillow, frowning. 'We know Charlie was definitely in Bournemouth by the evening because he attacked me.'

I counted the hours out on my fingers. 'Christ, the timing's tight. I mean, not impossible, but–'

Durand shot me a look, then moved away from the bed and perched on the edge of the table, nudging the pile of newspapers onto the floor.

'What is it, Sam?' I said, feeling the sharp edge of dread spike through me. Durand wasn't normally fidgety, and I could see the strain in his shoulders from my bed.

He bent down to pick the newspapers up. 'Between you and me, I still don't think Emily adds up.'

Something about his tone made me go cold.

'What are you thinking?' I asked, flatly.

Durand crossed his arms and gave me a long look. 'When the team went to search Emily's apartment things were missing. Clothes, her wallet, her phone. Her fertility medication. Almost as if–'

'She planned to disappear.' I sat up straighter.

Suddenly my phone rang and I glanced at the screen. 'It's the office. I should really take this.'

Durand stood up and rebuttoned his jacket. His voice sounded stilted. 'I've got to follow up on some things. Your car is still with forensics. Not that you should be driving anyway. I'm heading back to London in a couple of hours.' He cleared his throat, his eyes on a spot above my head. 'I'll give you a lift.'

'Thanks, Sam. I'd like that.'

Durand nodded once, then strode out.

I picked up the phone.

'Sophie, it's Philip Rowley. I'm here with the news team, and Austin and Helena Schriver from HR.' There was a pause. 'Let me assure you we're taking this very seriously. An attack on a *Herald* employee is an attack on all of us.' I raised my eyebrows, picturing Rowley and Lansdowne trying to contain themselves in front of HR.

'Soph? It's Kate. How are you, love?'

'I've been better,' I said, watching the rain slide down the glass.

Kate sighed. 'The Met gave us a heads-up on the forensics from your car. We know it was Charlie. Did he say anything to you?'

I closed my eyes and put a hand to my neck. 'It happened so fast. One minute I was starting the engine, the next ... I saw him, in the mirror. Only for a second.' The memory made me reach for my water cup.

'Do you know Emily's been kidnapped?' asked Kate, jumping into the silence.

'Guys,' I dragged my nail along the polystyrene surface, 'there's a possibility there's more to Emily's disappearance than meets the eye.'

I filled them in on Durand's suspicions about Emily.

'Do you think she's just had enough of the limelight and is lying low, or is this something else?' asked Rowley.

'Who knows? But at the press conference she was a woman on the edge.' I pictured Emily's ferocious expression, *without Sabrina, we can start again*. There was deluded, and there was plain unhinged.

Kate whistled. 'But her face is everywhere. Where the hell would she go?'

I flicked the corner of my blanket and sighed. 'I know Emily. She wouldn't run unless she had an iron-clad plan in place.'

'Which begs the question: does she have help?' said Rowley, 'And, if so, from whom?'

'Charlie?' I recognised Mack's voice. 'Come on, it's possible they're in this together, right?'

The room went quiet.

'In the meantime, it's blowing up out there,' said Kate. 'The media is blaming DCI Golden for putting Emily in the line of fire at the press conference. I doubt he'll be in the job much longer.'

Will Durand be reinstated? I considered the fact he was down in Bournemouth. Was he checking on me because he cared, or was I a route back to his old job? I shook the feeling away just as Lansdowne piped up.

'Kent, Austin here. Glad you're OK.' His voice was stilted and wooden. 'Can you give us your movements leading up to the attack? We need to file a report.'

I blinked, trying to clear the fog from my brain. 'Initially I went down to speak to Charlie's stepfather, Gordon. But then I followed a lead.' I filled them in about Christ Clan, pausing every now and again to sip water and catch my breath. 'Christ Clan sucked Charlie in and spat him out. He wasn't just a member. He was part of the inner circle. The source I interviewed identified Charlie as a kid they used to call the Starling. Bore the brunt of Marlon's cruelty.'

I stared at the Christ Clan leaflet I'd pulled out of my bag.

'When Vanessa's drink problem turned Charlie's home toxic, he had nowhere else to go. The reporter I met compared Christ Clan to *The Hunger Games*. Sadistic mind games. Systematic violence. Pitting the boys against each other. Brainwashed the kids in his group. Told them they had to purify their souls with water, fire and blood.'

'What do you mean?' said Rowley in his trademark nasal voice.

I told them what Fred revealed about the rituals: the bathing, the fires, the animal sacrifices. All the talking was taking its toll on my throat and I gulped down more water.

Lansdowne mumbled something, then he spoke up. 'Kent, I still don't see what this fucked-up cult,' he broke off to apologise to Helena for his language, 'has to do with Sabrina Hobbs.'

I sighed. 'One of the casualties of Christ Clan was a girl called Samantha Hartley. She and Charlie were in a relationship, until she cheated on him. She ended up face-down in a river. Marlon claimed it was an overdose but there were rumours she was drowned. And she had two triangles carved into her wrist. A sign of the Golden Flock. Sabrina, I think, had the same markings on her wrist.'

'Christ, this puts Charlie in context,' said Kate. 'All this time we've struggled to reconcile our version of Charlie with this cold-hearted killer. But when you factor in his childhood and the Christ Clan . . .'

'And this religious organisation is the one Charlie was researching?' asked Mack.

I nodded. 'I think he was reading up on Hector, the son. There's another link, too. Charlie's stepdad, Gordon, told me his mum changed her will right before she died. She left a chunk to Christ Clan.'

'Why?' asked Mack.

'I'm not sure yet but–' I thumped down my cup as a thought occurred to me. 'How have I not seen this before? Charlie's first wife, Lizzie, his mum, his mistress. All the women in Charlie's life are dead.'

Eventually Mack spoke. 'But Vanessa and Lizzie's deaths were accidental.'

'Were they?' I closed my eyes, willing the theory to tighten in my head. 'Marlon was a real piece of work; he blamed women for his shortcomings.' I told them what Jeff told me about Marlon's experimental cult in the seventies; when he tried, and failed, to spread his seed. 'His sadistic attitude towards women would have filtered through to the angry, vulnerable young men he led. What if it was indoctrinated into Charlie at a young age that women were the root of all evil?'

'You think Charlie is punishing the women in his life,' said Kate.

I leaned away from the pillow, yanking my tube with me. 'I think my source is wrong about Emily being involved. Think about it: Charlie's mum ruined his life. Samantha cheated on him, so did Lizzie. Sabrina aborted his child. Emily . . . well, we know things weren't good between them.'

'And you?' Kate's voice was quiet.

'Sophie got too close to the truth,' said Rowley.

A sharp, taut silence filled the room.

I pulled my hair into a ponytail, thinking out loud. 'Sacrifice. Purifying your soul. Fire, water, blood. Think about it: how did these women all die?'

'Samantha Hartley drowned,' said Kate, and I could picture her checking them off against her fingers. 'Lizzie drowned. So did Sabrina. But that doesn't fit because Vanessa fell down the stairs drunk and–'

'Vanessa was killed by a fire,' I said, quietly. 'All their deaths were caused by water or fire.'

There was a brief pause, then everyone started talking at once.

Rowley called order. 'Sophie, are you saying what I think you're saying?'

I gnawed on a fingernail, desperately trying to keep hold of my thread of thought. 'Listen, I've heard over and over about a fire that occurred when Charlie was a kid in 1988. Nearly gutted the house. After that Charlie moved out and wouldn't speak to his mum for years. What if that fire wasn't accidental?'

Kate cleared her throat. 'You mean, Charlie tried to kill his mum once already?'

I shrugged. 'It's possible. And when it didn't work he decided he was done with her. Disappeared from her life.'

'Why didn't Charlie try again if he failed to kill his mum in that fire?' said Mack.

I sighed. 'I don't know. Friends credit his stepfather with being a stable influence. Maybe the desire left him after–'

Kate cried out. 'Wait, when did you say the fire was?'

'April 1988.'

'Which is the same month Samantha Hartley died?'

I nodded, running my eyes down the page of my notebook. 'And the Christ Clan closed down that year, too.'

I heard the adrenaline in Kate's voice. 'All those things happened within months of each other. Don't you think –'

Mack cut Kate off. 'Earth to Bournemouth. I don't mean to be the harbinger of doom, but are you really suggesting that Charlie is responsible for four deaths spanning three decades?'

I leaned back against my pillow. 'Look, it's worth considering the possibility that this doesn't start and finish with Sabrina Hobbs. There are no notes on Samantha Hartley because there was no investigation, but we should take a look at Vanessa and Lizzie's post-mortems.' I pictured Dr Sonoma. 'I have a source. Let me see what I can do.'

'Will other people have drawn the link between Charlie and the Christ Clan?' asked Rowley, and I heard the pinch in his voice at the prospect of the new angle being snatched from under the *Herald*'s nose.

I shrugged. 'Not unless they had access to his internet search history. No one has got to my sources, yet. Not even the police.'

A phone rang in the background.

Rowley sniffed. 'Let's talk rundown. Sophie, see if you can get your hands on Vanessa and Lizzie's post-mortems. And do you feel up to writing a first-person piece on your attack?'

I swallowed thickly. 'Sure.'

'I still think we need to go big on Emily's disappearance,' said Lansdowne. 'People are invested in her now.' He paused. 'Although if what you're saying is true, Sophie, she's probably already dead.'

My hand tightened round my notebook. *Please no.*

'That was my source at the courthouse on the phone,' said Kate, sighing. 'The Rowntree jury have reconvened and are in deliberation.'

I frowned. 'I'd completely forgotten about that. Did Rahid get his petrol station source on the record?'

'Fucking right he did.' Lansdowne broke off again to apologise to Helena. 'We're tying up the loose ends now. Rahid's been trying to get hold of Bert Hughes all morning for a quote. No answer.'

There was a knock.

'Guys, I have to go,' I said as Dr Chatterjee reappeared holding his clipboard.

Rowley cleared his throat. 'Let's speak in a couple of hours.'

Dr Chatterjee curled his stethoscope, frowning. 'I can hear by the hoarseness in your voice that you've ignored my advice to take it easy. You know, it's not only the physical injuries we have to take into account.' Dr Chatterjee pressed the stethoscope against my back and the feel of cold metal against my skin helped me to focus.

'How long until I can leave?'

Dr Chatterjee sighed. 'Your vitals are good. The nurse will take the cannula out of your hand and then you're free to go. But, you're not leaving here alone.'

I shook my head.

After Dr Chatterjee left, I opened my laptop and stared at the white screen. Seconds later, I slammed the laptop closed and hurled it to the end of the bed.

Charlie wants me dead.

I'd never have believed it possible until I saw his eyes in the rear-view mirror. I knew hate when I saw it.

I rubbed my eyes, feeling wrung out. Outside the rain was easing. The sooty black clouds gave way to steady grey, casting a pale light over my room. My breathing gradually slowed, but I felt hollow and raw. I sighed and opened my bag, remembering the phone number for Les Miller, the father of the boy who was put in hospital by Christ Clan. I heard Jeff's strained voice: *Blow it apart. For those kids.*

My eyes landed on the letters I'd found at Vanessa's house. I untied the red and white string, grateful for the distraction.

The letters were written on white paper that had yellowed over the years. Each contained a couple of lines of childish scrawl. I unfolded the top letter and settled back against the pillow.

Mum,

    Are you happy at the way life has turned out for you? Is this what you wanted? I won't forgive you. Ever. I won't forgive you.

I read the next.

Mum,

    Let me come home. Please, just let me come home. I want to be a normal family. Why can't you see that?

And the next.

> Mum,
>
> I've done bad things because of you. I will do more bad things if you don't let me come home. No one you love will be safe. This is your fault. It's all your fault.

Ten minutes later, I'd read the lot. The letters alternated between despair, love and hate; Charlie's anger embedded in every pen line. I lay back on the pillow, listening to the sound of my pulse in my ears. All this time, the people who knew Charlie thought he'd broken off all contact with Vanessa. Here was proof they were wrong.

I turned the letters over in my hand, felt the weight of them, pictured Charlie, hunched over the desk, stabbing at each page with his pen, thrusting them into the postbox, wondering if this time his mum would respond. Is this why Charlie was so bitter towards his mum? Because she rejected him? I reread the final letter.

> Mum,
>
> You'll never be alone again. I'm watching you. I see everything. You can't see me, but I see you. Always.

I stared out the window as an idea began to form in my mind. Then I picked up my phone.

29

I closed the taxi door and stared through the trees at Vanessa's home, The Ridings. The cottage's white façade was scorched black, and all that was left of the thatched roof was a line of timber frames that poked out like a ribcage. The fire had mauled the right-hand side of the house so badly that I could see through the exterior to an upstairs bedroom. On the front lawn, a rusted sculpture of a boy on a swing lay on its side.

There was no sign of Gordon.

I sighed, then pulled out the scribbled number Jeff Johnson gave me in the pub. I sat down on a grimy brick wall underneath a large Horse Chestnut tree and dialled Mark Miller's dad, Les.

The phone rang and rang and I was about to hang up when a gruff voice answered.

'Yeah?'

'Is that Mr Les Miller?'

'Who's this?'

'My name is Sophie Kent. I'm calling from the *London Herald* newspaper. Do you have a moment to talk?' Silence. I folded the piece of paper in half and put it in my pocket. 'Mr Miller?'

The flick of a cigarette lighter, an inhale. 'What's this about?' he asked, expelling smoke.

'Your son, Mark.'

'What about him?'

I kicked the ground with my toe. 'I'm trying to track him down.'

Another inhale. 'Why?'

I licked my lips. As a reporter, you get a sense, a feeling. You learn to hear the different notes in a person's voice. An inflection that could lead to a quote, a piece of information. Or a flatness that means you're going to get nothing. Les's voice fell somewhere in between. Hostile but curious. I had one shot at this.

'Les, I've come across some information recently. In connection with a story I'm working on. Your son's name has come up and I wondered if you'd mind confirming a few details for me.'

'This going in the newspaper?'

'I can keep your name out of it, if you'd rather.'

I heard him suck on his cigarette. 'Go on.'

'Were you aware that Mark was a member of a religious organisation in the eighties?'

'So that's what this is about.' Les gave a thin laugh. 'Yes, I know all about Christ Clan.' A pause. 'What's your name again?'

'Sophie.'

'How old are you, Sophie?'

I bit down on my frustration, desperate to keep him sweet. 'Les, can we stick to the question?'

He gave a cruel laugh. 'I like a woman in charge.'

I tapped my thumb against the notebook, fearing Les was going to turn out to be what Lansdowne would call a Tart.

'Watch out for Tarts, Kent,' he once told me between bites of a banana. 'Tart are time-wasters; they'll lift their skirts up all the way, then leave you with nothing but a hard-on and a hole in your story.'

The sound of another cigarette being lit. 'Me and the kid, we never got along. The stress that boy caused us. I wanted to send him back–'

I frowned. 'What do you mean "send him back"?'

'But he got involved with that religious nuthouse and then he became ten times worse. We never knew where he was. And when he did turn up, he was covered in bruises. He was violent, always in fights. Angry.' I closed my eyes, picturing a confused, angry child lashing out at those around him in the only way he knew how. Jeff Johnson's words drifted into my head: *Miller used to get knocked about badly at home.* I clenched my jaw. Talking to morally dubious people was part of the job.

'And he killed my marriage,' said Les.

'What?'

'Pam, she left me. It was his fault, I'm sure of it. And after everything she did for that boy.' His voice dripped with hatred.

'Were you aware of the rumours about Christ Clan? The abuse that went on there?'

There was a pause. 'Yes.'

'And you weren't worried about Mark?'

Les sneered. 'It's because of him I lost my wife. As far as I was concerned, Mark was their problem.'

'Did you know Mark was hospitalised with severe injuries? In the late eighties?'

Les sniffed loudly. 'Don't know, don't care.'

I raised my eyebrows, struggling to comprehend the hostility. 'Did Mark ever mention a boy called Charlie Swift? Someone he knew at Christ Clan?'

Les sucked on his cigarette. 'Why do I know that name?'

Somewhere a dog barked and I looked round. 'He's the guy in the news. He's on the run. Killed his mistress.' The words still sounded ludicrous when I said them out loud.

Les laughed, a horrible high-pitched shriek. 'Sounds like the sort of person Mark would know.'

'When did you last see him?'

There was a long pause. Long enough that I wondered if the phone had cut out.

When Les spoke, his voice had dropped to a whisper. 'About ten years ago. I came home from the betting shop and Mark was sitting at the kitchen table. Said he'd been doing some soul-searching and had come to realise I was one of the reasons he was so unhappy. I told him to get out but he–'

I heard an odd noise. I pressed the phone to my ear and realised with a start that Les was crying.

'Mark said he wanted his face to be the last face I ever saw.'

'What do you mean?'

'I never saw it coming. The kettle, by his feet. He threw boiling water in my eyes.'

'You mean,' I chewed my lip as it dawned on me. 'You're blind?'

I heard footsteps and looked up to see Gordon shuffling towards me.

Les took a rasping breath. 'He got his wish. The last face I ever saw was my son. See, I told you he was a nasty little fucker.'

'Are you still in contact with Mark?' I asked, giving Gordon a wave.

'What do you think?'

The phone went dead and I let out a breath.

Gordon's eyebrows shot up. 'What happened to your eyes? They're very red.'

'Long story.' I blinked self-consciously, knowing how awful I looked.

Gordon was wearing the same grey cardigan as yesterday, although I noticed a new stain smeared along the chest. When he leaned forward to hug me, he smelt of cooking fat.

'I didn't realise Vanessa's house was so isolated,' I said.

Gordon looked over my shoulder at the two-mile lane that led back to civilisation. 'Ness liked it that way.'

We stepped over the debris of last night's storm and I followed Gordon past tangled flower beds, my feet sinking in the waterlogged grass.

Gordon stopped outside the charred front door and jangled a set of keys. I waited for him to unlock it but he didn't.

Eventually I stepped forwards. 'Would you like me to go first?'

Gordon shrugged. The key was stiff in the lock and it took both hands to open it. The door creaked loudly and I heard the scrabble of a creature darting across the hallway. I walked inside and was hit by a sooty stench that was ingrained in the walls.

Gordon limped straight over to a painting on the left-hand wall. 'I painted that for Ness.'

I gazed at an oil painting of a small dog. 'Wow, you're talented.'

'Couldn't do it anymore.' He held his hands out and I could see they were shaking. 'I'd like to have had a dog. Maybe one day.'

I left Gordon to his thoughts and scanned the narrow hall-way. I flicked a switch and wasn't surprised to find the electricity had been turned off. Pausing by the foot of the stairs, I stared down at the patch where Vanessa's body had lain, the skin on my neck puckering.

The acrid stench deepened in the kitchen and I covered my nose with my sleeve. The kitchen and the living area had borne the brunt of the fire. The low ceiling was studded with blackened beams, and ragged remains of a curtain hung limply against the grimy window. I ran my finger along the countertop surface, leaving a trail in the white ash. The fridge door was flecked with old bits of sellotape. A shopping list was tacked to the front, its edges curled and yellowing, the writing faded to nothing. I strolled over to the sink and looked out at the patch of grass outside. An empty washing line swung in the breeze. *You can't see me, but I can see you.*

I heard a noise behind me. Gordon hobbled across the kitchen and slumped down into a saggy red armchair.

He gazed around listlessly. 'Put the kettle on, dear.'

'The kettle isn't working, Gordon.'

Gordon fiddled with his cuff and his eyes filled with tears. I strode across the kitchen and gave him a hug.

'I taught Charlie to kick a ball out there,' he said, staring over my shoulder at the garden. 'Never liked to wear shoes. Used to trail mud through the kitchen. Feral he was.' Gordon tried to hide his face from me but I could see his cheeks were wet. 'Charlie was a good boy. I tried my best. I tried,' his words dissolved into sobs, 'but none of us could help Ness. No one could help her forget.'

I pulled a wooden chair over to Gordon and sat down. Gordon had said the same thing to me yesterday. 'What was Vanessa trying to forget?' I said, gently.

'Ness grew up here, you know. On this farmland. She was born upstairs in the pink bedroom. Her father was a wastrel. She got swept up in a local church group. Ran away with them. Travelled the country in the back of a minivan so the legend goes.' Gordon stared down at his feet. 'She was young, vulnerable. Got herself into a spot of bother with a man there.'

I frowned. 'What kind of trouble?'

Gordon tugged at his sleeve, his eyebrows knitting together. 'She never spoke to me about it, not sober anyway. But, well, you know. She was . . .'

'Raped?'

Gordon's eyes snapped towards mine. 'I think what happened set her up for a lifetime of misery. And there was nothing me, or Charlie, or anyone could do about it.'

A bird's high-pitched squawk cut through the air and Gordon flinched.

I leaned forward in my chair. 'Listen, that box in your house, the one with all Vanessa's things. I found letters.'

Gordon's gaze was so blank, I wondered if he'd heard me.

'You told me that Charlie cut all ties with his mum after the first fire but he didn't,' I said. 'He wrote her letters, stacks of them. He must have written them while he was living with you. He writes about watching Vanessa, spying on her here. The letters are bleak.'

'Well, what do you expect?'

'Did you know he used to come here?'

Gordon folded his arms and rocked forwards. His moustache twitched. 'Far as I knew, he was in his room most of the time. Used to spend hours in there. Locked the door.'

I nodded, keeping my face neutral. Lock the door, go out the window. Oldest trick in the book. I felt a wave of compassion for Gordon. He'd been woefully unprepared to take on an angry, scared child, but he'd done it anyway.

I looked around the room. Seeing Charlie's childhood home was depressing. The bare walls. The stark furniture. The dankness, the despair. No wonder Charlie craved something else. A community. Even if it was somewhere as toxic as Christ Clan.

My eyes landed on a wooden door in the corner. 'Where does that lead?'

Gordon was checking his watch again. 'It's 12.13 p.m. Help me up.' I hauled him out of the chair, and he shuffled over to his bag and pulled out a tiny silver radio. He switched it on and the kitchen filled with the crackling sound.

I left Gordon surfing the airwaves and crossed the kitchen to the wooden door. I unlatched it and pulled but it wouldn't open. It took my full weight to lift the door. As it scraped against the stone floor, a blast of icy, damp air hit me in the face. A rickety wooden staircase sloped away into the darkness. I darted back to my bag and grabbed my torch then picked my way down the steps, stumbling on a loose plank of wood. I hit the cellar floor hard, sending up a cloud of dust. As I sneezed, a jolt of pain ran through my neck.

The cellar was vast; it must have run the entire length of the house. I inched forwards, brushing cobwebs away from my face. As my eyes adjusted, shapes loomed into view. A water tank. A shelving unit laden with tools. An old lawnmower. A pile of boxes. As I neared the middle, a column of natural light spilled across the floor. I scanned the cellar trying to find the source. Tucked into the far right corner was a small window, brown with dirt.

I heard a noise behind me.

'Gordon?' I squinted into the darkness. 'Are you there?'

My pulse was loud in my ears. I turned back towards the window and gave it a shove. A piece of the wooden frame came off in my hand but the window didn't budge. It hadn't been opened for years. I sighed. What was I expecting? Evidence of a secret entrance that Charlie was using to hide in his mum's dilapidated cottage? It was too obvious; this was the last place Charlie would come. I threw the piece of wood on the ground and saw two mice scuttle away. I followed them with my torch beam and watched them disappear through a wall I hadn't noticed before. It was almost hidden from view behind the washing machine.

The cellar was creeping me out but I gritted my teeth and ploughed forwards. The wall was made of wood. I tapped it. *Hollow.* I ran my torch along it. In the top right corner was a hole just large enough to fit a hand. I dragged a crate over and climbed up. Then I put my hand through the hole and yanked the wood towards me. It came away in a cloud of dust.

It was a hole, no bigger than a large cupboard. A dirty mattress lay on the ground. Sweet wrappers littered the floor, juice cartons, an old newspaper. I kicked it with my foot. The date: 14 June 1990. I heard Fred's voice in my head: *He had a talent for stealing into people's homes. They never even knew he was there.* Charlie hadn't just spied on his mum, he'd been living here without her knowing.

I crouched down and ran my torch along the wall beside the mattress. Small triangles, the size of ten-pence coins, were scratched into the stone. There were hundreds of them. I ran my fingers along the surface. Each triangle was filled in with dark paint. I leaned in closer. Was it paint? Or was it . . . I stumbled backwards and collided with someone.

'What have you found?' Gordon was holding onto the wall, eyes invisible behind his glasses. He'd done up the buttons on his cardigan wrongly.

I blasted out a breath. 'Christ, you scared me.' I pointed my torch towards the shapes on the wall. 'I think it's blood.'

As I spoke, my torch beam landed on a brick that was sticking out further than the rest. I gave the brick a tug and it came out. I flashed my torch inside.

'Shit.' The torch slid out of my hand and landed on the floor with a thud.

'What is it?' Gordon's voice was weak.

I picked it up with a shaky hand and aimed it at the hole. It was a perfectly preserved skeleton of a bird.

'Any idea what type of bird that is?' I said, in a shaky voice.

Gordon was shifting his weight from one foot to the other. 'The long yellow beak. I'd say it's a blackbird or a starling.' I stared at Gordon, the hairs on my neck standing tall.

I reached forwards and prised out the brick next to it. More skeletons. Spindly legs, claws, beaks. 'How did they get in the wall?'

Gordon made a strange gurgling noise. He backed away, and I had to grab him to stop him collapsing. I half-dragged Gordon up the cellar steps and the feel of his spine through his cardigan made me think of the pile of twig-like bones in the cellar. I took a deep breath and helped Gordon over to the chair.

'I'd like to go home now, please.' Gordon's voice quivered and he slid his glasses up his nose revealing huge eyes.

I didn't blame him. I'd never wanted to leave somewhere so badly in my life. I helped Gordon pack away his radio and picked up my bag. As Gordon shuffled out of the kitchen, I shoved the cellar door closed, and that's when I saw it. A small hole right beside the handle. Large enough to peep through, small enough to remain unseen. *You can't see me, but I can see you.* This is where Charlie had stood, spying on his mum.

I locked the front door and went to join Gordon on the grass.

'What just happened in there?' Gordon's eyes were cartoon-large behind his thick glasses.

I led him towards his battered blue Golf. 'Are you going to be OK, Gordon?'

He stopped by the car, clutching his bag to his chest, taking short, sharp breaths. 'Ness was in so much pain. She tried to drink through it and she turned her son into a monster right in front of me. I never realised.' Tears spilled down his cheeks. 'What kind of stepfather am I?'

I pulled Gordon into a fierce hug. 'You were the only stable influence in Charlie's life. He mentioned you often. Why else do you think I badgered you so much when everything kicked off? You're the person I thought he'd turn to. I'm just surprised he hasn't.'

Gordon stiffened in my arms. My breathing tightened. 'Have you seen him?' I said, pulling back and staring at him.

'I wasn't lying yesterday. He hasn't come to my house. But I did see him once.'

'Where?'

'I came here Tuesday night to check on the place. Charlie was standing in the garden. I called out to him, but he ran.'

My mind was whirling. 'He was here Tuesday?'

The day after Sabrina's body was discovered.

Gordon faced me, his eyes red, his lip trembling. 'I've been leaving food out for him. He must be starving.'

I felt a prickle run through me and I glanced towards the wall of bushes swaying in the wind.

'Let's get out of here, Gordon.'

I opened the car door and helped him in. Then I raced round to the passenger side.

'Are you sure you're OK to drive?' I said, slamming the door.

Gordon nodded and started the engine. As he pulled away from The Ridings, I looked back over my shoulder wishing I could unsee the image burned on my vision forever.

Tiny, buried bones.

30

Durand opened the passenger door of his black Toyota and I sank gratefully into the car. The smell of coffee clung to the upholstery and, as I slung my bag on the back seat, I spotted a mountain of empty paper cups in the footwell.

I jabbed a thumb towards them. 'That's one hell of a caffeine habit you have there.'

Durand switched on the engine, shrugging slightly. 'Everyone needs a vice.'

He glanced in his mirror, then eased the car out of the Royal Bournemouth's car park. His auburn hair was brushed back off his face and the light softened his features. I wanted to ask why he was really here, visiting me in hospital, giving me lifts. *Business or pleasure, sir?* The weirdness of the last twenty-four hours hit me and I giggled.

Durand glanced at me, eyebrows raised. 'Something funny?'

I shook my head, and lay back against the seat. The leaden sky was still threatening rain; the atmosphere was oppressive, dank.

'When did you last eat?' said Durand, braking as we approached a roundabout.

'This morning. Unidentified brown sludge, courtesy of the hospital chef.' I ran my tongue over my teeth, grimacing as I realised I hadn't brushed them.

Durand leaned across me, then opened the glove box and threw me a KitKat. 'Lunch of champions.'

I wasn't hungry but I took a bite anyway, happy to replace the staleness in my mouth with a bunch of E-numbers.

Durand put his foot down and we joined the main road. A few drops of rain hit the windscreen, then stopped. 'How's your neck?'

I put a hand to the tender spot on either side. 'Sore. Is there any word on Emily?'

Durand's hands tightened on the steering wheel but he didn't respond. *I'll take that as a no.* 'Listen, I've been thinking about your Emily theory,' I said. 'I'm not sure she has it in her to pull the wool over everyone's eyes, not given how much attention she's received. She would have had to lie to all of us for such a long time.' I waited for Durand to speak and, when he didn't, I finished the last of the KitKat and scrunched the paper into a ball.

Durand's phone rang, and he reached out to hit 'answer', then obviously thought better of talking on speakerphone in front of me and shoved a Bluetooth bud into his ear instead.

I let my gaze wander to the green fields flashing past, tired of the constant push and pull. It was hard enough navigating the professional waters between us, but the personal stuff was starting to mess with my compass. Was I imagining a connection that wasn't there? I'd learned the hard way that crossing the

line with a work contact brings nothing but drama. An image of
Mack dropped into my head.

Sam's different, and you know it.

I yanked my phone out of my bag, swiping the stupid thought
from my head. I needed to focus. I scrolled through my inbox,
replying to urgent emails and shelving the rest. The reporter,
Jeff Johnson, wanted a quote from me to go in the piece he was
writing about rescuing Charlie Swift's latest victim. I replied to
Jeff that he was my hero, and to give me an hour to come up
with something good. I closed my eyes, feeling jittery. I couldn't
shake the memory of Vanessa's house: the filthy mattress, the
blood on the wall, the dead birds. I shuddered. All that time,
Charlie had been secretly living in the house, out of sight and . . .
I frowned as the seed of an idea took root in my head.

Durand hung up and tossed his phone onto the cup holder.
Then he turned on the radio. A Status Quo track was playing.

'Nice tunes, Granddad.'

'Don't diss the Quo,' he said, tapping the steering wheel
in time to the music. I rolled my eyes at him, just as the sun
emerged from behind a cloud. It flooded the car with light and
I noted the lines around Durand's eyes, the veil of stubble along
his jaw. He'd lost weight, a lot of weight.

I drummed my fingers on the armrest. 'Who was that on the
phone?'

'Where am I dropping you?' he said, ignoring my question.

Two can play at that game.

'The *Herald*, please.' Durand didn't need to know where I was
planning to go from there.

I felt his glance. 'Shouldn't you have an afternoon off?'

'There's no rest for the wicked.' My tone was light, but I could tell by Durand's silence that he didn't approve.

'Maybe it's time to rethink your priorities.'

'I'm happy with my priorities, actually,' I said, bristling at his tone.

Durand leaned forward to turn off the radio. 'Shouldn't your priority be staying alive?'

'Sam . . .' I fired off a warning shot, irritated by Durand's ability to go from sensitive to condescending in the blink of an eye.

'Listen to me, Sophie,' Durand's voice was studied, calm but I could see the tightness in his jaw. 'I care about you and I'm going to regret it if I don't say something. You never used to be so reckless. I've lost count of the number of times in the last few months I've had to–'

'What?' I said, breathing through the anger. 'Worry about me? No one asked you to.'

'You're no use to Tommy if you're dead,' he said quietly.

I wrenched my eyes away from Durand and forced them to my hands. I was holding my phone so tightly, my knuckles had turned white. 'You are such a hypocrite.'

'What's that supposed to mean?'

'So, my personal life is open to discussion but yours is off limits?' I bit down on my anger, but it was too late. The fury tasted sharp on my tongue. 'Clearly something is going on in your life at the moment, but I wouldn't know because you *don't budge an inch*. Well, you can't have it both ways. You don't get to comment on my baggage, just like I don't get to comment on yours. Because it's none of my business. And you've made fucking sure it stays that way.'

Outside the sky was darkening and the clouds looked as if they were going to break any moment. Up ahead a sea of red taillights greeted us. I swore under my breath at the prospect of being trapped in the car with Durand, when he finally spoke.

'A long time ago I made a mistake. My wife, Jen, and I were married for four years when it happened. A slip-up. One night only. I never saw the woman again.' Durand cleared his throat and focused on the road in front. 'Turns out I'm not a very good cheat. The choice I made sat with me until I couldn't bear it anymore. I confessed to Jen, who was devastated. But we found a way through. I worked harder at my marriage than I did at anything.' He broke off and stared out the window. 'Then, last October, the woman – the mistake – turned up at my office.'

Other than the steady tick of the engine, the car was completely silent.

'She said I had a daughter. *Have* a daughter.' Durand paused and took a breath. 'She never told me. Would never have told me, I don't think, if the little girl wasn't so ill.'

Durand raked a hand through his hair, then pulled on the steering wheel and turned sharply into the outside lane.

'My daughter has cancer. Ovarian. She's only six. Anyway, her mother wasn't happy with the care she was getting. She tracked me down to ask for help. It was a bolt out of the blue, obviously. I needed time, but that wasn't an option. She agreed to a paternity test and, when it came back positive, I transferred the funds. I didn't mention anything to Jen because I wanted to pick the right time. But she saw the bank transaction, and it all came out. While she had come to terms with my betrayal, she couldn't accept the permanent reminder of it. She – we – have struggled to have our own children . . .'

Durand's words trailed into nothing and a heavy silence stretched through the car.

Eventually I cleared my throat. 'What's her name? Your daughter.'

'Elodie.'

'Have you met her?'

'Twice. She's a redhead, too.' I heard the smile in Durand's voice. 'It was her birthday last week. I visited her in hospital. Took her a doll. She told me she's too old for dolls. Turns out I have a lot to learn about being a dad.' His voice caught on the last word and, before I could stop myself, I reached out and squeezed his arm.

'I'm sorry about Jen. About your marriage. But how lovely that you have a daughter. And a chance to help her.'

Durand looked at me uncertainly. 'You think?'

I gripped his arm harder. 'Sam, you're the most decent man I know. Elodie is lucky to have you in her life. Taste in music aside, obviously.'

Durand's laugh echoed around the car. The smile lingered on his lips for a second, then he seemed to remember himself. 'I've got so much time to make up. I worry Elodie thinks I don't care.'

'She'll understand.' My hand was still on Durand's arm; I pulled it away. 'Maybe not right now, but give it time. Just because you haven't been in her life until now, doesn't mean you can't make up for lost time. My father has been around since the day I was born and he's never given a shit about the whole parent thing. It's what you do now that counts.'

Durand glanced at me. 'Did you know your father has reached out to DCI Golden following your attack?'

I froze. 'He what?'

'He wants to know what measures Golden is taking to keep you safe. He's made the same call to your editor at the *Herald*.'

I shook my head in disbelief, feeling a complex mix of emotions. My father's instinct was to control, to pull strings, to influence. But he lacked the one thing I needed from him: love. It bothered me that after all this time he could still get under my skin. 'To the outside world, my father almost passes for human,' I said, under my breath.

Durand arched an eyebrow. 'You think he doesn't care?'

I heard the judgement and sharpened my voice. 'I think it's telling that my father spared the time to call the police and my boss, yet didn't get around to calling me. Hell, I'd have settled for a text. *Hi, daughter, heard you almost died. Thinking of you.*'

'I'm sure it comes from a good place.'

'Can we talk about something else?' I said, my eyes on the road. Ahead, the line of traffic started to move and Durand shifted the car into gear.

'Once Elodie's finished her next round of treatment, I've promised her a trip to EuroDisney.'

I smiled, in spite of myself. 'Will you wear the Mickey Mouse ears?'

'She says she wants me to dress up as Olaf from *Frozen*. I don't know what either of those things are.'

He looked so forlorn, I laughed. 'I will educate you in all matters of Disney, DCI Sam Durand.' Durand indicated right and slid into the outside lane. I waited a beat. 'What about Elodie's mum?'

'What about her?'

'Any chance of that relationship going anywhere?' I kept my voice light, eyes on the road.

'She's not really my type.'

'What is your type?'

Durand blinked. 'Stubborn.'

I felt the air grow heavy and cleared my throat, scouring my mind for a distraction. 'Sam, earlier. When I mentioned Emily, you shut me out. Has something happened?'

Durand tapped his thumb on the steering wheel, as if deliberating something, then he nodded towards his phone. 'Click on Videos and check out the latest one.'

I picked up the phone, my pulse quickening. When I pressed 'play', the screen went dark, then lit up to show a marble interior, with a waterfall in the corner.

'Wait, I recognise this . . . it's Hamilton Law?'

Durand nodded. 'The first few frames were caught by their security camera. The rest were picked up on the northern corner of Manchester Square.'

I watched as a red-haired woman in a cream mac crossed the lobby and pushed through the revolving doors. The footage cut to outside the building, where she hurried, head bowed low towards Hinde Street.

'When was this?' I said, watching Sabrina disappear from view.

'Two days before her murder.'

I waited, but nothing happened. I was just about to say something when I spotted movement. A blonde woman appeared from behind a parked car and darted after Sabrina.

I squinted at the screen, at her black exercise gear, her bright orange trainers.

Emily.

Durand checked his rear-view mirror and pulled out to overtake a coach. 'When Emily went missing, Waters and I went back to the drawing board and took another swing at all the evidence.'

'So, all this time Emily has known about Sabrina?'

'Of course, this doesn't mean anything on its own,' said Durand. 'Just because she lied about Sabrina doesn't mean she's guilty. But it raises more questions about her reliability.'

I shook my head in disbelief. 'Christ. What does Golden think abou—'

Durand's phone rang. He jammed in his earphone and grabbed it out of my hand.

I glanced out the window, trying to absorb what I'd just heard. If Emily was lying about Sabrina, what else was she lying about? With a start, I remembered Sinead's story about the girl at school who threatened to blow Emily's cover, her carefully constructed façade. Emily had pulled no punches when she got her revenge.

'Are the SOCOs there yet?' The strain in Durand's voice made me look up. He thumped his police emergency light on the dashboard. 'Tell Golden I'm on my way.'

'What's going on?' I said as Durand put his foot down and the car surged forward.

'We're making a detour.'

I could tell by the tension in his jaw that he'd crossed back into professional mode. I wouldn't get anything else out of him. I grabbed hold of the armrest as we weaved between cars, praying Durand was as good a driver as he was a detective.

Ten minutes later, Durand turned off the main road and we raced down a series of narrow streets that led to a collection of large grey warehouses. At the far end was a secluded car park, which was lit up with flashing blue lights. Police cars and fire trucks lined the outside. In the centre was the skeleton of a blue car; its tyres melted into nothing. Durand barrelled towards the police van that was parked at an angle behind it.

'Stay in the car,' he said, jamming on the brakes.

'But–'

'For once, do as I say, Sophie,' he growled, slamming the door.

As Durand strode towards the crowd, I cracked the window open. A thick burning smell spread through the car. A team of police were setting up a cordon around the blue car and I spotted the SOCOs pulling on white suits. Durand was deep in conversation with an ashen DCI Golden. I saw him point at the sky, then gesture towards the ground. Suddenly I realised the significance of the car. What was it Durand said in the hospital about Emily's disappearance? *A blue hatchback was seen speeding away.*

I squinted through the windscreen, trying to get a better look. Was this about Emily? My view was obscured by the line of police cars but I yanked out my phone and started taking photographs. I emailed the pictures to the news team, cc'ing Rowley.

Burned-out car found in Crystal Palace. Possible link to Emily's kidnap? Am sending photos.

A response came a moment later from Mack.

These pictures are shit, Kent. Can't you get any closer?

It would be impossible to creep closer without being seen. I didn't want to risk Durand's wrath, not when he'd been so open with me earlier. *Sometimes you have to lose the battle to win the war.*

I heard a loud crunch and glanced out the window. The SOCOs were easing off the car's metal door. The passenger side of the car had been mauled by fire, but the driver's side was intact. I looked at the front of the car.

Then I looked again.

I opened my door and stumbled forwards, slamming to a halt at the blue and white tape.

A thickset officer frowned in my direction. 'Can I help you, love?'

Over his shoulder Durand clocked me and his face darkened. He held a hand up to Golden, then stalked towards me, eyes blazing.

'I told you to stay–'

'What's that? In the car. It's a body, isn't it? Who–'

'Waters!' Durand called out over his shoulder. 'Please escort Sophie to the *Herald* immediately.'

'Sam, please,' I reached for his arm but he brushed me off, 'is it Emily?'

Durand nodded curtly at Waters. 'When you're done, head back here. It's going to be a long night.'

I glanced back at the car, my heart in my throat. 'Sam! Is it Emily?' I screamed.

Durand stormed off without a backwards glance.

I turned desperately to Waters and, as our eyes met through the cold police-blue light, I could tell by her face I was right.

31

Emily: The day before the murder

A bus sloshes past, kicking up a puddle of brown water that soaks Emily's feet. She stares mournfully down at her orange trainers, then crosses the road to the centre of Manchester Square, her feet squelching.

She spots a couple sitting on her bench ahead and feels a flicker of frustration in her chest. Emily finds an empty bench in the corner and pretends to stretch her calf muscles. The entrance to Hamilton Law is only partially visible from here. Emily throws an anguished look at the couple on her bench. They're both dressed in head-to-toe black and covered in piercings. Could she ask them to move? *Excuse me, can we switch benches? I'm waiting for my husband's mistress to come out of that building.*

A builder's drill goes off somewhere startling a flock of birds. As they scatter into the air, Emily pulls the baby scan out of her pocket and stares at it. She knows every smudge, every shadow, every line. She can see Charlie's profile in the fuzz of dots.

Emily's stomach twists. So, Charlie is finally going to be a dad. One woman married Charlie before her, another is having his baby. *Always the bridesmaid, never the bride.*

Emily grinds her heel into the dirt, just as a creepy sensation spreads through her. She glances over at the couple on the bench. The woman is resting her head on her boyfriend's shoulder and picking something out of her teeth. Emily's gaze continues round the square, looking for . . . what? Someone watching her? She snorts. *Don't be so dramatic.* Her mind is playing tricks on her again. Two days ago, she fell asleep in front of the TV and woke with a start, convinced she could smell a stranger's aftershave on her. Emily wonders if her subconscious is fabricating something for her to worry over, to distract her from her marriage.

It wouldn't be the first time she'd imagined things that weren't true.

Emily plucks an apple from her rucksack and gets to work, wincing as her teeth grate against a seed. At first it was enough just to see Sabrina with her own eyes. But yesterday curiosity got the better of her and she followed Sabrina, feeling the thrill as she ducked behind cars and lingered on street corners as if she was in a TV show. Sabrina had disappeared into Fit Fit Fit, a shiny white gym with a neon-pink sign outside, and Emily turned round and went home. Perhaps that would have been it, an end to her stalking career, she thinks, if hadn't been for last night.

Now everything is different.

Emily closes her eyes and allows the memory to swallow her up. She was running around Regent's Park, yesterday afternoon, the breeze warm across her shoulders. As she ran, she held onto an image of Charlie and herself on their wedding day: winter sunlight pouring over them as they pose for photographs outside the registry office. Charlie dipping towards her, brushing her cheek with his lips. Emily squeezing his hand as he whispers, 'Well, hello Mrs Swift.' Emily has always wished someone got a better picture of that moment. She'd hang it in the sitting room. No, the hallway. Somewhere public where people can see just how happy they are. Because they are happy, deep down. Really, really happy. All marriages go through tough times. This is nothing she can't fix. Emily sprinted up her apartment steps feeling faintly positive for the first time in days. But, by the time she set foot inside their flat, the image of their wedding day was replaced by another: Charlie, cradling a red-haired baby. The happy vibes abandoned her. Emily peeled off her clothes and climbed into a hot shower. She forced her head under the scalding water, letting it wash away her angry, exhausted tears.

Moments later, she heard something.

'Charlie?' Emily stuck her head out of the shower curtain but all was quiet. *I'm losing my bloody mind.*

Emily worked the shampoo through her hair then stepped onto the bathmat and grabbed a towel. She glanced at the mirror, and froze.

There, in the steam on the mirror, someone had scrawled the words:

BABY BABY BABY BABY BABY BABY BABY BABY BABY

The words covered every inch of the mirror's surface. Emily's knees buckled and she landed hard. Who wrote that? Charlie, when he last showered? Has he gone insane? His nightmares are off the charts. Only last night she heard his nightmare unfolding through the wall. For a brief moment, Emily's heart had gone out to him as she visualised Charlie hot, half-naked, tangled in the spare room sheets. Then she pictured Sabrina's pointy chin and swishy hair and her heart hardened.

Emily glanced back at the scrawled words and, just like that, she knew exactly who wrote them.

She shifts her weight on the bench and checks her watch: 12.49 p.m. Sabrina is like clockwork. She leaves Hamilton Law at exactly 1 p.m. every day. Emily pulls her laptop out of her rucksack and fires it up, then she clicks on her new obsession. The website has taken her mind off cutting herself in ways she could never have dreamed. What's the point of probing Bert for information on Sabrina if she isn't going to use it? She flexes her fingers waiting for LegalLens.com to load, then she starts to type.

Which flame-haired Partner has been overdosing on happy pills?

Emily's eyes flicker to the Hamilton Law entrance just as a woman appears, dressed in a mac and pointy black pumps. Emily stuffs her laptop into her backpack and springs to her feet so quickly, the goth-couple give her a quizzical look.

Emily has to run to keep up with Sabrina. She follows her up Thayer Street, careful to keep her distance. As Emily turns right onto Weymouth Street, she hears footsteps behind her.

She glances over her shoulder but she's alone. Shaking her head she puts on a spurt. Sabrina is fifty feet away. She stops at a pedestrian crossing and turns. Emily glares at Sabrina's stomach and her insides tighten. Sabrina pauses outside a stucco-fronted building, then runs up the steps.

Emily feels her mouth forming the word before she knows what she's doing. 'Sabrina!'

Her voice carries across the street and Sabrina spins round. Emily is about to raise her hand when a man collides with her, knocking her to the floor.

'Sorry, love. I didn't mean–'

'Get off me!' Emily claws him out of the way but, by the time she's on her feet, Sabrina is gone.

Emily's blood is pumping, like liquid fire, round her body. She stumbles towards the building and trips up the steps. Nailed to the wall is a gold sign:

Dr Anne Lack, Obstetrician

Emily limps towards the wall and collapses, feeling the adrenaline seep out of her. She pictures Sabrina, lying on a bed on the other side of that wall, the doctor's hands on her rounded belly.

That's my baby. My baby. My baby.

Emily is so tired. Of holding it together. Of working so hard on a marriage that's disintegrating.

A memory drops into her head: the moments before her Rolls-Royce pulled up to the registry office, just Emily and her dad.

'How are you feeling, kid?' he'd asked, squeezing her hand.

'Like I'm going into battle.' It was an odd thing to say but her dad hadn't remarked on it. He understood more than anyone what she meant.

'I'm going to let you in on a little secret.' He tweaked his buttonhole and picked a fleck of something off his lapel. 'No relationship is equal. You might have to make allowances every now and again for Charlie.'

'The way you do with Mum?' Emily's voice was soft.

'All marriages face challenges, Em. You need to decide: are you going to dig your heels in about every small detail, or are you going to look at the bigger picture?'

The car turned onto the King's Road and crawled to a stop outside Chelsea Registry Office.

Emily smoothed down her dress. 'Why have you stayed with her all these years?'

Her dad was quiet for a moment. 'Because, without her, I'm nothing.' He reached out to open the door, then stopped. 'You've always been resourceful, kid. Trust your gut. You'll know what to do when the time comes.'

Emily leans against the railings and pictures her dad's kind, blue eyes. Then other visions flit through her head: the silver earring, the baby scan, Sabrina's red hair and Lizzie's perfect smile, the perfume bottle. *Moonflower.* Emily can practically smell the vanilla scent, right here on the street.

Something shifts inside Emily and her dad's eyes give way to another set of eyes; hard and red and female.

Emily pulls out her phone and dials Charlie's number.

Pick up pick up pick up pick up pick up.

It goes to voicemail: *'You've reached Charlie Swift. Leave some words.'*

'Baby it's me. We need to talk.' Emily fingers the diamond pendant around her neck and takes a deep breath. 'I know what you've been hiding from me. I know about Sabrina, about the . . . baby,' Emily's voice cracks and she blinks up at the sky.

You'll know what to do when the time comes.

Emily glances over her shoulder at the white-stucco building and starts to walk away.

'I won't let you throw me away, Charlie. We made a vow. To love each other, until the bitter end. I still love you. Do you love me? No, don't answer that. Not yet. We can fix this.'

When the time comes.

'So I forgive you, Charlie Swift. You hear me? I forgive you.' An image of Sabrina's round, swollen tummy hits her between the eyes and Emily clenches her fists. 'But I'm warning you. Sabrina, the baby. They're gone. OK?'

The time has come.

Emily unclenches her fists, squares her shoulders. 'I don't care how you handle it, just handle it. Or I will.'

32

A cold burst of wind ruffled my hair, and I buried my chin in my jacket, grimacing as pain swept through my neck. I paced up and down the street outside 23 Delaware Street, willing Kate to hurry up. I didn't want to be alone, not after what I'd just seen. *The butchered car. The blackened corpse.* The smoke still clung to the back of my throat.

My phone vibrated in my pocket; I took a long breath and yanked it out, grateful for the distraction. It was an email from Jeff.

Subject: Life in the old dog yet

Hello Sophie, Jeff your hero, here. Take your time with that quote for my story. But, in the meantime, I've unearthed something I think you'll want to see.
The attachment shows Hector Marlon's membership database: every person registered at the new Christ Clan.
Look at entry 43.

The sound of footsteps. I tore my eyes away to find Kate storming towards me.

'All that work on the Rowntree exposé and now we can't find bloody Bert Hugh—' She stopped, sweeping her brown eyes over my face. 'What's the matter?'

It was only when I put a hand to my cheek that I realised I was crying. Then I took a deep breath. 'Emily's dead.'

'What?'

'I've just come from Crystal Palace.' My shrill voice rose into the night and I wiped my eyes. 'She was set alight, Kate. In a car.'

Kate stared at me as if she wasn't seeing me, her voice a whisper. 'Water and fire. You were right.'

A car sped past, kicking up a puddle of rainwater. It sloshed all over the pavement, splattering our shoes.

Kate shifted round and stared up at the building. 'So, why are we at Charlie and Emily's apartment?'

I leaned back against the railings and cleared my throat. 'Something's been bothering me ever since the day the police searched this place. Emily let me look round and I noticed something, in Charlie's wardrobe. Lizzie's wedding ring was hidden there.'

Kate flicked a loose curl behind her ear. 'I don't follow.'

'That ring was sacred to Charlie. If he really fled, I don't think he'd leave it behind.'

Kate narrowed her eyes. 'What do you mean "if he really fled"?'

I pulled out a tissue and blew my nose, giving myself a moment to order my thoughts. 'Look, the past forty-eight hours have painted a dark picture of Charlie. He was broken by his mum; desperate for somewhere to belong, and Laurence Marlon's twisted world provided it. We only ever knew Charlie as a husband, a friend, a colleague. A normal guy living his life like the rest of us.

But there's nothing normal about Charlie Swift.' I remembered Jeff Johnson's story about the killer who'd buried his childhood abuse dangerously deep. 'What happened to Charlie back then, that stuff doesn't just disappear. It lays dormant.'

I pointed at the townhouse. 'My Christ Clan source told me how the Golden Flock were taught to exploit a building's weak spot. When Charlie was sent out on missions, he could hide for days inside people's homes without them ever knowing he was there.'

I nodded towards the scaffolding where the wind was filling the tarpaulin sheet like a sail. 'This place has been decimated by builders over the past year. There have got to be weak spots, right?'

Kate chewed her thumbnail. 'What are you saying, that Charlie has been hiding here this whole time?'

I shrugged. 'It's a theory. But think about it: that night he attacked Emily. How did he get in? The police had a surveillance team parked outside. What if he's been here the whole time, spying on Emily, just like he spied on his mum when he was a kid?'

Kate frowned. 'Why not just run away? What's his endgame?'

'I don't know. He wants to stay close to the action?' I caught the scepticism on her face. 'Listen, I know it sounds nuts, but I keep coming back to Lizzie's ring. Charlie left it behind because he knew he could go back for it any time he wanted.'

Kate zipped her jacket up to her chin and huddled her arms round herself. 'So, what are we looking for exactly?'

'A weakness.' I hauled myself up and stretched out my legs to get the blood flowing. 'Anything that looks as if it might lead inside the building. The front of the building is too well-lit by the streetlamps. But there's an alleyway out back. Did you bring a torch?'

Kate stood up and cast her eyes over the building. 'What if Charlie's still here?' She said it matter-of-factly, but I could hear the anxiety in her voice.

'All we're looking for is the weak spot. Nothing more. If we find anything, we call the cops.'

Kate held my gaze, then she fished around in her bag and pulled out a torch. 'Let's go, Nancy Drew.'

We scurried round the edge of the building and into a narrow alleyway that ran the full length of the street. The buildings soared up either side of us, hemming us in and heightening the smell of wet tarmac and sour dustbins. I switched on my torch, nodding at Kate to do the same. As we crept along, I noticed that each numbered building had its own set of metal steps leading down to lower ground level and I ran my torch around each stairwell.

'I can't see anything,' said Kate in a low voice, as we passed a yellow skip piled high with planks of wood and rusty metal poles.

I fired my torch at the building, counting out the number of stairwells in my head. I trudged up to number 23 and leaned over the metal railings. As I flashed my torch into the darkness below, my beam hit something in the wall.

I climbed down the steps, my shoes slipping on the wet stone surface. 'Kate, look.'

Two feet off the ground, a metal grate was embedded in the brick exterior wall. I held the torch between my teeth, then hooked my fingers around the metal and gave it a tug. The grate came away from the wall and I stumbled backwards into Kate.

'Shit, sorry.'

Kate didn't respond; she was already aiming her torch into the hole. After a few seconds, she sat back on her heels and pushed her hair behind her ears. 'There's a tunnel. Not huge, but definitely big enough to crawl through.'

There was a bang as a blast of wind knocked over a plastic bin at the top of the steps and we both jumped.

I let out a nervous laugh, then nodded at the tunnel. 'Where do you think it leads?'

'I don't know. Could be an old sewer tunnel. Or–'

A faint tapping noise drifted through the tunnel. Kate stiffened and motioned for me to switch off my torch. I hit the button and we were plunged into darkness. We leaned towards the opening in the wall.

There it was again; a metallic tap-tap-tap. Then another noise. A low cough.

Kate stiffened. 'Weak spot. Let's call the cops.'

'But–'

'No buts. I'm pulling rank.' She moved away from the tunnel, and I saw a rectangle of light floating in the air as she unlocked her phone. 'Hang on, what if there's another way out at the front of the building? One of us should wait round there?' She sighed. 'I'll go. Can't get a bloody signal down in this stairwell anyway. Will you be all right?'

'Sure,' I said, hoping Kate couldn't tell I was lying.

I heard the sound of Kate's boots running up the steps and I tried to calm my breathing. I moved closer to the tunnel and strained my ears. The sounds had vanished. I shifted my weight and pressed a hand against the brick wall.

The brick wall.

I closed my eyes and all of a sudden I was back in Vanessa's cellar, surrounded by carvings and blood and tiny skeletons. A sour taste spread across my tongue. And then I saw myself slumped on Charlie's bed; drugged, vulnerable; could feel his hands on me, hot and probing. I refused to give in to the panic. I needed a distraction. I pulled out my phone and opened Jeff's email.

The attachment shows Hector Marlon's membership database; every person registered at the new Christ Clan.

Look at entry 43.

I clicked on the attachment and scanned the list of names. My eyes landed on number 43, and the air went out of my chest.

Name: Thomas Kent
Joined: 2013
Location: Bournemouth Clan Centre
Known family: Antony & Harriet Kent. Sister, Sophie (*The London Herald*).
Notes: drug-addiction, self-harmer, serial fantasist. Suicide risk. Deceased.

Tommy? Christ Clan? I slid to the ground in disbelief. It was like two worlds colliding. I should have known; I should have felt him there, in the fabric of the place. *How had I missed it?* Suddenly I realised why the graffiti cross logo felt oddly familiar. I'd seen it before: the blue keyring dangling from the zip of Tommy's beaten-up backpack the last time he showed up at my house. What was it Damo said that night in the bar? *Tommy bounced with different crowds. City, coast, wherever he could disappear to.*

I fell back against the wall.

The Post-It note with my name on it. This was the reason Charlie had drawn my attention to Christ Clan. He'd discovered the same thing about Tommy. My heart hammered in my chest. I stared down at my phone in disbelief.

Thomas Kent. Self-harmer. Serial fantasist. Deceased.

The black letters danced in front of my worn-out eyes. The walls seemed to close on me, shrinking the space, trapping me. *Like those tiny birds.*

I stood up and paced round the stairwell, desperately trying to count out my breaths and hold the panic attack off.

Help me, Soph. Tommy's voice was loud in my ear, broken and pleading, like it was in the voicemail he left me the day before he died. The phone call I never returned because I was so angry with him. If I'd answered the phone, would he still be alive?

Help me, Soph. I rocked backwards and forwards, trying to clear my head of Tommy's voice. Why hadn't he told me about his condition? Why hadn't he told me about Christ Clan? Images flew at me: Tommy, trapped behind six-foot gates. Tommy, dirty

and desperate. I blinked and the pin-sharp image of two figures plunging a syringe into Tommy's arm burned in the air. It
was supposed to look like an overdose. An accident, or suicide.
A homeless junkie. No one would care. As I doubled over, gulping down air, a thought knocked the breath out of my chest.
Samantha Hartley. She was injected with a fatal overdose, then
tossed in a river. The same thing happened to Tommy. Was it
a coincidence, or was this Christ Clan's method of getting rid
of people? Had Tommy unearthed something at Christ Clan?
Something that meant he had to be silenced?

I'm coming for you, Soph.

Tommy's voice again, only mean and thin. I heard a laugh.
I flinched as Tommy's face hovered in front of my eyes. It looked
so real. Silvery-white hair, eager smile, small nose bridged with
freckles. I could smell the peppermint on his skin. I reached out
to touch him and the vision shimmered. Then his eyes started to
rot in his skull and he held up a knife.

I'm coming for you, Soph.

I scrabbled backwards. Was this how it was going to be now?
The new knowledge twisting and shaping my memories of
Tommy?

The panic reared up and plunged its teeth deep into my skin.
My hands hit the stone floor. My ears filled with the sound of
laughter; a vicious laughter that sent me shooting forwards. I
was at the mouth of the tunnel, climbing, clawing, dragging
myself onwards. My chest was so tight I could hardly breathe.
Was Tommy really murdered? Was everyone lying to me? Had
Tommy really wanted me dead?

I could hear the sound of Tommy's ragged breathing. A thud thud thud. Rustling.

I froze. Those sounds weren't in my head.

Someone else was in the tunnel.

I breathed in a rancid smell, heard a grunting noise, something scraping against the floor. Then the sound was coming towards me.

What the fuck am I doing?

I squeezed back round and started to scrabble forwards. I'd crawled in so far, I couldn't see the tunnel opening anymore. My hands scraped along the sharp floor, kicking up dust. The noise grew louder. He was gaining on me. I clawed faster, the sharp stone floor cutting into my hands. My blood was on fire. I knew I was making a noise but I was desperate to get out before he caught up with me.

I threw a glance over my shoulder, not knowing how much space there was between us.

'Sophie?' Kate's urgent whisper echoed down the tunnel. I groped in the darkness, towards the sound of her voice.

'He's behind me, Kate!'

A white light flashed ahead. Kate's torch. A growl pierced the air over my shoulder. I was twenty feet away from the entrance. Fifteen feet. Ten.

I reached out to grab hold of the opening, when a hand closed around my ankle. It dragged me backwards and I screamed, hitting the stone hard. I felt the weight of him as he clambered over me. Then the sound of a sickening crack outside.

I lay still, my heart pounding in my ears. My ankle burned; I could taste the dust at the back of my throat.

'Kate,' my voice sounded like it was coming from far away. 'Are you OK?'

A faint groan. 'I'm bleeding. My head.'

I hauled myself forwards and squirmed out of the tunnel. Kate was lying in a heap at the bottom of the steps. I scrabbled towards her, switching on my torch with trembling hands.

Kate was grey and her teeth were chattering. 'He hit me. He fucking hit me.'

In the distance, a siren pierced the air. I pointed the light towards Kate and saw a trail of blood running down her face. I glanced back at the opening in the wall and licked my dry lips. 'Listen, do you think you can make it to the end of the alleyway by yourself?'

Blood was dripping onto Kate's jacket and she raised a hand to assess the damage. 'Why?'

I clenched my jaw and looked her in the eye. 'Don't you want to know where that tunnel leads? After everything that bastard's done to us, I'm damned if we're not getting the story.'

Kate held my gaze, then nodded once. 'We'd better get an award for this.'

She squeezed my arm, then crawled towards the steps. I clamped my torch between my teeth and ducked back inside the tunnel. The rancid smell I noticed before was stronger now. I crawled forwards, ignoring the cuts in my hands. Just after the point where I'd turned round, the tunnel veered sharply to the left. I followed it round and slammed to a halt, staring in amazement.

The tunnel had opened out into a space that was about six feet high and ten feet long. Along one wall was a grimy sleeping bag and a pile of clothes. I kicked the empty whisky bottles out of my way and edged forwards. In the corner stood a bucket that was filled to the brim with faeces. The stench was like nothing I'd smelt before. An upturned box stood next to it, with wires running along the floor. I shone the torch around the space. The walls were covered with tiny carvings. Triangles, painted a thick dark red. I knew blood when I saw it. I clamped a hand over my mouth, retching violently. With some effort I pulled myself together and grabbed my phone. I snapped pictures; my flash illuminating the space with a cold, white light. I turned to face the final corner, and spotted something on the floor. Plastic cords, crusted with blood. They'd been cut. Next to them were Emily's orange trainers.

I stumbled backwards and cried out as I half-fell through a hole in the wall. It was the tunnel, narrowing back into the same size as the one I'd crawled through. I swallowed thickly and forced myself through the gap. I had to know where it led. Seconds later I found myself at a dead end. I ran my hands over the surface of the wall. *It's made of wood.*

An image of Vanessa's cellar raced through my mind. *The fake wall.* I swivelled round onto my bottom, and kicked against the wood with both feet. It fell away and a cool, damp breeze hit me in the face. I slithered out of the tunnel and knocked into something. I dropped my torch and fumbled around in the darkness. It was a laundry basket. Next to it was a washing machine. I scrabbled past the shelves filled with tools and rusty paint tins and raced up the rickety wooden staircase. I stumbled towards it and groped for the door handle. One push and I was out.

I blinked as a soft, yellow light hit my eyes. Then I lurched forwards.

Into Charlie and Emily's hallway.

33

I woke up, jagged and raw, and fumbled for my phone: 5.01 a.m.

I lay back, forcing my breathing to slow and my muscles to soften. I'd barely managed four hours sleep. After giving the police a statement and accompanying Kate to hospital, my head finally hit the pillow at one in the morning. Kate had barely spoken to me at the hospital. I knew she was angry. I'd taken an unnecessary risk and she'd paid the price. Nine stitches along her hairline. I couldn't explain myself even if I'd wanted to. After Emily's death, and the bombshell about Tommy, my mind had dipped into its darkest hollows.

In that moment, I didn't care who came for me.

I shifted onto my side and saw two blue oblong pills sticking out from under my pillow. Last night I'd craved the artificial peace they'd bring. But, just as I was about to knock them back, I heard Durand's voice in my head: *You're no use to Tommy if you're dead.* I stuffed the pills under my pillow and lay there, forcing myself to feel everything. And I realised something. Despite his condition, Tommy had never hurt me. He managed to control his urges, and I owed it to him to do the same.

The watery dawn light lit my bedroom like a dreary painting. I pushed myself up to sitting and stretched my arms over my head. I needed caffeine and a shower. Today was going to take every ounce of strength I had. Rowley had emailed me late last night with a battle plan and I was determined to deliver the goods, not least because I was worried Kate would tell Rowley how reckless I was last night. I didn't want to give him an excuse to fire me again. Once Emily's death was made public, we'd be in the throes of a full-scale media storm. Given the *Herald*'s starring role, Rowley was gunning for blanket coverage. Legal were checking through the Rowntree/Bert Hughes exposé, and in the meantime Rowley wanted to go big on Emily. The fact that she was snatched leaving a police press conference only worsened the deal for the Met and Rowley wanted us to publicly call for Golden's resignation. He also wanted a spread on Charlie's life, boxouts on the Christ Clan, an updated timeline of events, and two double-page spreads on Emily: the woman who'd divided a nation. I pictured the scorched car and the silhouette on the front seat. A lump caught in my throat. I was supposed to be Emily's friend but the last time we saw each other, I'd called her a liar in front of a room full of people. I should never have listened to Durand, should never have put Emily through that.

Now I'd never get the chance to say sorry.

I sat cross-legged on my bed and spread out my notes, scouring everything I had: Sabrina's last known movements; the emails between her and Charlie; the derogatory comments on LegalLens.com, interview notes with Charlie's friend, Dominic, with Emily's friend, Sinead, with the reporter Jeff Johnson, and former Christ Clan member, Fred. I reread Charlie's letters to his mum, Emily's blog posts, the newspaper cuttings on Christ Clan. Then I started to type.

An hour later, I sagged against my pillows feeling drained. I glanced at my phone, half-expecting an update from the Met's press office to say Charlie had been arrested. But there was only an email from Rowley, asking if Emily's death was official.

I rubbed the grit out of my eyes, then glanced at the clock, wondering if 7 a.m. was too early to call Durand. Moments later my phone beeped with an email from the general patholo-gist, Dr David Sonoma. He'd attached Vanessa's post-mortem and said he'd call when he got to work. I opened the attachment and studied the report, my eyes drifting to the stark diagram. Vanessa's body was covered in abrasions and scars.

I took a swig of cold coffee just as my phone rang.

I picked it up.

'Have you learned nothing from me over the years?' The fury in Durand's voice made me flinch.

'Excuse me?'

'How dare you contaminate a crime scene.'

I blinked. 'You mean Charlie's flat. Look, I'm sorry, I needed–'

'To get the fucking story. Yes, I've heard that before.'

I raised my eyebrows; Durand never swore.

'Sam, I–'

'And next you'll want a favour from me. You don't get to trample anywhere you please, making my job ten times harder in the process, and then expect me to help you out.'

I could feel the anger building in my chest. I rubbed my eyes. I knew I should get off the phone as fast as possible. I was exhausted and ill-equipped for a fight. We'd broken new ground yesterday in the car and I didn't want it to go to waste. As a last-ditch attempt, I tried for conciliatory.

'Sam, you're right. It was stupid of me.'

'Damn right it was stupid.'

'Fine, I get the fucking message.'

'Not to mention dangerous, and unprofessional and–'

'Unprofessional. Don't make me laugh.'

Durand's voice hardened. 'What's that supposed to mean?'

I shook my head and glared at the ceiling. 'Thanks to you Emily died thinking no one believed her.'

'I hardly think that's–'

'Fair? You think I don't know what's been going on?' I clenched the duvet as a tide of adrenaline and exhaustion and stress and fury spilled out of me. 'You've been trying to undermine DCI Golden from the outset. You thought you could handle someone else being in charge, but you can't. I know exactly why Golden irritates you. Because he's young and successful and you can't fucking stand it.'

'Sophie.'

I ignored the warning in Durand's voice. 'The more I think about it, the dodgier that press conference feels. It was about undermining Golden, wasn't it? You could have gone to him with the evidence but you didn't.'

'That's because I genuinely believed Emily was hiding something. It was the most effective way for–'

'Bollocks,' I gave a shrill laugh. 'You were show-boating. Using me to go behind Golden's back. Pretending you gave a shit about me so I'd do your dirty work.'

'I haven't pretended anything. I do give a shit about you, although God knows why when you're such a pain in the arse.'

'You know what pisses me off the most?' I rocked onto my knees and shuffled towards the edge of the bed. 'You play the straight guy but you're wors—'

'You're being childish.' Durand's voice could have cut glass. 'I can't talk to you in this state. You need to calm dow—'

'Don't you dare tell me to calm down. Thanks to you, Emily is dead. Charlie is free, and he's probably coming for me next. For all I know he's watching me right–'

'Sophie!' Durand's shout stopped me in my tracks. He gave a sharp sigh. 'I wasn't going to do this over the phone. I thought you deserved to hear it in person.'

I punched the pillow next to me. 'Hear what?'

'Charlie isn't coming for you.'

I looked up. 'You've caught him?'

'Not exactly.'

I blinked furiously as my frazzled brain scrabbled to keep up. 'Sam, I don't foll—' As I started to speak, it hit me and the phone went heavy in my hand.

When Durand spoke, his voice had softened. 'Dental records confirmed it an hour ago. The body in the car: it's Charlie.'

I made a strangled noise, then doubled over, snatching down what little breaths I could from the airless room.

'There was a suicide note. In his flat,' said Durand.

I steadied myself against the bedside table as an image of the blackened car flashed across my vision. 'But that car was . . . *Charlie set himself alight*?'

'I can't go into details. Not yet.'

'Sam, please.' The agony in my voice reverberated down the phone. For a moment, neither of us spoke. I pictured Durand staring down at the ground, chewing his lip.

'All I can say is this: yesterday's storm meant the fire didn't burn for as long as it was supposed to.'

I looked up. 'What do you mean?'

'I mean, there's evidence this wasn't suicide. That Charlie might have been held captive somewhere.'

'He . . . what?' I tried to stand, but my legs went from under me. I thought back to the secret room. The restraints, the blood. I lurched to the window and yanked it open, desperate for air. 'But, the tunnel. If Charlie was already dead, who was that?'

There was a pause. 'That's what we've been working through the night to ascertain.'

As I hung out the window, breathing in the air that sliced through my tender throat, my mind screeched to a halt. 'What about Emily?'

A beat. Then Durand's voice, grim and flat. 'There's no sign of her. She's disappeared into thin air.'

34

As I ricocheted out of the lift, the newsroom lights flooded my vision like molten glass.

Kate folded her arms when she spotted me. 'Well, if it isn't our resident masochis—' She stopped dead as she noticed my expression. 'Are you OK?'

I shook my head, numbly. 'Charlie's dead.'

Kate froze. 'The police got him?'

I glanced towards Rowley's office. Through the open door, his bald head bobbed up and down behind piles of paper on his desk. The next thing I knew, I'd careened straight into his office without knocking.

Rowley opened his mouth to bawl me out, then he saw my face. 'What's happened?'

'Charlie. He's dead. And, fuck,' I collapsed on the chair opposite his desk and buried my head in my hands, 'fuck fuck fuck.'

Someone squeezed my shoulder and I peeped through my fingers to see Kate kneeling next to me, her dark eyes solemn. Behind her, Mack and Rahid had filed into the room and were filling the chairs, eyeing me warily.

Rowley peeled off his glasses. 'Rahid, close the door.'

'Kent, what the fu—' Mack began, then closed his mouth. I presumed Rowley was signalling him to shut up and I was grateful. My thoughts thrashed around my skull; I couldn't compute Durand's words. *Charlie was held captive.*

I pulled myself upwards, out of my own head, and stared at the window. 'The body, in the car last night. It's Charlie.'

A collective gasp, then everyone started talking at once.

Rowley raised a hand, his eyes never leaving my face. 'Let Sophie finish.'

With a shuddering breath, I related what Durand had told me. 'I don't know any more than that, but there must be some-thing concrete in the post-mortem that's pointing to the fact that Charl—' I pressed my lips together as I felt tears burn the back of my eyes.

Kate's grip tightened on my shoulder. 'But if Charlie was dead by the time we went to his apartment, who was that in the tunnel?'

I shook my head, unable to hold back the tears any longer.

Rowley leaned forwards, his leather chair creaking loudly, his face ashen. 'So, let me get this straight. The police think Charlie was murdered? That someone is setting him up? What about Emily? Do they know where she is?'

Emily.

I stared at Rowley. 'I haven't even updated you all. It didn't seem relevant when I thought Emily was dead but . . .' I filled them in on the CCTV footage from Hamilton Law.

'Emily knew about Sabrina this whole time . . .' Kate's hand flew to her mouth.

I nodded, trying desperately to tug at the corners of my flailing thoughts. 'I thought she was the body in the car, but . . .'

Rahid rattled his pen between his teeth and I glanced at him. 'What's the latest with Bert Hughes? Did you get hold of him?'

'He's disappeared into the ether,' said Rahid. 'Hasn't shown up to work, not answering his door, and his phone's switched off.'

My phone rang and I snatched it out of my pocket, then glanced round the room. 'I have to take this.'

I bolted across the newsroom and flung myself onto my chair.

Then I drew in a long, shaky breath and answered the phone.

'Morning, Sophie,' said Dr Sonoma.

'David, I – um . . .' My words came out in a hoarse whisper.

There was a pause. 'Are you all right?'

I closed my eyes. 'Charlie Swift.'

'Yes.' Sonoma cleared his throat. 'Unexpected.'

I lunged for the bottle of water on my desk and gulped it down. The shock was starting to subside and I had questions. I jabbed my fingernails into my palm, forcing myself to focus. 'What happened to Charlie?'

'Sophie, you know I'm not at liberty to speculate.'

I dug my teeth into my lip so hard I tasted blood. 'David, the past week has been . . .' I closed my eyes, focused on the metallic taste in my mouth. 'If there is a chance my friend didn't kill Sabrina, I need to know.' My voice dropped to a whisper. 'Please, I need to know.'

A long silence. I could sense Sonoma running through options in his head. I stared at my chipped nail varnish, saying a silent prayer that he would trust me enough to put me out of my misery.

'Charlie's body, Sophie. It was in bad shape. There wasn't much to go on. But,' Sonoma sighed heavily, 'there is evidence that he was restrained when the car was set on fire.'

'What do you mean?'

Sonoma's voice took on a detached, clinical quality. 'When a body is burned, the contraction of the muscles forces them into a pugilistic stance. A boxer's stance, if you will. But if a body is restrained when it's set alight, the bindings will prevent this muscle contraction. Well, for as long as the bindings remain intact.' I picked up my pen to take notes, but my hand was shaking so much I couldn't write. 'I was able to test parts of the right-hand side of the body, where the fire didn't fully catch. There were deep welts in the victim's wrist along with fragments of plastic. My forensic lab contact tells me the material is consistent with the plastic ties found in the cellar where Charlie was held.'

I raised my eyes to the ceiling, as tears spilled down my cheeks. 'Has Charlie been there this whole time?'

Sonoma softened his voice. 'As I said, there's not a whole lot to go on. But, given the abrasions and sores I've found on the areas of skin undamaged by the fire, I'd hazard a guess that the victim has been imprisoned for a considerable length of time.'

I closed my eyes, allowing the tears to drop onto my lap. An image of the putrid cellar burned in my mind. The stench, the blood, the blackness. What did Charlie go through down there, trapped, terrified, with no one to hear him?

Without thinking, my eyes drifted to Charlie's desk, as if I half-expected to see the heap of dark curls and everything would be OK. *Hey, Soph, want to grab a bite after this is all over?*

The pain was unbearable. I took a breath and my hand went to my neck. 'David, there's something I don't understand. If Charlie has been in the cellar this whole time, how did his hair end up in my car the day I was attacked?'

Sonoma gave a short, dry cough. 'As far as I can see there are two options. Secondary transfer is one. One of Charlie's hairs ended up on the killer's clothes and, when he attacked you, it was deposited in your car.'

'What's the second?'

'It's an even longer shot. According to the forensic report, the hair sample taken from your car comprised only the shaft of the hair, and not the follicle, or the root. Without the root, all you can test for is mitochondrial DNA, which is passed on to children through their mother's DNA.'

I shook my head, not following. 'Can you translate this?'

Sonoma chuckled. 'Sorry. I'm saying that the hair sample from your car could also match a sibling.'

'Except Charlie's an only child, so, great.' I slumped forwards in my chair and lay my forehead on the desk.

Sonoma drew in a breath. 'Listen, Sophie, we can talk about Vanessa's post-mortem later if you need some . . . time to yourself.'

I blinked, appreciating his tact. 'No, I'm fine.' I sat up straight and pulled my file towards me, determined to hold it together. 'I was looking for signs of foul play,' I said, sifting through my papers until I reached Vanessa's post-mortem, 'but that was obviously before I found out about Charlie.' The fact I had Vanessa post-mortem now felt like a betrayal.

'Look, as I'm on the line, I'll give you my thoughts,' said Sonoma. 'Vanessa's official cause of death was smoke inhalation. The level of alcohol in her bloodstream, coupled with the fall down the stairs, was certainly enough to render her unconscious. The only possible irregularity is the way that she landed when she fell.'

'What do you mean?'

'Well, according to the report, Vanessa's body cleared the bottom step entirely. I would have expected a shorter spillover.'

I drummed my fingers on the desk, picturing the narrow, dingy hallway. 'What are you saying? That someone pushed her?'

Sonoma took a long breath. 'Or she took a running jump, which isn't likely, not with that much alcohol in her system. But I didn't perform the PM so it's difficult to be certain.'

I heard people in the background and Sonoma must have covered the receiver with his hand because the voices turned muffled.

My eyes drifted across the crude diagram of Vanessa's body. I leaned forward.

That's odd.

Sonoma was back. 'Sorry, Sophie. The vultures are circling. I've got a meeting with the Board now. Is there anything else?'

'David, what's that marking on Vanessa's stomach?'

A pause. 'Judging by the position, I'd say it was the result of a C-section.' I heard a voice in the background and Sonoma sighed. 'I must go. Take care, Sophie. And my condolences for your loss.'

The line went dead and I sat there, staring at the space in front of my eyes. Something flickered at the back of my mind. I closed my eyes, trusting my instincts enough not to force it.

Charlie's voice drifted into my head. What was it he once told me about Vanessa? *The last favour she did me was four decades ago when she squeezed me out of her you-know-what.*

Charlie was a natural birth. He was born 7 August 1975. My hands went to the stack of items Gordon had given me. I rifled through until I found the two photographs of Vanessa in hospital, cradling Charlie in her arms. I raked my eyes over each photograph. The background was identical in both. Light grey curtains, custard-yellow walls. Vanessa was wearing the same checked-green hospital gown, her arms clutching a baby wrapped in blue. But in one photograph, a newspaper was folded on the bed. I squinted at the picture, trying to make out the headline. *Who killed the Owen girl?* I typed the words into my search engine and the *Herald*'s archives came up. I held my breath as I trawled through until I spotted it. I opened the front page and zoomed in on the date. *14 May 1973.*

I stared back at the photograph. At the two bundles of blue.

As I leaped up, my chair hit the floor with a thud.

35

Emily: present day

The cold shivers across her skin, burrows inside her pores. Emily curls up for warmth, covering her nose with her cardigan. The smell of sewage is so intense she can taste it. Emily blinks, trying to adjust her eyes to the gloom. It's silent other than the distant noise of birds. The floor beneath her is cold and jagged. She runs her palm along it. She tries to remember what happened. One minute she was running. The next she was being lifted off the ground. Dragged backwards. A sting in her arm.

How long have I been here?

She crawls forwards, feeling her way round the stone wall. She hears something. A cough?

Emily presses herself against the wall. Her breath jabs her ribs.

Footsteps. A jangling noise. Something scraping against the stone. Emily holds her breath. A torch beam hits her in the face. She scrambles her fists over her eyes as pain shoots through her head.

She can't see the figure behind the light.

'Please.' That's all she can muster. The light comes closer.

Emily looks up and, for a split-second, the torch beam wavers and Emily catches a glimpse of the man behind the light.

She doesn't see much.

She doesn't need to.

Emily starts to cry. He strides towards her and she thinks he's going to say something.

She doesn't see the fist coming until it's too late.

36

'This isn't about Emily at all.' I skidded through Rowley's door, my brain on fire, then spread Vanessa's post-mortem and the photographs of her in hospital on his desk. 'Vanessa had another child. In 1973; two years before Charlie was born. Same hospital, different baby.' I jabbed a finger at the desk. 'Charlie always said he was an only child.'

Four pairs of eyes stared at me in unison as I related what Dr Sonoma told me. 'The hair from my car, it was a match for Charlie. But my source said it could also have come from a sibling.'

Kate picked up the photograph of Vanessa cradling her baby. 'You think she gave her kid up for adoption?'

I grabbed her sleeve. 'You know what I'm going to ask.'

Kate pulled out her phone, heading for the door. 'I'll see what I can do.'

Kate had delved deep into the National Adoption Agency for a story she'd worked on two years ago when twelve-year-old Ayisha Nadim was kidnapped from her school in Balham. The city feared the worst for the little girl with dark pigtails and large, dark eyes. But nine agonising days later Ayisha was found unharmed in a council flat in Aldgate. The perpetrator was her birth mother, Radha Sabberwal, a distraught woman barely out of her teens, whose strict Muslim parents bullied her into giving away a baby born out of wedlock. Radha had watched Ayisha from a distance until, one day, she cracked. Covering herself in a lace-trimmed hijab, similar to the one she'd seen Ayisha's adoptive mum wear, Radha strolled into the playground and led the little girl out by the hand. Ayisha, assuming she was one of her mummy's friends, went willingly. Kate's inside source worked closely with the *Herald* to break the adoption story, which ultimately narrowed the field for the increasingly desperate police. The girl was reunited with her family and, in a happy twist, her adoptive parents reached out to her birth mother and offered to let her into their daughter's life. We all remembered the story because, in our line of work, happy endings are few and far between.

'So, where's Emily, then?' said Rahid, frowning.

Mack dismissed him and puffed up his chest, the way he always did when he was feeling overlooked. 'Look, I know this isn't going to make me popular, but is anyone else concerned that we've got six spreads ready to go on Charlie the killer? What the fuck are we going to do?'

I gave him an incredulous look. 'We're going to find out what really happ—' Kate appeared in the doorway with an odd expression on her face. 'What is it?'

She closed the door and ran a hand through her brown curls. 'You're right. There was an adoption. December 1973. The record shows the baby's mother as Vanessa Swift, father unknown.'

I chewed my fingernail, watching her closely. 'Does it say who the adoptive parents are?'

Kate perched on the edge of Rowley's desk. 'This is where it gets interesting. The baby's first name is registered as Mark. And he went to a local couple: Pamela and Les Miller.'

I froze. 'Miller? Mark Miller?'

The Christ Clan kid. I heard Jeff Johnson's rasping voice: *he was beaten to a pulp. Hospitalised.*

I shook my head at Kate. 'That doesn't make sense. I spoke to his dad, Les. He never said Mark was adopted.'

Kate shrugged, glancing at her notebook. 'Well, according to public record he is Vanessa's son.'

I thought back to my conversation with Les Miller. *The stress that boy caused us. I wanted to send him back.* At the time I thought it was an odd phrase.

My brain spun along in a vacuum. I had ingested so much information in the last few hours, I felt giddy. All of a sudden Rowley's office felt overbearingly hot and I yanked off my sweater. *Father unknown.* I thought back to what Gordon had told me about Vanessa's past.

I tossed my sweater on the chair, then paced to the window, trying to order my thoughts. 'OK, Charlie's stepfather, Gordon, told me that Vanessa was raped in the early seventies. What if she got pregnant?'

Kate chewed her pen. 'That would explain why she gave the baby away.'

I stared out of the window at the line of traffic snaking along Kensington High Street in the morning sun. The sun glinted off a bus's windscreen and I blinked.

'Shit, think about all the times in the past week Charlie has been spotted. CCTV picked him up at the bank in Bournemouth. Emily claimed she saw him in their apartment, Gordon saw him at Vanessa's house, I saw him in my car,' I whirled round to face Kate. 'Don't you see: Charlie was trapped in the cellar the whole time . . .'

'. . . so the man you all saw must look like Charlie,' she finished.

I lunged for my bag and dug out the Christ Clan leaflet. 'What if we've been barking up the wrong tree? What if Charlie had nothing to do with Christ Clan at all and the kid standing behind Laurence Marlon in this picture is his half-brother?' I thought back to my conversation in the Old Goat pub with Jeff and Fred. Fred had identified the boy in the photograph as the Starling. But he said none of them used their real names. I was the one who had made the leap and assumed the Starling was Charlie.

Rowley, who'd been silent up till now, cleared his throat. 'Sophie, tell us everything you know about Miller.'

I sat down. 'Well, up till now, I knew Miller as the kid who was hospitalised after one of Marlon's sadistic games went too far. I assumed the Starling was the one who put him there. It never occurred to me that Miller and the Starling could be the same person.' I recalled Fred's words: *Marlon loved him, but he gave him the roughest ride, too.*

'Do you think Mark knew he was adopted?' asked Rowley.

'I don't know. I mean Les never even mention—' The fog started to lift and I grabbed my file. *The letters.* I scattered them across the desk.

I won't forgive you. Let me come home. I want to be a normal family. Why can't you see that? No one you love will be safe. This is your fault.

'Charlie didn't write these,' my voice was breathless, 'Mark did.'

Mack tilted his chair back and scratched his head. 'OK, so say this kid Mark gets kicked out of his adoptive home, joins Christ Clan, grows up warped. And then what? Waits three decades then kills his half-brother's mistress, Sabrina Hobbs? That's ludicrous.'

'OK, let's look at the evidence,' I said, leaning against Rowley's desk. 'Start with Mark as a kid. His adoptive father is a fuckhead; Mark drifts into a sadistic cult where life gets even worse. He tracks down his birth mother and places his future happiness in her hands, but she doesn't want to know him.' I pictured the scene in Vanessa's cellar. 'He hides out in her home and spies on her.'

'And, as far as he's concerned, little brother, Charlie, has taken his place,' said Kate, frowning.

'So why not kill Charlie back then?' said Mack, dropping his chair down and fidgeting with his sleeve in an attempt to look at ease. 'I mean, if he's so–'

'Say that again,' I said, staring at Mack.

'If he hated Charlie so much, why not kill him back then?'

No one you love will be safe. I hadn't understood that line until now. I paced in front of Rowley's desk. 'Charlie's childhood accidents. They weren't accidents.'

Kate raised her eyebrows. 'Come again?'

'Think about it. In the space of eighteen months – at the period we know Mark is involved in Christ Clan – Charlie is concussed falling out of a tree, totals his bike, breaks his leg in a car crash, and almost dies in a fire. Charlie-Cat, his friends called him. Nine lives. Except Charlie wasn't accident-prone, he was being targeted.'

Mack touched a bony finger to his quiff. 'Forgive me, Kent. But that's four times Mark tries and fails to kill Charlie. I mean, there's shoddy work, and then there's just plain–'

'Perhaps the aim wasn't to kill Charlie.' I thought back to the birds in the cellar wall. *He buried them alive, because he could.* 'Perhaps the aim was to torment Vanessa, to remind her that he's there; that no one is safe.'

'Christ, no wonder she drank,' said Rahid.

Kate frowned. 'Why didn't Vanessa report him to the police?'

I shrugged. 'Lack of evidence? I don't know. Maybe she really was drunk enough not to care.'

Mack rolled his eyes. 'This still doesn't explain what triggered Mark off now. I mean, he's had three decades in between to fuck around with Charlie and Vanessa and he hasn't done so.'

I tapped my fingers on the desk, irritated as I realised Mack had a point.

I turned to Rahid. 'Can you run a search on psychiatric units across the country? See if Mark Miller was admitted anywhere.'

As Rahid bustled out of the room, my eyes landed back on the letters. Pages and pages scratched with black, spiky words. I pictured an angry, wounded teenager, struggling to find his place in the world.

Suddenly it hit me.

'Despite everything, Mark wanted to be close to his mum,' I said, picturing the cellar hideout; a whole life contained within ten square feet. 'When you've dedicated your life to obsessing over one person, what's the worst thing that can possibly happen to you?'

Kate's eyes widened. 'That person dies.'

I stood up so suddenly, I knocked a picture frame off Rowley's desk. '*That's* the trigger. Don't you see? All this time, Mark never gave up hope that one day his mum would open the door to him and they'd sail off into the sunset.' I bent down to pick up the picture. 'The moment Vanessa died, that hope died with her.'

Rowley pressed his elbows onto the desk and steepled his fingers together. 'So, with Vanessa gone, there's only one person he can take it out on?'

I nodded. 'The man who stole his life, and his mum's love. We already know Mark is capable of revenge. He blinded his adoptive father, for Christ's sake. And Charlie is everything Mark could never be: successful, popular, loved.' My voice cracked and I glared at the ceiling. 'What better way to exact revenge than dismantling his reputation? Making the world see him as a degenerate, a liar, a murderer. And then killing him.' I gripped hold of the picture frame. 'Mark buried himself so deeply in the walls of Vanessa's home, she never knew he was there. He did the same thing with Charlie and Emily. He's been toying with them ever since Vanessa died. Mark had access to everything; their phones, their clothes—'

'And the murder weapon,' said Kate.

Mack leaned forwards and narrowed his eyes. 'Then riddle me this, Kent. Why Sabrina? Why not go after Charlie's wife?'

I set the frame down on Rowley's desk. 'Because, by dragging Charlie's mistress into this, Mark is showing us that he's a cheat. That's already a black mark against his character.'

Mack shook his head and the light rippled off his shiny hair. 'For this Miller guy to have pulled this off, we're talking monumental levels of deception.'

I leaned forward. 'Stealing into people's houses; harassing, tormenting. It's what he does; it's all he's ever done.'

As I spoke, Rowley wandered across to a safe that was built into a walnut cupboard.

'There is one way we can settle this,' he said, punching in the code.

He pulled something out, then turned towards me. Our eyes locked in a shared understanding and I gave him a nod.

Rowley fiddled around at the back of his computer. I sat down next to Kate and clutched the arms of the chair, as if trying to anchor myself to something solid. The screen lit up and Rowley hit 'play'.

I tried to pretend it wasn't me lying on the bed. That it was some other blonde; comatose and moments away from a sexual assault. But the bitter taste in my mouth spread before I could stop it. I dug my nails into my palms and forced my eyes to stick with the screen.

A dark-haired figure crossed in front of the camera, tugged the sleeve of his hoody, then leaned over me. Mack and Kate knew its contents but they hadn't seen the footage.

Kate stiffened as the man began to undress me. Out of the corner of my eye, I saw Mack's head dip, his hand cover his mouth.

By the time the man unbuckled his belt, I knew.

'He doesn't show his face,' I said, flatly. 'He knows exactly where the camera is.'

A tense silence stretched through the room. I closed my eyes, trying to blot the image from my eyelids.

'Mark knew I was alone in the apartment. It was too good an opportunity to miss. He wore Charlie's hoody to make it look as if–' I stopped, folding over and stifling a sob. All this time I thought Charlie had betrayed me in the vilest way possible. 'He's been playing us all from the beginning. Hiding in plain sight this whole time.'

Mack was clenching his teeth so hard I could hear them grate against each other. 'Christ, Kent. That video. I should have – are you–' He sprang up and stood at the window with his back to us.

Kate put her arm around me and buried her face in my hair. 'We're going to get this fucker.'

'He hasn't put a foot wrong,' said Mack, as he raked a hand through his hair, sending it shooting in different directions.

'Not quite.' My voice was small but firm. 'That skirt is still hanging in my wardrobe. Mark's DNA will be all over it.'

Rowley's gaze flickered over me, and the edges of his face softened. 'I'll organise a car to take you home to get it.'

'I'll come with you,' said Kate, pocketing her phone.

There was a knock at the door and Rahid appeared, hopping from one foot to the other, too distracted to notice our tense faces. 'Sophie, your hunch was right. Miller's latest stint was at

Boscombe Mental Asylum. He left March last year. I just got off the phone with a health officer there and . . .' He paused, finally sensing the fraught atmosphere in the office. 'What's going on?'

I slid forward in my chair. 'What did the health officer say?'

Rahid's eyes ran over my face. 'She received a call from a guy who claimed to be Miller's brother, not long after Miller was discharged. He said he was trying to trace Mark.'

I stared at him. 'That must have been Charlie. So Mark *was* reunited with Vanessa?'

Rahid shook his head. 'That's just it. The health visitor felt there was something odd about the call. Charlie wouldn't give his name, you see. She knew Mark would agree to meet his brother – he'd written to his mum countless times over the years but never heard back, so she knew he was open to reconnecting with his biological family. But, because of Mark's fragile mental state, the approach would need to be made gently. Her gut told her she didn't have the full story. When Charlie rang again the following week for an update, the health visitor confirmed Mark's existence, but told Charlie she'd need to set up a face-to-face to discuss taking it forward. Apparently Charlie thanked her and told her he'd changed his mind and had no interest in taking it further.'

'Why would Charlie keep them apart?' said Kate. 'Finding her other son could have helped Vanessa straighten herself out. Was Charlie protecting her?'

'He was punishing her,' I said, quietly, starting to gather my things from Rowley's desk.

'Do we think Emily's still alive?' Mack's question came like a dart piercing the air.

'All the time there's no body, then there's hope,' I said. 'We just need to find–'

My notebook had fallen open on my interview notes with Fred. I read the scribbled blue words and blinked.

The place where it all began.

An explosion of images in my head.

Fire. Water. Blood. Christ Clan. Bones in the wall.

I stared around the room, my voice hoarse. 'Shit, I know where Emily is.'

37

Emily: present day

Emily leans back against the cold stone, her eyes pinned to the bottom of the door. As the bar of light fades, her windowless prison slides into darkness. She isn't sure how long she's been here but long enough to unpick the sounds outside. An animal bleating. The harsh cawing of a bird. The snarl of a lone motorbike. Emily shivers; the cold buckles around her like sheet metal. The man hasn't returned. When he left, Emily had screamed herself hoarse; crawled round her cell, scrabbling at the rock with numb hands, searching for a way out. The only thing she found was a rusty water trough; the stench of stagnant water had made her retch.

The man left her a bucket to use as a toilet, but it is filling up, and the air is growing even more putrid and sour. All she can do is wait. Her eyes grow heavy, she rests her head on her arms.

Sometime later – minutes? Hours? – Emily hears the low thrum of a car engine. It cuts out and the silence is piercing. Footsteps. Emily scrambles backwards into a corner, wishing she'd found something to use as a weapon.

The rusty screech of a key turning in a padlock. Suddenly the door scrapes open and a low hiss of terror comes from the back of her throat. The figure is holding a lantern and Emily squints into the light. She can see a lean, muscular build; dark jeans, a red woollen hat and a red scarf that obscures the lower half of his face.

Emily opens her mouth but all that comes out is a muffled squeak. The man sets the lantern in the corner then retraces his steps, walking high on his toes. He returns with a wheelbarrow that's filled with something Emily can't see. He is humming the same three notes over and over.

He stalks towards her. Emily tries to melt into the wall but he grabs her by the arm, drags her forwards, slams her hands together. She feels the cold bite of handcuffs; smells whisky and stale sweat, tinged with something else she recognises. As the man reaches for the lantern, his sleeve pulls back and she spies a tattoo: two red triangles, pointing in different directions. A memory stirs deep inside her.

She stares up at him. 'Wait, I know you.'

The tattoo. She closes her eyes as the memory sharpens: his hand on the back of her head, pressing her down, filling her mouth.

Emily snaps her eyes open and stares at him, her voice cracked and raw. 'The cinema. You're Sternus?'

The man cricks his neck and slides off his jacket. Underneath he's wearing a rumpled grey shirt with spots of sweat under his arms. Emily whimpers, not understanding. The man who called himself Sternus had messaged several times after the cinema, but she'd ignored him. Emily screws her eyes shut. How could she have been so reckless? What did she expect?

She takes a breath, searches for some common ground, a thread of some sort. 'Look, I'm sorry. About not replying to your messages. I'm married. I made a mistake. My husband, I love him and . . .' She tails off as the man straightens up and cracks his knuckles.

Emily can feel his eyes on her and she holds her breath. There is a dangerous stillness about him.

'What would you say if I told you we were going to start a new life together?' he says. The man's scarf muffles his voice and Emily has to lean towards him to hear properly. 'If I told you your clothes, your passport, are in the boot of my car. Everything you need is right here. Would you come with me?'

'Are you mad?' Emily clamps her arms over her knees, making herself as small as possible.

The man crouches down so he's level with her. The light from his lantern throws shadows over the part of his face that's visible. 'Your husband is a cheat, a liar, a killer. And you say you still love him. You sure I'm the one who's mad?'

Emily's eyes flicker to the ground and, as the man lifts his hat to scratch along his hairline, a tuft of dark hair escapes.

'Funny how there are never consequences for men like Charlie. We should have had the same chance in life. Except someone decided my life wasn't worth it, and his was.'

Emily's mouth is dust-dry and she runs a tongue over her teeth. 'What are you talking about?'

He laughs darkly. 'You've talked a good game in public about standing by your husband. But behind closed doors it's been a different story, hasn't it? How long did it take you to lose faith in him, days? Weeks? Even before I came on the scene the trust was fading.'

Anger creeps into her voice. 'You know nothing about my marriage.'

'I know everything about your marriage.'

He starts to hum, the same three notes, then reaches into his pocket, holds something up between filthy, nail-bitten fingers. 'Thanks for these, by the way.'

Emily's nostrils flare as she recognises her white knickers. 'How did you get those?'

The man rocks back on his heels, humming. Then he gives a thin smile. 'These have got me through many dark moments. And the other mementos I've taken. Do you know what you smell like?' He holds the knickers to his nose and inhales, his eyes never leaving her face.

Emily bites down on her fist. 'You've been in my flat?'

The man stuffs her knickers back in his pocket. 'Do you know how beautiful you look when you're asleep? Those silk pyjamas with the little bow on each strap.' Emily starts, as she remembers the day she came home from work to find them spread out on her bed. A muscle is twitching in his right cheek. 'Of course, it was easier to watch you once Charlie moved into the spare room.'

'Stop!' Emily screws her eyes shut. 'Why are you punishing me?'

'You?' The man blinks slowly, his eyes hardening. 'This has got nothing to do with you.'

He kneels down beside her; Emily recognises the same damp, peaty smell from the cinema. He clicks his tongue against his teeth. 'Do you know what it's like to be abandoned before you're barely old enough to open your eyes? Four hours. That's all I had with her. Then she handed me over for a lifetime of misery.'

Questions flood Emily's brain, but she bites her tongue, waits out the silence. Eventually, he reaches into his pocket. She hears a soft snick, the opening of a knife.

The man grips her arm, runs his finger along the milky skin on the inside of her wrist. 'Ssshhh,' he says. It sounds like a sigh. 'You should enjoy this. I've watched you slice into yourself for months.'

He lays the blade against her wrist and draws it sharply towards him. The pain is familiar and, in spite of herself, Emily feels a moment's peace. But he cuts too deep and she cries out. Eventually he sits back on his heels and Emily looks down through the blood. Two triangles, carved into her skin.

The man places a metal dish under her wrist. With a sickening jolt, Emily realises he is collecting her blood. She tries to snatch her hand away but he grips it more tightly. The pressure makes the blood run faster.

Emily's eyes roll back in their sockets and she moans. The man is watching her. His grip loosens round her arm and he sits, stretches his long legs out in front of him, eyes on the ground.

'The first time I saw my real family, I was hiding in the garden, behind the Horse Chestnut tree. My mum was cooking dinner; my brother was sitting at the table, colouring something in with a crayon. We looked the same, him and me. Except he was smiling. I watched her hug him; squeeze him half to death. No one had ever hugged me like that.' He shakes his head, hunches over his knees. 'I kept going back. I needed to know what was so special about him. By the time I moved into the cellar, I felt like I was almost part of the family. Except they never knew I was there.'

The man stares into the darkness. Suddenly he pulls off his hat and scarf.

Emily makes a strange choking sound.

The man's hair is curlier, his nose a fraction more crooked. Other than that, he looks just like Charlie.

'I thought if my mum knew how much I wanted to be part of their family, she'd let me come home. I tried to sort myself out; distance myself from the Clan. I even got myself a girlfriend, Samantha. She was about the only good thing in my life back then.' The man's voice hardens. 'But *he* had other ideas about her.'

'Who?'

He tears at the denim with his fingers. 'We called him the Shepherd. Laurence Marlon. The Clan leader. He was the one who told me about my real mum. But not the full picture. I figured that out myself later.' He clenches his teeth together, the corners of his mouth tightening. 'It was Samantha who suggested

I write to my mum. I put in the letter where she could find me. But she never came. So I wrote another, then another. You know where I found those letters? Stashed at the bottom of her wardrobe. You know what I also found? A letter she started writing to me. *You've made a mistake. I don't know who you are. Never contact me again.*'

He mimics her voice, and Emily watches his eyes flicker.

'She wanted to erase me from her life. Pretend I didn't exist. Well, two could play at that game. My only regret is that she didn't live long enough to see the son she loved fall from grace. I wanted to destroy her. So many times I came close. But then I found out what really happened and I–' He kicks his heels into the dirt. 'But my brother. He didn't deserve anything. Not after rejecting me.'

Emily frowns. 'Charlie knew about you?'

The man dabs a finger into the dish, then traces the tattoo on his wrist with her blood. 'When I found out his first wife had leukaemia and then drowned, it was like a sign from God. The Lord was punishing Charlie. Purifying his sins. An eye for an eye. The woman I loved drowned, too. The symmetry was breathtaking. For one exquisite moment, I thought Charlie would feel what I felt, suffer like I suffered. But men like Charlie always get a second shot at happiness. While some of us don't even get a first.'

Emily tries to focus on what the man is saying, but she's feeling weak, light-headed. She recognises the feeling; it happens sometimes, when you cut too deep, or let the blood flow for too long.

He looks at her, with flat blue eyes. 'And this time, you were going to be my blood sacrifice. But the more I watched you, the more I realised I could use you. You were the key to all of this. I would destroy him from the inside out. Tear him down, destroy his reputation. Make people hate him, the way they hated me. And you were his biggest supporter. If I could change your mind about him, the rest would follow.'

A throbbing was developing behind Emily's eyes. 'Why not just kill Charlie? Why torment him; why torment all of us?'

'Because I could.' The man shrugs and his smile sends a shiver down her neck. 'You don't think I wished someone had put me out of my misery?' He screws his eyes shut, his voice dropping to a whisper. 'You should try being locked in that space over there. Darkness so thick you can taste it.'

He nods his head towards a metal panel in the wall next to them, his voice deadly quiet.

'First night I spent in there, I was twelve. The things that happened in this hut; they'd make your head spin. You ever looked pure evil in the face?' He starts to beat his fist against his temple. 'The Shepherd pretended I was special, but I was nothing to him. When I found a sliver of happiness, he destroyed it, just because he could. I never wanted to kill Samantha. But the Shepherd had me tortured. I held out. Longer than he expected.' He gulped down a sob. 'But in the end, it was her or me. I had no choice. I went through hell and back. And the only reason I was there in the first place was because that woman chose Charlie over me.' He pushes himself up to standing, rocks back and forth on his heels for a moment.

'Where is he? What have you done with Charlie?'

He walks unsteadily over to the metal panel in the wall and Emily hears a strange clunking noise. She cranes her neck; he's opened it and is unscrewing the hinges.

'You know, I thought it would be much harder to knock Charlie off the pedestal; to break down the trust between you. But, in the end, all it took was a few little tricks.'

Emily's head pounds and the hut strobes in and out of focus. 'What do you mean?'

He hunches over the wall, concentrating on the job in hand. A rank smell is spreading through the hut. 'Oh you know, empty bottles stashed around your apartment. Planting the divorce lawyer's business card. Signs that Charlie was obsessing over his dead wife. The abortion pills were a particular stroke of genius.'

The ground seems to tilt and Emily presses her feet into the stone trying to brace herself. 'You mean, none of that was Charlie?' Her mind slowly starts piecing it together. The times she'd woken with a sense of unease. The sensation of being watched. The missing food, the strange aftershave, Lizzie's perfume, the writing on the mirror. All those times she'd accused Charlie and he'd been telling the truth. This monster had driven a wedge between them, so that when the time was right, Emily would suspect the worst of her husband.

'Charlie didn't kill Sabrina, did he?' she says, the tears falling silently down her cheeks.

The man wanders over to the wheelbarrow, lightly on his toes, and pushes it towards her. 'The best part about all of this was watching Charlie see his life implode. I kept him updated on every little twist. He was there the whole time, trapped under your apartment. So close, but so far. The agony on his face as he watched the people he loved lose faith in him. You, that reporter friend, his colleagues. Finally, perfect, untouchable Charlie understood what it was like at the bottom of the food chain. Where there's nothing but hate and fear.'

He tips up the wheelbarrow and an avalanche of rocks spill out. Emily visualises smashing one over his head.

'Charlie isn't perfect though, is he?' she says as an image of Sabrina's red hair splashes in front of her eyes. 'He is a cheat.'

She hears a strangled noise, and realises the man is laughing. 'If you say so.'

Emily stares at his back, then all of a sudden her vision narrows to a pinprick.

'No.' The word hisses from her lips.

He spins round, a cruel smile on his face. 'I had a lot of fun with their text messages. Bought the phones with a credit card I borrowed from Charlie's wallet.' He shrugs, turning back to the pile of rocks. 'Shocking, really, how quick people are to judge. Charlie's life was like a house of cards. Pull one out and the rest . . .' He flutters his fingers in the air.

Emily clamps a hand over her mouth. 'But the baby . . .'

'Was Bert's.' He pulls out his knife and starts to carve something on the wall. 'When I discovered the secret Bert was hiding, it wasn't hard to blackmail him into saying what I needed him to. That day he pitched up to your flat and told you about their affair? I was behind all of it. You ate it up. By that point you didn't trust Charlie as far as you could throw him.'

Emily squeezes her diamond pendant in her fist. 'But the video tape, on the phone I found. It showed Sabrina in our flat.'

A thin smile spread across the man's face. 'She was there. Only, with Bert. I made him take her there so I could film them. Sabrina didn't know whose flat it was. You never actually see your husband in the video.'

A draught swirls around her legs and Emily glances at the door. He's left it open a crack. Her heart starts to beat faster. Slowly, silently, she shifts forward onto her knees and flexes her feet to get the blood flowing. She needs to keep him talking.

'Why Sabrina?'

'I needed a victim, and she was perfect. Just enough of a link to Charlie to raise suspicions.'

Suddenly, he stops what he's doing and strides towards her. Emily freezes as he picks up the dish of her blood. She watches him dip in a finger and smear it on the wall. He's colouring in the carvings with her blood.

'Bert worked like a charm. The only thing I didn't bank on was what happened next. You spread your legs for him, when you shouldn't have. That was when I knew.'

'Knew what?'

'That some people are destined for happiness, and some aren't. I let myself get carried away. After all those months watching you, I allowed myself to believe something could happen between us. But after you betrayed me with Bert,' his shoulders hunch forwards and his voice grows quiet. 'Perhaps in another life.'

Emily edges forwards.

He stands back to eye his work. 'Still, we managed to have some fun, didn't we? That cinema trip kept me going for a while. And you should have seen Charlie's face when I showed him the photograph of the two of us. It was the last thing I showed him right before I kill—'

Emily staggers forwards and, with a strength she didn't know she had, picks up the rock and slams it into his head. The corner catches his temple and he lurches forwards. Without stopping to look, Emily drags herself towards the door.

Outside, the clouds have blotted out the stars and the night is black. Her feet crunch across the gravel and she looks wildly round for help. In the far distance a white building rears up out of the ground. Emily hobbles across the gravel. Then she's sinking in mud. She hears a growl behind her.

Suddenly she's running. Stumbling. Sinking. Falling. Scrabbling. To the left is a wooded area. If she can reach it, she can dive for cover. Her breath thunders through her ears. She daren't look behind her.

Emily's lungs are screaming. She knows she's slowing down. She's lost too much blood. White spots dance across her vision.

She is at the edge of the woods. She hears a grunt; he's gaining on her. Emily plunges forwards into the trees, her feet slipping and sliding in the mud. She clambers over a fallen trunk, then ducks down, clamping her hands over her mouth, vibrating with terror.

A torch beam slices through the blackness.

She closes her eyes, huddles her knees to her chest.

Then, footsteps. She can hear him the other side of the tree trunk. Emily presses herself against it willing him to move on.

For a moment, the silence is everywhere.

Then a hand grabs her by the throat.

Emily opens her mouth to scream, but nothing comes out.

38

'Can't you hurry up?'

The taxi driver glared at me over his shoulder. 'Are you blind, love?'

'Don't mind her, she's had a long day,' said Kate, shaking her head at me. 'Give him a break, he's doing his best.'

Outside, in the pitch darkness, the storm was raging. Thunder and lightning spat over our heads. I pressed my nose to the window, watching waves crash against the bleachers, dousing the coastal route in spray. Parts of the road were almost impassable. It wouldn't be long until it was completely flooded.

'Anything from your police source?' asked Kate, clinging on as the taxi swung a hard right into the road that led away from the coast, towards Christ Clan's remote hilltop.

I checked my phone. I'd left Durand two messages but he still hadn't responded. 'No, but Rowley's alerting Dorset Police. It's going to be fucking mayhem when we arrive. I only hope they've found Emily.'

An air-freshener shaped like a strawberry dangled from the rear-view mirror and its cloying scent filled my nostrils. I rested my head back, trying to breathe through my mouth, watching the wet road shimmer in the headlights.

Kate shifted in her seat and I could feel her staring at me. 'You haven't said much since we left London.'

I pressed my lips together and shook my head. I couldn't even begin to unpick the tangled threads of my emotions. For some reason, I kept thinking about Charlie in the office last week; his hair was too long and I'd called him Charlotte, and told him it was time to get the clippers out, and that I really should have pushed harder for the haircut because he looked ridiculous and that's what friends did for each other but now it didn't really matter because he was dead. *Dead dead dead.*

I fiddled with the zip on my jacket. 'If the tables were turned, Charlie would never have given up on me so quickly.'

Kate squeezed my arm. 'Stop, Sophie. This half-brother . . . he had us all fooled.'

'Not all of us.' I dug the zip into my thumb until it hurt. 'Emily stood by Charlie, didn't she? She was the only one.'

There was a pause and I sensed Kate trying to frame her words. 'Sophie, the last thing you need is to pile more guilt on yourself. Last night, in that tunnel,' she stopped, took a breath. 'You need help, Sophie. Proper human contact help. It's one thing putting yourself in the firing line for the story, but it's another if you're doing it out of some twisted desire to die. Especially when yours isn't the only life at risk.'

I gazed at my reflection in the window; my face was pale and ghostly. Kate's words hit home. She was right; I hadn't even considered her safety.

I opened my mouth to fob her off, when a crushing tiredness swept through me. I couldn't pretend anymore. I took a deep breath and turned to face Kate. 'Tommy was murdered.

A homeless friend saw it happen. Watched two guys hold Tommy down and inject him with a fatal dose of heroin.'

Kate's face tightened; she pulled at the collar of her blouse. 'How long have you known?'

'A month or two.'

'And you didn't say anything?

I shrugged as tears slid down my cheeks.

The taxi screeched to a halt. 'You want me to ring the buzzer?' said the driver, swinging round in his seat.

I wiped my cheeks and looked out the window at the vast iron gates. 'We'll just get out here.'

His brow creased. 'But, the storm . . .'

I handed him a tenner, grateful I didn't have to talk about Tommy anymore.

I forced the door open just as a bolt of lightning lit up the horizon and the sky went black. The wind screeched; throwing my hair around my face until I couldn't see. I could smell, though: salt and seaweed and pine trees.

As the taxi drove away, Kate cleared her throat. 'So, where's the cavalry?'

There were no flashing blue lights, no sirens. Just blackness, and the storm.

'I don't understand. Rowley said they'd be here.' I fished around for my phone and checked the screen. 'I'll give him a cal— Shit, I've got no service. Try yours.'

A few seconds later Kate swore. 'The storm must have knocked out a phone mast.' She tightened the belt on her mac and sized up the gates. 'No CCTV. What do you reckon, feeling nimble?'

I zipped my jacket up against the chill wind and raised my eyebrows. 'I thought we weren't being reckless.'

'That was before Emily's life was at stake.'

Kate put one foot on the railing and hitched up her skirt. I swung my bag over my shoulder and followed suit. Two undignified minutes later, we landed on the other side, into thick mud.

Kate stared down at her soggy ballet pumps. 'Glad I dressed for the occasion.'

I huddled close to her and pulled out my torch. 'OK, Fred, the former member I spoke to, mentioned a place called the Bunker. Marlon used to lock the kids inside as punishment. I think the Bunker is one of the stone huts.' I shone my torch around trying to get my bearings. Kate and I were standing at the edge of a wooded area. 'From what I can remember, the cluster of huts is quite a way past the main building. And the drive is long. It's basically fields, fields and more fields.' Kate threw another mournful glance down at her sodden shoes. 'Are you sure about this?'

'Nope.' She switched on her torch. 'Come on.'

We trudged through the forest, staying low, stumbling over tree roots, sinking into bogs. All around us, thickly scented pine trees arched and roared in the wind. Eventually the forest thinned and we came to a clearing. To the left stood the white Christ Clan building. I held Kate's arm, signalled for her to turn off her torch. We crept forwards, round the car park towards a hedge that ran along the back of the garden. Just as we reached the hedge, the back door of the building flew open and security lights lit up the garden like a stage. We dropped to the ground, hearts pounding. I heard the crunch of footsteps and peeked over my shoulder. A man, dragging a bin out to the shed. I let out a breath and waited until he'd returned to the building before crawling through a hole in the hedge.

The landscape opened out into a large, flat field and I pointed to the knot of buildings on the horizon.

Rain was coming down in sheets, and Kate shielded her eyes. 'What do you want to do?' she said.

I checked my phone again. Still no service. The storm filled my head, loud, raging.

I was too late to save Charlie's life, and I was damned if I was going to make the same mistake with Emily.

I locked eyes with Kate and she nodded, reading my mind. We trekked on through the waterlogged grass; the wind drove against us like a cliff. As we passed a flock of sheep sheltering under the branches of an oak tree, Kate lost a shoe and had to go back. Eventually we reached the other side of the field. Kate veered sharply to the left, shining her torch on the ground.

I raised my voice against the wind. 'What are you doing?'

She stooped over, face hardening with concentration. 'Looking for something to use if this gets ugly.' She stopped by a rock the size of a melon and picked it up. 'I suggest you do the same.'

I nodded, my lips pulled tight over my teeth. I seized a rock between ice-cold hands, then we hurried across the field towards the stone huts. As we got closer, the grass petered out and our shoes hit gravel.

We stopped at the first hut. A rotting wooden door hung on its hinges.

Kate peered inside. 'Nothing but cobwebs in here.'

We scoured the next hut, then the next. Kate skirted a puddle and opened her mouth to say something when we heard a noise: a bang, followed by a crunching sound. We ducked down behind the stone hut, fumbling with our torches.

A figure staggered past us, leaning into the wind. I held my breath until he disappeared from sight.

'Who was that?' said Kate, shivering against the granite wall.

I shrugged. 'I don't want to know. Come on, there are only three huts left.'

Kate nodded. 'I'll check the one over there.'

I wiped the rain from my eyes and lurched towards the hut nearest the forest. I ran my torch over the door; it was padlocked. I pressed my ear to the door but I couldn't hear anything over the wind. I did a circuit of the building; no windows, no other way in except through the door. My fingers tightened around the rock; I'd have to bash open the padlock.

'Kate!' I raked the darkness with my torch but I couldn't see her. My gaze fell on something on the ground and I crouched down for a closer look. Was that blood? I inched forwards, following the trail with my torch beam. It ran across the gravel, in the direction of the forest. I hesitated for a split-second then turned back towards the hut. As I did, my torch landed on a man, standing ten feet away from me, his hands jammed in the pockets of his waterproof.

'What are you doing?' The wind carried his gravelly voice towards me.

'I – I'm looking for someone. A woman. I think she's inside this hut.'

He edged towards me, on the tips of his toes. 'That's not possible, Miss. I've just been in that hut. Nothing but farming equipment in there.'

I tightened my grip round the rock and shone my torch in his face. I couldn't see much; he was wearing a woolly hat, and his chin was buried in a scarf. 'Then you won't mind showing me.'

He cocked his head to one side. 'And you are?'

I raised my voice, hoping Kate could hear me over the wind. 'My name is Sophie Kent. I'm a reporter from the *London Herald*.'

He wiped his nose with the back of his hand. 'You'd best talk to Hector. No one is allowed on Christ Clan property without speaking to him first. If you want, I'll take you to him.'

He took another step towards me and my light caught the trickle of blood running down his face.

A sense of unease swept through me. I edged backwards, scanning the darkness for Kate. 'No need to trouble Hector. I'm going now. Not really the weather for it, anyway.'

As if to make the point, a violent gust of wind blew across the field, blowing a flurry of leaves at us. One snagged on the rim of his hat and, as he swiped it off, he nudged the hat backwards and the wind carried it off.

For a moment, I just stared at him.

The thick, dark hair, the high forehead and chiselled cheek-bones. The similarity was so striking I let out a cry.

A slow, thin smile spread across his face.

I stumbled backwards. 'Mark, don't do this. You've made your point: Charlie is dead. Don't let Emily suffer too.'

Mark inched towards me and I could see the sticky patch in his hair oozing blood.

'I know things haven't been easy for you. Given up for adoption. Ending up in a place like this. But, your mum. It wasn't her fault. She was damaged, and traumatised, and young. She couldn't cope with a baby. That's why she gave you up. Not because she didn't love you.'

'What the fuck do you know about my life?'

'I know your mum was haunted by the choice she made over forty years ago.' Out of the corner of my eye I saw Kate dart silently between huts. 'She never forgot you, Mark. We've spoken to the health officer at Boscombe Asylum. She told us your mum was trying to track you down. She wanted to make amends.'

The colour drained from Mark's face. 'Liar!'

'It's the truth.' A little more digging had thrown up the stream of incoherent letters Vanessa had been sending the Bournemouth Adoption Service. Even though Vanessa never signed her name, the concerned clerk had kept them on file.

'Why didn't I hear from anyone, then?' Mark swayed slightly.

'Because Charlie chose to keep you and Vanessa apart. For reasons that were important to him but now seem . . .' I faltered, as the full impact of Charlie's decision hit me between the eyes.

The wind roared around us like a chained animal and I raised my voice. 'It doesn't change the fact that Vanessa cared. She left half her money to Christ Clan, Mark. She must have known they could find you.'

'What use is her fucking money?' He sagged against the wall and I thought he was going to be sick. 'So many times I've tried to make her see me. But she turned her back. And all the while I was two miles away, living in misery with adoptive parents who hated my guts.'

'I spoke to your dad, Les. Why didn't he tell me you were adopted?'

Mark blinked slowly. 'Because he's a fucking liar. He couldn't have kids of his own, but didn't want to admit it to the world. He's always kept up the pretence that I was his son. Even when things fell apart; even after Pam left and he kicked me out.'

'Even after you blinded him.' I kept my voice steady but Mark sneered.

'Payback,' he said, simply. 'Meanwhile my real mum showered all her love on Charlie.' He spat the name out. 'Well, the Golden Child got what he deserved in the end.'

'What he deserved?' My voice twisted with fury. 'You've been tormenting Charlie his entire life. And all because of a choice your mum made before he was born. Charlie couldn't control that any more than you could. He did nothing to you.'

'Wrong.' Mark pushed himself away from the wall, his eyes narrowing into slits. 'He stole my life. And then he stole her.'

Mark ran a hand through his hair and the gesture was so Charlie-like, my knees almost buckled.

'I was there the day Vanessa died. In the cellar. I watched them fight in the kitchen. Charlie was furious with her, for being so weak. She tried to run away from him, she made it up the stairs, but he followed her.'

Mark's breathing quickened and he let out a string of sobs like hiccups.

'When Charlie pushed her, he killed any chance I had to make things right with my mum. He deserved to pay.'

Charlie killed his mum? I blinked at him, forcing myself past his words. 'But Emily doesn't. Mark, you don't want her blood on your hands.'

Mark pressed a hand to his temple and winced. 'Women are the root of evil. My real dad always told me that. I should have believed him; he tried to teach me that at Christ Clan.'

'Your dad was at Christ Clan?'

A pause. 'He was the Shepherd.'

'Your biological dad is *Laurence Marlon*?' Gordon's words rang loud in my head: *Vanessa got swept up in a local church group, got herself into a spot of bother with a man there.* The realisation flew at me so fast, I could only stare at him. '*Marlon is Vanessa's rapist*?'

Mark's smile didn't reach his eyes. 'He didn't tell me about the rape, of course. He tracked me down when I was still living with my foster dad. He'd heard a rumour from someone that the bitch he'd raped all those years ago gave away his kid. He invited me to join Christ Clan, told me all about my real mum and how she'd kept me from him because she was evil. I thought I'd hit the jackpot with Marlon until he turned on me.' A bleak look crossed Mark's face and he rolled his eyes to the sky. 'And then I found out the truth about what he did to her.'

I hardened myself against the kernel of pity in my chest and cleared my throat. 'Where is Emily?'

Mark started to close the gap between us. 'Don't you see? I've purged them all. Water, fire, blood. My soul is finally clean.'

I stood my ground, injecting a hint of steel into my voice. 'Mark, where is she?'

Mark crept closer, until he was close enough that I could see the differences between the brothers. Mark's mouth was smaller, his dark eyebrows more pronounced. In another life, Mark's eyes could have been warm and laughing like Charlie's; instead they were dark and vicious. And trained on me.

'You'll never find her.'

He rose onto his toes and sprang at me. I slammed backwards into the wall of the hut. There was a crunch and Mark stumbled, hit the ground, the shock turning his face white.

Kate raised the rock again; her eyes blazing.

Mark mumbled something and I held out a hand to stop her. 'Wait! What's he saying?' I dropped to my knees and leaned towards him.

Mark made a strange gurgling noise; his lips quivering. 'If I die, your brother's secret dies with me.'

I froze. 'What are you talking about?'

Mark hacked up a cough and a torrent of blood poured down his face. 'Tommy's death ... it's tormenting you. I know–' he coughed again.

'What do you know?' I gripped his jacket so tightly my knuckles cracked. 'Do you know who killed him?'

He stretched his mouth into a smile. 'I've seen the whiteboard. In your house. You're wrong–'

I beat a fist against his chest. 'You've been *in my house*?'

'That little fag was hiding things from you.'

I didn't see it coming. The knife was inches from my head when Kate screamed. She slammed the rock into Mark's face again, shattering his nose.

He lay still and a keening noise pierced the air. It was coming from deep inside me.

I rounded on Kate. 'How could you? He was about to–'

'Fucking kill you.' Kate was breathing heavily; her wet curls plastered against her white face. She leaned across me and rooted around in Mark's jacket pocket. Then she held up a silver key.

I snatched it off her and lurched towards the hut. My hands were shaking so much I could barely get the key inside the lock. I tore the padlock off and fell through the door, bracing myself for a body.

All I could see was a water trough, an old wheelbarrow and some tools.

'Emily's not here.' I kicked the straw in panic.

Kate raced into the hut and we worked over every inch with our torches.

Suddenly, I pushed my hair out of my face. 'What's that smell?'

Kate frowned. 'Cement?'

I strode over to the wheelbarrow. 'Tools, gloves, cement. What was Mark doing in here?' I pointed my torch at the floor. The wind screeched through a gap in the roof. My mind spun. *Why would Mark need cement?*

I crouched down, staring into the darkness, trying to get inside Mark's head. I thought back to the hideout under Charlie's apartment, the filthy space in Vanessa's cellar, the carvings. The birds. A piercing thought took shape in my head.

'Kate, Vanessa's cellar. We found bird skeletons hidden in the wall. Loads of them. Perfectly formed. They were buried alive.' Kate shot me a look, her lip curling with distaste. 'Don't you see: Mark is the Starling. Those birds, they represent him.'

Kate shook her head. 'But why kill them if they represent him?'

'Because that's how he felt: trapped, helpless.' I blinked as the idea sharpened. 'This isn't the Bunker. We have to dig deeper to find the Bunker. The fabric of the building. The walls.'

'What?'

'Check the fucking walls!' It came out in a shriek, and I stumbled forward, running my hand along the rough rock. My palm came away wet. I aimed my torch at the wall. The grouting between the rocks was damp.

'Kate, quick.' I grabbed the trowel and tossed her my torch. I scraped away at the cement, but it was painstakingly slow.

Kate propped the torches up, then rifled around in her bag. She pulled out her house keys. 'I'll start this side.'

We worked in silence, as the storm surged around us. Chipping, scraping, digging, clawing. My fingers were raw with cold, my eyes gritty. Every so often I threw a glance over my shoulder to check that Mark was still unconscious by the door. Eventually my rock started to loosen.

'Help me out with this one.'

Between us, we eased it out of the wall. A rank smell blasted from the hole. Kate made a retching sound.

I covered my nose with my sleeve. 'Emily?'

Silence.

Kate pointed to the next rock along and we got to work. Eventually it came loose. I grabbed my torch, took a deep breath and plunged my head through.

There was something on the ground. I couldn't make out what. I pushed my head in further, aimed the torch downwards. The smell was deep in the back of my throat. Then I saw it, a heap of blonde hair.

'Emily? Can you hear me?' I scrabbled at the rock.

A loud bang pierced the air. I yanked my head out of the hole and looked at the door.

Mark was gone.

I gave a hiss of terror. 'Where is he?'

Kate grabbed the trowel off the ground and held it up.

A man's voice. A crackling noise.

I looked at Kate. 'Is that a radio?'

Kate fell against me and dropped the trowel. 'Halle-fucking-lujah.'

Seconds later, a figure appeared at the door. 'I'm Detective Inspector Morrison. Are either of you hurt?'

I pointed at the gap in the wall. 'Emily Swift. Please. Get her out.'

The DI pulled out his torch and shone it inside the wall. His jaw tightened and he strode to the door. 'Paramedics, now.'

Kate shivered beside me. 'There's a man, Mark Miller. He was he—'

'We've got him. He was trying to make his escape through the grounds.'

Two paramedics raced towards us with foil blankets. 'Put these round you. Let's get you checked out.'

We followed them into the night and I spotted a figure hovering by the ambulance and frowned. 'Hector?'

Hector Marlon's face was bathed in a cold, blue light. 'I'm so glad you're safe. When I heard what he'd done I–' He saw the expression on my face and gave a tight smile. 'Dolly Summerville. You met her. Turns out Miller has worked a number on her over the past few months. Has got her doing all sorts of things for him. Bringing him food and water out here. She even travelled round getting money out with Charlie's card to make police think he was alive and on the move.' He shook his head. 'Totally lovestruck. But when Mark asked Dolly to get the cement and tools, the scales fell away from her eyes and she freaked out. Came clean to me an hour ago.'

'It was you who called the police?' I shook my head, bewildered. What happened to Rowley?

A loud shout came from inside the hut. Kate and I hobbled to the doorway. The team of officers had ripped an opening big enough to climb through and were on their knees, examining something.

They lifted a blood-soaked figure on a stretcher and I clutched Kate's arm. 'Is she alive?'

'Boss, take a look at this,' said an officer.

DI Morrison strode past and was given a torch. He peered into the gap then handed the torch back to his Deputy. 'Get Forensics down here now.'

I raised my eyebrows as he came towards us. 'What's in the wall?'

'More like "who",' he said, blinking hard.

We hobbled back outside in time to see Miller being thrown into the back of a police car. The paramedics had patched his head up with a bandage. He must have felt me looking because he turned and stared at me. Then he licked his lips, raised his hands to his nose and inhaled deeply.

I stiffened and Kate nudged me. 'I know you want to take a running kick at him, but there's no need. I did it for you, after you ran into the hut. Three times in the bollocks. One for you, one for Emily and,' she faltered, her eyes damp with tears, 'one for Charlie.'

I leaned into Kate, not sure whether to laugh or cry.

'Let's go back to London.'

39

One week later

I stood with my back to St Mary's Church, looking at the view. Even two miles from the coast, you could taste the salt in the air. I smoothed down my black dress and glanced at the knot of people gathering in the churchyard. Rowley, tanned and trim in a double-breasted suit, was talking to Kate and Mack. I took a deep breath, and wandered over to them.

'All right, Kent,' said Mack, sucking on a cigarette; his gold watch glinting in the sunlight.

I raised my eyebrows. 'Since when do you smoke?'

He picked a piece of tobacco out of his teeth. 'I hate funerals.'

Rowley slid on his glasses and checked his phone. He couldn't spare much time away from the office; none of us could. Mark and Charlie's story had exploded. It had sparked off a national debate about nature versus nurture, and how our care system had failed the vulnerable. Rowley had dedicated pages and pages to the two half-brothers from different sides of the track; to the mum who drank to forget her past; to the catalogue of errors that led to tragedy.

Over the last week, I'd fought hard for space to be made for Sabrina Hobbs, whose murder set the ball in motion, and who was unlucky enough to be plucked from obscurity by a psychopath hell bent on revenge.

Rowley was concerned about Emily. It hadn't taken long for us to trace Emily's Tinder history. Or her relationship with Bert Hughes. It was Rahid who discovered Emily was sleeping with him. In his hunt for Bert, he came across CCTV footage of the pair kissing in the lobby of Bert's apartment block. I was amazed. All that time Emily pretended to take the moral high ground, she'd been cheating on Charlie.

'Don't judge her, Soph,' said Kate, sadly. 'She thought her husband was a monster.'

We'd agreed to let her alone; it was the least we could do for Charlie. But once the other press hounds caught her trail, God knows what would happen. The widow's secret life would be a hard exclusive to turn down.

Kate poked a stray curl under her hat. 'You OK?'

I shrugged, avoiding her eye. A car growled up the lane and I watched Dominic slide out. He was wearing a powder-blue suit and a fuschia bow-tie.

'Interesting funeral attire,' said Mack, stubbing his cigarette out on the paving stone. Then he gestured to the door. 'Shall we get this over with?'

'I'll join you in a minute,' I said.

I could feel Kate and Rowley's eyes on my back as I picked my way across the soggy grass to a bench beneath a beech tree. I sat down, running my tongue over my teeth, taking in the view. A silvery mist rolled across a landscape that was still blighted by last week's storms: fallen trees, ripped-out hedges, debris across the roads. In the far distance, I could see the blue shimmer of the sea.

At first I didn't see her, half-hidden behind the trunk. A twig snapped and I looked round.

Emily was dressed in a black satin coat and her blonde hair was pulled back into a low bun.

I half-rose. 'Sorry, I didn't realise anyone was over here.'

Emily hesitated, then sat down next to me, eyes forward. 'Thank you for coming.'

It sounded flat, rehearsed. I nodded, studying her out of the corner of my eye. She had the glazed look of someone on a Xanax-high. I'd heard from Rowley that the hospital weren't happy about discharging Emily, but she'd given them no choice.

My eyes dropped to the bandage round her wrist. 'Are you out for good?'

She pulled her sleeve down. 'The transfusion went well. But I have to take it easy.'

'Where are you staying?'

'With my parents.' She flicked her head towards a well-dressed couple, and I detected an edge to her voice.

A leaf fluttered onto the bench; I picked it up and turned it over in my fingers. 'I'm so sorry I didn't visit. The hospital staff were only allowing family in.'

Emily clasped her hands on her lap and stared at them. 'They were struggling with the media. Reporters dressing up as nurses and doctors.'

It was said without malice. For a moment, we sat in silence, listening to the breeze stir the leaves on the branches above. I tapped my thumb on the bench, unsure what to say next.

I shifted round to face her. 'I'm sorry I–'

'I really should–'

I smiled. 'Sorry, you go.'

Emily flicked me a glance, twisting her diamond 'E' pendant around her neck. 'Thank you. For . . . finding me in time.'

I nodded, gazing skywards as a lump caught in my throat. 'Emily, I'm sorry. The press conference. You have to understand, at the time–'

She held up a pale white hand. 'You were just doing your job. I get it, don't worry. They've got what they need to charge him, you know. Kidnap, murder . . . sexual assault.' She glanced in my direction and cleared her throat. 'I'm sorry you got dragged into all this.' It was as far as she went, and I was grateful.

There was so much I wanted to say to Emily but, all of a sudden, she stiffened. I followed her gaze to the vicar, who had just appeared in the church porch, his black robe swirling in the breeze.

Emily gave me a quick kiss. 'I need to talk to the vicar before Charlie gets here.'

Her choice of words made my throat constrict; as though Charlie was running late and would roll up any second, flustered, apologetic, grinning.

As she darted across the churchyard, I crushed the leaf between cold, angry fingers and tossed the shreds to the ground.

'Room for a tall one?' His deep, melodic voice loosened the knot in my stomach.

Durand sat down and uncurled his legs. His eyes were ringed with purple, and his cheeks hollowed out; hardly surprising, given the circumstances. The night of my Christ Clan showdown with Mark Miller, Durand was at University College Hospital, keeping vigil at his daughter's bedside. Elodie's mum called him, frantic, an hour before everything kicked off to say that Elodie had slipped into a coma. The prognosis wasn't good. She'd been moved to the ICU.

I glanced up at him. 'How are you?'

Durand ran a hand through his auburn hair and crossed his legs. 'Better now Miller has confessed.'

That wasn't what I meant, and he knew it.

'It's the most extraordinary story,' he said. 'Miller is about as screwed up as it's possible to be.'

I sighed. 'Can you blame him? What Laurence Marlon did to those kids . . .' I tailed off as a flock of seagulls circled overhead. Their squalls cut straight through me. 'I hope you're making Marlon a priority. The moron has probably been working on his golf handicap in the Costa del Sol all this time.'

Durand leaned forward and bowed his head. 'Marlon definitely didn't emigrate to the Costa del Sol.'

'How do you know?'

He gave me a look, and I saw the corners of his mouth twitch. 'Because he's spent the past fifteen years buried in the wall of that stone hut.' I blinked at him. 'One of the many crimes Miller confessed to. When he found out Marlon raped his mum, he snapped. After everything the man put him through . . .' Durand shrugged. 'He said he did it for Vanessa.'

I noticed a loose thread on my jacket button and wound it round my finger. 'During your interrogation with Miller, did he say anything about the day Vanessa died?'

Durand gave me a sideways glance. 'He might have mentioned it.'

'Do you believe Charlie killed his mum?'

'Do you really want to know?'

I pulled the thread until it snapped. The button spun onto the floor and landed by Durand's foot. His fingers brushed against mine as he handed me the button, and I felt a jolt. I could tell by the look on his face, he'd felt it too.

I cleared my throat and dragged my gaze to Emily, who was standing alone in the church portico. 'Does she know?'

Durand sighed. 'Not yet. And it's not as if Charlie can be charged with manslaughter.'

I nodded, feeling light with relief.

'What about Charlie's first wife, Lizzie? Do you think there was more to her death than everyone thought?'

'We considered it. Back when Charlie was a suspect. But there was nothing to suggest Lizzie's death was anything other than a tragic accident.' Durand picked a leaf off his trousers and flicked it onto the grass. 'We caught up with Bert Hughes this morning.'

I stared at him. 'He's reappeared?'

'He was hiding out this whole time; one of his dad's abandoned warehouses. Once Emily disappeared, Hughes wondered if being blackmailed was the least of his trouble. Anyway, he's come clean about the part he played in covering up the Rowntree evidence. We'll get him for perverting the course of justice.' He glanced at his watch. 'Service starts in five minutes we should–'

I put a hand out to stop him. 'Sam, if I don't ask this I'll always wonder . . .'

'It's a dead end.' Durand turned to face me, his gaze strong and steady. 'When Miller broke into your house, he went through your stuff and pieced together fragments of your life. He was lying about Tommy. Exploiting your weak spot.'

Disappointment stung my eyes and I nodded curtly, not trusting myself to speak.

Durand's voice softened. 'That said, we've spent the last week interviewing members of Christ Clan. Turns out Hector Marlon was in a relationship with a blond man. The boyfriend died recently, broke his heart.'

I whipped my head round. 'Hector . . . and Tommy?'

'You didn't hear that from me.' Durand buttoned up his jacket and stood up.

'How is Elodie?' The words were out before I could stop them.

'She's a fighter. She may surprise us all yet.' Durand looked up at the sky and smiled. 'Would you like to go for a drink once this is over? As friends, of course.'

His grey eyes darted across my face and I smiled. I was about to respond when I spotted the hearse pulling up to the kerb. I put a hand out to steady myself and Durand's eyes softened.

'Are you OK?'

I pressed my lips together and nodded, as my heart splintered in two.

Kate had saved me a spot near the front of the packed-out church. I squeezed into the pew and she gave my arm a squeeze, just as Gordon shuffled past in a creased grey suit that hung off his gaunt frame. I tried to catch his eye but he was gazing at the floor and muttering under his breath. He slid in the row next to Emily, and I made a note to speak to him after, to find out if there was anything I could do to help.

Suddenly the doors opened and a hush descended. As the organ broke into a sonorous version of 'Ave Maria', I stared up at the stained-glass window and bit down on my lip. I couldn't look at the coffin. No matter how many times Rowley told me we weren't to blame, I kept thinking about how Charlie was alive and under our noses the whole time. He was there the day I visited Emily, during the police searches, the press conferences, everything. He was alive, while we were chasing a ghost. *Or a Starling.* An image of Miller's haggard face drifted into my head. I couldn't blame Vanessa for pushing her rapist's son away. But it was all so fucking sad. I thought about that lost little boy who just needed to know that someone was rooting for him. To know that he was loved. But Vanessa's efforts came too late.

The vicar lumbered up to the lectern and I clutched Kate's hand, the corners of my mouth bunched tight.

My mind drifted back to Tommy's wake. After I'd smashed up the library, Charlie picked me up off the floor and propelled me into the garden. He held my hands under the outside tap and washed away the shards of glass. As the rain petered out, we sat on the high stone wall that ran round the terrace and Charlie handed me a glass of wine.

'Your dad's an arse, you know. For not showing up today.' Charlie kicked his legs against the wall and stared up at the slate-grey sky. 'My dad's dead, my step-dad's away with the fairies and my mum's a drunk. God knows who'd go to my funeral.'

I swigged my wine and punched him on the arm. 'I'd go.'

'Yes, but you'd be checking your emails. Or pretending to listen to the vicar, while sketching out headlines.' Charlie paused. 'Although, if I made you do a reading, you'd have to pay attention. Or a poem. Nothing major, just something about how unbelievably brilliant I am.'

'There was a young man called Swift, who viewed himself as God's gift–'

'Till a terrible drought, made his hair all fall out–'

'And for that he was terribly miffed.'

Charlie snorted. 'Forget it, Kent. Your services are not required.'

I smiled for the first time in days. 'I'd definitely mention how hair-obsessed you are. And your questionable taste in socks would need to be addressed.'

'What's wrong with these?' Charlie said, mock-indignantly, pulling up his trouser leg and flashing a poppy-red sock.

As we wandered back to the French windows, I turned to Charlie and my voice caught. 'I'd also mention how you got me through my darkest hours. For today, and all the other days like it, thank you.' I leaned up and kissed him on the cheek.

Charlie sighed. 'You're right. I really am a hero.'

The night air was punctured by the strains of a piano drifting out of an upstairs window.

'Who's the maestro?' he said, gazing up.

I rolled my eyes. 'That is the sound of my mum locking herself in for the night. Won't see her again until she's good and lubricated.' I couldn't keep the bitterness out of my voice. 'She can't even be there for Tommy at his own wake.'

Charlie turned to face me; and his face was cloaked in shadow. 'At least she showed up, Soph. Believe me, she could be a lot worse.'

She could be a lot worse. Hearing his words again, I realised he was talking about his own mum. By that time, Charlie knew about Vanessa's secret; the secret that had consumed her for forty-four years. When police went through Charlie's belongings, they found a letter, written in Vanessa's untidy scrawl.

My darling darling son, forgive me this letter is over forty years late and I'm sorry so sorry. I've thought of you every day, I haven't shown it but you've been in my heart every day.

At the time, police assumed the letter was Charlie's. They were wrong. The letter was meant for Mark. Between us all, we'd joined the dots. Vanessa had entrusted the letter to Charlie and begged him to help her find the son she lost. But Charlie buried that letter, along with any hope Vanessa had of seeing Mark again. It was a decision that would cost Charlie his life.

I marvelled at the irony. The son Vanessa gave away spent a lifetime trying to come home. And the son she kept, ended up abandoning her.

The fire changed everything. I heard Dominic's voice in my head. *All roads lead back to that fire.*

I dragged my eyes to the front of the church to where Charlie's coffin stood alone, covered in a blanket of lilies. We'd never find out what really happened that April night in 1988; Charlie had taken the secret to his grave. As the vicar's speech drew to a close, I smoothed down my dress and stood up.

Then I walked towards the lectern.

Epilogue

The last drops of wine are like hot nectar on her tongue. She staggers to the kitchen counter and rifles through the cupboards. *Empty.* Panic makes her palms itch. Vanessa heaves open the cellar door and blinks. The steps arch away from her into the gloom. Clutching the rail, she stumbles down, hitting the concrete hard. Then she snatches the lid off the laundry basket and rifles through the dank clothes. Her fingers touch ice-cold glass and she pulls the bottles out.

A noise behind her. She startles, tries to focus. 'Who's there?'

Silence.

Shivering, Vanessa crawls up the steps and pauses, straining her ears. Charlie is asleep. She pictures her dark-haired boy; wrapped in navy flannel pyjamas, smelling of sleep. The thought is almost enough to make her put the bottle down. But she knows she won't.

Vanessa collapses on the sofa and takes a long swig. Darkness is falling and she can't face turning on the light. She likes the dark. Then she can pretend she's somewhere else. *Anywhere but here.* The lines of the room blur and fade into nothing.

A noise pulls her out of the fog. She cracks open an eye. Can't see, can't move. A shadow passes. Footsteps. She blinks. *Charlie.* Her heart floods with love. What's he doing? She's confused. Somewhere, deep down, it dawns on her that Charlie doesn't own a grey tracksuit. Her head hurts. She can't think straight. All she wants to do is sleep.

The boy turns, and she realises the mistake.

He has come for her; like she's always known he would. Ever since that first letter, she's felt hunted. She screws her eyes shut; the red envelope is bright in her mind. The letters keep coming. Like drops of blood, they trickle onto her door-mat. How did he find her? This child that is half her, but also half him.

Without thinking, her hand moves to her stomach and traces the scar. For a second she gives in to the memory; feels the weight of the baby in her arms. When she first laid eyes on his black hair and velvet skin, she'd wavered. Then he looked at her and all she could think about was *him*. So she held her baby son out for the nurse, and his cries have haunted her dreams ever since. Now she doesn't know how to undo what she's done. He is just a child; it's not his fault. But every time she thinks about letting him into her life, she pictures his dad's face. Laurence Marlon kept her chained to his cellar wall for four days before she managed to escape. Every time he raped her, he told her it was the will of God. She'd clawed her way out of the darkness and when, four weeks later, she discovered she was pregnant, she almost ended her life. But, in the end, she couldn't do it. This tiny little human deserved a chance.

She knew she wouldn't be able to love it in the way a mother should. But she could let another couple do that for her.

She hears the snap of a lighter. Sees a trail of flames light up the carpet. The boy stands there, watching. He looks so much like Charlie her heart contracts. Then he scuttles into the darkness.

Vanessa coughs, hears the front door click. In the thick molasses of her brain, a thought stirs. The police will come. They'll know this wasn't an accident. His fingerprints will be all over the room. Her son will go to jail. His life will be in tatters. He can't spend his life paying for what she's done to him.

The smoke is filling her lungs; she covers her nose and mouth with her sleeve. Vanessa drags herself off the sofa, picks up one of the wine bottles she's stashed under the cushion and hurls it on the fire. The flames burn higher, but it's still not enough to destroy evidence of how the fire really started. She needs to burn this place to the ground. She reaches for the next bottle and uncaps it.

Hot tears run down her sooty cheeks. She is steaming drunk. One more bottle and she'll get Charlie. She'll take her boy away from this place; they'll start a new life together where the past can't find them. Her eldest son; she can't love him the way he needs her to, but she will do what she can to protect him.

As she throws the wine into the fire, the words punch out of her, loud and clear. 'Forgive me, son; forgive me, son; forgive me, son.'

She is crying so much that she doesn't see the shadow in the doorway, nor the pair of dark, solemn eyes taking in the scene.

As she tosses the bottle into the flames, the boy buries his face in his flannel pyjamas, choking back tears. He wants to pull his mum away from the fire, but she thinks he's asleep upstairs. He's terrified that if she sees him, she'll trap him in the burning room. She wants him dead. Why else would she set fire to their home?

The fire bursts through the far wall; the noise is deafening. He stands there, transfixed, his toes curling in his slippers. And that's when he hears her rallying cry: *Forgive me, son.*

The boy makes a run for it, staggers into the cold night.

Forgive me, son.

He hardens his heart.

Forgive me, son.

He stares back at his burning home and makes a silent promise.

No matter what, he will never, ever forgive.

Acknowledgements

Firstly, a heartfelt thank you to the folks at Hendrick's Gin. Without you, none of this would have been possible. Whilst I wouldn't necessarily recommend two transatlantic moves, a new baby, publishing a first, then writing a second, book within the space of eighteen months, it does wonders for your alcohol tolerance (shame the same can't be said about your liver. . .).

To my super-agent, Teresa Chris: apologies for being the most chaotic author on your books (see above). Your unwavering support and guidance mean everything . . . thank you!

I'm indebted to the team at Bonnier Zaffre. In particular, my fabulous editor, Katherine Armstrong. Thank you for your endless patience and for turning *The Perfect Victim* into a far better novel. Also, I am never drinking with you again (until the next time). Thanks also to my wonderful copy-editor Jon Appleton, proofreader Mary Chamberlain, cover designer Anneka Sandher; to Kate Parkin, Rebecca Farrell, Nico Poilblanc, and to my lovely publicist Emily Burns.

I wouldn't have got very far without the genius minds of Federal Forensic Investigator and Polygraph Examiner, Geoff Symon; retired Police Inspector and owner of Crime Writing Solutions, Kevin N. Robinson; and former police detective, Stuart Gibbon, at GIB Consultancy.

A special shout-out to anyone who has patiently answered my questions (aka dug me out of gaping plot holes): in particular

Dr Rini Chatterjee; crime-writer extraordinaire, Neil White; and Jana Pruden, award-winning reporter at Edmonton's *The Globe and Mail*.

I've been fortunate enough to meet many fabulous faces along the way: to the crime-blogger community, your support is hugely appreciated; to my fellow Bonnier authors, I miss you all hugely; and to the other crime scene writers, your boundless knowledge (and filthy jokes) have got me through many a dark night.

Thank you to my family: the Jacksons, Lanes, Bigmores and Butchers; and to my wildly supportive friends on both sides of the Atlantic. An extra-special thank you to my in-laws, Nick and Maggie, for keeping me upright when the world was spinning (and for answering my many childcare emergencies!).

To my daughter, Evelyn, who arrived just as I started writing *The Perfect Victim*. I apologise for breastfeeding you whilst on the phone to forensic experts, and for dedicating so much of your early life to plotting grisly murders. Any royalties will go towards your therapy.

To my son, Arthur: your hugs, laughs and Lego-building provided a welcome foil to the day job. I love you to the moon and back.

To my husband, James, who unknowingly inspired so many of the positive character traits in the book. You gave me space, gin and childcare in equal measure. What more could a wife ask for?! Seriously, without you this book wouldn't exist, and I thank you from the bottom of my heart.

A final thanks go to my wonderful parents, Peter & Gloria, who taught me to work hard and dream big. This one's for you . . .